SAINTS OF THE SHADOW BIBLE

Also by Ian Rankin

The Inspector Malcolm Fox Series
The Complaints
The Impossible Dead

The Detective Inspector Rebus Series

Knots & Crosses
Hide & Seek
Tooth & Nail (previously published as *Wolfman*)
A Good Hanging and Other Stories
Strip Jack
The Black Book
Mortal Causes
Let It Bleed
Black & Blue
The Hanging Garden
Death Is Not the End (a novella)
Dead Souls
Set in Darkness
The Falls
Resurrection Men
A Question of Blood
Fleshmarket Alley
The Naming of the Dead
Exit Music

Other Novels

Witch Hunt
Blood Hunt
Bleeding Hearts
Watchman
Doors Open
Dark Entries (graphic novel)

SAINTS OF THE SHADOW BIBLE

IAN RANKIN

LITTLE, BROWN AND COMPANY

NEW YORK   BOSTON   LONDON

Little, Brown and Company
Hachette Book Group
237 Park Avenue, New York, NY 10017
littlebrown.com

First United States Edition, January 2014
Originally published in Great Britain by Orion, November 2013

Little, Brown and Company is a division of Hachette Book Group, Inc. The Little,
Brown name and logo are trademarks of Hachette Book Group, Inc.
The publisher is not responsible for websites (or their content) that are not
owned by the publisher.

The Hachette Speakers Bureau provides a wide range of authors for speaking events.
To find out more, go to hachettespeakersbureau.com or call (866) 376-6591.
Lyrics from "One Man, One Guitar" by Jackie Leven reproduced with the permis-
sion of CV Publishing Limited

ISBN 978-0-316-22455-0
LCCN 2013955201

10 9 8 7 6 5 4 3 2 1

RRD-C

Printed in the United States of America

The saints of the shadow bible following me
From bar to bar into eternity...

Jackie Leven, "One Man, One Guitar"

PROLOGUE

Where are we going?"

"We're just driving."

"Driving where, though?"

Rebus turned to look at his passenger. The man's name was Peter Meikle. He had served almost half his adult life in various Scottish and English prisons and had the pallor and bearing common to ex-cons. His face needed a shave and his sunken eyes were black, wary pinholes. Rebus had picked him up from outside a betting shop on Clerk Street. A few sets of lights and they were heading past the Commonwealth Pool and into Holyrood Park.

"It's been a while," Rebus said. "What are you up to these days?"

"Nothing you lot need worry about."

"Do I look worried?"

"You look the same way you did when you laid me out in 1989."

"That far back?" Rebus made show of shaking his head in surprise. "But be fair, Peter, you were resisting arrest—and you had a temper on you."

"You're saying you didn't?" When Rebus made no answer, Meikle resumed staring through the windscreen. The Saab was on Queen's Drive now, skirting the cliff-like Salisbury Crags on the approach to St. Margaret's Loch. A few tourists were trying to feed bread to the ducks and swans, though a troop of swooping gulls seemed to be winning more than its fair share. Rebus was signaling right, beginning the climb that would snake around Arthur's Seat. They passed joggers and walkers, the city vanishing from view.

"Could be in the middle of the Highlands," Rebus commented. "Hard to believe Edinburgh's somewhere down below." He turned again towards his passenger. "Didn't you live around here at one time?"

"You know I did."

"Northfield, I seem to think." The car was slowing, Rebus pulling over and stopping. He nodded in the direction of a wall with an open gate. "That's the shortcut, isn't it? If you were coming into the park on foot? From Northfield?"

Meikle just shrugged. He was wearing a padded nylon jacket. It made noises when he twitched. He watched Rebus break open a new pack of cigarettes and light one with a match. Rebus exhaled a plume of smoke before offering the pack to Meikle.

"I stopped last year."

"News to me, Peter."

"Aye, I'll bet it is."

"Well, if I can't tempt you, let's just get out for a minute." Rebus turned off the ignition, undid his seat belt and pushed open his door.

"Why?" Meikle wasn't budging.

Rebus leaned back into the car. "Something to show you."

"What if I'm not interested?"

But Rebus just winked and closed the door, heading around the car and across the grass towards the gateway. The keys were still in the ignition, and Meikle studied them for a good twenty or thirty seconds before cursing under his breath, composing himself and opening the passenger-side door.

Rebus was the other side of the park's perimeter wall, the eastern suburbs of the city laid out below him.

"It's a steep climb," he was saying, shading his eyes with his free hand. "But you were younger then. Or maybe you weren't on foot—bound to be a mate's car you could borrow. All you had to tell them was you had something needed shifting."

"This is about Dorothy," Meikle stated.

"What else?" Rebus gave a thin smile. "Almost two weeks before she was reported missing."

"It was eleven years ago..."

"Two weeks," Rebus repeated. "Your story was you thought she'd gone to stay with her sister. Bit of a falling-out between the two of you. Well, there was no way you could deny that—neighbors couldn't help hearing the shouting matches. So you might as well turn it to your advantage." Only now did Rebus turn towards the man. "Two weeks, and even then it was her sister who had to contact us. Never a trace of Dorothy leaving the city—we asked at the train and bus stations. It was like you were a magician and you'd put her in one of those boxes. Open it up and she's not there." He paused and took half a step towards Meikle. "But she *is* there, Peter. She's somewhere in this city." He stamped his left foot against the ground. "Dead and buried."

"I was questioned at the time, remember?"

"Chief suspect," Rebus added with a slow nod.

"She could have gone out drinking, met the wrong man..."

"Hundreds of pubs we visited, Peter, showing her picture, asking the regulars."

"Tried thumbing a lift then—you can lose yourself in London."

"Where she had no friends? Never touching her bank account?" Rebus was shaking his head now.

"I didn't kill her."

Rebus made show of wincing. "This is just the two of us, Peter. I'm not wearing a wire or anything; it's for my own peace of mind, that's all. Once you've told me you brought her up here and buried her, that'll be the end of it."

"I thought you weren't working cold cases anymore."

"Where did you hear that?"

"Edinburgh's being shut down, transferred."

"True enough. But not everyone would be as informed as you seem to be."

Meikle gave a shrug. "I read the papers."

"Paying particular attention to police stories?"

"I know there's a reorganization."

"Why so interested, though?"

"You forgetting that I've a history with you lot? Come to that, why aren't you retired—you must be on full pension by now?"

"I *was* retired—that's what the Cold Case Unit was, a bunch of old hands still itching for answers. And you're right that our caseload has gone elsewhere." Rebus's face was by now only a couple of inches from Meikle's. "But *I've* not gone, Peter. I'm right here, and I was just getting started on reopening your case when it was taken away from me. Well, you know me, I like to finish what I start."

"I've got nothing to say."

"Sure about that?"

"You going to slam me into a wall, knock me out cold again? That's the way you and your lot always liked to operate..."

But Rebus wasn't listening. His attention had shifted to the mobile phone gripped in Meikle's right hand. He snatched at it and saw that its recording function was on. With a grim smile, he tossed it into a thicket of gorse. Meikle gave a little yelp of complaint.

"This the way you want it to go, Peter?" Rebus asked, stubbing the remains of his cigarette against the wall. "Always watching over your shoulder for someone like me? Waiting for the day a dog goes sniffing where it shouldn't and starts to dig?"

"You've got nothing and you *are* nothing," Meikle spat.

"You couldn't be more wrong. See, I've got *you*." A finger was stabbed into Meikle's chest. "And as long as you're unfinished business, that makes me something you need to worry about."

He turned and headed back through the gateway. Meikle watched him climb into the Saab and start the engine. The car sped off with a burst of smoke from its exhaust. Swearing under his breath, Meikle began trampling down the gorse in search of his phone.

The Chief Constable's leaving party took place at the canteen of Lothian and Borders Police HQ on Fettes Avenue. He was heading to a new post south of the border and no one seemed to know whether anyone would take over his role. The eight regional Scottish forces were soon to be amalgamated into something called Police Scotland. The Chief Constable of Strathclyde had been given the top job, leaving seven of his colleagues scratching around for fresh opportunities.

A perfunctory attempt had been made to turn the canteen into a festive location—meaning a couple of banners, some streamers and even a dozen or so party balloons. Tables had been covered with paper tablecloths. There were bowls of crisps and nuts, and bottles of wine and beer.

"Cake's arriving in half an hour," Siobhan Clarke told Rebus.

"Then I'm out of here in twenty."

"You don't like cake?"

"It's the speeches that'll no doubt accompany it."

Clarke smiled and sipped her orange juice. Rebus held an open bottle of lager, but had no intention of finishing it—too gassy, not cold enough.

"So, DS Rebus," she said, "what did you get up to this afternoon?"

He stared at her. "How long are we going to keep this up?" Meaning her use of his rank—detective sergeant to her inspector. A decade back, the roles had been reversed. But when Rebus had applied to rejoin, he'd been warned of a surfeit of DIs, meaning he would have to drop to DS.

"Take it or leave it," he'd been told.

So he'd taken it.

"I think I can string it out a little longer," Clarke was saying now, her smile widening. "And you haven't answered my question."

"I was looking up an old friend."

"You don't have any."

"I could point to a dozen in this very room."

Clarke scanned the faces. "And probably as many enemies."

Rebus seemed to ponder this. "Aye, maybe," he conceded. And he was lying anyway. A dozen friends? Not even close. Siobhan was a friend, perhaps the closest he'd ever had—despite the age gap and the fact she didn't like most of the music he played. He saw people he'd worked alongside, but almost no one he would have invited back to his flat for whisky and conversation. Then there were the few he would gladly give a kicking to—like the three officers from Professional Standards. They stood apart from the rest of the room, pariah status confirmed. Yet they had a haunted look—as with the Cold Case Unit, so too with their particular jobs: packed off elsewhere come reorganization. But then a face from the past was squeezing through the throng and heading in Rebus's direction. He stuck out a hand, which Rebus took.

"Bloody hell, I almost didn't recognize you there," Rebus admitted.

Eamonn Paterson patted what was left of his stomach. "Diet and exercise," he explained.

"Thank God for that—I thought you were going to tell me you had some sort of wasting disease." Rebus turned towards Clarke. "Siobhan, this is Eamonn Paterson. He was a DS when I was a DC." While the two shook hands, Rebus continued the introduction.

"Siobhan's a detective inspector, which has her under the cruel delusion she's my boss."

"Good luck with that," Paterson said. "When he was wet behind the ears I couldn't get him to take a telling, no matter how hard I kicked his backside."

"Some things never change," Clarke conceded.

"Eamonn here used to go by the name of Porkbelly," Rebus said. "Came back from a holiday in the States with the story he'd eaten so much of the stuff a restaurant had given him a T-shirt."

"I've still got it," Paterson said, raising his glass in a toast.

"How long have you been out of the game?" Clarke asked. Paterson was tall and slim, with a good head of hair; she wouldn't have said he was a day older than Rebus.

"Nearly fifteen years. Nice of them still to send me the invites." He waved his wineglass in the direction of the party.

"Maybe you're the poster boy for retirement."

"That could be part of it," he agreed with a laugh. "So this is the last rites for Lothian and Borders, eh?"

"As far as anyone knows." Rebus turned towards Clarke. "What's the new name again?"

"There'll be two divisions—Edinburgh, plus Lothians and Scottish Borders."

"Piece of nonsense," Paterson muttered. "Warrant cards will need changing, and so will the livery on the patrol cars—how the hell's that supposed to save money?" Then, to Rebus: "You going to manage along to Dod's?"

Rebus shrugged. "How about you?"

"Could be another case of last rites." Paterson turned towards Clarke. "We all worked together at Summerhall."

"Summerhall?"

"A cop shop next door to the vet school on Summerhall Place," Rebus explained. "They knocked it down and replaced it with St. Leonard's."

"Before my time," she admitted.

"Practically Stone Age," Paterson agreed. "Not many of us cavemen left, eh, John?"

"I've learned how to make fire," Rebus countered, taking the box of matches from his pocket and shaking it.

"You're not still smoking?"

"Someone has to."

"He likes the occasional drink, too," Clarke confided.

"I'm shocked." Paterson made show of studying Rebus's physique.

"Didn't realize I was auditioning for Mr. Universe."

"No," Clarke said, "but you've sucked your stomach in anyway."

"Busted," Paterson said with another laugh, slapping Rebus's shoulder. "So will you make it to Dod's or not? Stefan'll likely be there."

"Seems a bit ghoulish," Rebus said. He explained to Clarke that Dod Blantyre had suffered a recent stroke.

"He wants one last gathering of the old guard," Paterson added. He wagged a finger in Rebus's direction. "You don't want to disappoint him—or Maggie..."

"I'll see how I'm fixed."

Paterson tried staring Rebus out, then nodded slowly and patted his shoulder again. "Fine then," he said, moving off to greet another old face.

Five minutes later, as Rebus was readying his excuse that he needed to step out for a cigarette, a fresh group entered the canteen. They looked like lawyers because that was what they were—invitees from the Procurator Fiscal's office. Well dressed, with shiny, confident faces, and led by the Solicitor General for Scotland, Elinor Macari.

"Do we need to bow or anything?" Rebus murmured to Clarke, who was fixing her fringe. Macari was pecking the Chief Constable on both cheeks.

"Just don't say something you might regret."

"You're the boss."

Macari looked as though she'd made several stops on her way to the party: hairdresser, cosmetics counter and boutique. Her large black-framed glasses accentuated the sharpness of her gaze. Having swept the room in an instant, she knew who needed greeting and who could be dismissed. The councilor who headed the policing committee merited the same kiss as the Chief Constable. Other guests nearby had to make do with handshakes or a nod of the head. A glass of white wine had been fetched, but Rebus doubted it was anything other than a prop. He noticed too that his own bottle of lager was empty, though he'd vowed to save his thirst for something more deserving.

"Got a few words stored up in case she drifts this way?" he asked Clarke.

"I'd say we're well out of her orbit."

"Fair point. But now she's arrived, the presentations can't be far behind." Rebus held up the packet of cigarettes and gestured in the direction of the outside world.

"Are you coming back?" She saw his look and gave a twitch of the mouth, acknowledging the stupidity of the question. But as he made to leave the canteen, Macari spotted someone and made a beeline for them, so that Rebus had to swerve past her. She frowned, as if trying to place him, going so far as to glance at his retreating figure. But by then she had reached her prey. Siobhan Clarke watched as the most senior lawyer in Scotland took Malcolm Fox by the arm and led him away from his Professional Standards cohort. Whatever was about to be discussed, a modicum of privacy was required. One of the canteen staff had arrived in the doorway, holding the cake, but a gesture from the Chief Constable told her the ceremony would have to wait until the Solicitor General was ready...

DAY ONE

1

A flatbed lorry had arrived, the name of a local scrap yard stenciled on its doors. The previous night, a flimsy cordon had been erected, consisting of three-inch-wide tape with the word POLICE on it. The tape ran from an undamaged tree to a fence post and from there to another tree. The driver of the flatbed had sliced through it and was preparing to winch the crashed VW Golf up the slope towards the waiting ramp.

"Not a bad afternoon," Rebus said, lighting a cigarette and examining his surroundings. A stretch of narrow country road on the outskirts of Kirkliston. Edinburgh Airport wasn't far away, and the roar of approaching and departing passenger flights punctuated the rural scene. They had come in Clarke's Vauxhall Astra. It was parked on the opposite verge, flashers blinking in a warning to approaching drivers. Not that there seemed to be any.

"It's a straight road," Clarke was saying. "Surface wasn't icy or greasy. Must have been going at a fair clip, judging by the damage..."

True enough: the front of the Golf had become concertinaed on impact with the venerable oak tree. They made their way past the torn fencing and down the slope. The driver from the flatbed jutted out his chin in greeting but otherwise wasn't about to ask who they were or why they were there. Clarke carried a folder, which was good enough for him—meant they were official, and therefore probably best avoided.

"Is he okay?" Rebus asked.

"He's a she," Clarke corrected him. "Car's registered to Jessica Traynor. Address in southwest London. She's in the Infirmary."

Rebus was walking around the car. It was less than a year old, pearl-colored. From what he could see of the tires, there was plenty of tread on them. The windscreen was gone, driver's-side door and boot gaping, both airbags deployed.

"And we're here because...?"

Clarke opened the folder. "Mainly because her father seems to have friends. Word came down from on high: make sure we've not missed anything."

"What's to miss?"

"Hopefully nothing. But this area's notorious for boy racers."

"She's not a boy, though."

"She drives the kind of car they like."

"I wouldn't know."

"I think the Golf still qualifies as a 'hot hatch.'"

Rebus wandered over towards the flatbed. The man from the scrap yard was reeling out a cable with a large hook on the end. Rebus asked him how many Golfs ended up in the compactor.

"A few," he conceded. He sported oily blue overalls under a scuffed leather jacket, and dirt was ingrained on his palms and under his nails. The baseball cap he wore was so grubby the lettering on it was indecipherable, and a thick graying beard covered his chin and throat. Rebus offered him a cigarette, but the man shook his head.

"Roads around here used as racetracks?" Rebus continued.

"Sometimes."

"You on a diet or something?" The man looked at him. "Cutting back on your vocabulary," Rebus explained.

"I'm just here to do a job."

"But this isn't the first crash like this you've seen?"

"No."

"How regular?"

The man considered this. "Every couple of months. Though there was one last week, the other side of Broxburn."

"And it's cars racing each other? Any idea how it gets arranged?"

"No," the man stated.

"Well, thanks for sharing." Rebus walked back towards the Golf. Clarke was peering through the open door, examining the interior.

"Take a look," she said, handing Rebus a photograph. It showed a brown suede boot in what seemed a woman's size, framed against the floor of the car.

"I don't see any pedals."

"That's because it was in the passenger-side foot well."

"Okay." Rebus handed the photograph back. "So you're saying there was a passenger?"

Clarke shook her head. "It's one of a pair of Ugg boots belonging to Jessica Traynor. The other was on her left foot."

"Ugg?"

"That's what they're called."

"So it flew off on impact? Or came off when the medics pulled her out?"

"First patrol car on the scene, the officer took a few shots on his phone—including the boot. Jessica was still in the car at the time. Ambulance arrived a few minutes later."

Rebus pondered this. "Who found her?"

"A woman on her way home from Livingston. She works shifts at a supermarket there." Clarke was studying a typed sheet of paper from the folder. "Driver's-side door was open. Impact could have done that."

"Or the driver tried to get out."

"Unconscious. Head resting against the airbag. No seat belt."

Rebus took the photographs from Clarke and studied them while Clarke spoke. "The supermarket worker called 999 just after eight in the evening, no light left in the sky. No streetlamps either, just the distant glow from Edinburgh itself."

"Boot's closed," Rebus said, handing the photos back.

"Yes, it is," Clarke agreed.

"Not anymore, though." Rebus walked around to the back of the car. "Did you open this?" he asked the man from the scrap yard, receiving a shake of the head in answer. The boot was empty, except for a rudimentary tool kit.

"Scavengers, maybe?" Clarke suggested. "Car was here all night."

"Why not take the tool kit?"

"Don't suppose it's worth much. Anyone could have opened it, John—ambulance driver, our guy..."

"I suppose so." He tried closing the boot. It was undamaged, and stayed locked once shut. The key was in the ignition, and he pressed the button to unlock the boot again. A clunk told him he had been successful.

"Electrics still seem to work," he said.

"Sign of a well-made car." Clarke was sifting through the paperwork. "So what do we think?"

"We think a car was traveling too fast and came off the road. No sign of a prior collision. Was she maybe on her phone at the time? It's been known to happen."

"Worth checking," Clarke agreed. "And the Ugg?"

"Sometimes," Rebus said, "footwear is just footwear."

Clarke was checking a message on her phone. "Seems its owner is back in the land of the living."

"Do we want to speak to her?" Rebus asked.

The look Clarke gave him was all the answer he needed.

Jessica Traynor had a room to herself at the Royal Infirmary. The nurse explained that she had been lucky—a suspected fracture of one ankle, some bruised ribs, and other minor injuries consistent with whiplash.

"Her head and neck are in a brace."

"But she's able to talk?" Clarke asked.

"A little."

"Any sign of alcohol or drugs in her bloodstream?"

"Looks the clean-living type to me. She's on painkillers now, though, so she'll be woozy." The nurse paused. "Do you want to speak to her father first?"

"He's here?"

The nurse nodded again. "Arrived in the middle of the night. She was still in A and E at the time..." She had stopped by a window. It gave a view into Jessica Traynor's room. Her father was seated bedside, holding her hand in his and stroking her wrist. Her eyes were closed. The brace seemed to be constructed of thick squares of polystyrene foam, fixed in place with an array of metal clamps. Looking up, her father saw the faces at the window. He checked his daughter was asleep, then placed her hand gently on the bed and rose to his feet.

Exiting the room quietly, he ran his fingers through his mop of silver and black hair. He wore the trousers from a pinstripe suit—the jacket was draped over the back of the chair next to his daughter's bed. His white shirt was creased, and the cuff links had been removed so the sleeves could be rolled up. Rebus doubted the expensive-looking watch on his left wrist was a fake. He had taken off his tie at some point, and undone the top two buttons of his shirt, showing tufts of graying chest hair.

"Mr. Traynor," Clarke said, "we're police officers. How is Jessica doing?"

His large eyes were dark-ringed from lack of sleep and there was vending-machine coffee on his breath when he exhaled.

"She's all right," he eventually said. "Thank you."

Rebus wondered if Traynor's tan had come from a sun bed or a winter holiday. Probably the latter.

"Are we any clearer on what happened?" Clarke was being asked.

"We don't think another vehicle was involved, if that's what you mean. Maybe just a case of too much acceleration..."

"Jessica never drives fast. She's always been supercautious."

"It's a powerful car, sir," Rebus qualified.

But Traynor was shaking his head. "She wouldn't have been speeding, so let's rule that out right now."

Rebus glanced down at the man's shoes. Black brogues. Every inch the successful businessman. The accent was English, but not cut-glass. Rebus remembered Jessica's age from the notes in Clarke's folder: twenty-one.

"Your daughter's a student?" he surmised. Traynor nodded. "At the University of Edinburgh?" Another nod.

"What's her course?" Clarke added.

"Art history."

"Which year is she?"

"Second." Traynor seemed to be growing impatient. He was watching his daughter through the glass. Her chest rose and fell almost imperceptibly. "I have to go back in..."

"There are a couple of things we need to ask Jessica," Clarke told him.

He looked at her. "Such as?"

"Just to make sure we have all the facts."

"She's sleeping."

"Maybe you could try waking her up."

"She's sore all over."

"What did she tell you about the accident?"

"She said she was sorry about the Golf." Traynor's attention had shifted to the window again. "It was a birthday present. Insurance cost almost as much as the car..."

"Did she say anything about the accident itself, sir?"

Traynor shook his head. "I really do need to go back in."

"Mind if I ask where you're from, Mr. Traynor?" The question came from Rebus.

"Wimbledon."

"Southwest London?"

"Yes."

"And by the time you heard about Jessica, flights to Scotland would have finished for the day—did you take the train?"

"I have access to a private plane."

"So you've been awake all night and half of today? Might be you could use some shut-eye yourself."

"I managed an hour or two on the chair."

"Even so . . . Your wife wasn't able to join you?"

"We're divorced. She lives in Florida with someone half her age who calls himself a 'personal trainer.'"

"But you've told her about Jessica?" Clarke checked.

"Not yet."

"Don't you think she should know?"

"She walked out on us eight years ago—Jessica doesn't get so much as a phone call at Christmas." The words were tinged with bile. Traynor was exhausted, yes, but in no mood to forgive. He turned towards the two detectives. "Is this because I called in a favor?"

"Sir?" Clarke's eyes had narrowed at the question.

"I happen to know a couple of people in the Met—phoned from the plane to make sure everything up here was kosher. Thing is, as you said yourself, it was the kind of accident that could happen to anyone." His tone hardened. "So I don't see what's to be gained from you talking to her."

"We didn't *quite* say it could happen to anyone," Rebus broke in. "Straight stretch of deserted road—has to be a reason why the car decided not to stick to it. The locals out that way like to do a bit of racing once the sun's gone down . . ."

"I've already told you, Jessica was the safest driver imaginable."

"Then you've got to wonder what was causing her to do the speed she was doing. Was it maybe road rage? Was she trying to get away from someone tailgating her? Questions only *she* can answer, Mr. Traynor." Rebus paused. "Questions I'd have thought you'd want to have answered too."

He waited for this to sink in. Traynor ran his hand through his hair again, then gave a long sigh.

"Give me your number," he conceded. "I'll call you when she's awake."

"We were just going to grab something from the café," Rebus told him. "So if it's in the next twenty minutes or so, we'll still be here."

"We can bring you a sandwich, if you like," Clarke added, her face softening a little.

Traynor shook his head, but took her card when she offered it.

"Mobile's on the back," she said. "Oh, and one more thing—could we take a look at Jessica's phone?"

"What?"

"I'm assuming it'll be by her bedside somewhere..."

Traynor was starting to look annoyed again, but turned and went into the room, emerging moments later with the device.

"Thank you, sir," Clarke said, taking it from him and turning to lead Rebus back down the corridor.

Rebus headed outside for a cigarette while Clarke bought the drinks. When he returned, he brought a hacking cough with him.

"Should I see if they've a spare bed in the emphysema ward?" she asked.

"I wasn't lonely out there—hard to know if staff outnumbered patients or vice versa." He took a sip from the cardboard cup. "I'm going to guess tea."

She nodded, and they drank in silence for a moment. The café opened onto the hospital's central concourse. There was a shop across the way, people queuing for sweets and crisps. Further along, another concession specializing in health foods was doing no trade at all.

"What do you make of him?" Clarke asked.

"Who? The David Dickinson lookalike?"

Clarke smiled. "Bit more George Clooney than that."

Rebus shrugged. "He wears expensive suits and travels by private jet—I want to marry him, naturally."

"Join the queue." Her smile widened. "You have to say, though—he does love his daughter. Probably head of some big corporation, but drops everything to come north."

Rebus nodded his agreement and managed another mouthful of tea before pushing the cup away.

"What you said to him about road rage," Clarke went on, "was that off the top of your head?"

"Just trying to think of reasons why a careful driver would be putting the foot down."

"It's an idea. Reckon she lives in the city?"

"Bound to—maybe even in a flat bought by Mr. Pinstripe."

"So what was she doing out there in the first place? It's more or less a road to nowhere."

"Something else for us to ask her," Rebus agreed. "What did her phone offer up?"

"Unanswered calls and texts."

"No sign she was using it while driving?"

Clarke shook her head. "On the other hand, if her dad is as sharp as he dresses..."

"He might have decided to delete any evidence of her stupidity." Rebus nodded slowly.

Clarke's own phone pinged, alerting her to a message. "It's Page," she said, checking the screen. "Wants an update."

"That won't take long."

Another ping.

"And with perfect timing, Jessica's awake." Clarke started to rise from the table.

"Taking your tea with you?" Rebus asked.

"What do you think?" came the reply.

The same nurse was just leaving Jessica Traynor's room as they arrived.

"Go easy on her," she said in an undertone.

"We're famous for it," Rebus assured her.

The bed was still flat, the patient staring towards the ceiling. She moved her eyes, blinking a few times as she focused on the new arrivals. Her lips were moist, as though she'd just accepted some liquid from the beaker on the nearby tray. Her father was seated again, holding her hand as before.

"Jessica," Clarke began, "I'm Detective Inspector Clarke and this is Detective Sergeant Rebus. How are you feeling, or is that a stupid question?"

"Like I got hit by a car."

"I saw the state of your Golf. The airbag probably saved your life. Silly not to have your seat belt fastened."

Traynor stiffened as he took this in. Jessica's eyes widened. "I always do up my seat belt," she protested.

"The motorist who found you, the one who called for the cavalry, says you weren't strapped in."

"Couldn't it have come undone on impact?" Traynor asked.

"I've not heard of that happening," Clarke told him. Then, to his daughter: "Any idea why one of your boots ended up on the passenger-side floor?"

"I don't understand." Jessica Traynor's eyes flitted from one face to another.

"There you are in the driver's seat," Clarke obliged, "but one of your Uggs somehow lands the other side of the central console. Again, it's something I've not come across before."

Her father leaned in towards her. "The officers were asking me earlier if someone was maybe driving too fast behind you, causing you to do what you did."

"I don't know what happened." Tears were filling Jessica Traynor's eyes.

"Was there some sort of race going on?" Clarke asked. "Maybe you got in the way and they forced you off the road?"

"No…"

Traynor had risen from his chair. His daughter had her eyes screwed shut and he was asking her if she was in pain.

"I don't want to think about it," she told him. "I don't want to remember any of it. The car went off the road, that's all."

With her hand still in his, Traynor turned towards the two detectives. "Probably best if you leave now. Give her some time to recover." His eyes told them he would brook no argument. But still Clarke lingered. It was Rebus, however, who spoke.

"We just need Jessica's address here in Edinburgh."

"Why?" The question came from the bed. Jessica had balled her free hand into a fist. Her eyes were still closed but her face looked pained.

"We just do," Clarke said.

Traynor gestured towards the corridor. "Jessica," he said, "just try and relax. I'm going to show the officers out."

"I still don't understand why they're here."

"They're leaving right now." He gave her wrist a final squeeze, then let it go, extending an arm to indicate to Rebus that he should lead the way.

Once they were out in the corridor and the door was closed, he proffered the address. Clarke tapped it into her phone.

"Speaking of which..." Traynor held out a hand, palm up. Clarke dug his daughter's phone from her pocket and handed it over.

"Does Jessica have flatmates?" she asked.

"Another student. Her name's Alice or Alison—I only met her once."

"Does she know about Jessica?"

"I'm guessing she'd be here if she did."

Rebus had a question of his own. "Is Jessica seeing anyone?"

"A boyfriend? There was someone called Forbes. She hasn't mentioned him lately."

"Is Forbes a first name or a last?"

"I've really no idea." Traynor's eyes were trained on the window and the bed beyond. "I need to get back."

"If she confides anything..."

He turned to face Rebus, then nodded slowly before reentering his daughter's room. They watched him take his seat again.

"You don't think she was alone out there," Clarke suggested.

"I don't even think she was driving," Rebus replied.

2

In his cramped office—previously a storeroom off the main CID suite—Detective Chief Inspector James Page listened to their report. Gayfield Square police station was part of the city's B Division, but that designation would soon vanish, and Page feared that the station itself would be closed, knocked down and redeveloped. The "Square" outside was an area of grass which didn't get mowed enough. Traffic rumbled up and down Leith Walk, sometimes causing the windows at the front of the building to vibrate. Not that this affected Page, his office having no windows.

"So the boot ended up there how?" he asked. Rebus and Clarke were both standing, since there was no space for any chair other than the one their boss sat on.

"Whoever was driving fled the scene," Rebus explained. "That leaves two possibilities. One, she regained consciousness for a bit, realized she was alone, and dragged herself across to the driver's seat."

"Why?"

"To protect the other person. We would assume she'd been behind the wheel."

Page considered this. "And the second option?" he asked.

"Is that the driver either didn't black out or else came to before her. He or she panicked—for whatever reason—and hoofed it. But not before undoing her seat belt and hauling her across to the driver's side."

"Not bothering to do up her seat belt after," Clarke added.

"And you get all of this from the fact that a brown suede boot was in the wrong foot well?" Page looked from Clarke to Rebus and back again.

"Yes," she replied.

"Well, say you're right—what exactly does it change?"

"Driver could have been drunk or stoned," Rebus offered.

"Or taking part in an illegal race," Clarke said. "Or being chased—we really won't know unless we keep looking. Jessica has a flat in Great King Street, shares with someone called Alice or Alison. There was also mention of a boyfriend."

Page scratched at his nose while he thought.

"Don't want anyone thinking we were sloppy," Rebus prompted. "One quick visit to the flat should do it."

"We'd go this evening," Clarke confirmed. "This Alice or Alison is a student—might have classes during the day."

"All right then." Page had made up his mind. "But answer me this: why is it that nothing with you two is ever straightforward?"

"Blame her," Rebus said, pointing a finger.

"Blame him," Clarke said, at almost exactly the same time.

Out in the CID suite, they both took a series of deep breaths. It was always so airless in Page's little cupboard, yet somehow he thrived there, as if discomfort were as vital to his well-being as oxygen. Two detective constables, Christine Esson and Ronnie Ogilvie, were busy with paperwork. Clarke checked her phone for messages while Rebus made himself a coffee.

"Out of milk," Esson warned him.

"The amount we get through, we should chip in and buy a cow," Ogilvie added.

"It would keep the grass down," Rebus agreed, staring down onto Gayfield Square, the windowpane thrumming as a lorry rattled past the end of the road. He offered to boil the kettle for Clarke but she shook her head.

"Not if we've got no milk."

"I might have a sachet of powdered stuff in a drawer somewhere," Esson offered.

"Powdered?" Rebus said. "What is this, World War Two? I thought we were at the dawn of a shiny new country?"

"Only if you can be bothered to vote for it," Clarke chided him.

"I'll tell you the box I'm ready to mark my cross in—a couple of drinks after Great King Street."

But Clarke was shaking her head. "Dinner plans," she explained.

"I thought it was all over with..." Rebus gestured towards Page's office.

"It is."

Christine Esson decided that Rebus needed enlightening. "A single girl doesn't go hungry for long in this town."

"Is that you speaking from experience?" Ogilvie chipped in.

"Who is it then?" Rebus was asking Clarke from above the rim of his mug.

"Am I not allowed a private life?"

"Absolutely—just as soon as you convince me his intentions are honorable."

Clarke rolled her eyes and decided to busy herself making a coffee after all. Rebus stood his ground, mouth puckered, deep in thought. Then he ambled forward and leaned in towards her ear.

"A lawyer," he whispered.

She froze for a second before spooning granules into a clean mug.

"My, my," Rebus said. Her eyes were on him now, seeking an explanation. "It was when Macari and her team walked into the canteen," he obliged. "You straightened your back a little and checked your fringe. I thought maybe it was for *her* benefit. I don't remember any of the men looking particularly bright or beautiful."

"Then you're not much of a detective."

"It has been said. So is he taking you somewhere nice?"

"Why do you need to know?"

"Takes a bit of time to get gussied up—I was just thinking I could do Great King Street on my own..."

But Clarke was shaking her head. "You're still on 'probation,' remember? One screwup and you're back where you started."

"Yes, boss." He paused. "So he's not taking you anywhere posh? Means he's not very senior—don't tell me you've got yourself a toy boy?"

Clarke jabbed a finger into his chest. "Everybody has a breaking point, John." But she was smiling, and Rebus was smiling too. He turned towards Esson and Ogilvie.

"Either of you two up for a bit of surveillance tonight?"

"I'm warning you," Clarke said, jabbing him harder this time.

Great King Street was a wide thoroughfare in the New Town, stretching from Howe Street to Drummond Place. Three and four stories high, the terrace had probably all been houses when built in the early nineteenth century, but now many of these had been subdivided into flats. Rebus had never been a huge fan of the New Town. For one thing, you had to climb a steep incline to get back to the city center. There were also no front gardens, and parking was difficult. The door they were looking for had four buzzers beside it, with TRAYNOR/BELL at the top.

"Presumably meaning top floor," Rebus muttered.

"Maybe no one's home," Clarke offered by way of consolation. But when she pressed the button, a voice crackled through the intercom.

"Miss Bell?" Clarke guessed.

"Yes."

"It's the police. We need to talk to you about Jessica."

"I *knew* it! Door's unlocked—we're on the top floor."

"I knew it," Rebus echoed, turning the handle.

By the time they had climbed the first flight, he was breathing heavily, and Clarke was asking him to remind her how he'd passed the physical. He coughed a reply and watched as a head appeared over the banister.

"Up here," Alice or Alison Bell said. As she ushered the two detectives inside, Clarke decided to check.

"It's Alice," the student confirmed.

Rebus had expected high ceilings and airy rooms, but they seemed to be in the eaves. The hall was narrow, not helped by the presence of two bicycles. Alice Bell hadn't bothered to ask for ID. She was leading them past the galley-style kitchen into the living room. Music was playing from an MP3 player hooked up to a speaker. It was classical—unaccompanied cello. An actual cello sat on a stand in one corner.

"Yours or Jessica's?" Rebus asked, but Bell was concentrating on Siobhan Clarke.

"I'm almost afraid to ask," she blurted out.

"She's going to be fine," Clarke assured her. The young woman's knees seemed to buckle in relief and she sat down heavily on an armchair. Clarke and Rebus decided to settle themselves on the sofa. It was white and modern and just about up to the task.

"What happened?" Bell was asking.

"A car smash. You've been worried about her?"

"Texted her a few times—she missed a class this morning, and that's not like her."

"Do you study art history too, Alice?"

The young woman nodded. She was dressed in a T-shirt with an unbuttoned cardigan over it, and black denims. No piercings that Rebus could see, and no tattoos. Her face was round and her cheeks slightly puffy, reminding him of a cherub in a painting, an effect heightened by curly chestnut hair.

"How long have you known Jessica?" Rebus asked.

"Almost a year. She put adverts up around the department— room to rent—and I jumped at the chance." She paused. "She's really going to be okay?"

"Whiplash, sprains and bruises," Clarke explained. "Her father seems to think she's a careful driver."

"That's true."

"Not last night, though."

"What happened?"

"The crash was the other side of the airport, on a country road. Any idea why she'd be out that way?"

Bell shook her head. "Is her father here?"

"He's with her at the Infirmary," Rebus said.

"I should go see her."

"Any other friends who should be told?" Clarke asked.

"Her boyfriend, for example," Rebus added.

"Forbes?" Bell's voice lifted a little. "Has no one...?" She broke off, hands clasped between her knees, staring at the varnished wooden floor.

"We don't have his contact details," Clarke confided.

"I can phone him."

"That's fine, but we'd like a word with him too." Rebus cleared his throat. "When did you last see Jessica, Alice?"

"Yesterday. Around four or five."

"Here at the flat?"

"She was headed off out."

"Headed where?"

"Not sure."

"In her car, though?"

"I suppose so."

"And as far as you know, she hasn't got friends in Kirkliston or Broxburn?"

"I'm not even sure where those places are."

"Where are you from?"

"Stirling."

Rebus digested this and glanced towards Clarke, unsure where else to go.

"A number for Forbes," Clarke prompted the student. "And his surname."

"He's Forbes McCuskey."

"McCuskey," Clarke echoed, adding the name to her phone.

"As in Patrick McCuskey."

Clarke looked up at Alice Bell. "The politician?" Bell nodded, and Clarke turned her eyes towards Rebus, who gave a twitch of the mouth in response. Bell was digging her own phone out of a trouser pocket, finding Forbes McCuskey's number. She recited it for Clarke's benefit, then asked: "Should I ring him now?"

"If you like."

But Bell seemed to reconsider. She turned the phone over in her hand and said she would wait till she'd seen them out.

"You're still going to want to talk to him?" she checked. "And it's okay for me to warn him?"

Clarke was nodding her agreement.

"All right then." The student had risen to her feet. Clarke and Rebus followed suit and Bell led them back along the passageway. Rebus was half minded to ask to see Jessica's room, but knew he didn't have a good reason. At the door, Bell shook hands with both detectives. She was readying to close the door when Clarke remembered that she didn't have a contact number for Bell herself. The student reeled it off, then retreated into the flat.

"'Warn him'?" Rebus repeated.

"Yes, I noticed that."

"So what do we do?"

She looked at her watch. "I need to go home and get changed for this cut-price dinner."

"Having given me a lift first, obviously."

"Up the hill to the Oxford Bar?"

"We'll make a detective of you yet..."

Bia Bistrot was a small French-style restaurant on Colinton Road. Locals called the area Holy Corner due to a preponderance of churches at the intersection—Clarke counted four, though she couldn't be certain how many were still active. David Galvin was already at the table. He beamed a smile as he rose to greet her. Tall and slim, he was wearing a dark suit with a white shirt, open at the neck. As she leaned in for a peck on the cheek, she asked if this was as casual as he cared to dress.

"I was going for *Reservoir Dogs*," he explained. "Dapper but dangerous."

"Good try."

Galvin was only a couple of years younger than her and had been at the Procurator Fiscal's office since arriving in the city half a decade back. They'd worked together on a case the previous autumn and that was when he had asked her out for a drink, on the pretext of going over some notes. It was now their agreed code, and every week or so he would text to ask if she could spare an evening for "a consultation."

"I've not been here before," Clarke said, taking in her surroundings.

"I like it—and it's only five minutes from home."

"Not for me."

His smile faded. "I should have thought..."

"It's fine, David—plenty of cabs around." She accepted a menu and ordered a gin, lime and soda.

"I might try one of those," Galvin told the waiter. Then, to Clarke: "Busy day?"

"Not particularly. How about you?"

He offered a shrug. "Same old same old."

"What did you make of the Chief Constable's leaving do?"

"It was nice to be invited."

"Was that the Solicitor General's doing?"

"She does like to travel with a few bodies."

"To make her feel important?" Clarke guessed.

Another shrug. Galvin was concentrating on the menu. "Everything here's good," he said.

"Salmon rillettes, and then the lamb shoulder," Clarke decided.

"That didn't take long."

"I'm not one for dithering." Their drinks were arriving. They clinked glasses and sipped.

"How are things working out with your old sparring partner?" Galvin asked.

"John? He's doing okay so far."

"Toeing the line? Obeying orders?"

Clarke looked at him. "Something on your mind, David?"

Galvin shook his head. The waiter was hovering, so they ordered. There was bread on the table and Clarke tore at a chunk, realizing it had been some time since her last meal.

"Are we ordering wine?" her companion asked.

"A glass of white will do me."

"House?" the waiter asked.

"House," Clarke agreed.

"Small or large?"

"Large."

"Same for me," Galvin told him. Then he leaned back in his chair, closing his eyes for a second.

"Nice to switch off?" Clarke guessed.

"I'm not convinced the likes of you and me ever switch off, Siobhan. The motor is always idling."

"You wouldn't say that if you saw me slouched on the sofa with a tub of ice cream. But since we *do* seem to be talking shop..."

"Yes?"

"Have you ever met Patrick McCuskey?"

"The Justice Minister?" Galvin raised an eyebrow. "Well above my pay grade. I mean, I've been in rooms when he's been speaking."

"I looked him up on Google—Scottish National Party stalwart... face of the Yes campaign...married to a lawyer called Bethany..."

"She's American, I think. Practices commercial law in Glasgow."

"He's not got a legal background, though?"

"Studied it at university but ended up in politics instead—I dare say he did some cramming before taking on the Justice portfolio. What's this all about?"

"There's a son called Forbes. He goes out with a student called Jessica Traynor."

"No relation to Owen Traynor?" Galvin interrupted.

Clarke realized she didn't know Traynor's first name. "Who's Owen Traynor?"

"A businessman down south. There was a case a while back. It was in the papers."

"What happened?"

"One of his companies crashed and burned. A lot of angry investors."

"And?"

"The loudest and angriest investor got beaten up on his doorstep."

"This was where—in London?" Galvin nodded. "So what drew your attention?"

"It reminded me of a case we studied at university, that's all."

Clarke was picturing Jessica's father. "This Traynor has friends high up in the Met."

"Might not be him then. Anyway, you were telling me about Forbes McCuskey."

"Jessica Traynor was in a car smash. Found in the driver's seat, but we're not convinced she was driving at the time."

"Is she all right?"

"She will be."

Galvin was thoughtful. "Forbes did a runner?"

"We don't know that—we've not spoken to him yet."

"Wouldn't look good for his father."

"An embarrassment, certainly."

"Not to mention a possible criminal offense." Galvin sounded intrigued.

"We won't be bringing it to your lot for a while yet," Clarke cautioned. "Like I say, we've no real evidence—plus our boss doesn't like things messy."

"I know—I've met him. Is he still fretting about the future of Gayfield Square?"

"We all are."

"You'll be fine, Siobhan. It's mostly civilian posts you'll be losing."

"I'll have to do my own typing? And fingerprinting? Maybe train myself up to carry out autopsies...?"

They broke off as their starters arrived, and ate without saying much more. In the pause before the mains, Clarke took out her phone, thinking she might do a Google search for Owen Traynor, but she was getting no signal.

"Reception comes and goes," Galvin explained. "Hard to believe sometimes we're in the middle of a city."

"A capital city at that." She closed the phone down again. Their waiter had returned to ask how they were enjoying the wine. "It's fine," Clarke told him, though she noticed Galvin hadn't touched his. Nor had he made much headway with the aperitif.

"Keeping a clear head for the morning?" she chided him.

"Something like that," he replied.

Half an hour later, as the plates from their main courses were cleared, they were asked if they wanted to see the dessert list. Clarke looked at her companion and shook her head.

"Any teas or coffees?"

Clarke and Galvin shared another look. "There's coffee back at mine," he offered.

"And broadband?" she queried.

"And broadband," he confirmed. Then, after a pause: "Is this us continuing the consultation?"

"It is," Clarke said with a widening smile.

Rebus only had the one drink at the Oxford Bar, then took a cab back to the car park at Gayfield Square so he could pick up his Saab. He knew he could always change his mind, but knew too that he probably wouldn't. The lights were red at South Clerk Street. If he signaled right, he would be heading home. But when the light turned green he went straight ahead, towards Cameron Toll and Old Dalkeith Road. This time of night, the car parks at the Royal Infirmary were half empty, but Rebus pulled up at a double yellow line, sliding out the POLICE OFFICIAL BUSINESS sign from beneath the passenger seat and wedging it between dashboard and windscreen. He popped a stick of peppermint gum into his mouth, locked the car and walked into the hospital.

He was nearing Jessica's room when the door opened. He recognized Alice Bell. She was with a young man. He had tousled hair and wore faded baggy denims, plus a black V-neck T-shirt. Clean-shaven, with pale green eyes.

"Bit of a limp you've got there," Rebus said, indicating Forbes McCuskey's left leg.

"Twisted my ankle."

"Any whiplash to go with that?"

Bell was squeezing McCuskey's forearm. "This is the policeman," she told him.

"I'd kind of worked that out."

Rebus slid his hands into his pockets. "Any chance we could have a word, Forbes?"

"What about?"

"Jessica's accident."

"What do you need to speak to me for?"

"We usually like to interview witnesses—helps us compile an accurate picture..."

"But I wasn't there."

"And your ankle's just a coincidence?"

"Happened a few days back in the stairwell at Great King Street."

"That's true," Alice Bell confirmed hurriedly.

Rebus nodded slowly, eyes flitting between the two. "Coincidence, then. But we'd still like to get a few details from you."

"Tonight?"

"Tomorrow will do. You could come to Gayfield Square at ten."

McCuskey thought for a moment. "Ten should be okay," he decided.

Rebus handed him a card with his number on. "In case of complications. And if you need a lift back into town, I'll be heading that way in five minutes."

"We've got a taxi coming," Bell said.

"Tomorrow, then."

"Tomorrow," Forbes McCuskey agreed.

Jessica's father had appeared in the doorway. "Everything okay?" he asked.

"Fine, sir," Rebus assured him, watching as McCuskey and Bell headed for the exit. Rebus turned towards Traynor. "Still managing to stay awake, then?"

"I've found a hotel room in town. They're sending a car for me in half an hour or so."

They had made their way into the room. "Hello again," Rebus said by way of greeting to Jessica Traynor.

"Hello," she answered.

"Nice of your friends to drop in."

"Yes."

"Especially when it's such an effort for Forbes, him having hurt his leg and all."

She didn't bother replying.

"Is there something I should know?" Traynor asked.

Rebus shrugged. "Not really, sir. Just that there's a train of thought says maybe a careful driver wasn't behind the wheel." He turned towards the patient. She still lay flat on her back, and her hair needed a wash. "I'm thinking maybe he wasn't insured, or he had something in his system. All minor stuff as far as it goes, but fleeing the scene of an accident . . . and tampering with the scene . . ."

"Placing Jessica in the driver's seat, you mean?" The muscles in Traynor's face had tightened. He went to the side of the bed, looming over his daughter. "Is that what happened? Did that little shit leave you there, not even phoning an ambulance?"

But Jessica's eyes were closing. "He wasn't there," she said, her voice just above a whisper. "He wasn't there, he wasn't there."

Traynor saw Rebus out, walking with him all the way to the main foyer.

"We'll question him in the morning," Rebus explained. "See if we can move things along."

"And if not?"

"No huge harm done, I wouldn't have thought. I mean, you can blame him for speeding maybe, but unless one of them tells us the truth..." Rebus paused. "You know he's the son of a prominent politician?"

"Is he?"

Rebus smiled. "You pretended earlier you barely knew his name, but you seem the meticulous type to me—and you obviously dote on your daughter. I'd say you'd have checked up on any boyfriends she happened to mention."

"Okay," Traynor conceded, "maybe I do know who he is. Is this you telling me to let it drop?"

"Of course not."

"Because I know how it can be with the police and politicians..."

"Not around here, sir."

"Sure about that?"

Rebus nodded, and Traynor seemed to relax a little, staring past Rebus, eyes losing their focus. Then he blinked himself back awake, took Rebus's hand and shook it.

"Try to get some sleep, sir," Rebus advised. "And maybe buy Jessica a scooter next time."

This elicited the thinnest of smiles before Traynor turned and walked back into the hospital building. Rebus's phone was vibrating: a message from Siobhan. He opened the text.

Check out Owen Traynor's bio!

Owen Traynor's bio? Rebus watched as the tall, well-built figure receded, rounding a corner and disappearing from view. He tapped in Clarke's number but she wasn't answering, so he wandered outside, spat the chewing gum onto the roadway and lifted a cigarette from its packet.

DAY TWO

3

Forbes McCuskey was a few minutes early. He carried a Harris Tweed satchel over one shoulder and wore a three-quarter-length military-style coat, powder blue with brass buttons. Rebus led him to an interview room, where Siobhan Clarke was waiting. She had placed her folder—the one from the crash site—on the table in front of her. She gestured for McCuskey to sit down opposite. There was no chair for Rebus, but that was by agreement—he preferred to lean against a wall, always in the eye line of the person being questioned.

"I'm Detective Inspector Clarke. You've already met Detective Sergeant Rebus."

"So you're his superior?" McCuskey broke in.

"I'm the senior officer here, yes."

McCuskey nodded his understanding. He sat low in the metal chair with his legs splayed, as if he didn't find it uncomfortable in the least. Clarke had opened the folder. She positioned a photo of the VW Golf in front of the young man.

"Jessica was incredibly fortunate."

"I can see that," he said, nodding again.

"Lucky someone was driving past—they phoned for an ambulance."

"Right."

"If someone had been with her in the car, *they* could have called the ambulance sooner. Might have made all the difference."

"But she's going to be okay—she told me."

"It's still going to take her longer to recover," Clarke bluffed, giving the news time to sink in. "Odd place for her to be. Has she told you what she was doing there?"

"Said she just felt like a drive."

"Her father tells us she's not the kind to put her foot down..."

"Maybe she hit a patch of oil."

"Road looked fine when we checked." Clarke made show of searching the folder, pulling out another photo. "Then there's this."

"Yes?" McCuskey's eyes had narrowed in apparent concentration.

"It's one of her boots, found lying in the passenger-side foot well. Any notion how it might have ended up there?"

McCuskey gave a little pout, shaking his head.

"See, the obvious conclusion—obvious to us, that is—is that Jessica wasn't alone in the vehicle. She was the passenger. And after the smash, the driver hauled her across so it would look like her fault. Then he scarpered."

McCuskey's eyes met Clarke's. "And you think that was me?"

"Well, was it?"

"What does Jessica say?" When this received no answer, McCuskey barked out a short laugh. "I went to see her last night. If I'd run off and left her, would she have been so happy to see me? Would there have been tears in her eyes when we kissed?"

"How did you twist your ankle, Forbes?" The question had come from Rebus. McCuskey turned his attention towards him.

"I told you—I just got one of the steps wrong on Jessica's stairwell."

"Seen a doctor about it?"

"It'll be fine."

"Any other bruises or aches and pains?"

"I wasn't in the car with her. I don't even drive."

"You don't drive?" Clarke couldn't help glancing in Rebus's direction as McCuskey shook his head in confirmation.

"Do your parents know you're here?" Rebus asked into the silence.

"No."

"Haven't you told them about Jessica?"

"Not yet."

"How about her father—do you get on with him?"

"Only met him last night."

"He has a bit of a rep. You should Google him, that's what I did." Rebus had taken a few steps towards the table. "Not the sort of character you'd want to cross."

"Really?"

"An investor in one of his companies started bad-mouthing him. Ended up in intensive care. Afterwards, he kept tight-lipped about who'd thumped him. And that's just *one* of the stories." Rebus paused. "Which is why it's a shame I let slip our little theory—the one about you being responsible."

"What?" For the first time since entering the room, McCuskey looked nervous. Clarke was studying Rebus, trying to work out if he was telling the truth or bluffing. When he looked at her, his face didn't change. Truth, then.

"You have to tell him you're wrong," McCuskey was saying. "You've spoken to Jessica and me—why would we lie?"

"I don't know," Rebus said. "But something like this...it starts small but it can snowball, gathering up all kinds of crap as it rolls downhill."

"I can't confess to something I didn't do."

"Quite right," Clarke said, gathering together the photographs. "So that seems to be that. We just need an address for you, and you can be on your way."

McCuskey stared at her. "And then what?"

Clarke shrugged, closing the folder. "If we need to talk again, we'll let you know." She handed him a sheet of paper and a ballpoint pen. "Address, please." As he wrote, she asked if he was a student. He nodded. "Which subject?"

"Art history."

"Same as Jessica and her flatmate."

"We're all in second year."

"Is that how you met?"

"At a party." He had finished writing. The details were just about legible.

"Arden Street?" she checked.

"Yes."

"That's in Marchmont, isn't it?"

McCuskey nodded. Clarke and Rebus shared a look: same street as Rebus's flat. He glanced at the tenement number: about six doors up from him on the other side of the road.

"Thanks again for coming in," Clarke was saying, rising to her feet. McCuskey shook hands with both detectives and a uniform was summoned to show him out.

"Well?" Clarke asked, once he had gone.

"Girlfriend's covering for him."

"He's got a point, though—why would she do that?"

"Could be she's the forgiving type. He goes to her bedside, whispers a few sweet nothings and flutters those eyelashes—and that's when they prepare their story."

Clarke considered this, mouth a thin determined line. "And you really told Owen Traynor the whole story? After your little trip to the Ox, a few beers inside you...?"

"I just dropped in to see how the patient was doing. Coincided with McCuskey and Alice Bell leaving."

Clarke was shaking her head slowly. "This is exactly the kind of thing you shouldn't be doing..." She broke off as James Page appeared in the doorway.

"What shouldn't John be doing?" he inquired.

"Putting a bet on Raith Rovers for promotion," Rebus answered.

"I'm inclined to agree." Page paused. "So where are we with this car crash?"

"Not much further along," Clarke conceded.

"In which case, probably time to drop it, wouldn't you say? Nothing for us there, no point wasting effort."

"The boyfriend," Rebus said, "the one we think may have been in the car..."

"What about him?"

"He's the son of Pat McCuskey."

"Justice Minister?"

"And poster boy for an independent Scotland." Rebus knew his boss's feelings on the topic—like everyone else in the office, he'd had his ear bent by Page about the need for Scotland to remain part of the UK. "McCuskey heads the Yes campaign."

Page digested this information. "What's your thinking, John? A wee call to a friendly journalist?"

"Only if we can find something that will stick. Otherwise it looks *too* political."

"Agreed."

"Hang on," Clarke said. "You're planning to use the son to get at the father? Hardly seems fair."

"We all know how *you'll* be voting, Siobhan."

The blood rose to Clarke's cheeks. "I just don't think..."

But Page had turned his back and was marching away. "Another day or two," he called out. "See what you can find."

Clarke stared hard at Rebus. He spread his arms in a show of appeasement.

"It's not as if we have anything else to do," he argued.

"And that little game you just played..." She stabbed a finger in Page's direction.

"I knew damned fine he'd go for it."

"He might, but I won't."

"You're disappointed in me." Rebus tried to look contrite. "But you have to admit, it's not your typical setup—Pat McCuskey and Owen Traynor..."

"I do wonder how a dodgy businessman like Traynor ends up pulling favors with the Met."

"Met are still a law to themselves, Siobhan—way we used to be."

"A time you clearly yearn for. Meantime, this lets you stir stuff up for the hell of it."

"But sometimes that's how we find gold, too."

"And what sort of gold do you expect to find this time?" She folded her arms in a show of defiance.

"The stirring's the fun part," Rebus said. "You should have learned that by now."

"Your dad's not here?" Rebus asked.

Jessica Traynor looked better. The device around her head had been replaced by a simple neck brace, and the top of her bed had been raised a little, so that she no longer had to stare at the ceiling.

"What do you want?" she asked.

"Just thought I'd see how you're doing."

"I'm fine."

"Good to hear."

"My father's at his hotel."

Rebus noticed the mobile phone in her right hand. "Heard from Forbes today?"

"A couple of texts."

"He tells me you met at a party."

"That's right. I went there with Alice and got talking to Forbes in the kitchen."

"Just like the song, eh?"

"What song?"

"Before your time," Rebus admitted, gesturing towards her phone. "A couple of texts, you say—I'm guessing one before he came in to talk to us and one after?"

She ignored this. "I'm still not really sure why you're here..."

Rebus offered a shrug. "It just bugs me when people lie to my face. I start to wonder what it is they're afraid of. In your case, it might be something or nothing, but until I know for sure..."

"Would it really matter if Forbes was in the car?" She was staring at him.

"If he was in the car, that means he left you there. Didn't phone for help or flag down a passing motorist..."

"I don't see why the police would be interested in any of that."

Rebus gave another shrug. "What about your father? Won't he be interested?"

"It's not really any of his business, is it?"

"Fair enough." Rebus watched as she checked the screen of her phone. Maybe she had messages and maybe she didn't. "How long till you get to leave here?"

"I've got to talk to a physio first."

"They'll probably tell you to stay away from fast cars for a while." She managed a half-smile.

"And country roads at night," Rebus added. "West Lothian isn't called the Badlands for nothing."

She looked up at him. "Badlands?"

"Because it's largely lawless."

"That explains a lot." Rebus waited for more, but she pressed her lips together. A classic tell: she knew she'd let something slip.

"Jessica, if there's anything you feel you need to—"

"Get out!" she yelled, just as a nurse entered the room. "I want him to leave! Please!"

Rebus already had his hands up in a show of surrender. He walked past the nurse and into the corridor.

Badlands?

That explains a lot.

Explained what, though? Something had happened that evening. Rebus made a little mental note to check back—the comms room at Bilston Glen would have records of anything that had been reported. Illegal races? Locals trying to scare the tourists?

"Something or nothing," he muttered to himself, exiting the hospital and readying to light a cigarette. A black cab had pulled up. The passenger had left the backseat, preparing to pay the driver at the passenger-side window. Basic error by someone who was used to a different system—in Edinburgh you paid before getting out. Rebus walked over and waited behind Owen Traynor. He seemed to be wearing the same suit but a fresh shirt. The driver passed over some change and a receipt, and Traynor turned away, startled to find Rebus right in front of him.

"Bloody hell," he said.

"Sorry, sir. I was just leaving."

"You've been to see Jessica?"

Rebus nodded.

"And?"

"And what, Mr. Traynor?"

"Do you still think that boyfriend of hers was behind the steering wheel?"

"It's a scenario."

"Well maybe she'll tell me."

Rebus doubted it, but didn't say as much. "Probably simpler for everyone if we just drop it," he suggested instead. "Whatever the truth is, Jessica's standing by Mr. McCuskey."

"Yes, but if he did that to her…"

"Like I say, sir, better to just let it be. We don't want anyone doing something daft, do we?"

Traynor stared at him.

"You see what I'm saying?" Rebus went on.

"I'm not sure that I do," Traynor drawled.

"You have a reputation, Mr. Traynor. And I'm interested how you came by your friends in the Met."

"Maybe I'm just a member of the right clubs." Traynor began edging past Rebus, making for the hospital entrance.

"My town, my rules," Rebus called out. But Owen Traynor showed no sign of having heard.

"Thanks for meeting me," Malcolm Fox said, rising from the table and extending a hand towards Siobhan Clarke. "What can I get you?"

"Brian's already on it." She nodded towards the counter. The café owner was busy at the espresso machine. The place was only a hundred yards or so down Leith Walk from Gayfield Square, but she didn't know any other cops who frequented it. Making it a safe rendezvous, more or less.

Clarke slid onto the banquette opposite Fox. They'd met before, but just barely.

"I heard you were on your way out of the Complaints," she said. "That can't be comfortable."

"No," Fox agreed, rubbing a hand across the tabletop.

Reorganization again—internal-affairs officers were not exempt. Their Edinburgh office was about to be trimmed. Besides which, Fox had served his allotted time. He was being shipped back to CID, where he would work alongside men and women he'd investigated, in stations he'd investigated, stations where he would be mistrusted if not reviled.

The café owner brought over Clarke's cappuccino and asked Fox if he wanted a refill. Fox nodded.

"Black coffee, no sugar," he reminded the man.

"Because you're already too sweet?" Clarke pretended to guess, eliciting a wry smile. She leaned back a little and turned to watch the pedestrians on the pavement outside. "So why am I fraternizing with the enemy?" she asked.

"Maybe because you know I'm not the enemy. The Complaints exists so that cops like you—the good cops—can thrive."

"I bet you've said that before."

"Many times."

She turned towards him. He still had the same wry smile on his face.

"You need a favor?" she guessed, receiving a slow nod by way of reply. His coffee arrived and he touched the rim of the saucer with the tips of his fingers.

"It's to do with John Rebus," he stated.

"Of course it is."

"I've got to talk to him."

"I'm not stopping you."

"The thing is, Siobhan, I need him to talk. And if the request comes from me, he'll doubtless respond with a few choice words."

"Request?"

"Order, then. And it won't be coming from me, not ultimately..."

"The Solicitor General?" Clarke suggested. Fox tried not to look too surprised that she knew. "I saw her making a beeline for you at the Chief's leaving do."

"She's entrusted me with a job."

"A Complaints job?"

"My last," he said quietly, staring at his saucer.

"And if you break a sweat, she rewards you how? A big promotion? Something to lift you off the pitch and into the directors' box?"

"You're good at this." Fox's admiring tone sounded genuine enough.

Clarke knew now what David Galvin had been hinting at during dinner at Bia Bistrot. *How are things working out with your old sparring partner? Toeing the line? Obeying orders?*

"You really think I'm going to hand you John on a plate?"

"It's not Rebus I want—it's people he knows, or used to know. I'm going back thirty years."

"Summerhall?"

Fox paused and studied her. "He's talked about it?" She shook her head. "So how do you know?" But he had worked it out within a few seconds. "That leaving do," he said, almost to himself. "Eamonn Paterson was there. I saw him with Rebus..."

"Then you know as much about Summerhall as I do. And I'm still no further forward as to why I should help you."

"Whatever happens, I'm going to end up asking Rebus some questions. I just think it would smooth things a little if there was a referee of some kind."

"A referee?"

"To ensure fairness—on both sides."

She took a sip of coffee, then another. Fox did likewise, almost exactly mirroring her.

"Is that supposed to be an empathy thing?" she queried.

"What?"

"Aping me to make me think I'm the one with the power?"

He seemed to consider this. "You picking up your cup reminded me mine was there, that's all. But thanks for the tip—I'll bear it in mind."

She stared at him, trying to gauge the level of game being played.

"It's good coffee, by the way," he added, this time slurping from his cup. Clarke couldn't help but smile. She went back to watching pedestrians while she considered her options.

"Thirty years is a long time," she said eventually.

"It is."

"Something's supposed to have happened at Summerhall?"

"Possibly."

"And it involved John?"

"Tangentially—I don't think he'd been there that long. He was pretty junior..."

"You know he's not going to give up any of the men he worked with?"

"Unless I can persuade him otherwise."

"Good luck with that," Clarke said.

"My problem, not yours. I'd just like it if you could get him to sit down with me."

"So what are we talking about? A few statements altered? Lies told in court? Prisoners tripping and falling on their way to the cells?" She waited for him to answer.

"A bit more serious than that," he obliged, placing his cup back on its saucer with the utmost care. "So Rebus has never talked to you about it?"

"Summerhall, you mean?" She watched him nod. "Never a word."

"In which case," Fox said, lowering his voice despite the fact they were the café's only customers, "you maybe won't have heard of the Saints?"

"Only the band."

"This was a band of sorts too, I suppose. Saints of the Shadow Bible, they called themselves."

"Meaning what?"

"I'm not exactly sure—the files from the Solicitor General's office don't seem to be complete."

"Sounds vaguely Masonic."

"That might not be too wide of the mark."

"And officers at Summerhall were members?"

"They were the only members, Siobhan. If you worked there as a detective at that period, you were a Saint of the Shadow Bible..."

4

Rebus sat in his car, staring at the bungalow. Bringing the Saab meant he couldn't drink, but it would help if he felt the need to get away in a hurry. The sky was clear, the moon visible. Only a degree or so above zero, frost glinting on the surface of the road. Rebus's hands gripped the steering wheel. He hadn't seen anyone go in yet. There were lights on in both downstairs windows. Dormers built into the slate-tiled roof above, curtained and dark. Rebus eased his own window down and got a cigarette going. Maybe nobody was going to turn up. Seven, he'd been told, and it was now ten after. What if he went to the door and found it was just going to be him, Dod Blantyre and Maggie? Wouldn't that be cozy? He sucked on the cigarette, narrowing his eyes as the smoke stung them. Would Dod be bed-bound? Maybe in the living room, with a commode pushed against one wall? Maggie exhausted from coping with him, the life draining from her? Would she ask why Rebus never called round, never sent a Christmas card in exchange for the one she still always dispatched?

Hope to catch up soon. Love from Dod and Maggie.

Her husband's name first, but her handwriting. Did he really want to spend the evening confined with them? Did they have anything to talk about, other than the old days? Would she have made sandwiches or some kind of supper, so that he had to balance plate and fork and glass while he sat or stood?

"Bloody hell," he muttered, flicking ash out of the window.

"That's littering," a voice boomed, while a fist smashed down on the Saab's roof. Rebus nearly dropped his cigarette. Cursing, he stared out at the stooped, grinning figure of Eamonn Paterson.

"You trying to give me a heart attack?" Rebus pretended to complain.

"Old copper's trick—the ability to creep up on a suspect."

Rebus wound up the window, yanked the key from the ignition and opened his door.

"Don't tell me you walked?" he asked, climbing out.

"Caught the bus." Paterson nodded towards the Saab. "Is this you offering to be the designated driver?"

"Just like in Summerhall days."

"It was only once or twice you had to drop us all home."

"And clean the sick off the backseat."

"Not the same car, though?"

"Not quite."

"I seem to remember your wife complaining the smell wouldn't shift."

"Ended up selling it at a discount," Rebus said with a nod.

"The car or the wife?" Paterson gave a wink and patted Rebus's shoulder. "Feel up to visiting the invalid? Only it looked to me like you were getting cold feet there."

"Just worried I was going to be flying solo."

"As if the Saints would let that happen." Another pat of reassurance and Paterson led the way to the bungalow's front door.

It was a few moments before Maggie Blantyre answered the ring. Bathed in warmth and welcoming light, she didn't seem to have aged at all. Ash-blond hair falling to her bared neck, broad-shouldered but with a narrow waist. She wore plenty of expensive-looking jewelry and her makeup was immaculate.

"Boys," she said, opening her arms for an embrace from either man. "Come in out of the cold."

Paterson received a peck on both cheeks before stepping inside, then it was Rebus's turn. Her eyes lingered on his afterwards, and she pressed her fingers to his face, rubbing at the lipstick she'd left there.

"John," she said. "I was hoping you'd make it." Then she led him indoors by the arm, closing the door on the outside world.

"Divest yourselves." She nodded towards the banister, where a camel-colored woolen coat was already draped, a red scarf trailing from one pocket.

"Stefan's here?" Paterson surmised.

"You're the detective," Maggie Blantyre drawled. "You tell me."

"I always said camel makes him look like a used-car salesman." He hung up his padded jacket. Rebus wrestled with his own coat until Maggie helped him. He noticed a stairlift fixed to the wall at the foot of the stairs.

"I wasn't sure if we were expected to bring a bottle," he apologized.

"Nothing but yourselves," she assured him, touching his arm again. "Now follow me."

They passed a small dining room and entered the lounge. Dod Blantyre was seated in an ordinary-looking armchair, dressed and with a tumbler of orange liquid on an occasional table next to him. Stefan Gilmour had risen from the sofa, swapping his whisky from right hand to left.

"Hiya, Porkbelly," he said. The two men shook before Gilmour turned to Rebus. "John—it's been a while."

"Stefan." Rebus examined his old boss. The man was in his early seventies, but looked at least a decade younger. He wore a black T-shirt under a tailored jacket, with rust-colored cords and brown loafers. What hair he could boast had been engineered to cover as much of his scalp as possible. Piercing blue eyes and a healthy glow to his cheeks.

"You staying in town?" Paterson asked him. Gilmour shook his head.

"My driver will take me back."

"Driver, eh?" Paterson gestured towards Rebus. "I've got one of those tonight too." Then he headed to Dod Blantyre's corner of the room, squeezing a shoulder in greeting.

"You'll forgive me if I don't get up." One whole side of Blantyre's face hung lower than the other, making his words slightly slurred.

"You're fine, Dod," Paterson told him. Blantyre nodded and turned his attention to Rebus.

"And here's the prodigal," he said. "I reckoned the drink had got you, or you'd moved to Spain."

"Just working hard," Rebus replied with a shrug of apology.

"Well, you're here now. Maggie, are we going to let the man die of thirst?"

There was a drinks cabinet open. Maggie already seemed to know that Paterson would want a Highland Park.

"Same for you, John?" she asked.

"I better have one of those." Rebus nodded towards the glass of orange by Blantyre's side.

"With or without the three measures of vodka?"

"Without."

"Dod knows he shouldn't really be drinking." She began pouring juice from the liter-sized carton.

"Doctors try to drain all the fun out of life," Blantyre complained. Again Rebus had to strain to pick out his old colleague's words.

"Sit yourselves down," Maggie demanded, handing over the glasses. There was just about enough room on the sofa for the three visitors, Maggie settling herself on the spare armchair. "Here's to us," she said, toasting the room at large. Then, realizing her error, she got up again and went over to her husband's side, lifting his tumbler and helping him hold it while he drank through a straw. When a dribble settled on his chin, she brushed it off with the back of one ringed finger.

"Nice of you all to come," she said, sitting down again. "Isn't it, Dod?"

"Aye," he acknowledged. "The Saints of the Shadow Bible..."

"Been a while since I heard those words," Stefan Gilmour said with a smile.

"That's because you move in different circles these days," Paterson reminded him. "Footballers and film stars..."

"Not as many as you might think."

"Still got that hotel going up in Dubai, though?"

"Just about weathering the financial sandstorm," Gilmour conceded. Seated at the other end of the sofa, Rebus couldn't really see his old boss without leaning forward. Back in Summerhall, Gilmour had been the DI, with Paterson and Blantyre as DSs and Rebus as a lowly detective constable, alongside a younger DC called Frazer Spence. But Spence had died a decade back in a motorbike smash in Greece. The eventual funeral had been the last time all four remaining members of the Saints had been gathered in the same place.

"What are you thinking, John?" Maggie Blantyre asked, swirling her glass of white wine.

"I'm thinking I shouldn't have brought my car." He made show of examining his orange juice.

"Leave it where it is, then—drop by tomorrow and get it."

But he shook his head.

"I hear you're still working," Dod Blantyre said.

"I was retired for a while—did some civvy stuff for the Cold Case Unit."

"That the one set up by Gregor Magrath?"

"It's been wound up now. I reapplied for CID, and got lucky."

"Bit like the old codgers they take on at B and Q," Paterson joked.

"John was always a hard worker," Blantyre said.

"Did that stroke affect your memory, Dod?" Paterson asked with a snort. "John was about the laziest bugger going." He turned towards Rebus. "Back me up here, John!"

"You're confusing John with poor Frazer," Gilmour interrupted. "Frazer was the boy who'd always be nipping to the shops."

"Is that right?" Paterson was frowning as he tried to remember.

"Don't give Porkbelly any more whisky," Blantyre warned his wife. "He's got too few synapses left as it is."

There was a bit of laughter, after which they concentrated on their drinks. This is okay, Rebus thought to himself. But then he knew these men; the mood could change...

"Does anyone still have the Shadow Bible?" Gilmour asked into the silence.

"Don't know what happened to it," Blantyre said. "Maggie thinks it might have gone into a skip when we cleared out the garage."

"That's a shame."

Blantyre looked at Gilmour. "I'm betting you're glad you got out when you did—more money than us poor buggers will ever have."

"How many hotels have you got now, Stefan?" The question came from Maggie.

"They're not exactly mine. I just seem to have landed the job of heading the company."

"How many, though?"

"Seventeen at the last count."

"You must rack up the air miles."

"First-name terms with the staff at Emirates."

She smiled, seeming pleased for him. "And are you still dating that model?"

"She's not a model—she used to be on TV."

"Same sort of thing, though—you need the looks."

Gilmour nodded slowly. "We're still together," he acknowledged. "Not married, though."

"We read about you in the papers—all that stuff to do with the referendum."

"'Stefan Gilmour Says No,'" Paterson parroted. "This you pushing for your knighthood?"

"And what happened," Dod Blantyre added, "to that plan you and your football pal had to buy Tynecastle?"

"This is turning into an interrogation," Gilmour pretended to complain. "And we all know how those can turn nasty." He smiled and drank from his glass.

"How about you, John?" Maggie asked Rebus. "You split up with Rhona, didn't you? Just the one kid . . . ?"

"Leave the man in peace," Blantyre complained to his wife. Then, to Rebus: "Too many soap operas, John—that's the trouble."

"Should I pop the pies in the oven, then?" Maggie asked, starting to get to her feet. Her husband nodded.

"Pies?" Paterson queried.

"Dod thought it would be a nice touch. He says you lot ate nothing else for about two years."

"Certainly seemed that way." Paterson patted not his own stomach but Rebus's. "With John here and Frazer doing the fetching."

"I'll just be a minute then." She went over to her husband's armchair and kissed him on the forehead before making for the kitchen. As soon as she was gone, Blantyre asked that the door be closed. Stefan Gilmour obliged.

"All three of you, over here," Blantyre demanded. The three visitors approached his chair. "Means I don't have to talk too loud."

"What's going on, Dod?" Gilmour asked, keeping his own voice low.

"Last few times I've been to see the white coats, I've not let Maggie come with me. So she doesn't know things are as bad as they are. It's not just the stroke. There's plenty else wrong with the engine."

"Sorry to hear that," Paterson said.

"I've got a few months yet—at least I hope I have. But word's come to me that they may not be as pleasant as I'd like them to be." He looked at each man in turn. "Elinor Macari's on the warpath."

"Macari?" Gilmour queried.

"The Solicitor General," Rebus informed him.

"She wants the Saunders case looked at."

"What the hell for?"

"Because she can. Double jeopardy's been axed, if you hadn't heard."

"I hadn't," Gilmour admitted.

"Not axed exactly," Rebus felt it necessary to add. "But in certain cases a retrial can be requested."

"It was thirty years ago," Gilmour argued. "We can't be expected to remember..."

"Won't stop them asking." Paterson turned towards his friend. "Fancy seeing your photo in the papers, Stefan? And not in a clinch with a TV star but next to a mug shot of Billy Saunders?"

"Is Saunders even in the land of the living?" Gilmour inquired.

"Macari wouldn't go after him if he wasn't," Blantyre said. Then: "My throat's dry—can one of you...?"

Paterson lifted the tumbler and angled the straw towards Blantyre's lips. Gilmour produced a clean cotton handkerchief with which to dab the man's chin.

"So what do we do?" he asked.

"I'm just giving fair warning," Blantyre told him. "Few months from now, it won't matter a damn to me. You lot, on the other hand..."

Gilmour turned towards Rebus. "You're the only one of us with a finger in the CID pie, John—can you find out what's happening?"

"I can try," Rebus conceded.

"Without looking like there's something you're trying to keep covered up," Paterson added.

"Covered up?" Rebus echoed, as Maggie came back into the room.

"Oh!" she said, face growing fearful at the sight of all three guests huddled around her husband. "Has something...?"

"I'm fine," Blantyre assured her. "Just been taking a drink."

She pressed a hand to her chest. "You scared me there." Then she gestured back towards the kitchen. "About fifteen minutes for those pies—and I think I need to step out and have a cigarette."

"I might join you," Rebus said. He fixed his eyes on those of Dod Blantyre. "If that's okay...?"

"Fine," Blantyre agreed, after only a moment's hesitation.

Rebus followed Maggie through the small kitchen and into the back garden. There was a patio, its furniture covered, awaiting better weather, with a patch of lawn beyond. She lit her own cigarette before handing her gold lighter to Rebus. She had folded her arms in a show of keeping warm.

"Want me to fetch a coat?" he asked. But she shook her head.

"I get too hot in the house sometimes. Dod likes the thermostat turned up."

"The two of you have been managing okay?"

"What else can you do?" She flicked a strand of hair from one eye.

"Must be hard, though."

"Can we change the subject?"

"If you like."

She thought for a moment. "Actually, no, let's stick to that exact subject—why are you all here?"

"I'm not sure I follow."

"When was the last time the four of you were in the same room?"

"Frazer's funeral."

"And that was ten years back—so why now?" She held up a hand. "Don't bother trying any flannel. I've seen enough of it in my time to open a pajama factory." She took a step closer. He could smell her perfume. "It's because he's dying, right? He's dying and he thinks he can keep it from me?" She saw the answer in his eyes and turned away, sucking hard on her cigarette, exhaling through her nostrils so that her whole face was wreathed in smoke.

"Maggie," he began, but she was shaking her head. Eventually she took a deep breath and began to compose herself.

"Is that still your address?" she asked. "The one I send the card to every year?"

"Yes."

"You never bothered moving? Did you think Rhona was coming back?"

"Not especially." He shifted his feet.

"We like to stay tied to the past, though, don't we? Dod still talks about Summerhall. Sometimes I think it's a priest he needs rather than a wife." She saw his look and held up a hand. "He spares me whatever gory details there are. Different times, different rules, isn't that right?"

"It might be what we tell ourselves." Rebus examined the glowing tip of his cigarette.

"Something's got him worried, though, hasn't it—not just the cold hard fact that he's dying? And it's to do with the Saints?"

"You best ask him."

She smiled. "I'm asking you, John. I'm asking my old pal." And when he didn't answer she leaned in and kissed him on the lips, kissed him slowly, brushing away the evidence with a finger afterwards. "He never did find out," she said, her voice just above a whisper. "Not unless you told him."

Rebus shook his head, saying nothing.

"You were just boys, the lot of you. Boys playing at being cowboys." She ran a different finger down his cheek and neck.

"And what were you, Maggie?" he asked as she inspected the contours of his face.

"I was the same as I am now, John. No more, no less. You, on the other hand..."

"There's certainly a bit more of me."

"But you seem sadder, too. It makes me wonder why you think you need to keep doing the job you do."

"So what was I like back then?"

"There was an electric wire running through you."

"Lucky I got that seen to."

"I'm not so sure." She took one final draw on her cigarette and flicked it into a nearby pot. "Better get back indoors before tongues start wagging. Not that you Saints don't trust each other..."

Rebus finished his own cigarette and dropped it next to hers. "It was just a name we gave ourselves," he explained. "It doesn't mean anything."

"Try telling that to Dod." She paused at the back door, her hand turning the handle. "Far as he's concerned, you lot came straight from a comic book."

"I don't remember too many superheroes stoking up on pies," Rebus argued.

"You probably don't wear your underpants outside your trousers either," she agreed. "Unless there's something you want to tell me…"

Paterson's home was a semidetached Victorian property on Ferry Road. Most of his neighbors ran bed-and-breakfast operations, meaning gardens turned into rudimentary car parks. Paterson's frontage, however, was distinguished by mature trees and an established holly hedge. He had been a widower for seven years, but showed no sign of wishing to downsize.

"Kids are always nagging me," he confided to Rebus in the Saab. He had sunk enough whisky to make him sleepy, his sentences drifting off. "Less maintenance with a nice modern flat somewhere, but I like it fine where I am."

"Same goes for me," Rebus said. "Couple of spare rooms I'll never need."

"You get to our age, who can be bothered? Look at poor Dod— you never know what's waiting for you round the next corner. Best just to get on with things and not get too…" He couldn't find the right words, so spun his hands around one another instead.

"Wrapped up in stuff?" Rebus suggested.

"Aye, maybe." Paterson exhaled noisily. "Stefan's done well for himself though, eh? Millions in the bank and jetting around the place." Rebus nodded his agreement. "And Maggie's still a lovely woman—Dod got lucky there."

"That he did."

"She's still bonny and…" Paterson broke off, brow furrowing. "There's a poem I'm trying to remember—bonny and something and maybe something else after that."

"I'm on tenterhooks."

Paterson looked at him, trying to focus. "You're a cold man, John. You always were. I don't mean..." He thought for a moment. "What do I mean?"

"Cold as in standoffish?" Rebus suggested.

"Not that, no. It's more that you never liked to show emotion—afraid you might get the sympathy vote."

"And I didn't want that?"

"You did not," Paterson agreed. "We were battlers, the lot of us. That's who joined the police back then—not college graduates and the like. And if we had half a brain, we maybe made it to CID..." He paused, peering through the windscreen. "We're here."

"I know."

Paterson stared at him. "How?"

"Because we've been sat outside your house the past five minutes." Rebus held out a hand for Paterson to shake. "Good to see you again, Porkbelly."

"Are you glad now you went?"

"I'm not sure."

"And the thing Dod mentioned—do you think you can...?"

"Maybe. No promises, though."

Paterson released Rebus's hand. "Good man," he said, as though only now coming to a decision on this. Then he pushed open his door and started to get out.

"Helps if you unbuckle your seat belt," Rebus reminded him. A moment or two later and Paterson was free, weaving down the path towards his front door. A security light came on and he waved without looking back, letting Rebus know he could take it from here. With a tired smile, Rebus put the Saab into first and tried to calculate the simplest route home.

It took him twenty minutes, with a Mick Taylor CD playing on the stereo and traffic lights that seemed to turn green at his every approach. The phone in his pocket buzzed, but he waited until he was parked outside his tenement before taking it out and checking the text. It was from Siobhan Clarke.

Can we speak?

Rebus stayed in the car while he called her. She picked up straightaway.

"What is it?" he asked.

"I stopped by your flat a couple of times—wanted to do this face to face."

"Do what?"

"Intercede."

He wasn't sure he had heard her right. "Intercede?"

"On Malcolm Fox's behalf. He's requesting the pleasure of your company at some point in the next day or so."

"And he's too scared to ask me direct?"

"Something like that."

"And you're 'interceding' because...?"

"Because sometimes a friendly face helps." She paused. "But I know you're going to say no to him anyway."

"Am I?"

"He's the Complaints, John—you're hardwired to spit in his face."

Hardwired...He remembered Maggie's words: *there was an electric wire running through you...*

"Some truth in that," he said.

"So what should I tell him? Bearing in mind I'm a fragile flower of a soul."

"Your patter's pish, DI Clarke."

"But you're still going to say no?"

"I'm going to say tomorrow, the back room of the Ox, twelve noon."

There was silence on the line.

"You still there?" he asked.

"I'm not sure."

"Twelve tomorrow," he confirmed.

"Just like that?"

"Just like that."

"I'm never going to sleep now—not until you tell me why." She paused again. "It's almost as if you already knew."

"Is it?"

"Knew he was on his way," she went on. "But how is that possible? I'm the only one he told…"

"Magicians never reveal their secrets, Siobhan."

"You know it's to do with Summerhall? And the Saints of the Shadow Book?"

"Shadow Bible," Rebus corrected her.

"But you know?" she persisted.

"One thing I don't know, though…"

"Yes?"

"At this meeting tomorrow, will you be on my side or his?"

"What do you think?"

"Might be wiser not to be there at all."

"But then who would stop you lamping him?"

"I'm not going to lamp him, Shiv—I want to hear what he's got to say."

"It concerns a man called Billy Saunders."

"Well of course it does," Rebus said, ending the call and exiting the car.

DAY THREE

5

At twelve the next day, Rebus was seated at a corner table with a pint of IPA. The Oxford Bar consisted of two rooms—one containing the bar itself, and the other tables and chairs. The walls of the back room were lined with reclaimed church pews. A coal fire had been lit, and the place smelled of smoke, with undertones of bleach from the morning's sluicing. A large window gave onto Young Street, but the natural light was only ever fitful. Rebus had taken a couple of sips from his glass. There was no one else in the back room and only Kirsty the barmaid out front, the TV news keeping her company. When the door to the outside world rattled open, Rebus allowed himself a thin smile—of course Malcolm Fox would be punctual. The man himself appeared, spotting Rebus and moving towards the table. He drew out a chair and sat down, not bothering to find out if the offer of a handshake would be rejected. Siobhan Clarke was in the doorway, pointing towards Rebus's drink. He shook his head and she retreated to the bar, appearing again moments later with two glasses of sparkling water.

"Thanks for meeting me," Malcolm Fox said, fussing with the positioning of his glass on the beer mat. Clarke squeezed into the same pew as Rebus, but equidistant between the two men, saying nothing. "Mind if I ask: why here?"

"There's an old Edinburgh tradition of transacting business in pubs," Rebus explained. "Besides which, it shows how keen you are."

Fox looked at him. "Keen how?"

"You could have made it all official—summoning me to HQ—instead of which, here we are on my turf. Means you're keen, bordering on desperate."

Fox decided to let this go. "I'm here at the behest of the Solicitor General. She's looking at reopening some old cases."

"Now that the double jeopardy ruling's been tweaked."

"That's right."

"And she's got Billy Saunders in her sights?"

"For starters."

Rebus turned towards Clarke. "How much has he told you?"

"Thirty years back," Clarke answered, "Saunders was put on trial for beating a man to death. The case collapsed. Later on, he served time for another offense and admitted to a prisoner that he'd done it. Didn't matter, as he couldn't be tried a second time."

"But now he can," Fox added.

"Then what's Elinor Macari waiting for?" Rebus asked.

"The case against Saunders collapsed because of the actions of Summerhall CID. Evidence was tainted, interviews hadn't been conducted properly…"

"I seem to remember our DI at the time took the bullet."

"Stefan Gilmour, you mean? Eventually he did, yes. But there were some who said that was because he wanted to put a lid on it."

"A lid on what?"

"Billy Saunders had been a Summerhall snitch. You decided he was more use to you out on the street than behind bars. The guy he killed was a scumbag called Douglas Merchant—Merchant had been spending time with Saunders's partner. As far as Summerhall was concerned, Merchant was good riddance. So you made sure the case against your pal wouldn't stick."

"No one ever proved that."

"From what I can gather, no one really tried. Stefan Gilmour handed in his papers, then the station itself was condemned and the bulldozers got to work. No more Summerhall, no more Saints of the Shadow Bible."

"What's so funny?" Rebus asked, as Fox tried to stifle a smile.

"You don't think it's over the top? Who came up with the name anyway?"

Rebus shrugged. "It was around way before I got to Summerhall."

"So the seventies, or maybe even the sixties?"

Another shrug. "What is it you think you'll get from any of this—apart from a few of the Solicitor General's brownie points?"

"The notes on the case are being dusted off. Such evidence as still exists will be reexamined. Interviews with the main players..."

"That's not what I asked."

"I've been given a job and I'm doing it," Fox stated.

"George Blantyre's had a stroke—good luck getting him to answer your questions. And Frazer Spence died ten years back."

Fox nodded, letting Rebus know none of this was news. "But you're still here," he intoned. "As are Stefan Gilmour and Eamonn Paterson. Plus others connected to the case..."

"Billy Saunders?"

"Drives a private-hire taxi." Fox paused. "Have you ever happened to bump into him?"

"Not in quarter of a century."

"That sort of thing can be checked," Fox cautioned.

"So go check." Rebus rested his elbows on the table and leaned forward. "But don't expect to find much, other than cobwebs and dust."

"Can I assume you'll now pass word along to your ex-colleagues, let them know I'll be contacting them?"

"They'll tell you you're wasting your time, as well as a good chunk of taxpayers' money."

Fox ignored this. "I think I have the address for George Blantyre. Stefan Gilmour will be easy to track down—he's never out of the papers." He paused. "Does Eamonn Paterson still live on Ferry Road?"

"As far as I know."

"I doubt he's moved house since last night." Fox's eyes were fixed on Rebus's. "I was reconnoitering," he explained. "Saw you dropping him off. Good to see you're still close." Fox paused. "When the Saunders case flared up, you hadn't been part of the team at Summerhall very long?"

"About six months, maybe seven."

"Newest disciple to the ranks of the Saints?"

"Yes."

"Makes me think maybe you weren't involved—Gilmour and the others wouldn't have known how far they could trust you."

"Is that right?" Rebus leaned back, the pew creaking in complaint.

"You're just barely back on the force. Something like this could jeopardize that..."

"What you're saying is, if I help you, I can be written out of the story?"

"You know I can't make those sorts of promises." But Fox's tone of voice hinted otherwise.

"And all I'd have to do is grass up some of my oldest friends?"

"I'm not asking for that."

"You're a piece of work, Fox. And let me tell you something I *do* know." Rebus was edging out from the pew, getting to his feet. "You're a baw-hair away from having served your time in the Complaints. Means you'll be back in the fray soon, surrounded by people like me—fun and games ahead, Inspector. I hope you're not averse to a bit of ruck and maul..."

"Is that a threat?"

Rebus didn't bother answering. He was sliding his arms into his coat. The pint was where he'd left it, not even half finished.

"Formal interviews will commence in a day or two," Fox stated. "And trust me, those will be rigorous *and* recorded." He turned to watch as Rebus headed towards the doorway then through it, descending the few steps to the bar, the main door and the world outside.

There was silence at the table for a few moments, then Fox puffed out his cheeks and exhaled.

"Went well, I thought," Siobhan Clarke offered.

"Insofar as we didn't end up grappling on the floor, yes, I suppose it did."

Clarke had risen to her feet. Fox asked if she wanted a lift, but she shook her head. "Almost quicker to walk," she told him. "Plus it'll help clear all the fumes from my nose."

"The fire?" Fox inquired.

"The testosterone," she corrected him.

"Thanks for your help, anyway."

"I didn't really do anything."

"You got Rebus here."

"He actually didn't need any persuading."

Fox considered this for a moment. "Maybe he was warned by Eamonn Paterson..."

Clarke held out her hand and Fox shook it.

"Good luck," she told him.

"You really mean that?"

"Up to a point."

Left alone in the back room of the bar, Fox noticed that his glass wasn't quite centered on its mat. Slowly and carefully, he began the task of repositioning it.

Rebus had paused long enough at the North Castle Street junction to get a cigarette going and call Eamonn Paterson's home number.

"It's John," he said, when Paterson picked up.

"Last night was good, wasn't it? Thanks again for the lift."

"I've just been speaking to Malcolm Fox."

"Who's he?"

"Works Complaints, which makes him Macari's attack dog."

"That was quick."

"He's got us all in his sights. Reckons we banjaxed the Saunders case to keep a good snitch on the street."

"As if we'd do such a thing."

"But it wasn't that, was it?"

"How do you mean, John?"

"I mean, there was something else—something that had all of you twitchy. Doors that were pushed shut when I walked past...conversations that would stop dead when I stepped into the bar."

"You're imagining things."

"Whether I am or not, you're going to have to deal with Fox— and he might look like the sort of big soft bear you'd win at the fair, but he's got claws he's spent his whole life sharpening."

"And why would we even have to speak to him?"

"Because Elinor Macari will have made sure he has all the powers necessary. Right now, he's requisitioning files and evidence from thirty years back. He'll be well prepped when he comes calling."

"You said it yourself, John—thirty years...Maybe none of us can remember that far back."

"I doubt that's going to be much of a defense, Eamonn. Not if there's anything in those files for him to find." Rebus paused. "So let me ask you right now: *is* there?"

"You were there, John. You know how we worked."

"I know some of it." Rebus watched as Siobhan Clarke emerged from Young Street. She saw him and waved. "Anytime you want to fill in the blanks for me, I'd gladly listen—might mean I can help."

"John..."

"Think it over," Rebus snapped, ending the call. Then, to Clarke: "Hello, you."

"I was going to walk to Gayfield Square. You headed that way?"

"Why not?" The two crossed the road, mindful of traffic, and started along Hill Street.

"So what did you think?" she asked at last.

"You know me, Siobhan. I never give much thought to anything."

"Yet you seemed to have nailed Fox—this job's just deferring the evil hour when he's consigned to CID." She paused. "You don't mind me acting as go-between?" She watched him shrug.

"Actually," she corrected herself, "I think the word Fox used was 'referee.'"

"We were just a bunch of guys, Siobhan, typical of CID back then."

"Except that you had a name for your gang."

"I never had as much time for it as the others. When we went out on a job, we had this tape in the car—The Skids singing 'The Saints Are Coming.' It was mandatory to play it."

"And if you forgot?"

"Someone would get annoyed—Gilmour usually."

"He's a developer these days, isn't he?"

"Hotels mostly. Went into business with a big-name footballer."

"He's worth millions?"

"So the story goes."

"I've seen him on No campaign posters... You still know him?"

Rebus stopped walking and turned to face her. "I saw him last night."

"Oh?"

"At Dod Blantyre's house."

"The meeting your friend Porkbelly was telling you about?"

Rebus nodded, eyes boring into hers. "You can take that to Fox if you like. Bound to get his antennae twitching—a panicky reunion of the Saints."

"Is that what it was?"

Rebus scratched at his jaw. "I'm not sure," he confided. "The pretext was we wanted to catch up with Blantyre."

"Because he's had a stroke?"

"But he knew about Macari. And they wanted me to see what I could find out."

Clarke nodded her understanding. "Which is why you agreed to meet Fox? And that phone call you just made..."

"Was me reporting back to Paterson," Rebus confirmed. He had started to walk again, Clarke eventually catching up.

"You're trying to play both sides?" she guessed. "Meaning you really don't know what happened with Billy Saunders."

"I'm not sure it's as straightforward as Fox thinks."

"So tell him that."

"And drop the others in it?" Rebus shook his head. "Not until I'm certain."

"You're going to do some digging of your own? You know how that will look to Fox, don't you?"

"I don't give a damn *how* it looks to your friend Fox."

Clarke grabbed his arm. "You know whose friend I really am."

Rebus had stopped walking again. He looked down at his forearm, her hand clamped around it. "Of course I do," he said, almost gently. "You're Malcolm Fox's friend."

She looked furious for the two or three seconds before he burst into a grin.

"*You're* an absolute prick sometimes," she said, releasing her grip so she could curl her hand into a fist with which to punch him on the shoulder. Rebus winced and rubbed at the spot.

"You been training with weights?" he asked.

"More than you have," she snapped back.

"Same gym as your lawyer friend? Any more cheap dinners planned?"

"You're really not funny."

"Then why are you smiling?" Rebus asked as they set off again.

"Fox is taking charge of the files on the case," Clarke eventually commented.

"Yes, he is," Rebus agreed.

"So if you want to go digging…"

"All it'll cost is my dignity," Rebus told her.

"But back in the bar…"

"If I'd kowtowed straightaway, he'd have suspected something." He glanced in her direction. "Some people might mistake that look for grudging admiration."

"They might," Clarke acknowledged. But she kept on looking.

The comms center had gone through their logs for the night of the crash and found nothing from the western side of the city, other than the motorist who had called to report the crash itself. Rebus asked for those details anyway and jotted them down. He remembered the driver had been on her way home from her supermarket job in Livingston. He phoned her mobile and caught her at work. She asked how Jessica Traynor was doing.

"Recovering," Rebus told her. "Meantime, I've a couple of follow-up questions, if that's okay. When you stopped your car, you didn't see any other signs of life?"

"No."

"Nothing to indicate that she might not have been on her own at the time of the smash?"

"Was there someone else there?"

"We're just trying to establish a picture, Mrs. Muir."

"She was in the driver's seat."

"And her door was open?"

"I think so."

"What about the boot?"

"I've really no idea. I suppose the impact could have..."

"You don't remember whether it was open or closed?"

"No." She paused, then apologized and asked if it was important.

"Not really," Rebus assured her. "And you didn't see any other vehicle? No lights further down the road?"

"No."

"I know it's a lot to ask, but did you pass any cars traveling in the other direction in the minutes before you reached the scene?"

"I was thinking about my supper. And I had the radio on, singing along most likely."

"So you don't remember?"

"I don't."

Rebus thanked her and hung up. He reckoned she *would* have remembered if some boy racer had come roaring out of nowhere. He got up from his desk and walked across to Christine Esson's. "What have you got for me?" he asked.

She pointed towards the printer. "You being old school, I decided you'd want it on paper."

"Are we out of papyrus then?" He scooped up the thirty or so printed sheets.

"There was more," she told him. "But it was all mergers and acquisitions—and a lot of duplication."

"This'll do to start," Rebus said, returning to his desk and angling his chair so he could stretch his legs out. Then he began to read the Internet's version of Owen Traynor's life and times. Age fifty-two, married for seventeen years to Josephine Gray, acrimonious (and costly) divorce. Traynor had been declared bankrupt in his midtwenties but come good again within ten years. He was Croydon-born, and had told one interviewer that he'd attended the "university of hard knocks." More than one profile spoke of his rapid change of mood whenever a subject he didn't like was raised. An interviewer even confided that Traynor had threatened to hang him by the feet from the window—while making it sound like a joke. Not so much of a joke when that irate investor had started kicking up a fuss—attacked on his doorstep, ending up in intensive care. Charges never pressed. There had been other instances of flare-ups, Traynor's temper getting the better of him. Barred from at least one racecourse and one five-star hotel in London.

Quite the character, Mr. Owen Traynor.

Rebus tapped the number for the Infirmary into his phone and asked how Jessica Traynor was faring.

"She's been released," he was told.

"So soon?"

"There'll be a series of physio sessions and the like..."

"But she can manage stairs?" Rebus was thinking of the three steep flights to her Great King Street flat.

"Her father's booked her into a hotel for a few days."

In the room next to his, Rebus presumed. He thanked the nurse, ended the call and skimmed through the sheets of notes again. He realized the case was disappearing, as though it had been hoisted onto a trailer and was on its way for scrap. He looked around the office. Page was at some meeting, taking Clarke with him. Ronnie Ogilvie was prepping to give evidence at a trial. Christine Esson was studying statements. Was this what he had craved during his retirement? He had forgotten the lulls, the hours spent on paperwork, the hanging around. He thought of Charlie Watts—hadn't he said something about life as a Rolling Stone? Fifty years in the band, ten spent drumming and the other forty waiting for something to happen. Segue to Peggy Lee: "Is That All There Is?"

"Bollocks to that," Rebus muttered, getting to his feet. Probably just about enough time had passed. He patted his pockets, checking for cigarettes, matches, phone.

"Leaving so soon?" Esson teased him.

"Just for a few minutes."

"Acting as boss has taken its toll, eh?"

"I don't mind acting," Rebus told her, heading for the door. "In fact, I'm just heading to another audition..."

The small car park was a courtyard of sorts, the gray concrete cop shop hemming it in. Rebus was almost always the only smoker to use it. He called Police HQ and asked to be put through to Professional Standards—"or whatever they've decided to call it this week." The extension rang half a dozen times before being answered.

"Sergeant Kaye," the voice said by way of identification. Tony Kaye: Rebus had had dealings with him.

"Is your boyfriend there? Tell him John Rebus wants a word."

"He's in conference."

"He's not Alan fucking Sugar," Rebus complained.

"A meeting, then—sorry, I didn't realize grammar was your strong point."

"Vocabulary, you arsehole, not grammar."

"Mind and get a refund from that charm school, eh?"

"Soon as I've spoken to your generalissimo. Is this meeting of his with the fragrant Ms. Macari, by any chance?"

"How do you know that?"

"I'm a detective, son. A *proper* detective."

"You forget I've seen your files. Plenty six-letter words, but 'proper' got scratched from the dictionary the day you left the academy."

"I think I'm a little bit in love with you, Sergeant Kaye. Let me give you my vital statistics." He reeled off his mobile number. "Tell Fox I think I can help him. Have him call me once Macari unzips his gimp mask." He ended the call before Kaye could respond. Staring at the screen of his phone, he broke into a smile. He *did* like Kaye, didn't know what the hell the guy was doing in the Complaints. When a text arrived, he peered at it.

Blow me, it said, followed by three kisses. Dispatched, presumably, from Kaye's own mobile. Rebus added the number to his contacts and paced the space between the rows of cars, finishing his cigarette in peace.

6

It turned out the Solicitor General had given Fox his own little office within the Sheriff Court on Chambers Street, not half a minute's
walk from her own fiefdom.

"Cozy," Rebus said, examining his surroundings. The building
was relatively new, but he was struggling to remember what had
been there before. He had passed stressed lawyers outside, gabbling
into phones, plus, nearby, their devil-may-care clients, sharing cigarettes and war stories and comparing tattoos.

Fox was seated behind a desk that was too big for his immediate
needs, in a room that was a riot of wood paneling. He sat with a pen
gripped between both hands. To Rebus, it seemed like a pose the
man had spent too long preparing. Fox looked stiff and unconvinc-
ing, and maybe he sensed this himself—placing the pen on the desk
in front of him as Rebus took the seat opposite.

"So suddenly you can help me?" he asked. "Bit of a Damascene
conversion since lunchtime."

Rebus offered a shrug. "You plan to dump on my friends from a
great height; least I can do is make sure you've not got the squits."

"An arresting image."

"Are those the files?" Rebus gestured towards two large cardboard
boxes by Fox's side.

"Yes. Mid-'83, around the time Saunders killed Merchant."

"*Allegedly,*" Rebus countered. "You've already been through them?" He watched the other man nod. "And if my name was in the frame at any point, you wouldn't want me here?"

Fox nodded again. "Of course, until recently you worked for the Cold Case Unit. You could have accessed the files at any time, making sure nothing incriminating was left from your days at Summerhall."

"For the sake of argument, let's say I didn't do that and I'm clean."

"In this particular instance," Fox felt it necessary to qualify.

"In this particular instance," Rebus echoed. "And here I am, back in CID on sufferance..."

"Something you don't want to jeopardize."

"Which is why I'm offering my services—means I can keep an eye on you."

"If you had nothing to do with it, you've nothing to fear from me."

"Unless you start screwing up and I find myself lumped in with everyone else who ever worked at Summerhall."

Fox picked up the pen again. It was a cheap yellow ballpoint, but he handled it as if it were Montblanc's finest.

"So your idea of helping me is to doubt my abilities from the off?"

"Saves us the trouble of discussing it later," Rebus offered.

"And meantime I'm supposed to trust *you?* These are some of the first officers you bonded with, men you've known most of your professional life—why would you turn against them?"

"That's not why I'm here. I'm just making sure you don't start a firefight."

"Firefights aren't my style."

"That's good, because the Saints—retired as they might be—aren't lacking ammo."

"*You're* not retired, though."

Rebus nodded. "And they'll see me as part of their armory."

"But you won't be?"

"That's for you to decide—once we start work on those files."

Rebus gestured towards the boxes. Fox stared at him, then looked at the display on his phone.

"Only an hour or so left before going home."

"Depends what time you knock off," Rebus countered.

Another lengthy examination, and then a slow nod of the head.

"Okay, cowboy," Fox said, almost in a drawl. "Let's see what you've got." They lifted the boxes onto the desk and started to get to work.

Sandy Bell's wasn't the closest bar to the Sheriff Court, but it was Rebus's choice, and as Fox himself conceded: "You probably know better than I do." There was a small table near the back, so they grabbed it, Rebus fetching a cola for his newfound colleague and an IPA for himself. Fox was rubbing at his eyes and stifling a yawn. He insisted on chinking glasses. Rebus sank an inch of the pint and smacked his lips.

"You never touch the booze?" he asked. Fox shook his head. "Because you can't?"

Fox nodded, then looked at him. "I can't and you shouldn't."

Rebus toasted the sentiment and took another mouthful.

"Was it the drinking that made your wife leave you?" he inquired.

"I could ask the selfsame question," Fox shot back.

"And I'd have to tell you it was." Rebus thought for a moment. "Or maybe that was just part of it. Doing what we do...I couldn't let off steam at home—quite the opposite. So it got bottled up. And the only people I could talk to were other cops. That was the start of the distancing..." He exhaled, then shrugged.

"You could have knocked the booze on the head," Fox told him.

"Like you did, you mean? And that's why you're still happily married with a vibrant social life?"

Fox looked as if he might take offense, but then his shoulders loosened. "Touché," he said.

"We've all got different ways of dealing with the shit we deal with," Rebus offered.

"Which brings us back to the Saints," Fox stated. "Tight little grouping like that, you start to think your own rules are the only ones that matter."

"No argument with that."

"And back then, parameters were different, not as strict as they are now?"

"Leeway," Rebus agreed.

"Especially when you seemed to be getting result after result. The brass weren't about to start questioning your methods."

Rebus thought of Peter Meikle, the drive around Arthur's Seat. He pursed his lips and said nothing. Fox noted this but ploughed on.

"The whole system's changed, hasn't it? Used to be about snitches and contacts. You lost someone like Billy Saunders, suddenly you weren't closing cases and getting the respect of the Big House. Whatever he'd done, you had to keep him on the street."

"You keep saying 'you.'"

Fox held up a hand in apology. "I mean the Saints in general. But there had to be a hierarchy and I'm guessing that meant Gilmour— he was the DI after all. Was Saunders Gilmour's man?"

"You'd need to ask one or the other."

Fox glared at him. "You really don't know?"

"Let's say he was—what of it?"

Fox kept glaring. "Is there anything useful you *do* know?"

"Plenty."

"Such as?"

"That's for a later date." Rebus picked up his glass again.

"Suppose I tell you I need to know now."

"A later date," Rebus echoed.

"Then maybe I should just let you slink back to Gayfield Square."

"Maybe you should. But think about this first—you bring in each of the Saints for questioning and I'm seated there beside you. They're going to wonder if there's any point lying or twisting the truth."

"Unless you're acting as their spy all along."

"That's certainly a risk," Rebus agreed with a shrug. "But the job you do, you probably think you're good at reading people." He made eye contact with Fox and held it. "So ask yourself if I can be trusted or not."

"Let's see," Fox eventually said. "Let's just wait and see."

"But we start bringing them in tomorrow, yes?"

"We only question them when *I'm* ready," Fox qualified.

"Fair enough," Rebus said. Then, gesturing towards his empty glass, "Your round, by the way."

But Fox shook his head. "Some of us have got homes," he explained. "Meet in the Sheriff Court at ten?"

"You need to clear it with my boss."

"James Page?" Fox checked. "I'm fairly sure he can spare you, Detective Sergeant Rebus…"

"How long have you been here?"

"Not long. I was in the neighborhood." Clarke was standing in the doorway of Rebus's tenement. "Just sending you a text." She showed him her phone.

"Your flat's miles from here," he told her.

"I was having a drink with someone."

"Your lawyer?"

"In Morningside."

"The Canny Man?"

She shook her head. "Montpelier's." Rebus made a face: not his kind of place. "Where did you disappear to?" she was asking. "Came back from that meeting and Christine said you'd scarpered."

"I was in a meeting of my own."

She thought for a moment. "With Fox?" Rebus nodded. "And he doesn't suspect?"

"What's to suspect?" Rebus had dug out his key and was opening the door. "You coming in?"

"Is that all right?"

"Long as you're not after a white wine spritzer..." He led the way up two flights of stairs to the door to his flat. Unlocked it and scooped up the mail before switching on the hallway light. She followed him into the living room. The ashtray next to his armchair needed emptying. A couple of beer bottles sat alongside, plus an empty whisky glass.

"Cup of tea?" he asked her.

"Thanks."

While he was in the kitchen, she slid some of his LPs back into their sleeves. She was about to pick up the beer bottles when he reappeared.

"I'll do that," he said.

"I'll bring the ashtray."

She dumped its contents into the bin in the kitchen while he placed the bottles on the work surface next to the sink. He handed her a mug.

"You got lucky," he said. "Milk's only a day past its sell-by."

"I'll settle for that."

They went back through to the living room. "Is this okay for you now?" he asked. "Or does your OCD require any further action?"

She said nothing, settling herself on the sofa and resisting the urge to arrange the newspapers next to her into a neater pile. Rebus was putting an LP on, turning down the volume. Miles Davis, she thought—from the period before he got weird.

Rebus was about to lift a cigarette from its packet, but remembered she didn't like it.

"So you've got yourself seconded to Fox?" she asked eventually.

"In a manner of speaking."

"Access to the Saunders file?" She watched him nod. "And other cases relating to Summerhall?" A shrug this time. "Has it occurred to you that Fox could be playing a game of his own?"

"What sort of game?"

"Wondering if there's anything you'll try to cover up, any reports that could suddenly go AWOL..."

"It's a possibility."

"You've really persuaded him you're on his side?"

"Not completely—stands to reason he's got his suspicions."

She leaned forward on the sofa. "And *is* there anything for him to find? Anything that's going to end up incriminating you?"

Rebus considered this. "If he looks hard enough, there *might* be a skeleton or two. Thing is, a lot of the supporting cast have left the stage—gone walkies or been fitted for the wooden suit. So while he might find stuff, he'll have the devil's own job making it stick."

Clarke was staring at him. "How dirty was Summerhall?"

He studied the surface of his tea. "Dirty enough. You ever see that program *Life on Mars*? It felt like a documentary..."

"Beating a confession out of someone? Planting evidence? Making sure the bad guys got done for *something?*"

"You thinking of writing my biography?"

"This isn't a joke, John. Tell me what happened to Billy Saunders."

Rebus blew on the tea, took a sip, then shrugged. "It probably went down the way everyone seems to think."

"Botching the case so he'd stay out of jail and useful?"

Rebus nodded.

"And that's all going to have to come out in the wash for the Solicitor General to get her second prosecution," Clarke stated. "Though there *is* another scenario."

"I know," Rebus said. "Saunders cuts a deal. For a lesser charge, he grasses up Summerhall."

"Which would reflect badly on Stefan Gilmour."

"It would be like giving a cow a machine gun—bullets could go anywhere."

"You might take a ricochet?"

Rebus shrugged again. "I wasn't there but I was sort of there— you see what I'm saying?"

"You were in the team but not the room?"

Rebus rose slowly to his feet, walked over to the stereo and stared at the record as it revolved, the pickup arm traveling almost imperceptibly towards the center of the vinyl. "It was thirty years ago, Siobhan. Everything was..." He turned towards her. "Is it fair to bring it all up?"

She looked at him. "There's something else, isn't there? I mean, okay, the guy was a snitch, but he'd just pummeled someone to death. I'm guessing even back then your instinct would have been to wash your hands of him. A lesser crime...maybe you'd have asked for leniency...but murder?"

He returned to his chair, slumping into it.

"You know I'm right, don't you?" she asked quietly. "I think you knew it then too. Saunders had to have something on Stefan Gilmour. When you saw Gilmour the other night, how was he? When Blantyre told him about reopening the case, how did he react?"

"He was fine; he acted fine."

"Maybe acting is one of those things he does well. Have you seen him on TV, campaigning for Scotland to stay in the union?"

"I doubt that's an act."

"But it's a role he's playing."

"He resigned over the Saunders case."

"I know."

"He did the right thing."

"Does he still have any contact with Saunders?"

"Why would he?"

"If Saunders *did* have some hold over him..." She let this sink in. "And now Saunders knows Elinor Macari's coming gunning for him..."

"He might want to talk to Stefan."

"If nothing else, Gilmour probably knows a few sharp lawyers."

Rebus nodded slowly.

"If Saunders does have something on Stefan Gilmour—something big—do you have any inkling what it might be?"

"No."

"And if you dig down deep enough and hit the truth—do you

take it to Malcolm Fox, or do you arrange another meeting of the Saints?"

"I'd have to give it some thought."

"And you really think you can do all of this without Fox catching on?"

"I don't really give a damn if he catches on."

"No?"

Rebus shook his head. "But I know what Miles Davis would say if he did."

Clarke narrowed her eyes. "What would he say?"

"He'd say: *So what.*"

DAY FOUR

7

We can't question Saunders," Malcolm Fox stated.

He was in the office at the Sheriff Court, removing the lid from the tea Rebus had brought him. Rebus had arrived first, weaving his way through the concourse, past the mix of law officials and their clients—the two groups not easily confused—before finding the door to Fox's room firmly locked. By the time Fox arrived, Rebus had been out again to a café on George IV Bridge, returning with the gift of tea. He had asked if he could have a key, but Fox had shaken his head and Rebus had decided against pressing the point just yet. He had then thrown Saunders's name into the mix.

"Why not?" he asked now, trying his own tea and finding it wanting.

"Because the Solicitor General ruled it out from the off. I'm looking at Summerhall and Summerhall only."

"But surely Saunders is part of that."

"Elinor Macari's team will be questioning Mr. Saunders."

"But you must know that's going to make *your* job all the harder?" Rebus persisted.

"Nevertheless, it's what the Solicitor General wants."

"And you just left it at that?" Rebus sounded bemused.

"I'm not like you. Someone in authority tells me to do something, I don't question it." Fox slurped at the tea, savoring it.

"I still think it would help us ask the right questions of the Saints if we hear Saunders's side of the story first."

"I don't disagree. And once Saunders has been interviewed by Macari's team, we'll take a look at the transcripts."

"So we wait for that to happen before we bring them in?"

"I doubt it would be practical to 'bring in' George Blantyre."

"So we interview him at home?"

Fox fixed him with a look. "You're sure you can do this?"

Rebus nodded.

"And of course there's your own interview to consider."

"Of course."

"In fact, it might help if we got that out of the way..." Fox lifted his briefcase onto the desk and opened it, bringing out a pad of lined A4 paper.

"Shouldn't we finish going through the files first?" Rebus queried, nodding in their direction.

"I've been over them several times." Fox opened the pad, flicking through its pages. Dozens of them filled with his small, neat handwriting. Rebus saw a lot of question marks and a good deal of underlining. He was wondering if he had been huckled by Fox, reeled in like a greedy fish. Fox was staring at him, offering the thinnest of smiles.

"Might help me size you up," the man explained. "See how much use I can make of you."

"No tape recorders? No video?"

"Nothing so formal," Fox said with the same thin smile. "So..." He glanced towards the pad in front of him while removing the top from a ballpoint pen. "You were a detective constable when you went to Summerhall? And this was in October 1982?"

"November," Rebus corrected him.

"Of course."

Rebus watched as Fox made a little tick in the margin of a page. *You knew that already. You're just testing me, watching for when the lying starts...*

"And did you know any of the other CID officers before you arrived there?"

"I'd met one or two."

"Specifically?"

"Blantyre and Paterson."

"Both of them detective sergeants at this point?"

"Yes."

"How did you know them?"

"Probably from court—the *old* Sheriff Court. Hanging around waiting to give evidence."

"And then there was the Police Club?"

"I never went. Too much shop talk."

"You were already a regular at the Oxford Bar? A lot of cops used to drink there back in the day—anyone from Summerhall?"

"Not that I remember."

"The CID team was pretty well established when you arrived?"

"Was it?"

Fox allowed the question with yet another smile. He made show of checking his notes. "DI Gilmour had been there a couple of years, as had DS Blantyre. By the time you showed up, DS Paterson and DC Spence had the best part of eight months under their belts." Fox looked up. "Yet you were welcomed to the fold? They didn't treat you with any degree of suspicion?"

"They were fine."

"And how long was it before you were initiated?"

"You mean into the Saints?" It was Rebus's turn to smile. "You make it sound like a big deal."

"You're saying it wasn't?"

"It was just a name. Other CID units had their own versions—F Division were the Cowboys, C Division the Marooned."

"A lot more straightforward than 'Saints of the Shadow Bible'— you have to admit, it sounds more than a little portentous." Fox paused. "Or pretentious even."

"Were you never in a gang at school? Maybe you were shunned, kept on the outside, looking in?"

"I was asking how long you were part of the group before the Saints came up in conversation."

"Just a week or two."

"And there *was* an initiation?"

"What have you heard?"

"Everything from downing six pints to the slaughter of the innocent."

"Old wives' tales," Rebus stated.

"But the Saints *did* have a rep—not too many wanted to spend a
night in the cells or be taken in for questioning." Fox paused, turning the sheets of his lined pad. "Is it true about Interview Room B?"

"What about it?"

"Brown and red smears on the walls and floor? The smell of stale
urine? Words like 'help' scratched into the table?"

Rebus couldn't help but smile at the memory. "The smears were
courtesy of the local chip shop—brown sauce and ketchup. We
scored those words into the tabletop ourselves."

"So suspects would have something to read while they waited?"

"Got them twitchy."

"And the urine?"

"I forget now who was behind that. Made sure IRB was less than
welcoming—same went for the chair. Someone sawed half an inch
off one leg. No way you could start to relax in it..." Rebus looked
at Fox. "Not that I would condone anything like that these days."

"All the same," Fox said, scribbling a note to himself, "I can see
the attraction." He paused. "What was the Internal Affairs setup like
in those days?"

"The Complaints? Less than rigorous. As long as you got results,
blind eyes could be turned. Mind you, we still thought of your lot as
scum."

"I appreciate your candor."

"My pleasure." Rebus's phone was buzzing. He looked at the
screen. It was Siobhan Clarke. "Mind if I take this?" he asked Fox.
Fox didn't look happy, but Rebus wasn't about to wait for his answer anyway.

"What can I do for you?" he asked into the mouthpiece.

"McCuskey's at death's door," Clarke announced.

Rebus narrowed his eyes. "What?"

"Looks like a housebreaking gone badly wrong."

"Christ."

"He's being taken to the Infirmary."

"There's an irony."

"How do you mean?"

"Same place as his girlfriend."

"I'm not talking about the son—this is the father. *Pat* McCuskey. As in our beloved Justice Minister."

"Just a coincidence, then?"

"That's what I'm wondering. He was attacked at his home sometime this morning."

"And?"

"The home's just the other side of the airport from the city."

"Not far from the scene of the crash?"

"Not far at all," Clarke conceded.

"Are you on your way there now?" Rebus gestured for the loan of Fox's pen. As Clarke recited the address, he jotted it onto the side of his cardboard cup. Ending the call, he handed back the pen.

"Justice Minister's been attacked in his home," he explained.

"Oh?"

"I have to go."

Fox stared at him. "Why?"

"A case I've been working on with DI Clarke." Rebus broke off. "This isn't a ruse or anything—phone her back if you don't believe me."

"I'm not sure even *you* would stoop that low."

"A vote of confidence if ever I heard one." Rebus got to his feet and grabbed the cup with the address on.

Outside, he poured the cold tea down the first grating he saw.

The house was an extended two-story Edwardian property at the end of a gravel driveway and with no immediate neighbors. There seemed to be extensive grounds, including a paddock and stables. The road outside, narrow enough to start with, was already lined with vehicles belonging to journalists and the curious. Cameras were being hoisted, scripts checked, feeds established. A uniform stood guard at the wrought-iron gates and scrutinized Rebus's warrant card before letting him through. A low rumble indicated that a flight was leaving the airport. Rebus watched the passenger jet rise skywards, not half a mile away, then turned his attention back to the house. The gravel extended almost all the way to the front door, meaning approaching vehicles were bound to be heard. Same went for intruders on foot. But then he'd no idea of the layout to the rear—and housebreakers seldom used the front door.

A scene-of-crime van was parked next to four cars. Rebus guessed that the newish Land Rover probably belonged, while the others were just visiting. He ran a finger down the side of Clarke's Astra as he moved past it to the gaping front door. The wood-paneled hall reminded him of what they'd tried to do at the Sheriff Court, but this was the real thing. The suit of armor at the foot of the winding staircase was probably intended to show that the owner had a sense of humor. A vase had tumbled from its occasional table and now lay shattered on the parquet floor. There were muted voices in the sitting room and Rebus followed them until he was told to stop. A young woman in white overalls handed him a pair of elasticated paper shoes and warned him not to touch anything. Clarke stepped towards him. She was also in overalls and paper shoes, and was looking solemn. Video was being shot, photos snapped, surfaces dusted for prints.

"He was found on the floor in here," she explained. "His private secretary was worried when he couldn't be roused this morning. There was an eight-thirty meeting waiting for him. Usual driver had turned up but found the door locked and no sign of life." She saw his look. "They came in through the back— French doors with one pane punched out. Maybe they thought the house looked empty..."

Rebus scanned the room. Expensive flat-screen TV untouched. Paperwork strewn across the floor. A Persian rug rucked up.

"So what did they take?" he asked.

"Laptop, we think, plus both his mobile phones. Drawers have been opened in the bedroom—could be some jewelry's missing."

"The wife?"

"Is on her way back from Glasgow. She stayed there last night so she could take some clients to dinner and then see them again this morning."

"Clients?"

"She's a lawyer—American by birth." Clarke pointed out a framed photo of the couple. It had been knocked flat and now lay on top of the baby grand piano. Wedding day: low-cut off-white dress for her, traditional Highland outfit for her beaming partner.

"Has anyone told the son?"

"Left a message on his phone asking him to call back."

"He might not, if he thinks it's about the crash."

"I stressed that it isn't."

Rebus saw another photo—it showed McCuskey's wife on horseback. She was dressed informally—jeans and a checked shirt, and no headwear of any kind.

"What do the medics say?"

"He was either coshed or hit his head on something when they tried to grab him. Lump like an ostrich egg on the back of his skull and they're worried about internal bleeding."

"So there could be some damage?"

Clarke nodded slowly.

"If they came on foot, that would explain why they didn't take much. On the other hand..."

"We're hiking distance from civilization."

"So there might well have been a car waiting."

"I've got uniforms scouring the perimeter."

"How long before you talk to the media?"

"Won't be me—Page is on his way."

"Stopping off en route for a haircut and a new suit?" She couldn't help but smile. "Politicians are going to want a briefing," Rebus warned her. "This is one of their own, remember."

"I've already had the First Minister's office on the phone. He wants to visit the hospital, plus they're sending someone to check we're being thorough."

"Is there anything on the laptop the government wouldn't want getting out?"

"They're going to come back to me about that."

"He *was* the Justice Minister, after all."

"Plus leader of the Yes campaign."

"I doubt we can put unionists in the frame, Siobhan."

"Doesn't mean political capital can't be made out of it—same as Page wanted when we found out who Forbes was."

"I'd say that particular plan has just been put out with the bins. But let's stay focused on the main event—why do we think this morning rather than last night?"

"Mr. McCuskey spoke to his wife at eleven thirty, by which time he was tucked up in bed. When he was found this morning, he was wearing suit trousers and shirt but no jacket or tie. Pot of coffee in the kitchen and half a banana left on the worktop."

Rebus nodded his acceptance of this. "So where's this door they broke?" he asked. Clarke led him out into the hall and turned left. There were two doors, one leading to a modern kitchen, one to a formal dining room with French doors onto a large patio. Broken glass on the carpet, consistent with an attack from the outside.

"If McCuskey heard something," Rebus said, "wouldn't he come looking?"

"Maybe."

"But he was found in the sitting room? Could he have had the TV on? Catching the morning's headlines. Coffee and a banana, and next thing he knows there's someone walking in on him."

"Makes sense."

"But the TV was off? Who was first on the scene anyway?"

"The private secretary—she has a key."

"Maybe ask her about the TV."

Clarke nodded to let him know she was adding this to her list.

"Can't really know what else has gone AWOL until the wife arrives," Rebus mused. They locked eyes at the sound of another vehicle crunching its way towards the house. "As good as any guard dog," Rebus acknowledged.

But when they went to greet the new arrival, it was DCI James Page. "What's *he* doing here?" Page asked Clarke, stabbing a finger in Rebus's direction.

"I was just about to ask the same thing, sir," Rebus retorted.

"Off with you," Page ordered. "Nothing for you here."

"Aye aye, Captain." Rebus gave a mock salute before offering Clarke a sly wink. Page stomped past him into the house, followed by Clarke. Rebus had to admit, he'd been wrong about the man. No new suit and no haircut.

Just shoes freshly polished and the tang of shaving foam wafting after him.

Left to his own devices, Rebus knew he had two options. One was to head back to Fox's light grilling, which was why he removed his overshoes, stuffed them into his pocket, and went for a walk around the property instead.

There wasn't much to see at the rear of the house. Clarke was showing Page the broken pane of glass in the door. Rebus headed across an expanse of lawn towards where a line of venerable-looking trees hid the house from the country road beyond. Past the trees was a low stone wall topped with glossy black railings. Rebus peered through them. If a car had pulled over anywhere, it would have caused a minor obstruction—meaning anyone trying to squeeze past in their own vehicle would remember it. Three uniformed officers were probing the long grass forlornly.

"Anything?" Rebus asked.

"Not so far."

Rebus continued his tour of the perimeter. The thing was, once you'd scaled the fence and emerged from the tree line, you had to cross about eighty yards of highly visible lawn. Okay, it would have been dark first thing in the morning, but there were security lights at strategic points. Rebus checked and they all seemed to be motion sensitive. So maybe the intruders had come in through the front gate on foot—making almost no noise on the gravel, and hidden from the house by the dense shrubbery either side of the driveway. Still meant a car left somewhere in the vicinity. He headed back around to his starting point and set off down the driveway. There was movement at the gates, the media pack sensing he might have news for them. But he shook his head and pushed his way through. He was looking for a pull-in, a track, somewhere to hide a vehicle. He quickly found a couple of contenders, both now filled by journalists' cars, the ground churned up. A couple of reporters had followed him, asking questions without getting answers. But now there was a commotion at the gates; Rebus's disciples rejoined the pack as Page and Clarke came into view. The uniform on guard duty swung the gates open and everyone knew a statement was about to be made.

Before commencing, Page glanced down at his shoes, as if checking that their sheen was intact. As he started to speak, Clarke noticed Rebus and headed in his direction.

"Might keep them pacified for a while," she said under her breath.

"The wife's taking her time."

"Probably at the hospital as we speak."

"You heading there after?"

She nodded. "And meantime, I've sent Ronnie Ogilvie—just in case McCuskey wakes up."

"Any word on that front?"

She shook her head. "Wonder what room he's in—be a coincidence if it's the same one Jessica Traynor just left."

"Wouldn't be the end of the coincidences around here, Siobhan."

She looked at him. "No," she agreed.

"And yet neither of us has said the name yet..."

"Owen Traynor," she obliged. "With an investor who got thumped after a falling-out."

"Ending up in intensive care," Rebus added.

"Is Traynor still in the city, though?"

"Far as I know, he's moved Jessica into his hotel."

"Do we know which one?"

"A maximum of half a dozen phone calls would answer that."

"Want to make them?"

"Might as well, eh?"

"You'd not rather get back to working on Fox?"

"Working *with* him," Rebus corrected her.

"I know what I mean. Is that where you were when I phoned you?"

"Yes."

Clarke nodded to herself and watched as James Page got into his stride, taking questions, enunciating his answers clearly for the benefit of the microphones while he made sure the cameras caught his best angles.

"You have to admit, he's a pro," she commented.

"Pro everything I'm anti," Rebus retorted, taking out his phone and heading further along the road, seeking a quiet spot from where to make his calls.

8

The Caledonian Hotel wasn't really called that anymore. It was, according to the signs on either side of its entrance, the Waldorf Astoria, and had recently undergone a major refit. Sited at the west end of Princes Street, it currently looked onto a carnage of tramline construction. Both Shandwick Place and Queensferry Street were closed to traffic so as to allow the works to progress. Pedestrians were sent through the equivalent of laboratory mazes, squeezing down narrow passageways, hemmed in by high mesh fences behind which sat the tramlines themselves. Rebus had left his Saab out front, with the POLICE notice on its dashboard, the doorman warning him that it might not stop him getting a ticket.

"Saw a hearse get one once—and an ambulance."

"All part of Edinburgh's rich tapestry," Rebus had responded, stepping into the hotel foyer. They called up to Owen Traynor's room from the reception desk. Rebus was told to take the lift to the third floor. Traynor was waiting at his open door. He was in his shirtsleeves, the sleeves themselves rolled up, cuff links again dispensed with. No tie. Trousers held up with dark blue braces. Shiny black brogues.

"What is it now?" the man barked.

"Mind if I come in?"

Traynor hesitated, then led Rebus into not a bedroom but a suite, its living area turned into a makeshift office. The laptop computer was new—its box sat under the desk. On the sofa were bags from shops such as Ede & Ravenscroft and Marks & Spencer. From what Rebus could see of the computer screen, Traynor had been perusing spreadsheets.

"How is Jessica?" Rebus asked.

"She's in her room—physio's there with her."

"Could we maybe go talk to her?"

Traynor stared hard at Rebus, then checked his watch. "Five minutes till the session ends. I take it you've some news for us?"

Rebus gave a twitch of the mouth.

"You want a drink?" Traynor was gesturing towards the minibar.

"Bit early."

"Sure about that?"

Rebus looked at him. "You've been checking up on me?"

"Internet's a wonderful thing, Inspector."

"Detective Sergeant, actually."

"Why is that? I mean, you *used* to be an inspector—what did you do to piss them off?"

"I stuck around."

"Something you seem to be good at, judging by the stories. A lot of results down the years..."

"I didn't realize the web knew so much about me."

"Never know what to believe, though—I'm betting you've looked me up online. Not all of it is accurate." There was a hard gleam in Traynor's eye.

"Just most of it?" Rebus speculated.

"Ah, but which bits...?"

There was a knock at the door. Traynor answered and a young man stood there.

"How's she doing?" Traynor asked.

"I've given her some exercises I'd like her to try. Nothing too strenuous just yet."

Traynor nodded and reached into his back trouser pocket, pulling out a wallet. The physio held up a hand.

"We'll bill you, Mr. Traynor."

"Right." But Traynor pressed an English twenty-pound note on the man anyway. "Same time tomorrow?"

"Of course." And with a smile, stuffing the tip into his pocket, the physio headed down the corridor towards the lift.

"Not the NHS, then?" Rebus guessed.

"Not a bloody chance." Traynor turned to study him. "You sure you need to speak to Jessica? You can't just tell me?"

"Afraid not." Rebus could have added: *I want to see her reaction...*

Having checked he had key cards to both rooms, Traynor locked his door and knocked on his daughter's, before sliding the key in and out of its slot.

Her room was smaller, but still had space for a sofa and chairs. There were fresh flowers in a vase on a table. She was wearing a simple dress, bare legs showing bruising from the crash, one ankle strapped. She still wore the neck brace and was lying propped up on the bed, three huge pillows behind her. The TV was on—a channel playing music videos. She muted the volume, then noticed Rebus.

"Oh," she said.

"Hello again, Ms. Traynor."

"What do you want?"

"Something that apparently has to be said in front of both of us," her father explained, folding his arms in readiness. Rebus wasn't going to be invited to sit down, but that suited him fine. He made sure he had both father and daughter in his eye line before commencing.

"Earlier today," he said, "Patrick McCuskey was attacked in his home." He left it at that for the moment, content to gauge the reaction of the room. Jessica put a hand to her open mouth as if to stifle a gasp.

"Forbes McCuskey's father?" Owen Traynor asked. "The government guy?"

"The government guy," Rebus confirmed, his eyes on Jessica.

"Is he...all right?" she asked.

Rebus nodded towards the TV. "News channels probably know more than me."

She found one; the footage was a report from the Middle East, but a few words on the break-in ran along the bottom of the screen: *Scottish Justice Minister in hospital after burglary at his Edinburgh home…*

"Except we don't call it burglary up here," Rebus said by way of correction.

"Is Forbes okay?" Jessica Traynor asked. "Was he there when it…?"

"Father seems to have been on his own. Do you know the house, Ms. Traynor?"

"I've been there a few times." She paused. "How awful for Bethany."

"I've just come from the house—not too far from where your car went off the road. You weren't maybe headed there, or away from there…?"

"What are you saying?" Traynor had taken a step towards Rebus, fists clenching. Rebus held up both hands in a show of surrender.

"Dad, it's all right," Jessica Traynor intervened. "The officer's only doing his job…"

But Rebus was holding Owen Traynor's stare. "I don't suppose *you* know the house, do you?" he asked.

"No."

"Never been there?"

"No."

"Not tempted to have a word with young Forbes about the crash? Maybe you couldn't find him so decided to give his father a piece of your mind instead?"

"No."

"Only, you've not got a car, so I'm guessing it would have been a taxi or a rental, meaning a paper trail…"

Traynor was shaking his head, slowly and at length.

"Dad? What's he saying?"

"Nothing, Jessica." Then, to Rebus: "I don't even know where they live."

Rebus looked doubtful. "When you looked up your daughter's boyfriend online, a click or two would have taken you to Pat McCuskey. Such a public figure, I'm guessing his home address is out there somewhere."

A smile flitted across Traynor's face. He turned towards the bed. "He thinks maybe my blood was up and I went to give the McCuskey family a piece of my mind."

"But you didn't, did you, Dad?"

"I did not," Traynor confirmed, turning back to face Rebus. "I did not," he repeated.

"Then it's just a terrible coincidence, isn't it, Jessica?" Rebus had his eyes on Traynor's daughter. She was twisting the TV remote in her hand, staring at it.

"Coincidence," she echoed.

But Rebus could tell, all of a sudden, that she didn't believe it.

"He's in a coma," Fox said as Rebus walked back into their shared office. "Got him stabilized, though, and not as near to popping his clogs as he was."

Rebus blinked. "How do you know?"

Fox held up his phone, giving it a little wave. "The wonder of Wi-Fi," he explained.

"I barely get a signal on mine," Rebus muttered. He looked at the paperwork piled up on every available surface. "Someone's been busy."

"Did DCI Page decide you were surplus to requirements on the McCuskey case?"

"That hurts." Rebus studied the paperwork again. The two original boxes had been joined by about ten more. "So what have we got here?"

"Summerhall CID in its entirety, late seventies to mideighties."

"You sure this is everything?"

"You're saying stuff will have walked?"

"I'm saying filing wasn't always a priority."

"Neither was handwriting, judging by what I've seen."

Rebus had opened one file from 1983. He saw his own name at the top of an interview transcript. Domestic abuse at an address in Dumbiedykes. The names of victim and suspect meant nothing to him.

"So much ancient history," he said.

"Some of the procedures seem not to have changed since the Stone Age," Fox agreed.

"We're focusing on the Saunders case, though?"

"The murder of Douglas Merchant, yes." Fox placed a hand gently on one thick file.

"That's not the stuff we went through yesterday," Rebus stated.

"Freshly disinterred."

"Mind if I . . . ?"

"Be my guest."

Rebus picked the file up, feeling its heft. He sat with it, clearing space on the desk in front of him, and opened the cover. "Smells of mold," he commented.

"Some of the pages needed to be prized apart."

"You've taken a look at it, though?" He watched as Fox nodded. "And how often does my name come up?"

"Hardly at all."

"Which is why you don't mind me going through it?" Rebus paused. "See, if I were a betting man, I'd stick money on you having noted everything in here. That way, if I lift anything, you'll know— and that'll be the gen you really need."

Fox's face remained inscrutable. "Just take a read," he said. "Then we can talk about it."

"I hardly need to," Rebus said. "I'm not going to forget a case like Douglas Merchant. It near destroyed the Saints and put Stefan Gilmour out of a job."

"No harm done in the long run, though—for everyone except the dear departed Mr. Merchant." Fox pointed towards the file. "There are photos in there—family photos. Wife and kid. He had three sisters, too, all of them saying how he always looked after them, right from when they were little. Far as I know, they're all still with us. Maybe they think of him a few times a week, still missing him..."

"You auditioning for daytime TV?"

"I'm just looking at the reality of the situation. Someone ends up dead, there are ripples—lots of lives affected. It's not just about the Saints, John. The Saints got a slap on the wrist and that was that."

Rebus considered this for a moment, then asked when the Solicitor General was going to interview Billy Saunders.

"Soon. Very soon."

"He was a crook, remember—maybe he still is. How will anyone know if he's spinning them a story?"

Fox shrugged. "Not my problem."

Rebus was skimming the file at random. Some of the badly typed sheets had faded. He remembered the typewriter—the *o* was so fierce, it punched a hole through paper whenever you hit it. Handwriting was blotchy in some places where damp had got to it. He found a photo of the dead man—a glossy square with a white border. Taken in a pub somewhere, Merchant hoisting a tumbler of whisky, glassy-eyed and with a gap-toothed grin.

"Did you know him?" Fox was asking.

"Merchant?" Rebus shook his head, still studying the photograph.

"But you probably met Billy Saunders, him being the station's star pupil when it came to snitching?"

"That wasn't the way it worked," Rebus explained. "If you had a contact on the street, you kept him or her to yourself as much as you could. Otherwise one of your colleagues might try a bit of poaching. You'd arrange meetings in parks, or maybe you'd just happen to bump into them in a noisy bar, somewhere you couldn't be overheard. They'd ask you for a light and drop a name into your ear while you got the match struck. No mobile phones in those days, so meetings could be difficult to arrange. But it had to be face to face—that way you could look them in the eye."

"And why would you need to do that?" Fox sounded genuinely curious.

"Because usually, when they were giving you a name, there was a reason for it. Could be they just wanted to dump someone in the shit—a competitor maybe, or someone who'd crossed them."

"So it wasn't always just about the cash incentive?"

"There was never a lot of cash. That was the other thing—some of them did it just for the buzz it gave them. But sometimes that meant they gave you a story for the sake of it."

"In other words, fed you a pack of lies?"

Rebus nodded.

"And who was your snitch, back in those days?"

"I didn't really have one. I was just beginning to get the feel for who knew stuff and who didn't, and who might be willing to pass something my way."

"There was a reporter for the *Scotsman* called Albert Stout…"

"I remember him—bane of our lives."

"He worked hard on the Merchant case—and a few more besides."

"He hated the police."

"I get that impression from the stories I've read—the slant he puts on them."

"He can't be still alive?"

"Eighty-seven and living next to a golf course in Gullane."

"Bloody hell. He smoked forty a day." Rebus paused. "You're going to talk to him?"

"He's on my list. As is the pathologist who did the autopsy on Douglas Merchant."

Rebus sought his memory for the name. "Before Professor Gates?"

"His predecessor, yes—Professor Norman Cuttle, who also happens to be a spry eighty-seven."

"You're nothing if not thorough," Rebus said, making sure it didn't sound too much like a compliment. "Before or after you talk to Stefan Gilmour and the others?"

"Depends on availability. Speaking of which, we were just getting started this morning…"

"Were we?"

"Plenty more gaps I'd like you to help me fill." Fox was producing his A4 pad from a drawer. Rebus looked at his watch.

"Do we get time-and-a-half after five o'clock?"

"You *did* offer your services..."

"I did, didn't I?" Rebus acknowledged, leaning back in his chair.

That evening, in the back room of the Oxford Bar, Rebus was half-way down his first pint of IPA when Eamonn Paterson arrived and offered a top-up. Rebus shook his head, so Paterson returned from the bar with a pint of his own and a couple of packets of salted peanuts.

"Don't say I never treated you right," he said. They were seated in the same corner where Rebus had talked to Fox. "So you've managed to get your feet under the table, eh?"

Rebus had texted Paterson to say as much. He nodded slowly, pinching the bridge of his nose and swallowing back a yawn.

"Not quite got his trust yet, though," he said. "Everything's kept behind a locked door and Fox is the only one with a key."

"He's sent out invitations, you know. Wants me at three p.m. to-morrow."

"Guess who else he's asking."

"Who?"

"Albert Stout and Norman Cuttle."

"Bloody hell." Paterson puffed out his cheeks and exhaled.

"It's Stefan he's after."

"What makes you say that?"

"Saunders belonged to Stefan. Stands to reason Stefan would be the one pulling strings to get him off that murder charge." Rebus paused, studying Paterson over the rim of his glass. "Unless you know different."

"John..."

"Going through some of the old files reminded me that I was still earning your trust back then. Might be there's stuff you think needs keeping from me, even now. Walking into Fox's office was like wandering into a minefield—I'd hate to find out one of my old pals from the Saints had a map tucked away showing where all those explosives were buried."

"I'm keeping nothing from you, John," Paterson said quietly.

"And you can vouch for Stefan and Dod?"

Paterson considered this, then gave a shrug. "Everybody's got a skeleton or two—you should know that better than most. Can you hear them clanking, John? Because I can—but I'm not about to tell that to anyone else." Paterson's eyes had hardened. "Just find out what you can, and report back. That way we're *all* covered." Leaving the rest of his drink, he got to his feet and stuffed his hands into the pockets of his coat. "And don't forget to finish those nuts I bought—they cost enough..."

Rebus watched him leave. Thirty-odd years since he had been introduced to the man, and he was left wondering if he really knew him at all.

Easy to blame Fox.

Maybe too easy.

Rebus walked through to the main bar and stood with three or four other regulars. They were intent on a local news bulletin. Rebus saw Page give his ad hoc press conference. It was followed by footage of a car arriving at the McCuskey home, Bethany McCuskey in the passenger seat, her son Forbes driving. Both wore tense, worried faces.

"You *can* drive, you little bastard," Rebus muttered, finishing his drink and ordering another. While it was being poured, he stepped out into the street for a smoke. Behind him, on the TV, the First Minister was telling an interviewer of his "great shock and dismay."

"And what might this mean for the independence campaign?" the journalist asked, but the door had closed before Rebus could hear the answer. Clarke's car drew to a halt curbside as he was halfway down the cigarette.

"What are you drinking?" he asked her, but she shook her head.

"On my way somewhere," she explained.

"The lawyer again?"

"Maybe." She had changed into fresh clothes, maybe just a dab of makeup. And perfume—subtle but present. "So how did you get on with Owen Traynor?"

"He admitted everything," Rebus stated. Just for a moment she was taken in, but then she scowled. "Sorry to disappoint you, Shiv, but he says he had nothing to do with it."

"You asked him to his face?"

"In front of his daughter," Rebus added. "Hers was an interesting reaction."

"In what way?"

"I just sensed that cogs were turning; she wasn't sure what to make of it. Her dad meantime has created his own little office so he can keep on doing whatever it is he does."

"Meaning he's sticking around?"

"Looks like."

"Not running, the way someone guilty might?"

"There's something else—were you at the house when the wife arrived?"

"No."

"Young Forbes was behind the wheel."

She took a moment to consider this. "Can't really haul him in now, though, can we?"

"With his dad in intensive care, you mean?"

"Page would have kittens."

"Wouldn't want the media falling out of love with him."

"He's got half the office going through folders of housebreakings in the city. Old-timers dragged in and questioned..." She looked at him. "Doesn't *feel* like locals, though, does it?"

"The man just wants a quick result—that way the politicians will love him too."

"Can you put word out? See if anyone's heard anything?"

"I don't have the contacts I used to."

"Thing is, no one else I've spoken to has *any*. It's a skill that seems to have died out."

"Do we have a list of what was taken?"

"It's getting there."

"Get me a copy and I'll see what I can do."

"Thanks. Anything else I should know?"

"Just that me and Foxy are best buds now."

"Somehow I doubt that." She couldn't help smiling.

"Then let's just say he's thawing."

"Really?"

Rebus gave it three beats. "No, not really," he admitted. The smile was still there as she shifted the Astra's gearstick into first, giving him a little wave with the fingers of her right hand.

Back inside the bar, Rebus was asked if Alistair Darling was being brought in for questioning, since he was heading the No campaign.

"Aye, or that mate of his, Stefan Gilmour," someone else piped up.

"Guy like that can spend his way out of any amount of trouble," the first speaker argued. "See, when you back out of buying a football team, tends to leave you with a bit of spare cash—am I right, John?"

"Absolutely, Dennis," Rebus said, handing over his last five-pound note to the barman.

Alone in the flat in Great King Street, Alice Bell splashed water on her face and dried it with a towel, staring at her reflection in the bathroom mirror. Her eyes were reddened from crying, and she knew the pillow on her narrow single bed would be damp to the touch. She had closed the shutters in her room, aiming to blot out as much of the world as she could. Her knees were threatening to buckle as she made her way to the kitchen, hands brushing the hallway walls as if for support. With her mug of green tea, she settled at her desk in the living room. Her laptop, notes and books—what did any of these mean? Her throat felt cramped, heart pounding.

When her phone rang suddenly in the silence, she gave a little gasp of fright. Forbes's name was on the screen, so she answered.

"It's me," he said. "How are you?"

"I should be asking you that. I'm sorry about your dad. I tried calling earlier..."

"I know, thanks. Wasn't in a position to answer."

She listened to him exhale noisily.

"And your mum?" she asked.

"Soldiering on."

"It was a break-in...?"

"Of course it was."

"No connection...?"

"Let's not even get into that, Alice, okay?"

"If you're sure."

"Of course I'm not *sure!*" He paused, his voice calming. "Look, I need to go. Have you been to see Jess?"

"She was sleeping."

"You spoke to Owen? You know he blames me? He phoned me to tell me as much."

"You need to steer clear of him."

"I plan to. Jess should be home in a day or two, and with any luck he'll bugger off back south."

"This all feels like my fault," Alice said quietly.

"We're in it together, Alice. United we stand and all that. Talk to you tomorrow, yeah?"

"Okay," she said, listening as he ended the call. She placed the phone on the surface of the desk and stared at it.

"Divided we fall," she whispered to herself, closing the lid of her laptop.

DAY FIVE

9

Rebus's pub crawl started at opening time the next morning—not that he was on anything other than soft drinks. Clarke had sent a list of the stolen items to his phone, plus photographs provided by the McCuskeys' insurance company: pearl necklace, antique brooch, Rolex watches. The laptop was expensive, but whoever had taken it had left its cable behind. Same went for the missing mobile phones—both chargers still plugged into power points. Pat McCuskey himself had yet to regain consciousness, though the word "coma" was being avoided in the news bulletins. At least one tabloid was stirring up a debate on crime and punishment, and every paper Rebus had seen had run the story on its front page.

The pubs he visited were in unglamorous corners of the city, from Granton to Gorgie and the Inch to Sighthill. Some of the old places had closed. They were either boarded up or had been demolished and replaced by fast-food outlets. Rebus felt like an explorer returning to find that some wilderness had been tamed. Those haunts that did still exist were doing little or no business, the staff complaining about supermarket drink deals and the smoking ban.

"Lot of the old punters would rather stay at home, puffing away in front of the horse racing with a dozen cans of Special Offer..."

And that was another thing: lifestyle choices had hacked away at Rebus's network of faces. Some had passed away without him knowing; others had grown senile and moved in with family members in distant climes. *Hasn't been in for a while,* Rebus would be told. Or: *Never see him around these days.* In some pubs, the staff had no idea who he was talking about.

"Used to drink in here all the time," Rebus would persist. "Tall guy, thick mop of silver hair, worked on the buses..." Followed by yet another shake of the head. Even the hardened eleven a.m. regulars would struggle to recall "Big Tony," "Shug the Spit" and "Ecky Shake." Rebus would recite the list of stolen property to anyone who'd listen, and leave a card behind the bar with his number on it. He had texted Fox to ask if he was needed before the three p.m. interview with Eamonn Paterson. Fox had replied: *You've been talking to him then? No other way you'd know.*

"Nice work, John," Rebus had muttered to himself.

He was on his way to the final pub of his dispiriting tour when his phone rang. Not a number he recognized, but he answered anyway.

"Hello, you."

Maggie Blantyre's voice, instantly recognizable.

"Hi there, Maggie. Everything all right?"

"Fine. Are you in the car?"

"On my way to Silverknowes."

"For your sins, eh?"

"Something like that. I didn't know you had my number."

"Porkbelly gave it to me."

"Oh."

"Don't sound so worried—I told him you'd left something behind the other night."

"So how's Dod doing?"

"Same old." She paused. "It was fun seeing you at the house."

"Nice to catch up—just a shame about the circumstances."

"That man Fox has been on the phone, asking if Dod would be up for answering a few questions. Dod tells me you'll know about that."

"Sort of."

"And if he really doesn't want to talk...?"

"I suppose his doctor could write him a note."

"That's what I thought." Another pause. "It's not that he has any-thing to hide. It's just that he's not up to it."

"Understood."

"But will Fox see it that way?"

"Doesn't really matter, does it?"

"Dod doesn't want to go to his grave with a black mark against his whole career. Surely you can see that?"

"Of course."

She seemed to relax a little, as though relieved he was now sharing her burden. "Maybe we could meet for a coffee after Silverknowes — it would be lovely to see you."

"At the house, you mean?"

"There's a café on Roseburn Terrace. I sometimes take an hour out and sit there. Dod seems to manage without me..."

"Do they do food?" Rebus inquired.

"Just sandwiches and baked potatoes."

"Then I'll see you there at half-one."

"Always supposing you can bear to leave Silverknowes."

"Always supposing," Rebus echoed with a smile.

He was five minutes early, but she was already there, seated at a table by the window, the window itself opaque with condensation.

"John," she said in greeting, rising and pecking him on the cheek. Then the familiar touch of her thumb as she brushed away the lip-stick. "I ordered a pot of tea — is that okay?"

"Fine."

She didn't want anything to eat, but Rebus ordered a toasted ham sandwich. When he turned from the waitress, Maggie Blantyre was studying him intently.

"Have you left a mark on me?" he asked, rubbing at his left cheek.

"I was just thinking back. You were a lovely lot — a real gang of friends."

"The job does that to you."

"And a lot more besides."

"Despite which, here I am."

"Here you are," she said, lifting her teacup. But then her smile faltered. "There are times I wonder..."

"What?"

"How things might have turned out—if we'd been a little braver."

"You and me, you mean? At the time, I seem to remember we thought we'd taken leave of our senses."

"But thinking back..."

"The past's a dangerous place, Maggie."

"I know it is—look at what this man Fox is trying to do."

"It's not Fox, it's the Solicitor General—she wants to retry Billy Saunders, and for that to happen she needs to know nothing's going to bite her arse in the courtroom."

"You paint a lovely picture."

Rebus's phone was buzzing. "I need to take this," he apologized, seeing Clarke's name on the screen.

"Of course."

He got to his feet and exited the café. "Siobhan?" he said by way of greeting.

"Pat McCuskey just died," she said, no emotion in her voice.

"Shite."

"It's now a murder inquiry. A team's being assembled at Torphichen." Meaning the C Division HQ on Torphichen Place. Made sense: nearest manned station to the crime scene. Come reorganization, there'd be something called the Specialist Crime Division to investigate serious cases, but not yet.

"I can be there in five minutes," Rebus said.

"Your name's not been mentioned, John. I don't mean to say you won't be needed in future..."

"But *you're* in?"

"At the moment, yes."

"And Page?"

"No, not Page—and not Esson or Ogilvie either. Seems they only need an extra DI right now."

Rebus had taken the opportunity to get a cigarette lit. Through the window he could see his toastie being delivered. He indicated for it to be left there.

"How sure can we be that it's murder?"

"I agree—he could have fallen, smashed his head. Might have a better idea after the autopsy."

"On the other hand, calling it murder might stir things up a bit—put a bit of pressure on whoever did it. Small-timers, maybe not expecting to find anyone home..."

"Have you managed to get the word out around town?"

"As best I can." Rebus paused. "Media's going to be all over this."

"Not to mention McCuskey's colleagues. Speaking of which, his private secretary *did* switch off the TV—you were right about that."

"Anything sensitive on the laptop?"

"It's password-protected."

"Not exactly Fort Knox, then."

"Thing is, the Yes campaign isn't quite the same thing as the current government."

"So there could be stuff his office doesn't know about?"

"We're checking." Clarke paused. "I'm guessing it makes the son untouchable."

"Maybe, maybe not. I still think it's odd this should happen so soon after the crash."

"Lifting just enough in the way of valuables to make it look like a robbery?"

"Something like that."

"You think I should take it to DCI Ralph?"

"Nick Ralph's in charge at Torphichen?"

"His is the name I'm hearing."

"Good rep. And if he's asked for you, that consolidates it."

"Shucks."

"On the other hand, giving me a body-swerve has to count against him."

Inside the café, Maggie Blantyre seemed to be fretting that his lunch was getting cold. Rebus nodded for her benefit, took a final drag on the cigarette and flicked its remains into the gutter. "Got to go," he told Clarke.

"If you *do* hear anything about the stuff that got lifted..."

"I'll give it to you so you can get your gold star from teacher."

"You better had, or it'll be a Chinese burn next time I see you in the playground."

Rebus ended the call and went back indoors.

"Sorry about that," he said. But Maggie was on her feet, shrugging her arms back into the sleeves of her coat.

"I need to be getting back," she explained. "I've left money for my tea."

Rebus spotted the neat pile of coins next to her saucer.

"But we'd hardly got talking," he complained.

"Maybe it wasn't such a great idea." She smiled at him and touched his tie with the tips of her fingers. "But I'm sure Dod would like to see you, if you ever felt like visiting."

"Maggie..."

"Sit down and eat." She patted him on the chest and was gone.

Rebus stood there for a moment, wondering whether he was expected to follow, maybe be that bit more demonstrative. But his stomach was growling and he had to be at the Sheriff Court by three. The waitress was asking if everything was all right.

"Hunky-dory," Rebus told her, settling himself back down at the table. There was lipstick on Maggie's cup, and she had left enough money to pay the bill in full.

"Terrible news," Eamonn Paterson said.

"Terrible," Malcolm Fox agreed.

The three men were in the office at the Sheriff Court. Fox had set up a tape recorder but no video. Rebus noticed that no effort had been made to tidy away all the paperwork—quite the reverse, in fact. Fox had ensured the place looked good and messy, as if industry happened here, as if paperwork had been pored over time and again, evidence amassed. He had his A4 pad out—or maybe it was a different one. Reams of writing within, some sections capitalized or underlined. No doodles, not a thought wasted. Precision and diligence.

All of it to impress a man who knew tricks when he saw them. Paterson had even offered a wink towards Rebus as Fox fiddled with the cassette deck. If games were to be played, Paterson would prove a worthy competitor.

"Good to see the old technology still in use." Paterson gestured towards the tape recorder.

"Only when it's fit for purpose." Fox looked up. "I forgot to ask about tea or coffee—DS Rebus can nip out and get us something…?"

"I'm fine," Paterson said, giving Rebus another surreptitious wink. Fox had been letting them know where they stood. Rebus was the hired help here, Fox the master of the house.

"Shall we get started, then?"

"Ready when you are." Paterson clasped his hands across his chest, Fox started the machine, and the interview began with a few moments of staring before Fox lobbed his first question.

"Was the crossbow your idea?"

"Crossbow?"

"Didn't Summerhall have its own crossbow? Used for games of darts until the dartboard shattered?"

Paterson smiled at the memory. "I don't remember whose idea that was."

"You confiscated it after an arrest. Instead of forwarding it as evidence, you hung on to it for a while. It was only when it couldn't be located pretrial that anyone thought to come asking…"

"Okay, so you've done your homework, son—can we skip to the important stuff?"

"But this *is* the important stuff, Mr. Paterson. The lot of you seemed to run CID like it was your own little fiefdom—your rules and nobody else's. The red light in Interview Room B? If you had anyone gullible enough in there, you'd say it was a lie detector and switch it on. I wonder how many confessions you got that way..."

Paterson was still smiling benignly.

"The row of optics in DI Gilmour's office, hidden behind a bookcase—you even put the bookcase on castors so you could get at the booze quicker."

"You'd have to ask him about that."

"But I'm asking *you*." Fox glanced down at his notes again. "Or let's try this one—the practice of signing statements rather than writing them? Something you were supposed to have witnessed, but you weren't there at all. Or if you *were* there, Gilmour would have made sure everyone had the same story to tell—because he'd have written the version himself. All you lot had to do was go along with it."

Paterson's gaze shifted to Rebus. "John, tell the man..."

But Fox slapped his hand against the tabletop. "DS Rebus is here as an observer. I'm the one you need to convince."

"Convince of what?" Paterson's eyes were drilling into Fox's. "Sounds to me like you've already made your mind up—typical fucking Complaints. You should be thanking us and giving us medals—we were good at what we did. We got bad men off the streets. End of."

"You didn't get Billy Saunders off the streets. Evidence against him went missing. Statements were riddled with inaccuracies. Witnesses changed their stories after talking to you..."

"We can all agree that mistakes were made—and Stefan Gilmour walked the plank because of them."

Fox leaned back an inch or two. "What do you think Billy Saunders is going to say?"

"How do you mean?"

"Procurator Fiscal will be talking to him. Might be Saunders will want to cut a deal, looking for leniency."

"So what?"

"So he's kept his mouth shut for thirty years, but he might think it's time to spill what really happened."

"Confess, you mean?"

"Maybe not to the murder—but the cover-up after."

"Balls-up rather than cover-up."

"You reckon that's how he'll frame it?"

"I don't care what he does."

"When was the last time you set eyes on him?"

"Billy Saunders? Twenty, twenty-five years."

"Despite living in the same city?" Fox paused, making show of studying his notes. "When DI Gilmour resigned, who took control of Mr. Saunders?"

"You mean, whose snitch was he?" Paterson looked to Rebus. "He didn't warm to any of us, did he, John?"

"Not that I remember," Rebus felt obliged to answer.

"And here was I thinking he would have owed you," Fox commented. "I mean, whatever titbits he'd gifted you down the years, you got him off a murder charge..."

"Not intentionally," Paterson corrected him.

"Even so, he'd been useful to you and suddenly you just let him go?"

"Almost as if there was more to it than that," Rebus interjected.

"You were there, John," Paterson shot back. "What do you think?"

"It was another country."

"But that's where you're wrong, both of you," Fox said, turning from one man to the other. "It was the exact *same* country—you just treated it like you had the run of the place. A lot of bad habits were picked up, and the passing of time doesn't necessarily wipe the slate clean."

"It can play tricks on folks' memories, though," Paterson stressed. "Whatever story Saunders decides to tell, no way of knowing it's the truth."

"His short-term memory should be okay, though, eh?"

"What do you mean?" Paterson's eyes had narrowed.

"The Procurator's office set up a meeting with him this lunchtime. You sure it's been quarter of a century since either of you set eyes on him?" He waited until both Paterson and Rebus had nodded. "Well, according to Mr. Saunders, another of your number phoned him this very morning."

It took Rebus a moment to come up with the name. "Stefan Gilmour?"

"The same," Fox confirmed.

"What did he want?"

"He was wondering which particular beans Mr. Saunders might be about to spill."

"Stefan *spoke* to him?" Paterson sounded disbelieving, but Fox was nodding slowly.

"Seems some of those bad habits just never go away," he commented, flicking through his notes again.

After ten further stilted minutes, the interview concluded. Fox thanked Paterson and told him that Rebus would see him out.

"I'm sure the two of you will want a quick confab once I'm out of earshot."

Neither man bothered to deny it. Out on Chambers Street, Paterson pulled out his phone and called Stefan Gilmour's number.

"It's gone to voice mail," he muttered after a few seconds. He left a message anyway, telling Gilmour to phone him, adding, "You'll know what it's about, you daft bastard."

"Succinct," Rebus said. Paterson stared at the skies above and let out a sound that was on its way to being a growl.

"What does he think he's playing at, John?"

"You tell me."

"Does he really want all of us in it up to our necks?"

"Fox is right, though, isn't he? There's more to it than just keeping a good snitch on the street?"

Paterson jabbed a finger into Rebus's chest. "*You're* the one who said that, not Fox!"

"Only because he'd said it to me earlier."

"You're supposed to be on our side, John."

"Oh aye? And what about Stefan—how's he playing for the team when he's calling Billy Saunders behind our backs?"

"Christ alone knows," Paterson muttered, shoulders slumping.

"The Shadow Bible was a long time ago, Porkbelly," Rebus said quietly. "It made sense that we stuck up for one another back then—might not be so true now."

"You're asking me to side with you against Stefan?" Paterson was shaking his head slowly but determinedly.

"I'm saying we need to do what's right."

"And tell me, John—was it 'right' when you started seeing Dod Blantyre's wife? Was it 'right' that those of us who knew kept shtum?"

"That's not what we're talking about here." Blood had risen unbidden to Rebus's neck and cheeks.

"It is, though—secrets and lies and all the other crap we've dealt out and been dealt. I didn't see you owning up in there to signing your name to statements that weren't yours. But we both know it happened. A *lot* happened back then, and one crack in the dam might be all that's needed..." Paterson paused, looking Rebus up and down. "So make sure you know whose side you're on, John. And leave Stefan to me—I'll see to it he doesn't go near Saunders again."

Rebus noticed that Paterson's hand was outstretched. He took it and returned the firm shake, Paterson apparently reluctant to let go.

"All right then," Rebus said, finally extricating himself. He watched Paterson walk away, then returned indoors and headed to the toilets. Examining his face in the soap-spattered mirror, he saw that there was still a faint smudge of lipstick on his right cheek. Cursing, he rubbed it away. Maybe Fox had noticed it and decided not to say anything. But Paterson had certainly spotted it, and had surmised the identity of its bestower—hadn't she asked him for Rebus's phone number, after all?

Fox was in the office, tidying up now that the show was over.

"Much further forward?" Rebus asked him.

In place of an answer, Fox had a question of his own. "Did you reach Stefan Gilmour?"

"No," Rebus admitted. "Paterson left a message."

"Unbelievably stupid of him to contact Saunders."

"I'm not going to disagree," Rebus offered, slumping onto a chair.

"And have you come to any conclusions yourself, Detective Sergeant Rebus?"

"About what?"

"You're either my man or you're theirs. Up until now, maybe you've been thinking you can swap shirts as and when."

"Only conclusion I've been able to draw so far is that you're as sleekit as they come."

"I might have to pretend you mean that as a compliment."

"In some ways, it probably is." Rebus managed a tired smile.

"I'm sorry for threatening to turn you into the tea boy."

"You were just letting Paterson know who was boss."

"And you too, maybe."

Rebus nodded. "So what now?"

"Our first interview needs to be sent for transcribing. I'll leave that to you, if you don't mind—I'm meeting Elinor Macari at the top of the hour."

"To hear what else Billy Saunders has been saying?"

"That's right."

"So do you want me to lock up?"

Fox studied Rebus, then shook his head.

"Still don't trust me?" Rebus tried to sound hurt.

Fox didn't answer. He placed a thick file in his briefcase, where it joined his notepad. "It's good you finally got rid of that lipstick," he said, closing the clasps.

10

Some of the same faces Clarke had seen outside the McCuskeys' home were now huddled on the narrow pavement on Torphichen Place. Cars and vans parked illegally were being ticketed by wardens, but without the owners seeming to mind. Those same vehicles had narrowed the road from three lanes to one, and traffic was backed up, giving drivers plenty of time to stare at the media circus.

Once inside the police station, having ignored all the questions yelled in her direction, Clarke showed her ID and was buzzed through a locked door into the body of the building. Every bit of space on the first floor seemed to be in the process of being taken over by the Major Incident Team—desks moved, extra chairs sought, communications established. Clarke squeezed her way through the melee until she reached its still center and introduced herself to DCI Ralph. He was over six feet tall, his dark hair parted in the center, and sporting a neatly trimmed beard. He didn't bother with a handshake or words of welcome, telling her instead that there would be a briefing in ten minutes' time and she should make herself useful until then.

"Olivia will show you the ropes," he explained, nodding towards a young woman who was carrying a computer printer past him.

"Olivia Webster," the officer said by way of introduction, as Clarke followed her. "I'm a DC."

"I'm DI Clarke."

"Siobhan Clarke—I know who you are."

"Have we met before?"

Webster shook her head. She had long brown hair and gray eyes, her skin pale. "I've just heard you mentioned." She placed the printer on one of the desks, next to a monitor. "I've only been here six weeks—transferred from Dundee." She stared at the setup on the desk.

"Keyboard?" Clarke suggested.

Webster smiled. "Knew something wasn't quite right." She scanned the room. "Must be one around here somewhere..." Then she was off again, leaving Clarke without any sense of what she could or should be doing. She peered from a window until the press pack below noticed her and started waving.

"Not much room here for media conferences." DCI Ralph was standing next to her. "We're using the hotel on the corner instead."

"Good thinking."

He studied her. "You were at the scene soon after Mr. McCuskey was found." Statement rather than question. "That's why I want you focusing on the break-in itself—the nuts and bolts, if you like."

Clarke nodded her acceptance. "There's already an officer working on the stolen goods—putting word out."

"Good."

"Maybe we could bring him in?"

"As part of the team, you mean?" He wafted a hand in the general direction of the chaos behind him. "You think we're short-staffed?"

"Just seems rational, since he's been involved in the preliminary investigation."

"This wouldn't be your old friend, would it? The infamous John Rebus?"

"John not only has contacts, he was also with me when we attended the scene of a crash not far from the McCuskey home. The young woman pulled from the wreckage happens to be Forbes McCuskey's girlfriend. We're not sure she was alone in the car at the time."

Ralph grew thoughtful. "That's quite the coincidence."

"Our thinking exactly. Again, if DS Rebus is brought in, he's already done a lot of the groundwork…"

"Let me think about it, once I've got the pep talk out of the way." He glanced at his watch, then concentrated on the movement in the room, seeming pleased with the progress. Olivia Webster had located a grubby-looking keyboard and was plugging it in. Another officer, having wiped clean a large whiteboard, was attaching photos of the crime scene to it. McCuskey had been moved before any pictures could be taken of him, but there was a typed description of how he had been found on the sitting room floor, face down and with his legs at an awkward angle. There was a close-up of the smashed patio door, and another of the ransacked bedroom. Two bedrooms, in fact. Clarke walked over and studied the photograph of what had to be the son's old room—she hadn't checked it at the time, and chided herself now. There were band posters on its walls, shelves of novels, a double bed with a bright red duvet. The duvet had been thrown to the floor, some of the books scattered, one poster torn in half. Drawers sat half open. Yet there had been nothing in the room worth taking. Was this evidence of anger? As if Forbes McCuskey were as much of a target as his parents? Clarke thought back to Owen Traynor again. Did they need to bring him in for a more formal chat?

DCI Ralph was clapping his hands, calling out for everyone to stop what they were doing. All eyes turned towards him. Officers filed in from the corridor and the other rooms off. Clarke found herself with her back pressed against the whiteboard, unable to see anything except the very top of Nick Ralph's head. Around her, phones were pinging and vibrating.

"Maybe we could have those off," Ralph ordered.

She slid her own from her pocket. She had a message from Malcolm Fox, but she could read it later. For now, she powered down the phone and concentrated on the job at hand.

"Let's begin," Nick Ralph said.

*   *   *

Early evening, Rebus left his tenement flat and headed for a shop on Marchmont Road where he could buy cigarettes and bacon. He was almost at the top of Arden Street when he spotted Forbes McCuskey on the other side of the road. McCuskey had recognized him. He stood there for a moment, then strode towards Rebus.

"You following me? Stalking me?"

"Just passing," Rebus said, reluctant to let him know they lived on the same street.

"I could call this harassment."

"It's not. Sorry to hear about your dad, by the way."

The young man's anger abated a little, good manners taking over. "Thanks," he said.

"We'll be doing everything we can to find his attacker."

Forbes McCuskey nodded distractedly. Now that he had confronted the detective, he seemed not to know what to do next.

"Including interviewing Jessica's father," Rebus continued matter-of-factly.

"What for?"

"Because his daughter had just been in a car smash and he wasn't convinced it was her fault. Because, historically, he has a temper on him."

"So he attacks *my* father in revenge?"

"Only when he fails to find *you* at home."

McCuskey started to shake his head, but then stopped. "Well," he said, "I suppose you have to explore all the avenues…"

"You can be sure we'll do that." Rebus gestured towards McCuskey's building. "I'd have thought your mum might be needing you."

"Aunt Dorothy's with her. I'm just collecting some of my stuff."

"Your mum's okay, being in the house…?"

"I did suggest a hotel."

"Not the Caledonian?" Rebus cautioned.

McCuskey nodded his understanding. "Jessica's there..."

"Next door to her father. Have you been to see her?"

McCuskey shook his head.

"She'll have been in touch, though, having heard...?"

"I've talked to her, yes." McCuskey's eyes locked on Rebus. "Were you really just passing?"

"I live down the road," Rebus admitted, seeing no harm in it. "On my way to Margiotta's. I'm at number seventeen, second floor—if you ever want to talk."

"Talk? What about?"

"Maybe why you lied to us."

"Did I lie?"

"You said you couldn't drive, yet I saw you behind the wheel, with your mum in the passenger seat."

The young man was shaking his head. "I said I *don't* drive, I never said I couldn't if I have to."

"You were attempting to mislead us, Mr. McCuskey. And all it's done is made me even more curious about the night of the smash."

"You can't still be going on about that?"

"It's unfinished business—and with what happened to your dad..." Rebus left the end of the sentence hanging and started on his way. "Number seventeen," he reminded McCuskey. "My name's on the bell..."

Once inside his flat, Forbes McCuskey dug his phone from his pocket and made a call.

"It's me," he said. Then, in response to a question: "Yeah, I'm all right, I suppose. A bit numb, to be honest. But I've just been talking to that guy Rebus." He listened for a moment, wandering through to the kitchen and opening the fridge, in search of something to drink. "Apparently he lives on my street, which is a nuisance, and he's still harping on about the crash. But here's the thing—the thinking seems to be that Jess's father might have been behind the break-in. That could play well for us, take a bit of the heat off." He paused again to listen, glugging milk from a carton. "No, not *that* heat. Speaking of which, I better try ringing Jess..."

He ended the call and went through to his room, falling back onto the bed and staring at the ceiling. There was some dope under the mattress and he would smoke it in a little while. Maybe he'd drink some wine, too, or neat tequila. Anything to stop him thinking about his father and what had happened—what *might* have happened.

"You dickhead," he muttered to himself, covering his eyes with his forearm. "What the hell have you gone and done...?"

Slowly, the tears began to come.

"Can I come up?"

"Where are you?" Siobhan Clarke asked.

"Standing outside."

She went to the window to take a look. Her flat was on the first floor of a utilitarian block just off Broughton Street. Fox was standing in the middle of the road, his phone pressed to his ear.

"What's going on?" she asked him.

"I'd rather tell you in person."

She scanned her living room. It was presentable—*more* than presentable. But still, she didn't want to share it with Fox. "I'll come down," she said into the phone. "There's a bar around the corner we can go to."

"I don't drink," Fox reminded her. "And this isn't really a social visit."

"Two minutes," she said, ending the call and wondering whether to bother making herself presentable.

The bar was called The Basement because it was in a basement, reached by a short flight of stone steps from the pavement. It was gloomy and the furniture looked like props from the *Alien* films. There was a traditional pub almost the same distance away in the other direction, but Clarke had chosen this place because she sensed Fox would be less at ease in it. The drinkers were young, the music as jagged as the seats and tables. Clarke ordered a glass of white wine and Fox a spiced tomato juice.

"Can't hear myself think," he complained, so Clarke relented and led them back outdoors to the tiny courtyard where smokers could usually be found. There was a bench attached to the wall and a couple of slatted tables, plus a scattering of wicker chairs. They sat opposite one another with their drinks. The night was chill, and Clarke wrapped her coat around her, pleased to see that she was better prepared than Fox, who wore only a thin dark blue suit, shirt and tie.

"Better?" she inquired.

"Quieter, certainly." He buttoned his suit jacket as he spoke. "I'll make this brief—it's about you and David Galvin." He watched for her reaction and she couldn't help but give one, her eyes widening slightly, glass stopping halfway to her mouth.

"What about him?"

"He works as a fiscal depute."

"I know that."

"On the Procurator Fiscal's staff."

"To state the blindingly obvious."

"And the two of you are an item?"

"What the hell has that got to do with you?"

Fox held up a hand to appease her. "It shouldn't have *anything* to do with me—except that Professional Standards has been contacted anonymously, and that communication has been passed along."

"Anonymous?"

Fox nodded. "But obviously from someone Galvin works beside. Maybe someone with a grudge."

"So what does the message say?"

"It simply informs Professional Standards that the two of you are spending a lot of time together and that you know one another intimately..."

Had she been any less furious and irritated, she might have found his language amusing. Instead of which, her face remained stony as she told him to go on.

"There's not much more," he admitted with a shrug. "Messenger says we should maybe look into your relationship, in case there's any element of impropriety to be found."

"Such as me influencing David and vice versa?"

"I suppose so." Fox shifted a little, his drink untouched as yet. "Do many people know about you and Mr. Galvin?"

"I've not told anyone." She gave him a hard stare. "It's not that I think we've got anything to hide..."

"Of course." Fox paused. "And on his part...?"

"Sounds as if he might have told *one* person at least." She lifted her phone. "I better talk to him." But then she studied the illuminated screen. "Soon as I can get a signal."

"Maybe leave it till morning," Fox advised. "Give yourself time to reflect."

"Always erring on the side of caution, eh? Never doing anything in the heat of the moment?"

"Goes with the job," he said with a shrug.

After a moment, Clarke put her phone down again and lifted her drink. She took a couple of sips, before asking him how things were going with Rebus.

"Hard to say."

"Because you can't tell me, or because you don't know?"

"More the latter than the former. I'm just not sure where I stand with him. There's so much happening behind his eyes..."

"I know that feeling." Clarke hoisted her glass again. "He's like one of those chess wizards, the ones who play a dozen boards at the same time."

"Not a bad analogy," Fox agreed with a smile. "And if he looks like losing even one of those games..."

"Time to duck before the pieces go flying."

Now they were both smiling, and the cold didn't seem as bad as all that.

"Thanks for letting me know," Clarke said into the silence. "About the mystery message, I mean. What's the next step?"

"It goes to the bottom of a rather crowded in-tray. Might be it never comes up for air. With reorganization, a lot of paperwork could end up in the vaults."

"Is that ethical?"

"You think a bit of Rebus has rubbed off on me already?"

"He can have that effect." Clarke noticed her glass was empty. "Another?" she asked.

"I've not started this one yet. But look…and don't take this the wrong way or anything…"

"Go on," she prompted.

"I was wondering if you'd eaten—because I haven't and I'm starving."

"Broughton Street's got everything you need," Clarke said. "And to tell you the truth, a curry might just hit the spot…"

DAY SIX

11

Next morning, Rebus dropped into Gayfield Square. There was no point arriving at the Sheriff Court before Fox and finding a locked door. DCs Esson and Ogilvie had a pot of coffee on the go, and—as a bonus—there was no sign of James Page.

"He's in the huff," Esson explained.

"Because Nick Ralph got given the sweeties?" Rebus guessed.

"Plus he can't even take it out on you, since the Solicitor General stole you from us."

"I almost feel sorry for the man." Rebus took a slurp of coffee, then made a face.

"Ronnie bought it," Esson explained. Rebus looked to Ronnie Ogilvie.

"I didn't see 'decaf' on the packet."

"Or the words 'cheap and nasty,'" Rebus added. "That's some hattrick, son." Rebus's mobile phone alerted him to a call. He saw Ogilvie and Esson exchange a look.

"That ringtone's BB King, by the way," he informed them. "So don't even start." Then, into the phone itself: "Good morning, Inspector Fox—what can I do for you?"

"Elinor Macari wants to see us. How soon can you get here?"

"The Sheriff Court? Ten minutes with a headwind. What's up?"

"You remember that your friend had a word with Billy Saunders?"

"According to Saunders," Rebus felt it necessary to qualify. "We've not heard Stefan Gilmour's version yet."

"Well, that's going to happen sooner rather than later. Billy Saunders has vanished."

"Vanished?"

"His car was found this morning on a patch of wasteland in Niddrie. Guy who runs the minicab office hadn't heard from him all through the night shift. Apparently his last job was from a pub called the Gimlet..."

"Just off Calder Road?"

"Might have guessed you'd know it."

"I was in there asking about the stuff taken from the McCuskey house."

"Well, the destination was Niddrie Marischal Road."

"Bandit country," Rebus commented. "Does the passenger have a name?"

"Robinson."

"Probably fake."

Fox had to ask: "What makes you say that?"

"If he drinks in the Gimlet, chances are he's dodgy to start with. And people don't go to Niddrie at night for the Michelin restaurants. So Mr. Dodgy was probably about to *do* something dodgy."

"And wouldn't want his name cropping up if we ran a check?" Rebus could almost hear Fox nodding his acceptance of the argument. "Ten minutes, you say?"

"Will there be coffee?"

"If we're talking the Solicitor General's inner sanctum, I think there's one of those Nespresso machines."

"You silver-tongued bastard. I'm on my way..."

Elinor Macari's assistant brought the tray through.

"Smells great," Rebus said, accepting one of the small white mugs. There were even biscuits, and he selected one from the plate. Macari was seated behind her desk and didn't want coffee. She drank from a bottle of still water and looked as though she'd spent at least an hour of the morning at some gym or other. Her skin glowed. When the assistant left, she asked Fox for his report.

"DS Rebus should probably do the talking," Fox told her, so that was what Rebus did, giving his view of the Gimlet and its clientele. Afterwards, the Solicitor General tossed her empty bottle into a waste basket and pressed her hands together.

"Plan of action?" Her eyes drilled into Rebus's.

"He's not been gone long. Might be he's got a lumber somewhere or will wander back home after a day or two, having bankrupted himself at a casino or card game."

"Or he's been paid to make himself scarce—would we happen to know of anyone with money enough to make that happen?"

"We'll be talking to Stefan Gilmour," Fox interrupted. "We'll also track down Saunders's last fare, just in case it ties in."

"What else?" the Solicitor General demanded.

"We can question family and friends, ask his mobile provider for a list of calls made and received..."

She nodded, as if finally just about satisfied.

"Mind if I ask something?"

"What is it, DS Rebus?"

"You interviewed Saunders, didn't you? Could that have spooked him?"

"It's possible," Macari conceded. "A follow-up session was due later today."

"Might be why he ran, then." Rebus paused. "Did he give you anything?"

"He was reticent."

"Were you prepared to offer him a deal?"

"Not immediately. But if you're concerned, I'm happy to reassure you your own name didn't come up—that's the only reason you're sitting here. Malcolm has explained his thinking to me, and I can see why he might find you useful...up to a point."

"I'm guessing I'll know when that point is reached?"

"Believe me, you will."

"Fine then. But meantime, have we earned our coffee and biscuit?"

For his efforts, Rebus received the sort of look she would have given a busted rowing machine. Fox was rising to his feet, placing his mug back on the tray.

"We've taken enough of your time," he was saying.

Rebus followed suit, pausing just long enough to lift a second digestive. Macari said nothing, but kept her eyes on them as they exited the office. Once the door was closed, she reached forward and took the one remaining biscuit, studying it for the best part of thirty seconds before indulging in a large, satisfying bite.

The Gimlet wouldn't open for another hour, so they took Rebus's Saab to Niddrie. The worst of the housing stock had been ripped down and replaced. Gap sites existed, and it was on one of these that the Ford Sierra had been abandoned.

"Key left in the ignition," Fox explained as they parked next to the spot. "Lucky the local kids didn't decide to take it for a spin."

"Why didn't they?"

Fox just shrugged. "Anyway, the owner of the minicab company sent someone this morning to rescue it."

"Meaning any evidence will have been contaminated," Rebus commented.

"Evidence?"

"It's the stuff we collect to make a case that can go to trial."

Fox glared at him. "You think something could have happened to Saunders?"

"Not really."

"But there's a chance?"

"If someone's going to do a runner, they'd normally head for a train or bus station. Saunders didn't do that. He left his car in the back of beyond."

"To throw us off his scent?"

"Or it could be he's got a pal nearby who could fix him up." Rebus narrowed his eyes against the smoke from his cigarette.

"So we talk to family and friends?"

"And his boss—see what else he might know about the booking from the Gimlet."

"And the Gimlet itself—someone there is bound to know who the pickup was for."

"Getting them to tell us might be the problem. It's not exactly G and Ts and cashmere jumpers in there."

"But you're a known face?"

"Doesn't make me a *liked* face."

"Then maybe I should do the talking."

"That I'd like to see."

"My pleasure," Malcolm Fox said, doing everything but puffing out his chest.

But first they visited Billy Saunders's home, an unassuming mid-terrace pebble-dash in Blackhall. Saunders was still married to Bettina, the woman Douglas Merchant had been killed over.

"Best if you don't introduce me," Rebus told Fox.

"In case he's mentioned you to her?"

Rebus nodded.

The woman was at home, but showed no great enthusiasm to see them. They stood in the living room, since every chair was covered in cats or laundry, including some with cats on top. She was sure Billy would turn up. Reckoned he was just sickened with working nights. He'd be sleeping it off somewhere.

Did he have friends in Niddrie?

He did not.

And things were okay at home?

If they were asking about other women, who would be daft enough?

She knew that a case against Billy was being prepared? Had he seemed worried about that?

Wouldn't they be?

Any addresses where they might try looking for him? And a copy of his latest mobile bill...

They didn't ask for much, did they?

Then Rebus cleared his throat and asked her about Douglas Merchant.

"What about him?"

"Billy's supposed to have done him in for sleeping with you."

Bettina Saunders gave a piglike snort. "That was a lot of pish—some rumor got started and Billy saw red."

"He *did* kill Merchant, then?" Fox interrupted.

"I'm not saying that." She glowered at him. "Billy might get angry, but he wouldn't hurt anyone—that's why the trial collapsed in the first place. Wrong man was in the dock."

"Yet he admitted his guilt to a cellmate."

"Men in jail say all sorts, don't they? You let the story get round that you've done someone in, you get less grief from the other cons."

"You seem to know all about it."

"Years of my life spent visiting him inside."

"If and when he gets in touch, you'll let us know?"

"You're right at the top of my list."

"I'm not entirely sure I believe that." But Fox thanked her anyway.

Similar line of questioning at the minicab office. The Ford was parked down the lane, so they were even able to give it the once-over. No signs of damage; nothing to indicate any sort of struggle.

"My way of thinking," Saunders's boss said, folding his bare meaty arms across his chest, "is that the punter hasn't any cash, so takes off. Billy goes after him—and that's when something happens. Not the fittest of guys, so he could have keeled over somewhere. Alternatively, he ends up being led into an ambush." He shrugged his shoulders as if such eventualities were written into the job description.

Back in the Saab, Fox asked Rebus if it was time for them to try the Gimlet.

"I think you're ready," Rebus said, starting the engine. "Place used to be under the ownership of a thug called Frank Hammell. Good spot to visit if you were in the market for a stolen telly or hi-fi."

"Where's Hammell these days?"

"Out of the game."

"You make it sound like a decision taken out of his hands."

"You might say that..."

When they reached their destination, Fox walked in ahead of Rebus. Rebus placed a hand on his arm.

"Slight change of plan—maybe let me do the talking to start with."

He had already been recognized—not by the tattooed barwoman but by the young, well-dressed man seated on a stool, who broke off his conversation with her as Rebus walked in.

"Darryl Christie," Rebus said.

"Mr. Rebus." Christie didn't budge from the stool. He looked Rebus up and down. "Something I can do for you?"

Rebus ignored the question and turned towards Fox. "This young streak of piss is the reason Frank Hammell gave up this place, and plenty of others like it. I know what you're thinking—he can't be long out of school—but don't let that fool you."

As if to reinforce the point, Christie rubbed his hand along the acne on his jaw line, offering a grin which still seemed to contain some milk teeth. Rebus was searching the room for muscle.

"Not got your boys with you?" he asked. "Unless the old lad in the corner with the tot of rum is a master of disguise."

"City's nice and calm, Mr. Rebus. And personnel come expensive."

"Did you happen to be here last night, Mr. Christie?" Fox interrupted. "Around eight forty-five one of your clients rang for a cab. We're trying to trace the driver."

"Ask Lavinia here," Christie advised, indicating the barwoman.

"I'm only on days," she corrected him.

"So you are." Christie tutted at his mistake. "It would have been Colin or Johnny."

"Plus someone manning the door?" Rebus asked.

Christie thought for a moment. "That would have been Deano. You're thinking he would have clocked the cab? What's the story with the driver anyway?"

"Not your concern, Mr. Christie," Fox said, sounding apologetic.

"I like you," Christie told him. "You've got the right attitude—probably means you've not been chumming Rebus long. And because you've made an impression..." Christie took out his phone and made three calls: both barmen, plus the bouncer. He drew a blank.

"Nobody saw anything," he announced with a thin smile.

"Now there's a surprise," Rebus muttered.

"Maybe if you felt able to trust me with a bit more information..." Christie was speaking to Fox, and Fox eventually opened his mouth to respond.

"Tell him nothing," Rebus snapped. "We'll do this the hard way. It's not as if he owes me anything..."

"Because you put away Kenny Magrath?" Christie had risen from the bar stool. "I'm supposed to thank you for that?"

But Rebus was already turning away, his hand on Fox's arm again. "Let's go," he said.

Outside, he got into the car, slamming shut the door and choking the steering wheel with both fists.

"A bit of history?" Fox surmised.

"His sister was Annette McKie. Kenny Magrath killed her and I put him away."

"And he doesn't owe you anything?"

"Because he wanted Magrath dead—probably still does."

Fox nodded his understanding. "Maybe if I'd gone in there on my own..."

"He'd have played the same game he just did. You heard his tone when he made those calls—no way he wanted them telling you any-thing useful."

"You think he had something to do with Saunders's disappear-ance?"

Rebus stared hard at the pub's uninviting frontage. "I wish," he said.

"But you don't think so—which takes us back to where we started."

"We're just doing it the hard way, like I said."

"Meaning?"

"Meaning we put in a request to check Saunders's phone calls."

"And then sit on our hands?"

"What do you think?"

"I think we go to Glasgow and invite ourselves in for a chat with an extremely well-connected businessman by the name of Stefan Gilmour."

"Bingo," Rebus said.

Fox gave a final glance towards the Gimlet. "You're really telling me that kid's a player in the city?"

"World's changing, Malcolm. Out with the old, as they say."

"Present company excepted, naturally."

"Naturally," Rebus said, starting the engine.

"Do I need a lawyer?"

"You're not under caution, Mr. Traynor."

Ralph and Clarke had brought Owen Traynor to one of the smaller, tidier offices on the first floor of Torphichen Place. Members of the Major Incident Team could be heard behind the closed door, pretending to traverse the corridor but really hoping to over-hear some titbit or other.

"Had to run the bloody gauntlet coming in," Traynor com-plained. He was wearing his suit, but no tie. "If this is about Jessica's crash..."

"In a way it is," Nick Ralph interrupted. "DI Clarke tells me your daughter is recovering?"

Traynor nodded.

"But there's still some confusion over the cause of the crash."

"She skidded on a patch of ice or something."

"So she *was* driving?"

"That's the story."

"Interesting choice of words," Clarke broke in. "Sounds to me like you don't totally believe her."

"Blame your pal Rebus—he's the one who tried stirring things up, bringing in Forbes McCuskey's name. Next thing I know, he's asking if I had anything to do with the break-in at the parents' place."

"And did you?"

Traynor stared hard at Clarke. "I *knew* that was what this was about," he growled. "You're desperate to put some mug in the frame—any mug!"

"We're just interested in the coincidence, Mr. Traynor," DCI Ralph said, all calmness and reason.

"As far as I know, the only thing that links the two events is the son, but I don't see *him* being questioned. Wouldn't look good in the papers, would it? So now *my* photo's going to be in them instead!"

"Just to be clear, then," Ralph went on, ignoring the outburst, "you've never met Patrick and Bethany McCuskey? Never been to their house?"

"Didn't even know where it was until I saw it on the news."

"And you don't blame Forbes McCuskey for what happened to Jessica?" Clarke added.

Traynor stared at her again. "Not at all," he stated, though she could tell he was lying, his eyes shifting away from her as he spoke.

"I believe you have friends in the Met?" Nick Ralph said, leaning back a little in his chair.

"Amazing who you bump into when you play golf." Traynor tugged at one of his shirt cuffs.

"Yet you've been in a bit of trouble in the past."

"Says who?"

"There's been a certain amount of insolvency."

"I've always bounced back."

"Unlike some of your investors."

"What's that got to do with anything?"

"Just that you're a man with a temper."

"Doesn't mean I go around walloping politicians. Besides which, I was in my hotel all morning and plenty of staff can vouch for me." Traynor looked from one detective to the other, as if daring them to doubt him. "So you're wasting your time, and—more importantly—mine."

"Do you like Forbes McCuskey?" Clarke asked into the silence.

"Kid seems all right."

"And if it were the case that he caused the crash rather than Jessica, and fled the scene without helping her . . . ?"

"That's not what she says happened."

"Maybe she's just scared what you'd do if you discovered the truth."

Traynor glared at her, then turned his attention to Ralph. "We about done here?"

"Unless there's anything you want to add."

"Nothing," Traynor stated.

Olivia Webster was summoned to lead Traynor out. Clarke and Ralph stood together in the corridor, watching him leave.

"Wouldn't want to get on the wrong side of him," Nick Ralph commented. "On the other hand, I've seen nothing to suggest that breaking into someone's house is his style." He rubbed his chin thoughtfully. "Any word on the stolen property?"

"Not yet."

An officer had appeared in one of the doorways, waving to catch Ralph's attention. "Call from the First Minister's office," he explained.

"Wonderful," Ralph muttered, stalking down the hall.

12

Footage from the police station was playing on the TV news channel in Rebus and Fox's café of choice. They were in the Glasgow suburbs, and thankful for the satnav on Fox's phone.

"Never really got to grips with the roads here," Fox commented, as his Scotch broth was delivered.

"Join the club." Rebus sat back a little, so that the waiter could place the steak pie in front of him. It came with chips, salad and a roll and butter.

"Help me out," Rebus said to Fox.

"You're on your own, pal," Fox replied, tucking his napkin into his waistband. Then, after a glance at the wall clock: "And you've got about twenty minutes before we need to be elsewhere." Having said which, he picked up his spoon and got to work.

"Did you always think you'd end up in the Complaints?" Rebus asked.

"Does anybody?"

"Maybe not, but you seem to be good at it—judging by the number of cops who hate your guts."

"Yourself included?"

"Maybe less so than before."

Fox added some white pepper to the soup. "Somebody's got to make sure we don't take liberties—pun intended."

"And used many times before, I don't doubt." Rebus removed some gristle from between his teeth. "But now that we're getting to know one another, would that make you feel any worse if you had to bust me?"

Fox glanced up at him. "Maybe," he conceded.

"You'd bust me anyway, though?"

"If I needed to."

"Some bloody job that. Say I was trying to get some bawbag to confess, and they *did* end up confessing but I'd had to finesse a procedure or two...?"

Fox smiled. "You think that puts you on the side of the angels?"

"And you don't?"

"I'm not some bean-counter, John. Every situation is different, and circumstances are taken into account."

"Sounds like bean-counter talk to me." But Rebus was smiling too.

Fox checked the clock again.

"You don't think Stefan will grant us a few minutes' leeway?" Rebus asked.

"Would you?"

"Good point," Rebus was forced to agree, digging into the steak pie again.

"Hey, take a look." Fox was gesturing towards the TV. Rebus saw the media outside Torphichen police station becoming restive as a man maneuvered his way past them to get inside. The shot then cut to the same man leaving the building, while the newsreader explained that he was "businessman Owen Traynor from southwest London, whose daughter Jessica is the girlfriend of Patrick McCuskey's son..."

"Good for you, Siobhan," Rebus muttered under his breath, before giving up on the pie and starting on the chips instead.

It was a three-story hotel, all smoked glass and chrome, sited within easy reach of the M8 and M74—a place where business traffic could stop for meetings or food or a bed for the night. Stefan Gilmour and his partner, the ex-footballer Barney Frewin, had built the place from scratch, and it had only been open three weeks. There were framed photos on a wall in the lobby showing guests at the official opening party, including Frewin and a few of his footballing cronies past and present, plus Gilmour's girlfriend and some of her showbiz friends.

"She's still a beauty," Fox was forced to admit. Then, sensing Rebus's look: "Used to see her on TV..."

They were about to announce themselves at the reception desk, but Stefan Gilmour himself was walking towards them, calling out a greeting to Rebus. The two men shook hands, and Rebus introduced Fox.

"Let's make this quick," Gilmour said, sounding impatient. He was in shirtsleeves, no sign of a jacket. He summoned the lift, and once all three were inside, slipped a key card in and out of the slot before pressing the button marked PH.

"Penthouse," he explained. "Not booked today, so we might as well."

The doors slid open, and they were in a private hallway, doors leading off to living room, bathroom and bedroom. Floor-to-ceiling windows gave views towards the center of Glasgow and the hills beyond. On the other hand, what Rebus mostly saw were motorway lanes and industrial units.

"Impressive," Fox said, as Gilmour settled himself on one of the room's two sofas, stretching his arms out along the back of it.

"I just saw Owen Traynor on TV," Gilmour said. "What's that all about?"

"You know him?" Rebus asked.

"We were planning a hotel in Croydon—never quite happened, but Traynor was part of the syndicate. Now he pops up in Edinburgh..."

"He's from Croydon originally," Rebus commented.

"Hence his usefulness, John."

"Fascinating as all that may be," Fox broke in, "it's not why we're here."

"So why are you?" Gilmour crossed one leg over the other.

Rebus stayed standing by a window, while Fox took an armchair. "It's to do with Billy Saunders," Fox said.

"I know—it was daft of me to phone him." Gilmour held up his hands, arms still stretched.

"How did you get his number?" Rebus asked.

"Guy drives a minicab, John—how hard do you think it was?"

"I'm guessing maybe money changed hands."

"No comment."

"Well," Fox interrupted, "maybe you'd care to 'comment' on Mr. Saunders's sudden disappearance?"

Gilmour looked bemused.

"His car was found abandoned on waste ground," Rebus explained. "Just when the Solicitor General was readying to question him more thoroughly."

"Whoa there." Gilmour leaned forward, elbows now resting on knees, hands clasped together. "You're not going to blame *me* for that!"

"What exactly did you say to him?" Fox inquired.

"I just wanted to know…" Gilmour broke off, fixing Fox with a look. "I'm not a cop anymore, haven't been for thirty years. Nothing to stop me wanting to ask the man what he was going to say to an investigation."

"Asking rather than threatening?"

"Threats aren't my style." Gilmour leaped to his feet. Pointing at Fox, he aimed his question at Rebus. "How can you hang around with this skid mark?"

"So you asked Billy Saunders what he was going to say?"

Gilmour stood not three feet from Rebus, and eventually nodded by way of answer.

"And?" Rebus nudged.

"And nothing—he didn't want to talk to me. I doubt our little chat lasted twenty seconds." Gilmour paused. "I'm willing to bet you've applied to see his phone records—they'll show I'm not lying."

"Did you call him back?" Rebus asked.

"Tried, but he wouldn't pick up."

"And at no point did you offer an inducement?" Fox added from his chair.

"A bribe, you mean?" Gilmour shook his head. "Tell you what I think, though—I think you lot scared him off. Thirty years after the fact and suddenly he's going to be in the dock again. I'd probably have scarpered too."

"Nevertheless, Mr. Gilmour," Fox commented, "it can't be easy for you. You've got all of this now." He waved a hand, taking in the room and everything around it. "Stuff you did in the past, you think of it as long forgotten. *This* is your life now—unless Billy Saunders stands up in court and tells the world about the person you used to be."

"A good cop is who I used to be, the kind that put his neck on the line, the kind that made the public feel that little bit safer in their beds at night." Gilmour walked over and planted himself in front of Fox's chair. "Whereas what I hear about you is you could never cut it in CID, near as dammit got down on your knees and *begged* for a Complaints posting."

Fox got slowly to his feet, blood rising to his cheeks. "You know this doesn't end it? Case can go ahead with or without Billy Saunders. I'm still going to be picking apart your little gang."

"He means us, John," Gilmour called to Rebus.

"But you above all," Fox felt the need to clarify. "Saunders was *your* snitch and I reckon you're the one who got him off. Whether you had any help is neither here nor there."

"Douglas Merchant was a scumbag who got what was coming to him. We should be looking at a commendation rather than a jail sentence."

"Keep telling yourself that," Fox advised. "The more often you and your pal Paterson say it, the less convinced you sound."

"Are we about done here? Because I'm hearing nothing that's going to cause me even a sleepless five minutes. Billy Saunders can tell any story he wants; it's going to be his word against Summerhall CID. Hearsay's all you're ever going to have." Gilmour jutted out his chin, almost toe to toe with Fox. Fox was opening his mouth, readying a response, when the lift doors shuddered open.

"You here yet, Big Boy?" A woman's singsong voice. "Reception told me to come up and wait..." She walked into the room and came to a stop, lips opening into an O.

"Your next appointment?" Fox pretended to guess, eyes on Gilmour.

"I think you should leave," Gilmour said, his words edged with frost.

The woman was young—midtwenties maybe. Dyed red hair and a short coat below which was a presumably shorter dress. Rebus thought he recognized her from one of the photos in the lobby. She'd had a footballer's arm draped around her. Perfume was filling the room, replacing the oxygen.

"We're going," Rebus stated, making his way towards the hall. Gilmour was avoiding eye contact, but that was just fine. Maybe there was some parting shot from Fox, but if so Rebus didn't hear it. The two men stood together as the lift doors closed and they began their descent. Nothing was said until Rebus paused by the display from the party, checking that he was right about the visitor.

"Cheating on a woman like that," Fox commented, shaking his head as he pressed the tip of a finger to Gilmour's girlfriend's face.

Up in the penthouse, there was a call on Gilmour's phone. He was going to ignore it until he checked the name on the screen.

"Back in a minute," he barked to his visitor, retreating to the bathroom and closing the door. "Long time no hear."

"Took you long enough to pick up."

"I'm rushed off my feet. What can I do for you?"

"I'm after a favor. Do you still know anyone on the force in Edinburgh?"

"I might."

"Only a friendly face wouldn't hurt."

"What's this about, Owen?"

"I want to know what really happened the night Jessica had her smash."

"Enlighten me."

"My daughter, Stefan. Her car went off the road and the cops seem to think her boyfriend was behind the wheel. Next thing, his dad's attacked in his home and they pull me in."

"The dad in question being Pat McCuskey?"

"I just need someone who can keep me in the picture."

"Best guy I can think of is called John Rebus."

"Anyone but that bastard!" Traynor snarled.

"You've met him, then?"

"Enough to know I want to smack his face. So can you help me out?"

"I'm not sure."

"You were a prick back in the day, Stefan, and you're *still* being a prick."

"I suppose I can ask around, maybe pull some strings."

"Try not to sound too thrilled about it. And call me when you get news."

The phone went dead and Gilmour stared at it. "Don't bother thanking me," he scolded it. He could hear his visitor putting on some music in the living room. Instead of joining her, he locked the bathroom door and settled himself on the toilet pan, head in hands, wondering what to do about Billy Saunders.

When Rebus's phone rang that evening, he knew who it would be. He could still feel the steak pie like a solid weight in his stomach, so had decided on a liquid dinner of a couple of bottles of IPA. He was starting the second of them as he answered.

"I want to apologize," Stefan Gilmour said.

"For what?"

"It isn't what you think, John."

"Does she qualify as one of those WAGs I read about in the red-tops?"

"She's got a knack for getting herself on guest lists."

"Your secret's safe with me."

There was silence on the line.

"I mean it," Rebus said. "On the other hand, I can't vouch for Fox."

He listened as Gilmour drew in breath through his teeth. "I need to know whose side you're on, John."

"Aye, it seems to be a popular question these days."

"I can't believe you'd want a piece of pond life like Fox cutting me off at the knees." Statement rather than question.

"A bit of trust might help," Rebus retorted. "So how about you telling me what sort of hold Saunders had over you? See, my guess is *that's* why you were phoning him—maybe to tell him it was no longer relevant, or that *you* had something on *him*."

"There was never any 'hold,' John."

"I think you're lying."

"Then there's not much more to say." Gilmour paused. "And probably no point me asking you to intercede with your new friend Fox?"

"You mean ask him to forget about the WAG?"

"It would be worth a case or two of malt—you still like a whisky now and then, don't you?"

"You can't buy *every*body, Stefan. And if you considered me a pal, you wouldn't even feel the need to try..."

"Fair enough." Gilmour sounded beaten. "I just think it's crazy to waste time and money on a case that's going to go nowhere. And even if it *did* go to trial, all it would do is fluff up Elinor Macari's feathers. Because this is one big ego trip for her—her way of telling the world she was right to bring in the double jeopardy clause. Nothing to do with justice, John—we're just the same pawns we always were."

"You're not exactly a pawn these days, Stefan."

"But she wants to make me one. Know why? Because of the No campaign. She's an SNP appointment and a lifelong supporter. And suddenly she has the chance to chuck a couple of darts at the No campaign's public face."

"You, in other words?"

"Of course!"

"Have you been asked to comment on Pat McCuskey?"

Gilmour seemed disconcerted by the change of tack. "Yes," he eventually conceded.

"You must have sparred with him a bit?"

"All the time. Lovely guy, though. Once we'd finished the public debate, he was always game for a private drink and a bit of a laugh."

"Sounds like you knew him pretty well. The family too?"

"Family were kept out of it." Gilmour paused. "I *did* meet Bethany a couple of times."

"Have you sent your condolences?"

"Of course. My point is—*that's* what the police should be focusing resources on, not the likes of Billy Saunders."

"Can you think of a reason why anyone would want to attack Pat McCuskey?" Rebus asked.

"It was a housebreaking, wasn't it?"

"We're not a hundred percent sure."

Gilmour seemed to think for a moment. "You don't seriously believe Owen Traynor might be in the frame for it, though?"

"We're ruling nothing out."

"Breaking into a man's house? Smacking him just for being someone's dad?"

"Stranger things have happened. So tell me what you know of Pat McCuskey."

"Like I say, he was a nice guy."

"No skeletons in his closet?"

"Not that I can think of." Gilmour paused. "You planning to mark a cross in that independence box, John? If the Yes campaign gets hold of Susanna…"

"Your penthouse guest?"

"I'll know it had to come from you or Fox."

"How about the receptionist who sent her up without checking? Is he or she still in a job? Because if you've fired them, you'll have to add them to your little list too. That's how it is, Stefan, when we start lying and cheating and concealing—it creates a lot of work, and nothing but."

"No skeletons in *your* cupboard, John?" Gilmour managed a sour chuckle. "You'd need a space the size of IKEA to store them all."

The line went dead, Gilmour determined to have the last word. Rebus sucked on his beer and went to turn the vinyl over. Rory Gallagher: "Sinner Boy." He toasted the guitarist and slumped back on his chair to do some thinking. Then he picked up his phone and called Clarke.

"What?" she snapped.

"Bad timing?"

"I'll call you back in half an hour."

The phone went dead again. "Doing well tonight, John," he said to himself, lifting the bottle to his lips.

Clarke waited for David Galvin to come back from the toilet. It was a bar in the New Town—her choice, her patch. They had been polite at first, Galvin seeking to apologize. But then he'd thrown up his hands and asked what he was apologizing *for:* "It's not like I'm the one who called the Complaints!" After which the arguing had commenced—albeit with voices never raised; that wasn't the done thing in the New Town.

Pushing the table away from him, so that its edge jabbed her in the midriff, Galvin had then had to answer a call of nature. Or, Clarke reckoned, had gone to gather his thoughts in peace. While he was away, she thought back to the meeting she'd recently come from, held at Bute House on Charlotte Square. Just Nick Ralph and her, plus the First Minister and one of his special advisers. The First Minister had wanted updates—even though he seemed to have been briefed on everything the inquiry knew. He'd demanded "swift and decisive action." He'd worn a tie covered in tiny saltire flags and hadn't offered them anything to drink. Every thirty seconds or so a staffer would knock and enter, handing slips of paper to the First Minister for him to read. Sometimes he'd nod, and other times he would fold the note into his pocket. Couldn't be easy, running a country while trying to plan for a future more than half its constituents didn't yet seem to want.

"Swift and decisive," the First Minister had repeated. "Let's show the world what Scottish policing can do now the new model is in effect."

"Not quite in effect," Ralph had corrected him, receiving a hard stare for his efforts.

Clarke watched now as Galvin emerged, rubbing his hands together as if to reassure the room that he had remembered to wash them. He walked up to the table and just stood there, shaking his head slowly, as though disappointed in her. Then he exited the bar, never looking back.

"Prick," Clarke said under her breath. She took another slug of wine and called Rebus. "Sorry about that," she said.

"Anything I need to know about?"

"Definitely not."

"You sound like you're in a pub."

"Sharp as ever."

"Alone?"

"As of thirty seconds ago." She sighed and rubbed at her eyebrows. "So what can I do for you, John?"

"I saw Owen Traynor on the telly—nice work, bringing him in."

"Just seemed to make him angry."

"Angry is good. Angry means unthinking."

"Well we didn't get anything out of him. How about you?"

"Billy Saunders has gone AWOL."

"Interesting."

"Fox thinks maybe Stefan Gilmour slipped him a few quid to make himself scarce."

"And?"

"Stefan denies it."

"What about you and Malcolm—not come to blows yet?"

"We seem to be managing." Rebus paused. "Can I toss another tiny grenade into your foxhole?"

"If you must."

"Stefan Gilmour knew Pat McCuskey—knew him well, I mean."

"Stands to reason." It was her turn to pause. "You're not suggesting...?"

"Of course not. Though it did get me thinking. I know we discounted a political angle from the get-go, but on the other hand, politics in Scotland has never been so ugly. Lots of hotheads out there, and most of them nursing some grievance or other. Your boss doesn't strike me as the type who'd want to disregard a possible motive..."

"I'll mention it to him." She was still rubbing at her eyebrows.

"Sure you don't want my company? I can do witty repartee."

"I'm fine, John."

"Something to do with your lawyer friend?"

"I said I'm fine."

"Well, if you ever need a shoulder to drink on..."

She was smiling tiredly as she ended the call. The wine was finished. She'd had just the one glass and didn't want any more. It was churning sourly inside her. Five or ten minutes' walk and she'd be back at her flat. She paid the bill and headed outside. The air was crisp, the night sky clear. She remembered Rebus telling her that he used to drive through the city whenever he couldn't sleep. Not with any great purpose in mind, just enjoying the feel of the journey. She could do that. Or she could veg out on the sofa with whatever was on TV. A book—when had she last picked up a book? But as she turned the corner into her street, a car door opened.

"Siobhan?"

Clarke flinched, her eyes darting to left and right. You could never be too careful. But she recognized the owner of the voice, and walked towards the sporty Alfa Romeo.

"What are you doing here?" she asked.

"What do you think?"

The smile accompanying the question was warm but professional. Laura Smith—petite, with short brown hair—was the *Scotsman* newspaper's chief crime reporter, and also, since recent cutbacks, its *only* crime reporter.

"Hop in," Smith said. And before Clarke could demur, the journalist had ducked back into the car and closed the door. Music was playing from the stereo. The engine, however, was turned off and the interior was losing heat.

"How long have you been here?" Clarke asked, sliding into the passenger seat.

"Maybe half an hour."

"You could have been waiting half the night."

"Comes with the job."

"I'd no idea you had my address."

When Smith raised an eyebrow, Clarke knew she'd said something stupid. Smith worked the crime beat—she was obviously equipped with the resources.

"You want to ask me about the McCuskey case," Clarke guessed.

"You brought Owen Traynor in."

"Can't fault your powers of observation."

"He's a man with a past."

"He is indeed." Clarke watched as Smith drummed her fingers against the steering wheel in time to the music. She didn't recognize the tune, would have classed it as "disco" if such a thing still existed.

"And he has a daughter called Jessica," Smith went on, "who wrote off her VW Golf only a few days back. Nice straight stretch of road and somehow she loses control."

"Again, you're scarily well informed."

"No need to be sarky." Smith switched off the music and twisted her body towards Clarke. "Jessica's boyfriend is Forbes McCuskey, whose father then ends up dead after a break-in at the family home." She paused. "And you bring in Owen Traynor for questioning. Let me guess what his motive might have been..."

"We were just checking a few details, Laura."

"I'm sure you were. How did it go with the First Minister, by the way?" Pleased with the look of surprise on Clarke's face, Smith smiled again. "I have spies everywhere," she explained.

"He wants us to find whoever did it."

"Understandable. Meantime, he has to find a new face to front the Yes campaign without looking callous. Is Rebus keeping his nose clean?"

"I'm not his mother."

"How has he managed to wangle his way into the Saunders inquiry?"

Clarke gave Smith a glower. "You're in danger of coming across as smug, Laura."

"Just well informed, as you say," Smith corrected her. "You know Stefan Gilmour left the force because of Saunders? And now he helms the good ship No..."

"Are you going to print any of this?"

Smith looked thoughtful. "A few hard facts wouldn't go amiss. Way things are, post-Leveson, the lawyers will redact anything that can't be corroborated."

"I'm too close to the inquiry," Clarke said, shaking her head. "Fingers would point straight at me..."

"You know I can make sure that doesn't happen—it's all in the phrasing."

"Right now, I'm not sure I know much more than you do," Clarke argued.

"But there'll come a point when you do. The paper's constantly updated online—if I'm even ten minutes ahead of the pack, it means I publish first."

Clarke was shaking her head again. Smith stuck out her bottom lip in a show of mock unhappiness.

"I've not come to the table empty-handed," she announced. "Might be something or nothing, but as a show of good faith..."

"What?" Clarke asked.

"And you won't just go away and forget about me?"

"Spit it out."

Smith paused for a few moments, then took a deep breath. "Word is," she said, "Forbes McCuskey's the go-to guy if you want a better class of illegal substance. Posh student parties in all those flats bought by mumsy and dadsy."

"The son of the Justice Minister?"

"Delicious, isn't it? I heard it from two normally reliable sources. Even set up a bit of a surveillance—had a photographer with me and everything. Never caught him, though."

"So we're talking unsubstantiated rumors?" Clarke, while sounding skeptical, still had a question. "Where's he getting it?"

Smith offered a shrug. "Not sure it originates in Edinburgh—do your lot know of any dealers who could be sending stuff down the chain?"

"I'll look into it."

"A note of caution—this is a son grieving for his father, remember."

"Meaning there's nothing *you* can do with it?"

Smith shook her head. "Would I be trading it otherwise?" she asked, with that same sweet, professional smile.

Rebus was asleep in his chair when his phone woke him. He didn't recognize the number, but answered anyway, massaging his eyes back into focus with his free hand.

"John Rebus," he said.

"You've got to stop hassling my dad!"

"Jessica?" Rebus walked over to the record deck and lifted the stylus from the run-out groove. Side two of *Beggars Banquet*—how had he managed to sleep through so much of that? "I didn't know you had my number."

"You gave Forbes your card."

"So I did."

"Now listen to me—just leave him alone!"

"Forbes or your dad?"

"Dad's not *done* anything—he doesn't deserve this..." She seemed to be trying to control a sob.

"Has he taken it out on you, Jessica?" Rebus asked.

"Of course not—but I can see it's eating him up. They named him on TV, and now people keep phoning him."

"You're still at the hotel?"

"Checking out tomorrow."

"You'll go back to your flat? What about your father?"

"He needs to be in London. What he *doesn't* need is this hanging over him."

"Then tell me what happened," Rebus said.

"What do you mean?"

"The night of the crash..."

There was silence on the line. He thought for a moment she'd hung up. But then came a crackling sound as she exhaled noisily.

"I can't," she said. "They'll kill me."

"Who'll kill you?" He gave her time to answer, but none came. "You're Owen Traynor's daughter—no one's going to kill you."

"I just can't. Don't ask me again."

"You can expect to see me at your door tomorrow. Does it involve Forbes? Or maybe his father?"

But this time she really had ended the call. Rebus rang back, but her messaging service picked up. He added her number to the contacts list on his phone, then patted the phone against his cheek as he went back over the conversation.

They'll kill me.

Who the hell were *they?*

No mention of Forbes McCuskey, just this plural threat. Did Owen Traynor know or suspect? If someone were menacing his daughter, what would he do? Would the red mist descend? Did he have friends he could call on?

Expect to see me at your door...

His mind flashed to the doorway of Dod Blantyre's bungalow, and Maggie standing there, looking radiant. Her words to him at the

café: *How things might have turned out—if we'd been a little braver.*
And Stefan Gilmour: *No skeletons in* your *cupboard, John?*

We start lying and cheating and concealing…

His brain felt foggy: too many connections, too much loose, frayed wiring.

He made himself a mug of tea, stuck *Solid Air* on the turntable, and slumped back in his chair, ready for a long night's thinking.

DAY SEVEN

13

This Laura Smith, she wouldn't be spinning you a line?" Rebus was seated in a café on Morrison Street, halfway between Torphichen Place and Haymarket railway station. It was an area of town he tried to avoid—the tram works seemed to have shut half the roads. He'd found the last space in an over ground car park off the West Approach Road and walked from there to the café.

Midmorning and the place was doling out coffee and buns to visitors fresh off the train. There were no tables as such, just a long shelf by the window and a row of tall narrow stools. Siobhan Clarke was perched on one, while Rebus opted to stand. He had removed the lid from his coffee and was blowing on it while Clarke plucked gobbets of damp pastry from her croissant and popped them into her mouth.

"Could be," she conceded. "But why would she bother?"

"And all she knows is Forbes McCuskey flogs drugs to his fellow students? We don't know quantities or whether we're talking weed or heroin?"

Clarke shook her head. "I'm wondering what to do with it," she said eventually.

"You mean: is it worth taking to Nick Ralph in its current doodle-like state, or should you try to add a few recognizable features?"

"Something like that." She checked the time on her phone.

"Press conference?"

She nodded. "Hotel along the street in twenty minutes."

"Autopsy results?"

"I don't think we're seeing those until later." She looked at him. "Rough night?"

"Not particularly."

"Get to bed at all?"

"In time for the dawn chorus." He told her about Jessica Traynor's phone call.

"A drug deal gone wrong?" Clarke speculated, seeming to wake up a little. Her drink of choice—a three-shot espresso—was already finished, and one of her knees was bouncing.

"Possibly. Remember the car boot? Closed in the initial photos from the crash scene..."

"But wide open by the time we got there. Meaning someone took something?"

"Forbes McCuskey panics and does a runner. But then he has second thoughts, hangs around nearby. Once the ambulance has taken Jessica away and the patrol car has gone..."

"He comes back, opens the boot and takes whatever was inside?" Clarke's eyes had opened a little wider. "And he's walking distance from his parents' place, so he takes the drugs there?"

Rebus nodded. "Maybe the original owners wanted them back—if the deal had gone sour."

"Forbes isn't there, but they find his father instead?"

"It's guesswork at best, Siobhan," Rebus warned her. He knew this because he had spent half the night piecing it together.

"We really need to talk to Forbes, don't we?"

"Might be easier starting with his girlfriend. She's back in her flat as of today, with her dad nowhere in sight."

"Making her the weaker link?" Clarke nodded, without looking especially convinced. She saw that there was no longer a queue at the counter. "I need another coffee to take with me."

"You sure about that?" He nodded towards her knee. "I'd say you're already shakier than a Neil Young tribute band."

"He's playing Glasgow, you know—Neil Young, I mean."

"June the thirteenth," Rebus confirmed.

"You've got a ticket?"

He shook his head. "They only had standing."

"And at your age you need a nice comfy seat?" Clarke was smiling.

"There are just some things I won't stand for," Rebus replied. "You should know that by now..."

He walked with her to the hotel, and stood at the back of the room for the first few minutes of DCI Ralph's presentation. A couple of political hacks seemed to have joined the usual newshounds. Rebus recognized their faces from late-night TV discussions. He had no idea what they sounded like—he always had the sound muted, an album playing in its place. They held phones or iPads rather than actual notebooks, and the look they affected was world-weary. Maybe they yearned for the bright lights of Westminster, Big Ben chiming the hours. Rebus almost felt sorry for them as he exited the hotel and returned to his car. He called Fox to make sure the office wasn't locked.

"Thought we might make a day of it," Fox told him. "I've fixed those interviews with Albert Stout and Norman Cuttle."

"Want me to bring anything for them—an ear trumpet or a bag of pan drops?"

"They both sounded spry when I phoned them."

"So where are you just now?"

"Elinor Macari's office. She's been updating me on Billy Saunders."

"And?"

"Craigmillar police station are running the show—without any apparent enthusiasm."

"Guy's been missing no time at all," Rebus argued.

"Even so, Macari has got one of her fiscals to go gee them up. Poor bugger's to stick to the investigation like glue."

"Glue used to be a currency in Craigmillar," Rebus commented.

"So shall I meet you at Macari's."

"Why not?" Malcolm Fox said.

Why not indeed? Rebus thought to himself, ending the call and turning left at the lights.

Albert Stout lived on his own in an Edwardian house with uninterrupted views across Muirfield golf course. The place would be worth a few bob, but would also need gutting and updating by any new owners. The central heating radiators were the same age as the building, and emitted as much heat as a Bluebell match. There was a pervasive smell of damp, the window frames were crumbling, and the carpets were moldering at their edges. There were books and newspapers everywhere, Stout having explained that he was writing his memoirs.

"The industry's on its last legs, so this is by way of *ave atque vale*."

"Do you know Laura Smith?" Rebus inquired.

"I hear she does a good enough job—under the circumstances." Stout shuffled along in carpet slippers, leading them into the lounge. More clutter—unopened mail, boxes of photographs, cups and plates. "Someone comes and cleans once a week," he apologized.

"Do you have any other help?" Fox asked.

"Council tried matching me with someone, but I'm too set in my ways. They did install a button I can press if there's an emergency…" Stout looked around in vain for the device.

There were grease stains on his cardigan and brown cord trousers. He was jowly, and hadn't shaved in a couple of days. What hair he had left was silver and unruly, but his eyes were alert. As the three men sat down, he wagged a finger in Rebus's direction.

"I remember you now," he said. "Gave me more than a few column inches down the years."

"I hope that's not a euphemism," Rebus retorted. Then: "Do you still smoke a couple of packs a day?"

Stout made a face. "Doctor told me I should call a halt."

"We want to talk to you about a particular case," Fox broke in, perching on the edge of the sofa rather than move the heaps of magazines behind him. "Summerhall CID and the death of Douglas Merchant. You wrote about it several times..."

"Because it was a scandal—the police back then were like little tyrants." He paused and glanced in Rebus's direction. "No offense."

"None taken," Rebus assured him, coldly.

"They faked confessions, framed the innocent, planted evidence— we all knew it went on, but there was nothing we could do about it."

"The press knew, you mean?"

"Very straightforward procedure—you bought a desk sergeant or someone from the custody suite a drink, and they poured out all the gossip. Almost none of it made the news pages."

"Why not?"

"Editors would spike it. They'd be on the phone to someone high up at HQ, there'd be a few quiet words, and the piece would fail to appear."

"Editors in cahoots with the upper echelons?"

Stout nodded, stuffing his hands into the pockets of his cardigan.

"But the pieces you wrote about the Merchant killing made it into the *Scotsman*," Fox nudged.

"By no means all of them, but some, yes. It was safe by then, you see? A senior officer had already resigned."

"Stefan Gilmour?" Fox watched the old man nod.

"Did him no harm in the long run, did it?" Stout grumbled. "On his way to a knighthood, I shouldn't wonder."

"The officers at Summerhall contend that it was a simple matter of errors being made."

"Nonsense," Stout snapped back at Fox. "Billy Saunders had to be protected."

"Because he was Stefan Gilmour's snitch? Or do you think there was more to it than that?"

"It did cross my mind. Plenty of men around like Saunders at that time—losing one snitch to jail would hardly have shaken Gilmour's world."

"So what do you make of it?"

"Have you tried asking him?" Stout gestured towards Rebus. "I seem to recall you were at Summerhall same time as Gilmour."

"I'm in the dark as much as anyone," Rebus commented. "But we're talking to Eamonn Paterson and George Blantyre."

"And Gilmour himself, of course," Fox added.

"Not Frazer Spence, though," Stout said quietly. "Poor little bugger. He was one of mine, you know."

"One of the officers who'd take a drink from you?" Fox checked.

Stout was nodding again. "Not until a few years after the Merchant case, but yes…" He seemed lost in thought for a moment. "Reluctant to talk about Summerhall though. And clammed up completely whenever Merchant was mentioned."

"He knew something?"

"He was scared, or maybe haunted is a better word—like there was something he'd stuffed into a locker and he didn't ever want it opening."

"Will Summerhall feature in your memoirs, Mr. Stout?" Rebus asked. Fox looked annoyed at the interruption.

"Maybe as a postscript to be published after my death—that way nobody can sue." There was a glint in the old journalist's eye.

"You worked with Frazer Spence, John," Fox was saying. "Do you know why he'd feel 'haunted'?"

"No idea."

"Nobody in that police station was totally clean," Stout said sourly, his eyes on Rebus.

"And we know that journalists have always been paragons of virtue," Rebus responded.

"One or two of us were scumbags," Stout allowed. "But with your lot it was institutionalized lying, institutionalized violence and threats."

"You're one to talk, you old—"

"DS Rebus," Fox broke in, his voice rising. "Maybe you need a breath of air."

After a staring match of a few seconds, Rebus got to his feet. "Maybe I do at that. The atmosphere in here's getting a bit too fucking pious for me. I'll leave you and this old hypocrite to it…"

Outside, he paced the short gravel driveway, sucking on a cigarette. It was a good five or six minutes before Fox emerged. Stout hadn't bothered coming to the door to wave him off.

"You okay?" Fox asked.

"Sanctimonious prick of a man," Rebus began. "You can be sure there'll be no shortage of lies and half-truths in his book. Albert Stout wasn't above groping a typist or offering someone a deal if they'd rat on their lover."

Fox unlocked his Volvo and got in. Rebus wished he'd brought his Saab, but it was parked on Chambers Street. He paused for a few more seconds, draining the life from his cigarette before flicking it towards Stout's front door. Then he climbed into the passenger seat.

"Got it off your chest?" Fox said. He didn't look displeased to see Rebus fired up.

"Let's just get going, eh?"

Fox started the car. Rebus had already noticed that the man never quite broke the speed limit. In a 40 zone, he'd keep to 39; in a 30, he'd do 29. The one time Rebus had suggested putting the foot down, Fox had actually eased off the accelerator instead. So he kept quiet as they drove back into the city, headed for Colinton and the home of Professor Norman Cuttle. Fox stuck the Scottish news on, but switched the radio off again almost immediately.

"All you seem to hear about is the referendum," he complained. Then: "Mr. Stout was interesting about that actually—after you left. He's got a whole chapter in his book about the '79 vote and the years that followed. SNP were at a low ebb then. Some of them decided to take matters a little further. I had a case a couple of years back…"

"A Complaints case?"

"Started off that way. You ever heard of the Dark Harvest Commando? The SNLA? They got hold of weapons, sent firebombs to politicians and Princess Di—even posted anthrax to the government in London."

"I vaguely remember."

"Stout covered a few of the trials. He's an interesting man."

"He's an arsehole, and the fact that you can't tell the difference says a lot about you, if you don't mind me saying."

"Do you think it was true, though, what he said about editors spiking stories?"

"Is that going to be your next archaeological dig—brass who were too close to the men who ran the papers?"

"I'd assume they're all dead by now."

"I'm not sure that would stop you."

"This is my last work for Professional Standards."

"Unless you can persuade the Solicitor General that you need to be kept on in some capacity."

"That could work for you too, you know."

Rebus turned towards Fox. "How do you mean?"

"Until recently you were working cold cases. If the double jeopardy verdict goes, there'll be a lot of 'archaeological digs' to be organized. Who better than someone with cold-case experience?"

"I prefer my bodies with a bit of warmth in them."

Fox gave a shrug. "Your funeral," he said.

"Meaning what?"

"Meaning you're back in CID but the clock is against you—two or three more years and you'll hit the retirement wall again. That wouldn't matter if you were working for the Solicitor General."

"I know plenty of ex-cops who work for lawyers—they never seem particularly happy about it."

"Doing precognitions, you mean? That's not what this would be like."

"It would be like death," Rebus stated, switching the radio back on.

"Something you should refrain from saying at our next destination," Fox advised, as a Waterboys song started playing.

*   *   *

Professor Norman Cuttle was resident in a care home overlooking the greenery of Colinton Dell. A trolley was serving tea and biscuits in the TV room. Cuttle rose slowly from his chair to greet his two visitors, then suggested they "repair" to the garden, where it would be quieter.

Quieter and chillier. Not that Rebus was complaining. He'd had to remove both coat and jacket upon entering the care home's reception area, a member of staff explaining that the heating had to be kept full blast or there were complaints. He remembered the suffocating warmth of Dod Blantyre's bungalow, and Maggie's occasional need to escape.

The same staff member provided a tartan travel rug for Professor Cuttle, wrapping it around his legs and chest. The professor was seated on a new-looking wooden bench. There was a plaque on it, identifying the donor as someone who had lived at the care home.

And died there, Rebus presumed.

Cuttle was a bit stiffer than Albert Stout, and required a hearing aid. He was a lot more skeletal, too, his skull all but visible through his paper-thin blue-veined skin. Rebus remembered him as a gentle man who took great care with the cadavers in his possession, respecting them as though family members were gathered at his shoulder. He apologized for not remembering Rebus.

"We didn't meet often," Rebus said. "I got to know your successor a bit better."

"Professor Gates?"

Rebus nodded and buttoned up his coat. There was a stiff breeze from the north, the cloud thickening. With Fox and Cuttle taking up the bench, there was nowhere for him to sit, so he was standing to one side, leaving the woodland view unobstructed.

"We're here about Douglas Merchant," Fox nudged.

"Yes, I've been thinking about him. It was on the news about Billy Saunders disappearing."

"You did the postmortem examination."

"With Professor Donner—he was the senior pathologist."

"I don't suppose you recall the details..." Fox opened the briefcase he'd been holding and slid out a thin brown folder. Inside was the report from the autopsy. Cuttle peered at the sheets, seemingly engrossed.

"These were written by Donner," he said. "Such tiny handwriting, yet perfectly legible. I'd no idea we kept paperwork for this number of years."

"We're lucky it survived," Fox said.

"Indeed, yes."

"You gave evidence at the trial?"

"I did. But then the case fell apart."

"A question of contamination?"

Cuttle nodded. "The victim's blood was found on clothing owned by Billy Saunders." He paused. "Unfortunately, that clothing had apparently been stored in an evidence bag alongside items belonging to the victim."

"Meaning the blood could have been transferred from one to the other?"

"That was the fear."

"Pretty basic error." Fox watched Cuttle as he sifted through more of the paperwork, including photos of the deceased from both the scene of the attack and the autopsy slab. "Merchant was killed in the alleyway behind the pub he'd been drinking in. He'd had an argument an hour or two before with Billy Saunders. Saunders had then left the pub. He was apprehended, drunk and blood-spattered, in a street half a mile away. His story was that he'd stumbled over the body, and been so horrified he'd staggered off down the road. He told police he'd no idea the body had belonged to Douglas Merchant."

"Mmm," Cuttle said, managing to inject huge skepticism into the single syllable. "The man had grazed knuckles and a burst lip, consistent with a fight. Plus a few nicks that could have been received from an opponent's blows. DNA collection was not as advanced as it is these days—we never matched skin from under either man's fingernails..."

"But you're pretty sure Billy Saunders did it?"

"Mmm," Cuttle said again.

"And was helped in beating the charge by officers at Summerhall CID?"

"I can't comment on that."

Rebus cleared his throat. "When Inspector Fox asked if Saunders had done it, you didn't sound wholly convinced—or are my ears playing tricks on me?"

"His story had a certain plausibility. People jumped to the obvious conclusion—the two men had been arguing; Merchant had been sleeping with Saunders's wife..." Cuttle gave a shrug and pulled the rug a little tighter around himself. "The iron bar found at the scene provided no usable fingerprints."

"Story is, someone wiped it," Fox interrupted.

"Never proven, though—so much of what we're talking about here will remain always in the realm of conjecture."

"If Billy Saunders didn't do it, who did?" Fox asked.

"A question for the police, unless of course..."

Fox leaned in towards the old man. "Unless the police did it, you mean?"

"It would explain the need to doctor evidence, and maybe feelings of guilt meant no one wanted an innocent man to go to prison for the crime..."

Fox snatched the report from Cuttle's hands. "Why is none of that thinking in here?"

"Because," Cuttle replied calmly, "I wasn't the one who wrote it up."

"But you spoke to Professor Donner? You told him you had reservations?"

"I may have done."

"And he chose to ignore them?"

Cuttle offered another shrug. "We were so busy during that period: a lot of lowlifes dropping dead or succumbing to injuries; not enough staff to assist in the mortuary—I can't recall now if industrial action or sickness was to blame. The mortuary had to close soon after, you know? They found asbestos in the walls…" His eyes lost focus for a moment. Then he blinked and looked up at Rebus. "Is Professor Gates still alive, do you know?"

Rebus shook his head. "I think I saw you at his funeral—quite a few years back now."

"I don't remember. It's funny, usually I'm fine with the far past— just don't quiz me on what I had for dinner yesterday."

"I need to ask you rather an awkward question, Professor," Fox said, pressing the palms of his hands together. "Did anyone at Summerhall try to pressure you in any way?"

"Pressure?"

"Ask you to change anything in the report, or try your best in the witness box to help the defense rather than the prosecution?"

"Nothing like that." Cuttle shook his head defiantly. "Never anything like that."

Fox pressed the point, but Cuttle kept shaking his head, so that Rebus feared the man might do himself an injury.

"Is everything all right?" Another staff member had come into the garden. The sun wasn't far off setting, the daylight fading. "Might be an idea to come back indoors, eh?"

"Yes," the professor said, as Fox and the aide helped him to his feet. "I'm beginning to feel it now in my bones."

"Nice cup of tea when we get you in. *Pointless* will be on the TV soon—you like that one, don't you?"

"Do I?"

"Well, let's find out…"

Rebus and Fox lingered by the bench.

"Got enough?" Rebus asked.

Fox was stuffing the report back into his case. "You heard what the man said—might not even have been Saunders."

"You can't be serious?"

Fox turned to face him. "We've been looking for a reason why Gilmour would work so hard on a snitch's behalf. This theory's as good as any I've heard."

"Why would Gilmour kill Merchant? Why would anyone other than Billy Saunders kill Merchant?"

"You're right—might not be Stefan Gilmour. Might have been someone close to Stefan Gilmour."

Rebus rolled his eyes. "You know how stupid you sound right now?"

"I can see why you'd want to think that. Because if Gilmour was protecting someone, that puts all the Saints back in the picture...including you, John."

Rebus stuck out a hand to grab a fistful of Fox's coat, but the man's reflexes were sharp. He caught the hand and pushed it away, then stood his ground, going up on his tiptoes.

"You really want to do this?" he asked. "You're twenty years older than me and couldn't climb the Scotsman Steps unless there was a drink at the top."

"And you're in peak physical condition, I suppose?"

"Not necessary, John—I just need to be that little bit fitter than you..."

Rebus took a moment to ponder this, then he managed a resigned smile. "Okay then, Action Man," he said. "Stand down the mission..."

"You know that in my shoes you'd be considering the selfsame hypotheses."

"I wouldn't be in your shoes, though."

Fox's eyes narrowed. "Why not?"

Rebus glanced down at Fox's footwear of choice. "They're brown," he stated. "One thing I learned from Uncle Frank..."

"No brown shoes?"

"No brown shoes," Rebus agreed.

"And Uncle Frank is...?"

"Frank Zappa." Rebus saw the blank look on Fox's face. "The musician."

"I hardly ever listen to music."

"That's one more strike against you, then," Rebus stated with a slow shake of the head.

That evening, Rebus and Clarke rendezvoused at Great King Street.

"Autopsy result is in," she told him. "No signs of a physical assault on McCuskey. He cracked his head against the corner of the stone fireplace and bleeding to the brain did the rest."

"So is it still being treated as murder?"

She gave a shrug. "Procurator Fiscal's office hasn't decided yet. But whoever broke in, their defense could be that he was already unconscious when they arrived. He tripped and fell, maybe having just heard the glass breaking."

Rebus nodded. "No marks on the body at all?"

"Nothing conclusive." Clarke paused. "You ready?"

When he nodded, she pressed the buzzer for Jessica Traynor's flat.

"Hello?" The voice on the intercom was Alice Bell's.

"It's Detective Inspector Clarke. Is Jessica there?"

"What do you want?"

"We need a word with her."

"She's supposed to be convalescing."

"This'll only take five minutes, Alice."

A few seconds later, the buzzer sounded as the door was unlocked. Clarke pushed it open and Rebus followed her up the winding stairs.

Alice Bell stood in the open doorway of the flat. Clarke offered a smile and asked how Jessica was doing.

"All right, I suppose."

"She's managing the stairs?"

"I doubt she'll be using them much for the next week or so." Bell led them inside. Jessica Traynor—minus neck brace—was stretched out on the sofa in the living room, one ankle still strapped, with the TV remote, an iPad and her mobile phone close to her.

Books lay open on the room's only table, next to a laptop whose screen seemed to show the opening paragraph of an essay. Bell sat down at the table while Rebus and Clarke stayed standing.

"If you could just give us a minute to ourselves," Rebus said to Bell.

"I want her to stay," Jessica Traynor protested.

"Some things are best said in private," Rebus warned her, but Traynor shook her head.

"Are you on the mend?" Clarke asked.

"Supposedly. I'm taking co-codamol for the pain. Makes things nicely spacey."

"Is that a prescription?" Rebus inquired. "Or are you getting it from your boyfriend?"

"What's that supposed to mean?"

"We hear he sells drugs, Jessica," Clarke explained.

"Rubbish!" Traynor barked. "Who told you that?"

"You're saying it isn't true?"

"Of course it's not true," Alice Bell interrupted. "And we'd know, wouldn't we?"

"You probably would, yes," Clarke agreed. "But I can appreciate you might not want to admit it."

"It may come as news to you," Jessica Traynor said, "but Forbes's father has just died. You're really going to drag him to a police station and accuse him of dealing drugs? All because somebody spun you a bullshit story?"

Rebus took a step towards the sofa. "When you called me last night, Jessica, you were on the verge of telling me something. 'They'll kill me,' you said. Sounds as if there are people out there you're afraid of, people your father can't protect you from."

"She's already told you," Alice Bell said, rising from the table. "She's taking painkillers. Half the time she doesn't know what she's saying." She had settled herself on the arm of the sofa, next to Jessica Traynor's head. Reaching down, she stroked her flatmate's hair. "She shouldn't even be talking to you now."

Rebus's stare was directed at Traynor. "Who are they, Jessica?" he asked. "Who is it that'll punish you if you talk to us? Were they there the night of the crash? Are they after Forbes too?"

"Time for another of these, I think." She produced a bottle of pills which had been tucked beneath her on the sofa. "Fetch me some water, will you?"

Alice Bell got up and headed for the kitchen. Once she'd left the room, Rebus approached Traynor, crouching down in front of her, his face inches from hers.

"We can help, Jessica. Maybe we're the only ones who can. You just need to trust us."

The student's eyes were glassy, but she was listening.

"Talk to Forbes," Rebus went on. "Let him know we're on your side. Then give us a call…"

He was getting back to his feet again as Alice Bell returned with a half-filled glass.

"I think it's time for you to leave," Bell said, determination in her voice. The childproof cap on the pill bottle was defeating her friend, so she took it from her and opened it.

"You need to go easy on those," Clarke advised.

"Then I won't." Traynor shook three small tablets into the palm of her hand and scooped them into her mouth, taking the glass from Bell and drinking from it. Afterwards, she gave a satisfied sigh and laid her head down on the sofa, closing her eyes.

"Don't let her take too many," Clarke warned.

"Time for you to leave," Alice Bell repeated, pointing towards the door.

Siobhan Clarke was stretched along her own sofa, a cookery program on TV and a microwave meal on a tray on her lap, when her mobile rang. It was Laura Smith, wanting an update.

"The office is closed for the night," Clarke told her, stabbing at a forkful of food.

"I hear the postmortem result was inconclusive."

"Then you know as much as I do."

"You can really switch off? At home, I mean?"

"I'd be a sad case otherwise."

"That must be me, then. Working days seem to get longer all the time."

"Poor you. Editor running you ragged?"

"It's not him; it's just the job."

"Then put the phone down and go for a walk, maybe catch a film..."

"Chance would be a fine thing. Have you done anything with that tip I gave you?"

"Forbes and his drugs? Everyone seems to be denying it."

"There's a surprise. And the interview with Owen Traynor...?"

"Was a matter of routine."

"I had a chat with the political desk here—you know he's friends with Stefan Gilmour, don't you?"

"Of course," Clarke lied, suddenly interested but hoping it didn't show in her voice. "But I'm impressed your political desk knows."

"Since he's prominent in the No camp, the Yes supporters have a little file on Gilmour. Traynor's name is in there. Some business venture from a few years back."

"Not really relevant," Clarke said, scribbling a note in the front-page margin of an old *Evening News*.

"There could still be political capital to be made out of it. With Pat McCuskey gone, the Yes people would love some dirt on his equivalent in the No camp."

"I dare say they would."

There was silence on the line, then a sigh from the journalist. "I'm wasting my breath, aren't I?"

"It's yours to waste, Laura."

"I gave you Forbes McCuskey—don't forget that."

"I won't." Clarke ended the call and compared the dish on the TV screen with the food on her plate. "No contest," she said, scooping up another forkful.

DAY EIGHT

14

Something Professor Cuttle had said—*we were so busy... lowlifes dropping dead or succumbing to injuries*—took Rebus to the Summerhall files the following morning. Malcolm Fox had been summoned to a meeting with Elinor Macari elsewhere in the building. It was raining outside, the sky black. Rebus had hung his coat up to dry and slipped his shoes off, balancing them on a radiator. He padded across the office in his damp socks, opening box files and ledgers, seeking out anything from the days and weeks leading up to Douglas Merchant's murder.

"Not interrupting, am I?" Fox said on his return. He was carrying two cardboard beakers of tea. "Do you take sugar? I can't remember." He dug some sachets from his jacket pocket.

"Thanks," Rebus said, prizing the lid from the proffered beaker. "Macari's coffee machine on the blink?"

"I just prefer tea." Fox took a sip, wincing at the scalding temperature.

"You left the door open."

"Maybe I just forgot to lock it."

"Or it could be that you're starting to trust me?"

Fox blew across the surface of his drink. "Here's the thing, John—you wanted back on the force at any cost. They told you you'd be bumped down the ranks and you said okay. It's not about status with you; it's about the job itself. Am I right?"

"More or less. So you *are* beginning to trust me?"

"Trust works both ways." Fox gestured towards the paperwork in front of Rebus. "So tell me what's keeping you busy."

"Working on a timeline," Rebus explained, hoping he could keep things nice and vague. "What did the Solicitor General want?"

"Billy Saunders is still missing. His phone hasn't been used, but two hundred pounds was taken from a cash machine with his card."

"When?"

"Night he disappeared. From a Bank of Scotland in Newington."

"So he's either alive and running, or..."

"Someone took his card and made him hand over the PIN."

"Does Macari have a preference?"

Fox's mouth twitched. "She wants Stefan Gilmour formally questioned."

"Because he had words with Saunders?" Rebus watched Fox nod. "So do we bring him in?"

"It'll just be me, John, plus one of the fiscals. You're too close to Gilmour."

"Thanks for the vote of confidence."

"You know I'm right, though." He paused, his attention shifting to the box files. "Remind me why we need a timeline..."

"I thought you asked for one."

"Did I?" Fox's brow furrowed.

"I reckoned maybe you wanted me kept busy," Rebus lied blithely.

"Fine then," Fox said eventually. He noticed that Rebus was in socks, and looked towards the radiator. "At least brown shoes keep out the water," he commented.

Rebus opened another ledger and started reading.

He remembered most of the cases, but not all of them. An arson attack in Craigmillar...a series of corner shops held up by a drug addict armed with a syringe...several sexual assaults late at night in the Meadows (never officially linked, never solved). An off-duty constable had been attacked by a mob of football fans in a pub on Forrest

Road. A tramp had been found dead in Grayfriars Kirkyard, bearing the signs of a beating. Cashpoint muggings, aggressive beggars, a pickpocket gang from Eastern Europe. The cells at Summerhall had been overflowing some nights. Then there was the cannabis haul from a lockup in Dumbiedykes, and the stolen car that was used to ram-raid an off-license.

All fun and games.

Rebus's own name cropped up occasionally, as did his signature—at the bottom of reports he might or might not have typed. Cross-referencing the custody ledger against suspects arrested, he found that the bottom half of a page had been torn out.

"Just for the record," he said, motioning for Fox to take a look, "it was like this when I opened it."

Fox nodded. "I noticed that a while back."

The last entry on the half-page still remaining gave details of a suspect detained a week before Merchant's murder, while the first entry on the next page was from the same day.

"Four hours or so missing," Fox commented. "Late afternoon to midevening."

"What do you think happened?"

"If the custody sergeant were still around, I'd ask him."

"Deceased?" Rebus guessed.

"Name of Magnus Henderson."

"I remember him," Rebus said. "Red-faced cheery-looking chap, but when he put someone in a headlock they soon realized he wasn't Father Christmas."

"Retired to the Costa del Sol. Died a couple of years back from a coronary." Fox prodded at the ledger with a finger. "You think there's something there that needed to be got rid of?"

"I'm pretty sure that would have been your first reaction."

"You're right, but unless you or one of the other Saints is about to confess…"

Rebus offered a shrug. "There are arrest records, other bits of paperwork that might provide an answer."

"Or else the custody sergeant just got a name wrong and tore the page out to save embarrassment."

"Maybe the prisoner got shirty, made a grab for the book," Rebus suggested. "I could ask around."

"Your old buddies? You really think Stefan Gilmour would own up? Or Eamonn Paterson?"

"Probably not." Rebus's phone was ringing.

"Morning, DI Clarke," he said, answering. "Enjoying the weather?"

"Have you heard?" she asked.

Rebus's jaw tightened. He fixed Fox with a stare. "Heard what?"

"Body fished from the canal this morning. Bank card in his pocket has the name William Saunders."

"Billy Saunders is dead?"

Fox took out his own phone and tapped in a number.

"Looks like," Clarke was saying. "Body's not been formally iden-tified yet."

"Pulled from the canal?"

"A quiet stretch near Dumbryden—not far from Wester Hailes police station."

Fox was giving the news to the Solicitor General. He kept his eyes on Rebus, ready to pass on any wisdom.

"Near Dumbryden," Rebus dutifully repeated.

"And there's another thing, John..."

"Did he jump, fall, or was he maybe pushed?" Rebus interrupted her.

"That's what I'm trying to tell you. Word is he'd been shot."

"Shot?"

"Shot," Fox said into his phone, eyes widening a little further.

"Shot," Siobhan Clarke confirmed.

It had been decided to base the investigation at Wester Hailes. With the Pat McCuskey case in the process of being downgraded, officers were being moved from that team to the new one. By the time Rebus and Fox arrived at the canal, Clarke had been put in charge of the inquiry. DC Olivia Webster was with her, Clarke making the introductions from beneath a large black umbrella. Droplets of rain were dripping into Rebus's eyes from his hair. Crime-scene tape had been strung across the canal path, onlookers gathering on the opposite bank. There wasn't much in the vicinity other than an industrial estate and some wasteland. Ducks were sheltering between the thick reeds, heads tucked under their wings.

"Grim," Rebus stated, taking in everything.

The canal was cleaner these days than in times past, but litter still floated on its oily surface, and nearby walls had become a sprawling canvas for the neighborhood taggers.

"Any CCTV?" Fox asked.

"On the industrial estate," Clarke told him. "We'll be taking a look."

"What was he doing here?"

"Your guess is as good as mine."

"There can't be many guns in the city."

"One more than we thought," Clarke commented.

"What I mean is, where did it come from? Someone must know."

She nodded. Miserable-looking uniformed officers were combing the ground in all directions. They wore waterproofs, and Rebus thought he recognized one or two from the perimeter search of Pat McCuskey's homestead.

"The diver's going to have fun," he said to Clarke. "Hope his shots are up to date."

"Not the best turn of phrase, under the circumstances."

"You think the gun's in there?" Rebus gestured towards the canal.

"Maybe."

"How many bullets?"

"Just the one. Close range, middle of the chest."

Rebus examined the path beneath their feet. "Bloodstains?"

"Not found any yet."

"So the impact probably propelled him into the water. Any casings?"

"Christ, John, we've only just got started." Clarke's voice was brittle.

"Room for any more on the team?" he asked. "Malcolm and me know as much about Saunders as anyone..."

"We already have a job," Fox reminded him.

"You don't think the two just became one?"

"We'd have to clear it with the Solicitor General."

"Don't bother," Clarke broke in. "Neither one of you is coming on board."

"Dive team's just arrived," a uniform announced from beyond the cordon. Clarke headed off in that direction, Olivia Webster at her heels. Rebus yanked his raincoat over his head, creating a little tent within which he could get a cigarette going.

"You know why you're not wanted?" Fox was asking.

"I think so," Rebus replied. "The Summerhall connection."

Fox nodded slowly. "We need to talk to Macari. With Saunders out of the picture, her case is..." He swallowed back the conclusion of the sentence.

"Dead in the water?" Rebus obliged.

"Which probably means I'll be on CID duties sooner than expected."

"The whole force rejoices," Rebus said, before sucking on his cigarette. Clarke was coming back, brolly still held aloft, shoes muddied.

"A change of heart?" Rebus guessed.

"We'll need your notes," she said, her eyes on Fox. "Everything you've got on Saunders."

"Just as soon as you clear it with the Solicitor General's office," Fox agreed.

"I'll add it to the list," she grumbled.

"Malcolm would be an asset to you, you know," Rebus told her. "And he just happens to be between jobs..."

Clarke studied Rebus, as though seeking the catch or waiting for a punch line. Then she nodded stiffly.

"Fine," she said, turning to leave again.

"Don't say I never give you anything," Rebus said to Fox, patting him on the arm.

At the mortuary, Clarke and Fox changed into protective clothing, but at the door to the autopsy suite Clarke paused, eyes on Fox.

"You sure you're up to this?" she asked.

"It'll be my first in a while."

There was a sudden wailing from somewhere in the building.

"The widow," Fox surmised.

Clarke nodded. "Change of plan," she decided. "You've met her before—go see if you can get anything out of her."

"Afraid I'm going to embarrass you in there?" Fox gestured towards the door.

"I'm sure you'd do fine, Malcolm. It's a question of what's most useful."

"You're the boss, Siobhan."

"Thanks." Having said which, she pushed open the door and disappeared inside, leaving Fox with a glimpse of steel trolleys and gleaming instruments. Back in the changing room, he dispensed with the protective clothing and headed for the waiting area, where Saunders's widow Bettina was keening and being comforted by a female friend.

"They won't even give her his things," the friend complained to Fox.

"They'll be returned as soon as possible," Fox said, unsure whether this was true or not. The mortuary was an anonymous slab of a building on Cowgate, and Cowgate itself a narrow, claustrophobic canyon which only came alive at night, thanks to its bars and clubs. Fox hadn't been inside the mortuary in several years, the remit of the Complaints falling short of unexplained deaths. As a young beat officer he had attended a couple of postmortem examinations, but with his eyes averted and trying not to inhale the various aromas.

"My name's Fox, by the way," he told the friend.

"I'm Taylor—Taylor Craddock."

"We've met before, Bettina," he was saying to the widow. There was an untouched beaker of tea at her feet.

"I remember," she said, rubbing at her eyes and sniffing. There were blue smudges on her knuckles, the remnants of ancient tattoos.

Craddock was explaining that the identification process had been traumatic. "Though he did look at peace, Bett, you have to say he didn't suffer..."

More platitudes followed, but Bettina Saunders was hearing none of them. She concentrated, red-eyed and blinking, on the wall across from her. There was nothing on it but a framed color poster of a heathery landscape, puffy clouds and blue sky above. Fox decided to make Taylor Craddock the focus of his questions.

"Billy didn't make contact after he disappeared?"

She shook her head.

"It's just that we need to try to piece together his movements, maybe find out why he acted the way he did."

"Can't this wait?" Craddock chided him. "The woman's in shock."

"I appreciate that, but the sooner we can get started, the better."

"Better for you or better for her?" Craddock's hackles were rising. Bettina Saunders placed a hand around her friend's wrist.

"It's all right, Taylor. The man's only trying to help." She fixed her eyes on Fox. "Billy was worried about going to court. Stands to reason that's why he ran."

"But he didn't exactly run, did he?" Fox went on quietly. "He stayed in the city."

"Where else could he go? He was Edinburgh born and bred."

"Did he have friends nearby? Near that stretch of the canal, I mean?"

She thought for a moment, then shook her head.

"And he never called you? Not even a text so you wouldn't worry?"

"Nothing." She looked down into her lap. "But he was up to high doh. Somebody phoned him one morning—that was the start of it."

Stefan Gilmour, stood to reason . . .

One of the mortuary attendants was standing in the doorway.

"Inspector Fox?" he inquired. "Got a minute?"

Fox smiled an apology towards the two women, hoping the relief on his face wasn't too evident. The attendant led him to a small office, where a clear polythene bag sat on a desk.

"Deceased's possessions," the attendant explained. "Need you to sign for them."

Fox studied the contents of the bag. There was a sheet of printout next to it, listing the individual items. Fox made sure it tallied.

"Hundred and fifty in cash," he commented.

"Despite which, judging by the state of his clothes, he was sleeping rough."

"Oh?"

"Grubby, you might say."

"Speaking of which, where are they?"

"Off to Forensics." The attendant paused. "We didn't lift any of the money, if that's what's on your mind."

Fox shook his head. "Last cashpoint he visited, he took out two hundred. Didn't get through much of it, which tallies with sleeping rough." He lifted the bag. "Did the water bugger the phone?"

"Might be okay when it's dried out."

There wasn't much else—a handkerchief, chewing gum, house keys, loose change and the Bank of Scotland debit card, plus loyalty cards from Costa Coffee and Tesco.

"No watch?" Fox queried.

"No watch."

He double-checked the list before signing his name to the bottom of the sheet. "Autopsy finished yet?"

"Might be another half-hour. They got the bullet though. Wedged between two of the vertebrae. You need to put the date."

Fox added the date beneath his signature, which seemed to satisfy the attendant.

"Were you there for the identification?" he asked.

The attendant nodded.

"How did the widow seem?"

"She managed."

"Did she say anything?"

"Nothing out of the ordinary. You think she did it—crime of passion and all that? You should be swabbing her hands for gunpowder..."

Fox studied the young man. "You watch too many films."

The attendant shrugged. "Not much excitement around here—though we've still got the Justice Minister on the premises. Body's due to be released to the family today."

"Counts as a busy week, does it?"

"Place has been in the news and everything. Mind you, still doesn't make for much of a chat-up line, saying you work here."

"I imagine not."

"Unless you're into Goths, I suppose..."

15

The bullet is undergoing analysis," Siobhan Clarke announced to her team. They were gathered around her in an open-plan office on the first floor of Wester Hailes police station. There was a bit less room than any of them would have liked—competition had been fierce for the few comfortable-looking chairs. Hot-desking was necessary and no one had yet found a kettle. There were journalists outside on Dumbryden Drive, but not many. Shootings were rare in Scotland's capital, but the demise of a minicab driver couldn't compete with that of a senior politician. Fox didn't doubt that the foul weather was also a factor. With a new cold front making itself felt, the rain was turning to sleet. And Dumbryden was not exactly salubrious—mesh grilles protected the cop shop's ground-floor windows—meaning there would be no press conferences in new-build hotels... not until such hotels were constructed.

"I can't tell you a lot more than that at present. It's a nine-millimeter caliber, probably from a handgun. Pathologist commented that it didn't look shiny new, but I'm not sure what that tells us. Until Ballistics and Forensics get back to us, therefore, I want to concentrate on the victim's movements from the night he went missing until he ended up in the canal. He must have eaten—most recent intake comprised a cheese and onion sandwich and a packet of ready-salted crisps, plus a bottle of Irn Bru..."

"Sounds like a meal deal," Olivia Webster interrupted. "Sort of thing a garage or supermarket would sell."

Clarke sought out Fox. "Any receipts among his possessions?"

Fox shook his head. "We don't have his clothes, though—I suppose there could be something in one of the pockets."

"Can you check that?" Clarke asked. Then, to the room at large: "We need door-to-door, starting at the locus and radiating out. The industrial estate will be part of that. They're bound to have camera footage, or else nighttime security we can talk to. Shops and petrol stations in the vicinity—get photos of Saunders out there."

"Local media?" someone else asked.

Clarke nodded. "Newspapers and Internet—TV if we can get it. Putting out a plea for anyone to come forward."

"There might be something on his phone," Fox said. "Doubtful—we already checked once with his mobile phone provider—but worth taking another look."

Clarke nodded her agreement. "Inspector Fox here," she explained to the room, "has been helping the Solicitor General's office form a case against William Saunders. Thirty years ago, Mr. Saunders was charged with the murder of a man called Douglas Merchant. The case fell apart due to police incompetence..."

"Incompetence or collusion," Fox corrected her.

"Anyway," Clarke went on, "those files will be coming here as soon as I've cleared it with Elinor Macari. And as Inspector Fox is the expert, he'll be the one to answer any questions you might have."

"A good starting point," Fox added, "might be the detectives who were responsible for the collapse of the case against Saunders. One of them, Stefan Gilmour, contacted Saunders by phone. We've questioned him once, but now that a murder has been committed..."

Clarke had been nodding throughout. "We'll bring him in," she stated.

"*The* Stefan Gilmour?" someone asked.

"The only one I know of," Clarke confirmed.

*   *   *

Fox was impressed.

Clarke had stamped her authority on the group, giving an immediate sense of order and purpose to the inquiry. There had been room for some levity—just enough so that everyone could relax into their given tasks. Afterwards, she squeezed through the throng towards the desk he was sharing.

"You'll get me those files from the Solicitor General?" she prompted.

"I've put in a call. Waiting for her to respond."

"Or we could just go and fetch them…"

"Best not to get on the wrong side of her—not this early in the game."

Clarke seemed to sense the truth of this.

"I'll track her down," Fox said. "You think it ties in, don't you?"

"Rule nothing in and nothing out."

"I didn't really glean anything from the widow."

"I hope you don't think I was going easy on you?"

"I think we both know you really were."

"You'd met her before, making you the obvious candidate."

Fox nodded and decided to drop the subject. "It's good the bullet was found," he said.

"And the casing," Olivia Webster interrupted, coming towards them and waving her phone. "It was in the water."

"Anything else?"

"Not so far."

"Evidence suggests he was sleeping rough," Fox said. "Maybe not too far from where he ended up."

"The industrial estate?" Clarke suggested. "Maybe we should go take a look—as soon as you've tried the Solicitor General's office again."

For want of anything better to do, Rebus returned to Gayfield Square, where DCI James Page had been left with only a skeleton crew. He was seething, prowling a line from his cupboard-sized office across the floor of the CID room and back again.

"It's not that I don't think Siobhan's perfectly capable," he commented.

"Agreed," Rebus said. "Always annoying, though, when the action's elsewhere."

Page glowered at him, trying to work out whether sympathy or mockery was being offered. Rebus's face gave nothing away.

"I suppose your own little adventure with Malcolm Fox is coming to an abrupt halt?" Page eventually countered.

"A few ends to trim off first," Rebus lied, checking his watch. "In fact, I should get over there and give him a hand…"

"So we can expect you back at your desk here bright and early tomorrow?"

"Of course." Rebus gave a little salute before turning to leave.

Outside, he stood in the car park, smoking a cigarette. There were no messages on his phone, and no point in heading to the office at the Sheriff Court—Fox had locked up on their departure, and Rebus hadn't bothered asking for the key. Instead, he tapped in Stefan Gilmour's number. It went to an answering machine, so Rebus hung up. But a moment later a text popped up on his screen. It was from Gilmour—*In a meeting. I've heard about S. Don't worry.*

S for Saunders. What was it Rebus wasn't supposed to worry about? The threat to all the Saints, or just to Gilmour? Was he saying that he didn't blame Rebus for the increased attention?

"Bloody hell, John," Rebus muttered to himself as he crushed the remains of the cigarette underfoot.

He got into his Saab and drove to Torphichen Place. The media presence had lessened—maybe they'd heard the results of the autopsy. Inside, DCI Ralph nodded a greeting. He seemed flustered, which probably explained why he didn't question a stranger's arrival in his midst. There was a heavy, almost drowsy atmosphere in the office. Rebus recognized it from dozens of previous investigations. Adrenaline and process carried you through the initial stages of an inquiry, but if progress stalled, there came a creeping inertia. All the phone calls had been made, all the interviews conducted. You were going over old ground constantly, for want of anything else to do. Or you headed down unpromising paths which led to dead end after dead end. All of it sapping the strength and the spirit. Especially galling when the team had become fragmented—Rebus sensed that the loss of Clarke and the few others she'd taken with her weighed heavily. Many hours of effort had been expended, and by now, answers were expected. Without them, self-worth would deflate, team morale flag.

One short tour of the main room told Rebus all of this. He headed into a smaller office where a solitary detective constable, jacket over the back of his chair and sleeves rolled up, was working away at a computer. There was a kettle, and Rebus asked if it was all right to make himself a brew.

"Long as you've got a pound for the kitty," the young man said.

Rebus nodded, noticing the tin tea caddy with the slot in its top and the word MONEY taped on one side. He switched the kettle on and asked the officer if he wanted anything.

"My shout."

"Coffee, thanks. One sugar, no milk."

Rebus nodded again and got to work. He sifted through some change from his jacket, then, with back turned, lifted the caddy and gave it a shake, so that its contents rattled, before returning the coins to his pocket.

"No milk, one sugar," he said, placing the mug on the corner of the desk. Then he asked the young man's name.

"Alan Drake."

"Pleased to meet you." Rebus stuck out his hand. "I'm John Rebus."

"I know."

"Probably been warned off talking to me, eh? Big bad wolf and all that."

"No, it's just . . . well, *everybody* knows you."

"You can ignore most of what you've heard." Rebus picked up his mug and scooped the tea bag into a bin.

"You mentored DI Clarke," the young man stated.

"No one 'mentors' Siobhan—all she ever learned from me was what *not* to do." Rebus had come around to the side of the desk, so he could see what Drake was working on.

"Deceased's diary," the young officer obliged. "His office has been helpful..."

"The Justice Minister was a busy man," Rebus commented. "What about the night prior to his death? Have we anything on that?"

"A rare evening off," Drake conceded. "Watched a couple of episodes of a TV show called *Spiral*. Supper from the freezer and some preparatory work for the next day. Replied to a dozen e-mails—personal as well as business—and made a few calls."

"I see you've got the records." Rebus gestured towards the printouts.

Drake nodded. "Landline and mobile. I've got names for everyone he spoke to or texted."

"And they've been interviewed?"

"Sometimes just by phone."

"Including this one?" Rebus tapped a finger against Alice Bell's name.

"Shares a flat with the deceased's son's girlfriend. She's studying art history and Mr. McCuskey had arranged a tour of the Parliament for her—big collection there, apparently. Have you ever been?"

Rebus nodded slowly. "Years back, not long after it opened. Official business, though, I don't recall seeing any paintings." He paused. "Any more calls between the two of them?"

"Three or four over the space of a month."

"Setting up the Parliament tour?"

"That's right—have you spotted something I missed?"

"Not at all—seems very thorough," Rebus said. "And you've shown the results to...?"

"DCI Ralph. It would have been DI Clarke, only she's not here." Drake looked up at Rebus. "They've put her in charge of a *real* murder case."

"You never know, son—this might turn into one again." Rebus placed his half-empty mug on the nearest window ledge. "You just have to keep panning for gold..."

Rebus spent the rest of the late afternoon in the Central Library on George IV Bridge. A librarian showed him how to use the microfilm reader in the Edinburgh Room. He was interested in the local daily and evening papers for the four weeks leading up to Billy Saunders's attack on Douglas Merchant. Having been through the police logs, he'd found nothing surprising or out of place—excepting that torn page from the custody ledger. As he spooled each day's news across the large screen in front of him, he tried not to become distracted; difficult when there were so many reports and stories that triggered memories. Margaret Thatcher was planning a June general election, and Jimmy Savile was fronting an advertising campaign for train travel. Alex Ferguson's Aberdeen beat Real Madrid in extra time to lift the Cup Winners' Cup. British Leyland was in trouble, as were Timex and Ravenscraig. There were moves to ban smoking from the upper decks of buses, and *Annie* was showing at the Playhouse—Rebus remembered Rhona and Sammy dragging him along so he could sleep through it. An ad for a Kensitas gift book reminded him that some of Sammy's Christmas presents would have come from his cigarette coupons. Meantime, the Balmoral Hotel was still the North British and pirate videos were being seized. He thought he could recall a stash of them doing the rounds at Summerhall—*Gandhi* a popular choice. A business computer cost almost the same as a new car, and Bowie was due to play Murrayfield. Stefan Gilmour had blagged the Saints into the eventual gig, Rebus watching and listening through a haze of alcohol on a wet, gray June evening...

On the verge of taking a break and stepping outside for a cigarette, he noticed that the room was emptying, the students unplugging their laptops and packing their bags. Rebus walked across to the desk, and asked what time the place closed.

"Five," he was told.

Giving him only another ten minutes. Instead of the break, he speeded up his reading. He had been doing little more than glancing at each day's obituaries, concentrating instead on news stories. But then he saw a name he recognized.

Philip Kennedy.

Suddenly but peacefully at home . . . Funeral service . . . Family flowers only, please . . .

Wee Phil Kennedy. Slippery Phil. Rebus thought he remembered Stefan Gilmour at the time brushing his hands together at the news—one more scumbag who wouldn't be clogging their in-tray. From the date of birth, he calculated that Kennedy had died just shy of his forty-third birthday. Rebus could see his face—pockmarked and florid and freckled. It was the sort of face you used to see in kids' comics: slightly exaggerated, an overgrown child. Toothy and nervous and bad news. A housebreaker who always carried a knife with him on jobs, scaring the daylights out of anyone he happened to find at home. The elderly and frail a specialty; sheltered housing was never quite sheltered enough from one of Kennedy's nocturnal visits. He would often follow his victims home from the post office on pension day, scope the place out, and then return later, a balaclava over his face and six inches of blade gripped tight. One woman died of fright, and another fell and broke her hip, leaving her in pain as well as fear for the rest of her days.

Suddenly but peacefully at home . . .

Some justice in that, perhaps. He skimmed back a few days, but found no reports of Kennedy's body being found. Rebus gnawed at his bottom lip. Was it Frazer Spence who had come in one day, a bounce in his step, and announced the news? And had Stefan Gilmour really brushed his hands together, quite content to have heard it? Was Porkbelly Paterson in the office at the time? How had he reacted? Rebus couldn't remember. But all of them would have pulled Kennedy in for questioning at one time or another, and some of them would have given evidence against him in court. He had passed away six days prior to the attack on Douglas Merchant—their bodies might well have lain in adjacent drawers at the mortuary. Professor Cuttle's words again: *we were so busy...a lot of lowlifes dropping dead...*Rebus wondered what had happened to Slippery Phil. He could think of one man who might well have the answers. The same man who very probably had sliced him open on a slab...

It was dark by the time Clarke and Fox arrived at the canal bank, ducking below the crime-scene tape. The rain had finally stopped and the sky was clear, the temperature dropping rapidly. Arc lights had been set up to illuminate the area where the dive team were still searching. The bullet casing had been recovered from the water, but no weapon as yet. From their time in front of various streams of CCTV footage from the businesses based on the industrial estate, they now had a good notion that Saunders had been sleeping in an alley, covered by a roll of felt underlay and some flattened cardboard boxes. In the alley itself they had found scraps and wrappers indicating that he had indeed been eating from a local supermarket— whose CCTV was also now being checked for sightings. His phone had been dried out and was working. Once charged, it showed that he had made no calls, and had received only a few—predominantly from his wife and the Solicitor General's office, both leaving messages asking him to get in touch.

"Why didn't he use it?" Clarke had asked.

"Because he was worried it could help trace him?" Fox had suggested. "We have the technology to do that."

"You're saying it was us he was afraid of?"

To which Fox had offered only a noncommittal shrug. "Before he vanished, he had a call one morning—number withheld, and lasting all of half a minute. I'm guessing that was Stefan Gilmour. Certainly chimes with what Gilmour told Rebus and me."

"I need a full report from you, Malcolm—everything you can tell me about Summerhall and Saunders."

"Including John Rebus?"

"Yes. No room for favors here, understood?"

"Understood. Do you mind me asking something?"

"What?"

"Is this your first time in charge of a Major Incident Team?"

"What if it is?"

"Nothing—I just want to thank you for making me feel useful."

"You'll be useful once I get that report." They were clambering up the bank towards the canal path, but Clarke stopped suddenly, turning to face him. "Summerhall *was* dirty, wasn't it?" She watched him nod, his eyes on hers. "And John?"

"I'm not sure," he admitted. "He might not be implicated at all."

"You're not just saying that because he's my friend?"

"We both know Rebus has sailed close to the wind—more times than either of us can count. I'm sure you've helped him out of a few jams, as have a lot of his other colleagues down the years, and some of them came to grief. I don't know what kind of body armor Rebus wears, but it's done its job up to now. Could be that when he arrived at Summerhall he took with him the idealism of youth. But by the time he left, he'd learned bad lessons."

"From Gilmour, Blantyre and Paterson?"

Fox nodded again, and watched as Clarke let out a hissed exhalation between gritted teeth. "The question is," he asked, "how much of all that Saints mumbo-jumbo does he still believe? Is he going to cover up for them?"

"Misguided loyalty, you mean?" It was Clarke's turn to nod. Her phone buzzed and she checked the screen. It was a text from Laura Smith: *We'll call it quits if you brief me on William Saunders.*

"Something important?" Fox inquired.

"Absolutely not."

"David Galvin?"

Clarke glared at him. "He's history, Malcolm."

She turned her head sharply, alerted by a cry from the canal. One of the frogmen was standing in the water, which reached only to his chest. He was waving something, a small, dark shape draped with strands of slimy green weed.

"That looks to me very like a gun," Fox commented. Then watched as a relieved smile broke across Siobhan Clarke's face.

DAY NINE

16

Next morning, Rebus went back to the nursing home in Colinton. Professor Cuttle, he was told, was under the weather, staff fearing he had caught a chill from too much time spent in the garden.

"He had visitors the other day," the staff member informed Rebus. "They kept him outside longer than they should."

"Some people, eh?" Rebus sympathized, making a tutting sound and shaking his head.

"He's in his room, tucked up in bed. Can I fetch you a cup of tea…?"

Rebus said he would be fine, and followed her along a corridor which held the faint aroma of talcum powder. She knocked on a door and opened it.

"Visitor for you," she trilled, stepping back to allow Rebus past her. He nodded his thanks and, once inside, closed the door gently on her.

Cuttle looked paler and thinner than ever. It took him a moment to place Rebus.

"Seems Inspector Fox and me kept you too long in the cold," Rebus apologized, lowering himself onto a folding chair next to the bed.

"Fresh air is supposed to be good for a body," Cuttle said with a shrug. He had been reading a tabloid newspaper with the help of a magnifying glass.

"Anything interesting?" Rebus asked, gesturing towards the paper.

"That shooting in the city—they've found the gun."

Rebus nodded. "They've certainly fished out *a* gun—I dare say a few items of interest have been tossed into the canal down the years." He crossed one leg over the other, trying to get comfortable on a chair ill suited to the task. "Did you ever have to deal with shootings?" he inquired.

Cuttle grew thoughtful. "Once or twice—the first when I was still a young pup. Professor Donner was very much my teacher in those days." He paused. "Is my memory playing tricks, or did *you* once end up with a bullet in you?"

"Lucky I didn't end up on a slab," Rebus acknowledged. "That was 1987—I'd not long been promoted detective sergeant. Took a bullet to the shoulder."

"Donner and I did the autopsy on the shooter." Cuttle was nodding to himself.

"I'm impressed you remember so many of the bodies."

"That's because they were never just 'bodies'—they were human beings, each one with a life story, an identity."

"Well I'm hoping you'll maybe be able to tell me about one more—Philip Kennedy. He died suddenly at home in Moredun at the age of forty-two. This was the week before you had Douglas Merchant in your mortuary."

"Suddenly at home?" Cuttle echoed. "Kennedy, Kennedy, Kennedy..." He was searching for the memory.

"Also known as Slippery Phil."

"Ah, yes. Known to the Lothian and Borders Police. I'm pretty sure CID attended that particular postmortem exam. They wanted to make sure the man really was dead and wouldn't be slipping out of their clutches again."

"CID meaning...?"

"DI Gilmour, I believe. And probably DS Blantyre. Victim had fallen down a flight of stairs at his home. Head injuries and, I think, a broken neck. Professor Donner did the cutting that day. I was on hand for corroboration." Cuttle broke off, eyes narrowing.

"What is it?"

But Cuttle shook his head. "The man had been drinking heavily. Fumes from his stomach had us reeling." He broke off again, lost in thought. "He'd been a housebreaker, hadn't he? With violence— 'hamesucken,' as the law has it. DI Gilmour was glad to see the back of him..."

Rebus's phone was vibrating. He took it out and checked caller ID: DCI James Page. Doubtless wondering why Rebus had failed to turn up for work. Rebus put the phone away again.

"That man Fox," Cuttle was saying, "the one who was with you the other day..."

"Yes?"

"He's investigating Summerhall?"

"He is."

"Specifically the death of Douglas Merchant at the hands of William Saunders?" Cuttle watched Rebus nod. "So why *your* interest in Philip Kennedy? You wouldn't be trying to wrong-foot him?"

"Not at all."

"Because Saunders has turned up dead, hasn't he? Hard not to see a connection."

Rebus glared at the old man. "Would your report of the Kennedy autopsy be held somewhere?"

"Professor Donner wrote it up, not me. And to answer your question, it's very doubtful. Accidental death—not likely to be of interest to posterity."

"Then I'm wasting my time, aren't I?" Rebus rose to his feet.

"Glad I could be of help in that, Detective Inspector Rebus."

"Detective Sergeant, actually."

"Same rank as 1987?" Cuttle asked with a cold smile. The question sliced into Rebus like a scalpel.

Stefan Gilmour had been brought from Glasgow to Wester Hailes police station in a patrol car. He'd looked furious as he was led into the building, past the stunned journalists and trigger-happy photographers.

"The Yes campaign will have a field day with this," he had complained to anyone who would listen, including, eventually, Siobhan Clarke and Malcolm Fox. All three sat in a makeshift interview room, with recording equipment standing by. They were awaiting the arrival of Gilmour's expensive lawyer.

"You're not being cautioned or anything," Clarke had sought to reassure him.

"Nevertheless," Gilmour had replied. He kept casting looks towards Malcolm Fox, as if wondering how much Fox might have told Clarke about the meeting in Glasgow.

The solicitor, when he arrived, introduced himself as Alasdair Traquair and apologized for his "tardiness," before handing an embossed business card to both Clarke and Fox. The cards smelled of sandalwood aftershave.

"Bit of a circus out there," he commented. "Not particularly helpful—and such a charming part of town..."

Traquair rested a black leather-bound notebook on the table and opened it, unscrewing the top from a fountain pen before checking his watch and marking the time.

"Let's make a start, shall we?" he suggested.

"Your client," Clarke obliged, "has already been questioned—in a more informal manner—concerning the disappearance of a former acquaintance called William Saunders. Mr. Saunders has since turned up dead, so we thought it would make sense to have an official record of events."

"As I understand it, Detective Inspector," Traquair drawled, "there *are* no events—merely a single, abbreviated phone call from Mr. Gilmour to the deceased."

"Is that correct, Mr. Gilmour?" Clarke asked. Gilmour glanced towards the solicitor before answering.

"It is," he said.

"You had William Saunders's number?"

"Hard to make the call otherwise."

"How did you happen to have it? I was under the impression the two of you had lost touch..."

Another glance towards the lawyer, who merely indicated with a twitch of the mouth that Gilmour could answer if he wished.

"It wasn't hard," Gilmour conceded. "There's a company I use." He leaned forward in his seat, as if to take them into his confidence. "In business, sometimes it helps to have an edge over whoever you happen to be dealing with."

"And this company helps with that?"

Gilmour nodded. "They're private investigators. Give them a name, a car license plate or a business address and it's quite gobsmacking what they can dig up."

"What did they 'dig up' on William Saunders?"

"All I wanted was a phone number."

"Did they know why?"

Gilmour shook his head. "Look, it's all pretty straightforward." He rested his elbows on the table, so that the lawyer had to move the notebook a little. "I'd heard that the Solicitor General was hoping to reopen an old case, one that involved both Billy Saunders and the CID unit I happened to run at the time. The mishandling of that investigation had led me to resign from the force. Stands to reason the Yes campaign would want to tar me—don't think they've not got people of their own trying to dig up dirt on me." Another glance in Fox's direction, accompanied by the licking of dry lips. "We all know the Solicitor General's leanings, and her camp know they're way behind in the polls..."

"You're saying this is all politically motivated?"

"Why else would it be coming up now?"

"Because the double jeopardy law has changed."

"And you don't think the timing of *that* is pretty convenient? Macari rushed that legislation through specifically so she could have a go at me—a blind man could see it!" Gilmour sat back in his chair so violently that it creaked a complaint.

"Did you bring any of this up with William Saunders?" Clarke asked.

Gilmour ran a hand through his hair and shook his head. "I just asked him what he was going to say to Macari's inquiry."

"And?"

"And nothing—he ended the call right there."

"You didn't threaten him?"

"Absolutely not."

"Or offer an inducement of any kind?"

"Don't answer that," the lawyer drawled. Traquair stopped writing and beamed a professional smile across the table. "My client has told you the extent of his conversation with William Saunders. He has cooperated fully with you. I don't see that this dialogue need continue any further."

"Did you meet him, Mr. Gilmour?" Clarke was asking.

"Really, DI Clarke, I must insist..." Traquair had placed a hand on his client's forearm, as if to warn him against answering.

"I want the name of that firm of investigators," Clarke went on. "I want to hear from them that all you got was a phone number."

"Any objection?" Traquair asked Gilmour.

"No," Gilmour said, staring hard at Clarke. Then: "Will John Rebus merit the same treatment? Dragged here in a squad car, with the media primed and ready? How about Blantyre and Paterson? Or am I the only one that'll help you get your face on TV, DI Clarke?"

"We'll need contact details for those snoopers," Clarke said to the lawyer, as she rose to her feet. "And they'll need to be told they can speak to us—no 'client privilege' smokescreen."

"Understood," Traquair said, closing his notebook and beginning to screw the top back on his fat black pen.

"This firm of investigators," Fox interrupted. "Ever used them to dig dirt on the Yes campaign?"

Gilmour just glowered, as did his lawyer.

Before leaving, Gilmour slapped his fist against the interview room door. It was only afterwards that Clarke realized what he'd done. She pointed out the sticker to Fox. BETTER TOGETHER, it read. VOTE NO.

"The man has a sense of humor," Fox said, peeling it off with a fingernail. "I wonder how big a bill he's just run up with that lawyer of his."

"Whatever it is, it won't be funny. And by the way, that parting shot of yours?"

"Yes?"

"Worthy of Rebus himself."

"Is that a good thing, do you think?"

They returned to the office and watched as a taxi drew up, lawyer and client fighting their way through the melee and the questions before clambering into the back. One particularly stubborn photographer ran down the road after the cab, firing off a few more shots through its rear window.

"Those private investigators will only give us whatever story Gilmour tells them to," Fox cautioned.

Clarke nodded her agreement. "Do you think we let him off too lightly?" she asked.

"No," Fox reassured her. "But is he right about the others—will they merit the same attention?"

"None of them spoke to Billy Saunders," Clarke stated.

"Not on his phone, at any rate," Fox added by way of qualification. "But whoever met him on the canal path that night, they didn't just stumble upon him. It was an arrangement."

"Arranged how?"

"I suppose a few of the public phone boxes in the city still work."

"Needle-in-a-haystack stuff," Clarke said.

"Needle in a haystack," Fox agreed.

An hour later, the team crammed into the office so Clarke could inform them of the initial findings regarding the firearm found in the canal. She was reading from a printed e-mail, sent from the ballistics unit in Glasgow. A rush job had been ordered, so the report was not comprehensive. But it did include the crucial information that the bullet removed from Billy Saunders's spine had been fired from the gun.

"The gun itself," Clarke intoned, "is a Browning L9A1 nine-millimeter pistol, probably dating back to the early 1980s. Standard British Army issue from the 1950s until just recently. Apparently a lot of them went walkies after the Falklands War. The serial number has been filed off, and no usable prints have been found on the grip or barrel. Three bullets remain in the clip and again these seem to date back a few decades. The gun hasn't been kept in the best condition, and probably hadn't been used in quite some time. Accurate only at short range." Clarke looked up from the sheet and realized Fox had ducked out of the room at some point. The other members of the team were jotting notes to themselves or frowning in a show of concentration.

"Thoughts, please," she said, scanning the faces in front of her.

"We need to trace the gun back..."

"Someone must know where it came from..."

"Worth contacting army bases in the city...?"

"Do we know who the underworld would go to if they needed firearms...?"

"Are we treating the shooting as an assassination? If it was a pro, they could be ex-army themselves..."

"Except a pro wouldn't just chuck the weapon, would they? They'd break it up, dispose of it in bits and pieces..."

"Could the gun have belonged to the victim...?"

"Any further tests we could run...?"

After listening, arms folded, for a few minutes, Clarke broke the meeting up, handing out fresh chores to those who needed them. Then she went in search of Fox, and found him in an adjoining room, going through boxes of folders.

"What's all this?" she asked.

"The Summerhall files," he explained. "They arrived this morning with the Solicitor General's blessing."

"And?"

"And this." He had found what he was looking for. He placed the relevant documents on the nearest desk. "It was when you mentioned the Falklands."

Clarke peered at the report. It was dated October 1982 and concerned an army veteran who had been making too much noise late at night in his council flat. Neighbors had complained and—not for the first time—police officers had arrived to deal with the disturbance. The officers had found a small amount of cannabis and, lying on the coffee table in full view, a Browning pistol.

Clarke stopped and looked at Fox. Fox nodded and gestured for her to read on. The ex-soldier's name was Laurie Martin. He was eventually charged with possession of drugs, but let off with a caution and the advice that he should enter a course of counseling.

"Don't suppose anyone had heard of posttraumatic stress back then," Fox commented.

"Am I missing something?" Clarke had turned the sheet over, but it was blank. "The gun didn't make it onto the charge sheet."

"No," Fox said.

"How come?"

He offered only a shrug. "Coincidence?" he suggested.

"You obviously don't think so. A pistol—same make and probable vintage as the one used to kill Billy Saunders..." She was shaking her head slowly.

"Should we bring Stefan Gilmour back in?"

"What's the point? I don't see his name here." Clarke scanned the report again. "This is all there is? No record of the weapon going into an evidence locker? No mention of it in the courtroom?"

"I could try doing a bit more digging—courts will have their own records..."

"Sounds like another haystack to me." She had taken out her phone and was finding a number on it.

"Let me guess," Malcolm Fox said.

*   *   *

Rebus was seated in his car on Great King Street when he got the call.

"Hiya, Siobhan," he said.

"Where are you?"

"The car park at Gayfield Square," he lied. "Trying to work up the energy for an hour or two of DCI Page's company."

"Have you heard we found the weapon?"

"The one used on Billy Saunders? Yes, congratulations and all that..."

"It's a Browning pistol, probably brought home from the Falklands War. Ring any bells?"

"Should it?"

"Serial number has been removed at some point too, if that helps jog the memory."

"I'm not sure I..."

"Laurie Martin, John. Ex-army and failing to fit back into Civvy Street. He was brought to Summerhall by two patrol officers after a disturbance."

"Hang on, when was this?"

"October '82."

"I didn't start at Summerhall until November."

"Laurie Martin's name means nothing to you?"

"No."

"He was being disruptive, so officers went to his door. He let them in and they found the pistol sitting in his living room."

"So?"

"At some point in the story, the gun stops being a character. Doesn't even look as though it was marked as evidence."

"Bit of a stretch to say the same gun was used on Saunders."

"And this is all coming as news to you?"

"Scout's honor."

"Is it worth me bringing it up with any of the others?"

"The Saints, you mean?"

"We had Gilmour in here earlier."

"Oh aye?"

"He's sticking to his version of events."

"That's his privilege, I suppose."

"John..."

"I'm not the enemy here, Siobhan. Whatever happens, bear that in mind."

"What are you saying?"

"Fox is all over this, isn't he? He's been through every bit of paperwork from Summerhall and memorized the lot. Be careful he doesn't lead you a dance..."

Rebus ended the call and got a cigarette lit, flicking ash from the window. Then he called Eamonn Paterson.

"It's John," he said. "Can you talk?"

"At a loose end, as per," Paterson replied. "What's troubling you?"

"They took Stefan in for questioning."

"About Billy Saunders? Stands to reason."

"Thing is, they've got the gun."

"Yes, I heard on the radio."

"What you didn't hear is that they think it originally belonged to an old soldier called Laurie Martin." Rebus listened for a response, but there was silence on the line. "Now, Laurie Martin was before my time, but I *do* remember the Browning. It sat in your drawer and after a few drinks it might come out for a bit of a joke. Laurie Martin's handgun, yes?"

"The man was a war hero, John. Yomped halfway across those bloody islands and got almost no thanks for it. He told us the stories that night—the custody sergeant came and fetched us so we could listen. Man needed psychiatric help more than anything, and he wasn't going to get much of that in the clink."

"So you spirited away the gun? Shame you forgot to scratch it from the arrest report."

"What do you want me to say, John?"

"I want you to tell me what happened to it."

"The gun? I haven't the faintest notion. When we were leaving Summerhall, it just wasn't in my drawer anymore."

"Someone took it?"

"I don't know." Paterson paused. "There's no way they can tie it to Saunders's murder, is there?"

"You tell me. Even if it's circumstantial, it's another piece of the jigsaw as far as Fox is concerned. And it's a murder inquiry now, Eamonn—so don't think it isn't serious."

"I'm not stupid."

"Neither am I. You'd be wise to remember that. Okay, change of subject—fill me in on Slippery Phil Kennedy."

"Now there's a name from the vaults. What's Kennedy got to do with anything?"

"You tell me."

"There's nothing to tell—died in his house after a day's boozing. Sleekit wee shite, too. We should have put him away, but we didn't. 'Not proven' was the verdict, that one time we got him to trial."

Not proven: the "bastard verdict" available to a Scottish jury when they thought the Crown had not done quite enough to convince of the accused's guilt. You walked out of court a free man, no official stain on your character. The words stuck in every detective's craw: *you nearly got me, but not quite.* Rebus had seen absolute villains swaggering from court after a not proven, with a grin and a wink for the law officers who had racked up hundreds of hours building the case—the case that didn't quite stack up in the jury's collective mind.

Better luck next time, those grins and winks said.

"Were you at the autopsy?" Rebus asked.

"No."

"How about Gilmour or Blantyre?"

"It was a long time ago, John." Paterson fell silent, as though thinking. "I'm fairly sure it was Frazer Spence. Aye, Frazer drew the short straw that day."

Liar, thought Rebus. *Why do that?* Professor Cuttle had already supplied the names—Gilmour and Blantyre—names Paterson was choosing to ignore.

"I still don't see where Kennedy fits into anything, though," Paterson was now saying.

"I don't think he does." *Here, have one of mine—fair exchange is no robbery.*

Rebus ended the call and finished his cigarette, flicking it from the car window. He stared up towards the top floor of the building across from him, then got out, marched to its front door, and pressed the bell marked TRAYNOR/BELL.

"Hello?"

He recognized the voice, and leaned in towards the intercom. "It's Detective Sergeant Rebus," he announced.

"Jessica doesn't want to see you."

"It's not her I'm here to talk to, Alice—it's you."

"What do you mean?"

"If Jessica's up there, probably best if you come down here."

"Why? What have I done?"

"Does she know about you and our dear-departed Justice Minister? Come to that, does Forbes know you were seeing his old man?"

"You bastard," she said. "Just go away and leave us alone."

"Can't do that, Alice. Not until I get a few answers."

"Just—sod—off!" A click told him the intercom had died. He stood up straight, waited a few seconds, then retreated to his car, making himself comfortable behind the steering wheel. He was about to occupy himself with a fresh cigarette when Alice Bell yanked open the door to her building, stepped out and looked up and down the street. She was fretting, hands clasped. When she saw the Saab, her eyes narrowed, her lips forming a thin determined line. Rebus gestured for her to come join him, and she did, opening the passenger-side door and getting in, slamming the door closed after her.

"You're vile," she said.

"When the investigation team called you, you told them Forbes's dad was showing you around the Scottish Parliament. As far as I know, they've accepted that story." He paused. "I wasn't so sure, and you sitting here seals it for me." Another pause. "So do you want to tell me?"

"Tell you what?"

Rebus leaned back against the headrest, face half turned towards hers. "So far they've only been looking at Pat McCuskey's most recent phone records. I can go back a bit further and work out when it started . . ."

"Three months," she eventually said. "Three and a half."

"How did the two of you meet?"

"Forbes took Jessica and me to the house. His parents were there. When I said I was interested in Alison Watt, Pat told me there was a painting by her hanging in the Parliament building." It was Alice Bell's turn to pause. "That was the start, I suppose."

"Forbes and Jessica . . . ?"

"Don't know anything about it."

"How often did you meet, you and him?"

"Eight times." She sounded almost proud that she could be so specific.

"At his house?"

She shook her head. "Never there."

"Where, then?"

"He has a friend with a flat on Holyrood Road. The friend is away in London a lot . . ." She had begun to blush. "I know he's a lot older than me, and . . . and he's Forbes's dad and everything, but . . ."

"You're not in the confessional, Alice."

"You don't think . . . ?"

"That his death had anything to do with you?" Rebus shook his head. "Not unless you want to tell me otherwise."

"Then I don't see . . ."

Rebus twisted his body towards her. "I need information, Alice. I need to know what happened the night of the crash. My gut tells me Jessica will have confided in you."

"She hasn't."

"I think you're lying."

"I'm not!"

"Well if that's how we're playing this, I might have to share your little secret with a few mutual friends—Jessica and Forbes to start with, then the team investigating Mr. McCuskey's demise…"

Her eyes had grown fiery. "You *are* vile," she said, voice trembling with rage.

"I prefer the phrase 'hard but fair.'"

"What's fair about *this?*"

"Look, I'll make it easy for you. Forbes was the go-to guy for student drugs. My theory is a deal went bad that night and he totaled the car getting away. Then he kept on running, leaving Jessica in the lurch. Now I ask you: is *that* fair, do you think?"

"I don't know what to think." She blinked a few times, as though having trouble bringing the immediate world into focus. Then she took a deep breath, composing herself. Rebus bided his time, knowing she was about to offer him something.

"Forbes gets the stuff from a bar."

"In the city center?"

She shook her head. "It's called the Gimlet. I think it's in Gorgie or nearby."

"Nearby," Rebus agreed quietly. "Who's his contact? The owner? A man named Darryl Christie?"

She was still shaking her head. "One of the doormen. Deano? A name like that."

"Deano," Rebus agreed.

"That's as much as I know."

"No whispered conversations between Forbes and Jessica since the crash? No muffled phone calls when she doesn't know you're listening?"

"Nothing," Alice Bell said, her eyes drilling into his.

"Is she upstairs just now?"

Bell nodded. "On the phone to her father—talking about tomorrow's funeral."

"What about it?"

"Her father wanted to put in an appearance. Jessica's persuading him otherwise. Apparently he called Forbes and accused him of nearly killing Jess. She's worried he'd make a scene..." Her look hardened. "It was *you* who put the idea in his head."

"We both know Forbes was driving that car, Alice."

She had reached for the door handle, pushing it outwards. "You're hacking your way through a lot of innocent lives, you know. And I sense you get a kick out of it, too." She was on the pavement now. He watched her cross the street and enter her building. Once she was inside, he noticed she had left the passenger-side door wide open. No way he could reach that far. He would have to get out and walk around to close it. As payback went, it was petty but effective.

Rebus couldn't help but admire her for it.

17

You Deano?"

"Who's asking?"

It was eight p.m. and music was blaring from within the Gimlet. A chalkboard outside announced that it was 80s Night. The bouncer on the door wore a long black woolen coat and a black polo neck. His hands were in his coat pockets and his feet were splayed.

"Detective Sergeant Rebus," Rebus said, flipping open his warrant card. "Is your boss indoors?"

"Not tonight."

"Any idea where I can catch him?"

"No."

Rebus pretended to be stymied, even going so far as to scratch his head.

"Looks like you're out of luck," the bouncer stated.

"Not me, Deano," Rebus replied. "*You.*"

The man was a couple of inches taller than Rebus and carried a similar amount of heft, the difference being one of muscle tone. One look at Deano's neck told Rebus he was a gym regular. Nicks to both eyebrows meant he had probably boxed at one time, or still did. The small, wary eyes met Rebus's.

"How's that then?" he asked.

"I was going to talk to Darryl in person, but I suppose a phone call will have to do. We go way back, me and your boss. Thought it only fair to warn him . . ."

A couple of regulars were arriving, men only a few years younger than Rebus.

"All right, Deano?" one of them said.

Deano nodded, taking a step to the side so they could get past. As the door opened, Rebus caught a blast of Duran Duran. Someone was singing along, though the band wouldn't have thanked them for it. The door closed again and Deano resumed his staring match with Rebus.

"Warn him of what?" he asked.

"Someone's using the Gimlet for drug deals. Like I say, I know Darryl and he's not that stupid. I'm not saying he wouldn't get involved, but I doubt he'd let it happen anywhere that could connect so sharply to him." Rebus paused. "See what I'm saying?"

The bouncer was trying not to show it in his face, but he couldn't help balling his fists and shifting his feet. Little tics that told Rebus the man was unnerved.

"Darryl's going to want to know," Rebus pressed on. "It's happening right *here* without his say-so. That means you're not doing your job. In fact, story is, the one doing the dealing might be an employee. Darryl's going to want to know one of his own is in danger of bringing the Drug Squad down on him. Who knows what they'll turn up once they start looking?"

"I haven't a clue what you're talking about."

"Then there's no problem." Rebus took the liberty of stretching out a hand and patting the bouncer's shoulder. "I'll just call Darryl and give him the story."

"Could be a punter," Deano blurted out.

"What's that?"

"Selling the dope—could be one of the punters."

Rebus shook his head and tried for a soulful look. "What I've heard is it's someone closer to home. Someone very like yourself . . ." He had lifted his phone to his face, making show of scrolling down the names in his contact list. "Here we are," he said, pressing the phone to his ear.

"Hang on a minute," Deano said.

"What?"

"Just put the phone down."

Rebus did so, and waited while the cogs turned inside the bouncer's head.

"If you're so sure it's me, why piss around? Why let me know you know?"

"Because Darryl never needs to find out. You help me, I help you."

"I'm nobody's snitch."

"Don't fret—it's not your boss's secrets I'm interested in."

"What then?"

"You sell to a young guy called Forbes McCuskey."

"Do I? Who says?"

"I don't have time for this, Deano." Rebus lifted the phone again. The bouncer gripped him by the wrist.

"Okay, okay," he said, looking up and down the street. "I know who Forbes McCuskey is."

"Now we're getting somewhere. You heard about the car crash?"

Deano looked genuinely puzzled. "He was in a crash?"

"His girlfriend was with him at the time. Out Kirkliston way, other side of the airport."

"And what does that have to do with me?"

"You didn't happen to be in the vicinity?"

Deano shook his head.

"So how does it work when Forbes buys from you?"

"He parks across the road there." The bouncer nodded towards the spot where Rebus's Saab sat. "Winds the window down. I go over, he tells me what he needs and I give him a price."

"Bit of a markup, him being a posh student and all?"

"I play fair." The man actually sounded aggrieved by the accusation.

"You know he's the Justice Minister's son?" Rebus watched Deano nod. "Never tempted to use that?"

"I didn't find out until his dad died. Saw his photo on the front of the paper."

"You sure that was the first of you twigging? Only, a few papers might pay good money for the story."

"Hard to give them a story without being put in the frame myself."

"True enough," Rebus agreed. "And if Darryl were to find out you were conducting a bit of business without his okay..."

Deano stiffened, squaring his shoulders.

"How much were you selling to McCuskey?"

"Enough for him to share with friends."

"Coke? Ecstasy?"

"As and when required, plus a bit of blaw."

"And where do *you* source the stuff?"

The bouncer shook his head slowly and determinedly. "You've got what you're getting."

"I've hardly started, son." Rebus took a moment to gather his thoughts. "Forbes was freelance? He wasn't working for you?"

"No."

"When was the last time you saw him?"

"A couple of weeks."

"Is that normal?"

"He might have other stuff on his plate right now."

"True, but I'm wondering how often he used to come see you. Maybe he's found another outlet."

"You think that's what he was doing the night of the crash?"

Rebus offered a shrug. A car was slowing as it passed the bar. A cheap model with a modified exhaust. Two young men in front, two in the back. Hip-hop blaring. They saw that Deano had company and seemed to recognize what kind of company it was. With a growl from the engine, the car sped off.

"I maybe just lost you a sale," Rebus apologized.

"They'll be back," Deano said. "Are we done here?"

"Just one last thing." Rebus lit a cigarette, offering one but receiving a shake of the head. "Cab driver called Billy Saunders had a pickup here four nights back. That was the last anyone saw of him until he turned up with a bullet in his chest, floating in the canal."

"I heard."

"And I'm guessing by now you've been interviewed?" Rebus watched as the bouncer nodded. "What did you tell them?"

"I said I'd no idea who it was got picked up that night—or even if a cab ever arrived."

"As I thought," Rebus said. "But now you're going to tell *me* the truth. See, Darryl already told me you were on the door that night. And a cab was ordered from here to go to Niddrie—and Niddrie is where the car ended up. So someone from this pub was in the back of that cab and they had to walk right past you when they left."

"Maybe I was on my break."

Rebus squinted through a cloud of cigarette smoke, leaning back a little in a show of disbelief. "Lying might be in your job description, Deano, but you're really bad at it. Care to try again?" "What if the cab was for someone I know? Would they be in the frame for the driver's murder?" Rebus shook his head. "Saunders was a worried man. He abandoned the cab and slept rough for a couple of nights. Nobody thinks it had anything to do with his passenger. We just need to know if he said anything, or seemed edgy, or maybe took a call on his mobile..."

"The answer is no," Deano said. The door of the bar burst open and a man and woman stumbled out, arms around one another, giggling like the teenagers they no longer were. Ignoring Rebus and the bouncer, they headed off towards the flats behind the Gimlet, the woman pausing to remove her high heels, hanging on to the man for support as she did so.

"You were the passenger?" Rebus asked quietly. Deano eventually nodded.

"An urgent delivery, maybe?" Rebus guessed. "Or maybe stocks were low and you needed a top-up?"

"He was supposed to wait. I told him I'd be five minutes, maybe ten. Handed him a twenty as down payment. But when I came out, he was nowhere to be seen."

"Did he know what was going on?"

"No."

"You hadn't used him before?"

"Not that I know of."

"And he seemed fine?"

"I was texting most of the way."

"When you handed him the money and told him to wait…"

"He just nodded." Deano paused. "Maybe that *was* a bit odd. I mean, he didn't say anything, like he was distracted. Just stared at the windscreen while I flicked the twenty onto the passenger seat." He fixed Rebus with a look. "No way I'm telling this to anyone else."

"I'll need to think about that."

"I'll deny everything. It'll be your word against mine."

"I wonder whose story your boss would be likely to believe, Deano. Could be the police will be the least of your troubles."

Rebus crossed the road and got into his car. Turned the ignition and gave a little wave in the bouncer's direction before moving off.

Deano watched the car all the way to the T-junction. Even when it was lost to view he kept staring, as if there might be something around the corner that would emerge suddenly, changing his life utterly and forever. A distant roar told him that the hip-hop car was somewhere in the vicinity. He turned and headed into the Gimlet, knowing that the sanctuary it offered might be fleeting and deceptive.

"Anyone would think you have no social life," Rebus said. He had recognized Clarke's Astra parked directly outside his tenement. She was getting out of the car now, smiling tiredly.

"You don't exactly look as if you've been partying," she responded.

"The law never sleeps, Siobhan. But in your case, I might make an exception. Workload getting to you?"

"I don't want any foul-ups."

"They're more likely to happen when the boss hasn't had enough shut-eye." Rebus was finding the key for the main door. "You coming up?"

"How strong can you make a cup of tea?"

Rebus tutted. "Warm milk for you, young lady. And a lift home after, if you're too tired to drive..."

The flat was chilly, and Rebus turned up the radiators in the living room. He plugged his phone in to charge while he made tea. Clarke wandered into the kitchen and opened the fridge.

"You hungry?" he asked.

"I may have just lost my appetite." She closed the door on the dried-up cheese and gray-pallored sausages.

"We could call for a delivery."

But she shook her head and watched him remove the tea bags from either mug. Back in the living room, she rested her head against the back of the sofa, eyes closed.

"Stretch out, if you like," Rebus said, settling into his own armchair. "Then tell me all your troubles."

"Like I'm in therapy, you mean?" She smiled, eyes still closed. "I'll tell you mine if you tell me yours."

"Do I sound like a man with problems?"

She angled her head and looked at him. "You are, though. Let's start with the gun. You know something about it, scout's honor or not, so spit it out."

Rebus stared back at her above the rim of the mug. "There *was* a gun like it," he admitted. "Doesn't make it the *same* gun, mind."

"Taken from an ex-army veteran? And then what? Kept lying around Summerhall for anyone to borrow?"

"As far as the Saints were concerned, they were repaying a debt. That soldier had served his country, so they decided to keep him out of jail."

"It wasn't their decision to make, John."

"I know."

"Who did you speak to? Paterson?" She watched him nod. "What did he say?"

"Gun was kept in his desk drawer. Then one day, just before we all got moved out, it wasn't there anymore."

"Only a handful of people had access to it," Clarke stated.

"Can we be sure it was the same gun?" He saw the look she was giving him. "Okay, it's a good bet, but it's no more than that."

"Whoever shot Saunders, they'll have gunpowder residue on their skin and clothes."

"And if they're ex-police, they'll know that and have dealt with it." He held up his right hand, waggling his fingers. "Want a quick sniff, Inspector?"

"Don't be revolting." She lifted her mug and drank from it.

"Look, I'm sorry I didn't tell you. I wanted to do a bit of checking first."

"So you phoned Paterson and warned him?"

"I wasn't warning him..."

"Could be construed as such by someone who doesn't know you like I do. But I'm running a murder case here, John, and the last thing I need is you placing hurdles in the way."

"Understood."

"You were in the army, weren't you? Ever carry a Browning?"

"Thirteen rounds, and you never knew when one might go off and you'd end up shooting yourself in the thigh or ankle."

"How so?"

"Safety catch was far from foolproof. You never kept a round in the chamber."

"Easy to use, though? Could someone who'd never fired a shot in their life find their way around one?"

Rebus nodded, then asked how the questioning of Stefan Gilmour had gone.

"He brought along a shiny lawyer."

"Only to be expected."

"Doesn't make him look any less guilty."

"I'm guessing that's what the media pack are thinking now too."

Clarke's phone had sounded, letting her know she had a text. She looked at the screen.

"Uncanny," she commented. "That's one of them now. Laura Smith."

"The *Scotsman*'s crime reporter?"

Clarke nodded. "She thinks I owe her for the gen on Forbes McCuskey and his dealing."

"She'd be happy enough if you told her you've connected Summerhall to the murder weapon."

"I'm not at that stage just yet." She looked at him again. "What's happening about McCuskey?"

"Father or son?"

"Both, I suppose."

Rebus got up and headed over to the bay window, pulling it open and crouching down so he could light a cigarette and blow the smoke outside.

"I appreciate the thought," Clarke said. "Now, about the McCuskeys . . ."

"You probably know as much as I do when it comes to the break-in."

"Managed to link it to the son yet?"

"No . . ."

"That sounds like you're getting closer, though."

"Just from the way I said 'no'?"

She nodded. "So here's where we find out if you think you can trust me."

"I trust you."

"Then share."

Rebus held up a finger. "You have to go first—how is Fox working out?"

"He's okay. A sharp mind, even if his CID skills are a bit rusty."

"Do you trust *him?*"

"I think so, yes."

"Even though he could still be playing for Elinor Macari's team?"

"I trust him," Clarke stated. "Now it's your turn."

Rebus blew smoke through the gap in the window. "Forbes McCuskey isn't a big player. My guess is he just buys enough to sell on to his immediate circle—probably reckons it makes him look big and important. He gets the stuff from a doorman at the Gimlet."

"Darryl Christie's pub?"

"The same. Not that Christie knows anything about it." Rebus paused. "So when you question the doorman—name's Deano, by the way—keep it low-key. He might be useful to us some day, but not if Christie's booted him off the park."

"And why would I be questioning this Deano character?"

"Because he was the passenger in Billy Saunders's minicab. Needed to go to Niddrie for a bit of shopping. Says Saunders didn't seem particularly antsy. The car was supposed to wait, but it didn't."

"Anything else?"

Rebus shook his head.

"And you were going to bring this to me first thing in the morning?"

"Of course." He gestured towards her mug. "How's the tea?" "I think the milk's past it."

"Past it sometimes still does the job." He paused. "If you want to leave your car here, I can run you home. Don't want you nodding off at the wheel."

She was stifling a yawn, but shaking her head at the same time. "You know that your pal Gilmour connects to Owen Traynor?"

"Yes."

"Been keeping that to yourself too?"

"Obviously not—who told you?"

"Laura."

"Another favor owed."

"The shining knight of the Better Together campaign is beginning to look pretty tarnished."

"This is why I don't vote. My ex campaigned for devolution back in '79. Drove me demented."

"But we've got the chance for a fresh start," Clarke teased him.

"Thing about fresh starts, though, Siobhan..."

"What?"

"They usually turn out to be same old in disguise."

As Malcolm Fox sat by his father's bedside, he thought of Professor Norman Cuttle. It had been on the tip of his tongue to reveal to Rebus that his own father was in a home not unlike the one in Colinton. Mitch Fox was dozing. Malcolm looked around the room, seeing the few select pieces of furniture from the old house, the ones Mitch had decided to keep. Everything else had either been split between Malcolm and his sister, or else sold. A line of saliva had dried to a salty crust on Mitch's unshaven chin. The skin looked red and sore. Malcolm would mention it to the staff. They would have an excuse ready—they always did—but he would ask anyway, just so they'd know he was paying attention.

Fox was tired, but he wanted to stay until his father roused himself. That way he could say a proper goodbye. They'd been discussing the latest travails of Hearts FC, along with small talk about the weather and the trams. With a single snore, Mitch Fox blinked back to wakefulness.

"I nodded off there," he confessed.

"Testament to my conversational skills."

"Pass me the glass, will you?"

It wasn't actually glass, but a toughened translucent plastic which would bounce if dropped. There was an inch of tepid water left in it, and Mitch drained it, shaking his head when his son offered a refill. He lay back against his bunched pillows and studied Malcolm.

"Is that you finished in the Complaints?"

"More or less."

"And they'll have you back in CID?"

"You don't think I'm up to it?"

"It'll be hard going."

"I'm armor-plated."

"That's the problem, though—you're anything but. It's why Complaints suited you. Paper-pushing rather than blood and guts."

"Is it that time again?"

"What time?"

"Whenever I visit these days, you always feel the need to stick the knife in."

"Do I?"

"You know you do." Fox had risen to his feet so he could pace what floor space there was. He'd had a letter a few weeks back informing him that money could be saved were his father to share with another of the home's clients. He'd been tempted, not because he couldn't afford the fees but just to see the look on Mitch's face—a small, cruel victory of sorts.

"What are you smiling at?" his father asked now.

"Nothing wrong with your eyesight."

"That doesn't answer my question."

"I was just wondering whether I'd stop off for a Chinese on the way home."

"You don't feed yourself properly."

"Better than some. Speaking of which, have you seen Jude?"

"Your sister's another one who's worried about you."

"Tell her not to bother."

"She says you've had a falling-out."

"I handed her fifty quid last week, went round a day later and she'd stocked up on booze and fags rather than food. Not a penny of it left."

"She needs looking after."

"Thanks, but I'll pass."

"Who else will do it if you don't?"

"You don't think I've tried?"

"Oh, you're good at dishing out the money, but sometimes a little more is required."

"I come see you when I can. Though God knows why, since we always seem to end up like this."

"It would just give me a bit of solace if I knew the two of you were going to be all right."

"We're getting by." Fox stretched out his arms and gave a shrug. "I wish I could say we're both on course for our Nobel prizes, but there you are."

Mitch Fox smiled sourly. "The pair of you were always this way. It drove your mother up the wall."

"I don't remember that."

"No, butter wouldn't melt in *your* mouth. You'd carry the shopping, set the table... But if you ever did something, you'd be quick to lay the blame on poor Jude, keeping your face straight as you lied through your teeth."

"Will this character assassination take long?" Fox made show of checking his watch. "Only I've an appointment with a carryout menu..."

"You really think you'll cope when they drop you back into CID?"

"I'm working a murder case right now—nobody's scrawled any graffiti about me in the toilets."

"That's something, I suppose." Mitch Fox's eyelids were drooping again, his mouth hanging open half an inch.

"I better be off, Dad," Fox said, returning to the bed and touching the back of his father's hand. "Fancy an ice cream on the seafront this weekend?"

"Will it be bracing?"

"In Portobello? I think I can guarantee that."

"And is Jude invited?"

"I'll ask her," Fox said, giving the mottled hand a final squeeze, and feeling the pressure returned.

DAY TEN

18

Mortonhall Crematorium had seldom been busier. Nobody lined the streets nearby, but journalists and camera crews had parked their cars and vans curbside and were being corralled behind metal barriers on the other side of the road from the entrance to the crematorium grounds. The car park was full and mourners were awaiting the arrival of the hearse carrying Patrick McCuskey. Rebus doubted a tenth as many would turn out for Billy Saunders's obsequies. They'd be lucky to fill the front two rows of the small chapel, whereas today, in warming sunshine, the large chapel had been reserved for family and close friends, with everyone else asked to pay their respects outside. A PA system had been erected so that the service could be relayed. Some of the mourners were asking each other if they qualified for a seat indoors. They broke off to watch as a fleet of official cars arrived, bearing senior politicians of all parties, plus police brass and the Lord Provost. A liveried chauffeur opened the back door of one Jaguar and Stefan Gilmour stepped out. He had traveled alone, and Rebus wondered if this was a message from the No campaign. Freshly interviewed as part of a murder inquiry, he might have become damaged goods. Most eyes were on the First Minister and his deputy, but Rebus watched Gilmour. Crisp dark blue suit, white shirt, black tie, sunglasses. Gilmour adjusted his cuffs and buttoned his jacket. Then he saw Rebus. As the politicians filed into the chapel, he headed in the opposite direction. Rebus was standing on the pavement next to a row of covered benches. He nodded a greeting at his old colleague.

"What are you doing here?" Gilmour asked in an undertone, removing the sunglasses and pocketing them.

"Paying my respects."

"He was a good man, regardless of politics. Any closer to finding out who killed him?"

"Not as far as I know. Bit of progress on Billy Saunders, though."

"Oh?"

Both men were pretending to be interested in the doors to the chapel and the people milling there.

"The gun's turned up."

"I heard."

"Might turn out to be the Browning that Porkbelly kept in his desk drawer."

"Won't be easy to prove."

"Nevertheless, you might find yourself being interviewed again."

"Just what I need," Gilmour muttered.

"Thing is, Stefan, it did disappear around the time you were getting your jotters."

"I *resigned*," Gilmour said by way of correction. "And lost out on a healthy chunk of pension as a result."

"If you hadn't, the Complaints would have crawled all over us."

"And found plenty—don't forget that, John."

"How can I?"

Gilmour turned his head to study Rebus. "Please tell me you don't think one of us killed Saunders?"

"Why not? Back then we were capable of just about anything— might still be true today." Rebus held Gilmour's stare. "We were bad cops, Stefan. That's the truth of it. And out of all of us, I'd say you've got most to lose."

"Maybe so, but I didn't do it. What if I were to tell you Frazer Spence took that gun home?"

"I'd think you were lying. The one Saint who's not in the frame for this is Frazer."

"I doubt Dod Blantyre could have made it to the canal under his own steam."

"Which leaves me, you and Porkbelly—and I know it wasn't me."

"What if it wasn't any of us? Saunders had served time, knew more than a few nutcases. There could be any number of people out there with a grudge. You're *assuming* it's the same gun, but I'm not hearing any proof."

"The time you phoned him, did you try a bribe?"

"Didn't think it would work. I mean, he'd have taken the cash but then come back for more."

"In other words, you'd never have been free of him?"

"Right."

"An admission that doesn't really help your case." Rebus paused. "What is it he had, Stefan? What could he tell Macari and her team? I've been through the custody ledger and there's half a page missing from the week before Saunders killed Merchant. It got me think-ing—could there be something Saunders knew? He comes to you, tells you he'll do a deal—forget all about it if you get him off next time he's arrested. You couldn't know he was going to bludgeon some poor sod to death, so you shook hands on it."

"The hearse is arriving," Gilmour said, nodding in the direction of the gates. A slow-moving procession of vehicles, the engines al-most silent. Wreaths shrouding the coffin, allowing only glimpses of gleaming brass handles, varnished pale wood. In the car behind, the Justice Minister's widow and son. The First Minister and his deputy had reemerged from the chapel and were flanking the door, hands clasped as if in prayer, heads bowed.

"Nothing to say, Stefan?" Rebus whispered into his neighbor's ear. Gilmour's jaw was jutting as he watched the vehicles pull to a halt. The First Minister offered his condolences to the widow, along with a peck on the cheek. She was dressed in black, and wore sun-glasses which obscured half her face.

"Only that you're making a mistake, John. Sounds very much as if you've decided you're not part of the Saints anymore."

"Let me tell you something, Stefan. I spoke to Porkbelly and he was all for letting Frazer take the rap for that gun, same as you just did. Seems to me you'll shit on anyone to save your own necks."

"Maybe *you* think you're clean, but you're not," Gilmour retorted. "You knew we hung on to that gun—why didn't you take it to the bosses at the time? Remember Interview Room B, that time I walked in and you had your hands around a suspect's throat? I forget the name now, but it'll come back to me if necessary. The drugs we planted on that barman we didn't like? The prossies we let off after an hour in the holding cell, once they'd slipped us a few quid or a promise? The restaurant tabs that never arrived at the end of a meal? Two hundred cigarettes here, a case of malt there... The stories we could tell, eh?"

Gilmour's eyes were boring into Rebus's.

"I took the fall, John," he went on. "And I did it for all of us. Remember that, when you've got the tin-opener poised above the can marked 'worms.'"

He started walking towards the chapel, maneuvering his way delicately but determinedly through the throng. Finding himself in front of Forbes McCuskey, he shook the young man's hand and said a few words. McCuskey turned his head and seemed to recognize Rebus. But by then Gilmour was working the crowd, knowing which flesh deserved to be pressed. A pat on the shoulder from the First Minister, even though they were adversaries. A slight bow of the head from the Lord Provost. A warm smile from the outgoing Chief Constable. And then everyone was heading indoors, organ music beginning to emerge from the PA. Rebus backed away towards the memorial garden and lit a cigarette. He spotted a pair of crutches amongst the mourners. Jessica Traynor was making for the chapel, with the help of Alice Bell. Neither of them noticed Rebus, but when they reached Forbes McCuskey, Jessica burst into tears, resting her head on his shoulder. Her boyfriend ran a hand through her hair, and seemed to mouth a few words, words very like "Don't worry."

Don't worry.

And with his eyes focused not on Jessica Traynor but Alice Bell.

Rebus arrived at Wester Hailes police station to find that they'd just brought in Deano. He was being taken from reception to the interview room.

"Thanks for nothing," he spat, seeing Rebus.

"Just say your piece and don't worry about anything," Rebus advised.

He showed his ID to the desk and asked for directions to the Major Incident Team.

"Whole station's the Major Incident Team," came the terse reply.

He poked his head around the doors of a couple of rooms before finding what he was looking for—the Summerhall boxes. They were on a desk in a small office. One of the boxes was open, and Rebus reckoned it was the one he wanted. The custody ledger sat open at the same torn page, other paperwork piled atop it. Rebus closed the door quietly, so he would have some privacy. Then he got to work.

After only a few minutes the door swung open and Malcolm Fox stood there, transfixed.

"Couldn't keep away?" he eventually commented.

"Just something I need to check."

"Without anyone knowing?"

Rebus stopped reading and looked up. "Siobhan says you might be okay. I'm going to see if she's right."

"By taking me into your confidence?"

"Slippery Phil Kennedy," Rebus stated.

Fox's eyes narrowed. "That name's in the Summerhall records."

"Vicious wee bugger we never quite managed to put away. Charged and taken to trial, but the jury couldn't be convinced."

"Not proven?" Fox guessed.

"Which pissed some of us off mightily."

"Stefan Gilmour?"

Rebus nodded. "Week before Douglas Merchant was killed, Kennedy took a tumble down the stairs at home."

"Natural causes, then?"

"Our old friend Professor Cuttle performed the autopsy." Rebus broke off, remembering his conversation. "Or rather, he helped out. It was Professor Donner who did the slicing..." He broke off again. Something Cuttle had said? Or hadn't said?

I was on hand for corroboration...

Fumes from his stomach had us reeling...

"I went back to see Cuttle," Rebus admitted. "To ask him about the autopsy. I'm not sure now I got everything out of him that I could have."

"Want a return bout? With me in the corner?"

"Fixing my cuts?" Rebus said with a smile, playing along. "You sure Siobhan can spare you?"

"She's busy with Dean Grant."

"That's Deano's real name? I never thought to ask."

Fox raised an eyebrow. "You're the one who got him to talk?"

"I have my uses."

"So it would seem."

"But for what it's worth, I don't think he had anything to do with Billy Saunders's vanishing act."

"Which means we're stuck with the double jeopardy inquiry as the main suspect."

"And the Summerhall connection," Rebus added. "That what you're doing here?" He patted the paperwork on the desk. "Still looking for the elusive golden thread?"

"Cotton would do just as well," Fox replied. "So do we go talk to Cuttle or what?"

"I suppose we could," Rebus said.

*   *   *

They took Rebus's Saab. Exiting the high-fenced car park, Rebus warned Fox that the nursing-home staff reckoned the pair of them had nearly given Cuttle pneumonia.

"Was it our idea to talk in the garden?" Fox asked.

"I think it was his. Can't say I blame him—cooped up in that place all day and night..."

"My father's in a place not unlike it," Fox admitted.

Rebus glanced towards him. "I don't think I knew that."

"No reason why you should."

"Is he still compos mentis?"

"Enough that he can have regular digs at me for wasting my life. Are either of your parents still with us?"

Rebus shook his head. "Long gone," he stated. "And my brother with them."

"I've got a sister, Jude. We don't really get on..."

"I was like that with my brother. Believe it or not, *he* was the black sheep of the family—got in a bit of trouble, served some time."

"I know—it's in your files."

"I keep forgetting you worked for the dark side." Rebus shifted into fourth, the high-rises of Dumbryden shrinking in his rear-view mirror.

"Did Siobhan really say she trusted me?" Fox asked.

"She said you might be all right."

"Well I suppose I'll settle for that. She's good at her job, isn't she?"

"Despite my best efforts, you mean?"

"Maybe," Fox replied with a smile. "But it means she'll probably get to the truth of the shooting. And that might prove distinctly uncomfortable..."

"I saw Stefan Gilmour at the Justice Minister's funeral this morning—he's adamant he didn't do it."

"Someone did, though. And Saunders *had* been running scared."

"How likely is it he could have been traced? Sleeping rough the way he was?"

"Meaning what?"

"It had to be Saunders who arranged the meeting with his killer. Or else the shooter found out about it and invited himself along."

"Who might Saunders have needed to see?"

Rebus shook his head. "How much of a background check is Siobhan doing?"

"Friends and family interviewed, mail, computer and phone records gone through. We're tracing as many of his fares as we can, even speaking to convicts he might have got to know during his time inside."

"Not too many holes there."

"DI Clarke is nothing if not thorough. At one point I thought she would make a great Complaints officer, but that would be CID's loss."

"Implying that you weren't," Rebus couldn't help saying.

"Now you sound like my dad..." Fox turned to look out of the window at the passing parade of shops and offices.

For the rest of the drive Rebus considered apologizing for the barb.

But he kept his mouth shut.

Professor Cuttle was feeling a little better. He was out of bed and watching TV in the lounge with three other residents, not one of whom was actually awake.

"You again," he complained, recognizing Rebus.

"Remember me?" Fox asked. "Inspector Fox?"

Cuttle nodded while still scowling. "Is this going to be a regular thing? Visits to the aging and infirm?"

"Just a couple of points that need clarifying," Rebus assured him, dragging a vacant chair over and settling himself on its arm. "If you don't mind casting your mind back to that Phil Kennedy autopsy..."

"You're persistent, Detective Sergeant."

"Sorry about that, sir." But Rebus didn't manage to sound it.

"You said that DI Gilmour and DS Blantyre were in the room when the deceased was being examined?"

"Nothing unusual in that."

"Nobody else from CID was there? DS Paterson, DC Spence?"

The pathologist shook his head. "And no DS Rebus either."

"I was still a detective constable back then."

"And you've soared through the ranks since."

Rebus glanced towards Fox and noted that the man was enjoying his discomfort—perhaps understandably.

"When I asked yesterday, I think you said you weren't a hundred percent sure about DS Blantyre being present?"

"Ninety-five percent," Cuttle stated.

"But you doubt we'd find any paperwork after all this time?"

"I suppose Professor Donner's family might have kept copies of his reports."

"You sound skeptical."

"Comes with the territory." Cuttle looked at Fox. "I did say to DS Rebus here, last time he saw fit to disrupt my daily routine, that I wondered if all this might not be a diversion from the Merchant killing."

"Don't think I've not harbored the same thoughts, sir," Fox commented.

"But to get back to the autopsy itself," Rebus pressed. "When you told me Professor Donner was in charge that day, you hesitated..."

"Did I?"

"As if you'd remembered something."

Cuttle looked from one detective to the other. "Professor Donner is not here to defend himself, and I won't speak ill of the dead."

"He made a mistake?"

Cuttle shook his head slowly and rested his hands across his stomach. "The Y incision had been made, the ribcage prized open. Organs were in the process of being removed and weighed..."

"Yes?"

"We were short-staffed. The autopsy had been fast-tracked for some reason, when we could just as easily have left the cadaver in cold storage."

"A lack of technicians?"

The old man nodded. "Meaning I took on the more menial role—fetching and carrying."

Rebus felt like reaching across and shaking the pathologist. But he balled his fists instead and waited.

"I had to leave the room for a moment. Professor Donner had need of a clamp. It was in a room across the hall. While I was out, the postmortem examination continued."

"There are supposed to be two pathologists present at all times," Rebus said. "Scots law requires corroboration."

"Does it really? Well, thanks for the lesson."

"You knew at the time, and so did Donner."

"Nevertheless, he chose not to wait. By the time I returned, the stomach had been cut open. The smell of spirits was over-powering."

"To be expected in a man who'd been on a binge," Fox stated.

"But his mouth had been examined, no hint of anything on his breath. And the smell was...there had been no reaction with the other chemicals in the stomach."

"You're saying it was too fresh?" Rebus asked.

"As if it had just been poured from the bottle," Cuttle replied.

"Poured from the bottle?" Rebus echoed, eyes on Fox. "Did you mention that at the time?"

Cuttle shook his head. "I was probably too busy wondering about that clamp."

"What about it?"

"Well, the fact of the matter is, it wasn't needed at all. It just sat there while the rest of the examination went on. No question about the cause of death—the man had sustained lethal injuries consistent with a fall of some kind. One or two anomalies weren't going to change that."

Rebus thought for a moment. "All the times you worked with

Professor Donner...was this the only occasion something like that happened?"

Cuttle looked down at his hands. "More or less," he eventually confided.

"More or less? And the other times were always when Summerhall CID were on hand?"

Cuttle nodded slowly.

Fox made show of clearing his throat before asking a question of his own. "Would you say that Professor Donner was on friendly terms with anyone from Summerhall in particular?"

Cuttle looked up at him. "The man is not here to defend himself."

"So you say. But that also gives us a certain freedom to be frank with each other, doesn't it?"

Cuttle considered this, then took a deep breath. "There were occasional invitations from DI Gilmour—to dinners, social functions, boxing bouts..."

"And were you included in these invitations, Professor?"

"I was, but I seldom said yes to them."

"And Professor Donner?"

"He'd known Stefan Gilmour for longer."

"And saw him as a friend, maybe?"

"Perhaps," Cuttle conceded.

"Someone he might do a favor for now and then...?"

"I won't speak ill of the dead," the old man repeated.

"You knew it happened, though?"

Cuttle was shaking his head again.

"Okay," Fox persisted. "Then let's say you had your suspicions."

"Professor Donner was one of this country's most distinguished pathologists."

"Who just happened to enjoy hanging out with CID of a night." Fox shifted his attention to Rebus. "Did you know any of this?"

"No."

"Is that the truth?"

Rebus's jaw tightened. "Yes," he said.

One of the sleepers had awoken. She leaned forward and told Cuttle how lovely it was that he had visitors.

"They're just leaving," the old man said.

"Your pal Stefan, eh?" Fox said as Rebus drove them back to Wester Hailes. "Splashing the cash, showing Professor Donner a good time..."

"He was the generous sort," Rebus intoned. He was remembering back to nights at the pub—Gilmour tipping the bar staff even in the seediest dive. Same went for clubs and restaurants.

Means they remember me kindly, Gilmour would explain. *And that's good for business...*

"So how do you think it went down?" Fox was asking now. "Hip flask in a back pocket? They get Cuttle out of the room and tip the contents into the open stomach to make it look as though Kennedy had been drinking. Blood tests would have told a different story, but there were no blood tests."

"You're saying it wasn't an accident?"

"John." Fox leaned in towards him. "I think I'm saying it was murder. He was thrown down those stairs, wasn't he? Because Gilmour was so riled by that not-proven verdict. Needed to make sure it was recorded as accidental death, and luckily he had a friendly pathologist to hand." He paused. "That sound about right to you?"

"You know none of it will stand up in court. In fact it wouldn't even get that far, because the Procurator Fiscal will ask for evidence—not theories or character assassination, but a few cold, hard facts. And I'm not seeing any. On top of which, I'm guessing you think that's the hold Saunders had over Gilmour—but Saunders didn't know Phil Kennedy."

"Are we sure about that?"

"You're the one who's working the Saunders murder—has Phil Kennedy's name ever come up?"

"We've been digging for *recent* friends rather than ghosts. But I think if we give all of this to Siobhan Clarke, she'll decide the circumstantial evidence goes way beyond theory."

"How about character assassination? Stefan Gilmour's a huge success story. He brings lawyers and PR people with him. You can bet he'll twist it round to make it look like a political plot. The Yes campaign have lost their big beast, so the No camp's equivalent has to be brought down."

Fox was silent for a moment. "It's a good point," he admitted at last. "But it doesn't change anything." He slapped the palm of his hand against the dashboard. "We should have taped our talk with Cuttle."

"There were two of us," Rebus reminded him. "We've got corroboration..."

19

Siobhan Clarke was starving.

She'd been to Fettes HQ to give a report to her bosses—the incoming head of Police Scotland was taking an interest. Shootings were not as yet a common occurrence in the country and he didn't want his tenure of the new setup to coincide with a rise in gun crime.

She rendezvoused with Rebus and Fox at a burger bar next to the cinema complex in Wester Hailes, where she worked her way through a double cheeseburger and told them about the interview with Dean Grant.

"I'm with John," she concluded. "The guy's a hundred percent dodgy, but there's nothing he knows that can help us with Saunders."

"Meantime, we've got news of our own," Fox informed her. He had decided against any food and was nursing a weak tea, while Rebus demolished a helping of onion rings.

"I'm listening," Clarke said.

Fox laid out for her the conversation with Professor Cuttle and the story of the autopsy. Halfway through, Rebus's phone alerted him to an incoming call. He checked the screen and maneuvered his way out of the booth.

"Got to take this," he said, pressing the phone to his ear and heading for the door.

"Stefan?" he said. The day had grown overcast, threatening sleet.

There were picnic-style tables outside, but no diners. The drive-through window had a queue, and beyond it Rebus could see traffic growing heavier on the commuter route out of town. For some, the working day was over.

"I hear you've pulled in the bouncer from some drug den of a pub," Gilmour stated.

"News travels fast," Rebus said, his thumbnail working a sliver of onion free from his teeth.

"He's got to be a better candidate, surely."

"We don't think so."

"Bit of effort might make all the difference."

"You want me to pin Billy Saunders's murder on anyone I see fit?"

"Used to be the way of it, John—get the scumbags off the street by hook or by crook."

"Things have changed, Stefan. But since you're on the line, let me ask you a question."

"Make it quick—I've a wake to get back to."

"What's this I hear about Slippery Phil Kennedy?"

"I doubt you're hearing anything about that turd. He died decades back."

"The week before Douglas Merchant, actually."

"Is that right?"

"I seem to remember you rubbing your hands with glee at the time."

"No surprises there."

"What *did* come as a surprise was the news that the autopsy may have been got at."

"Got at?"

"You used to carry a hip flask…"

"Nestling in my pocket right now. What are you saying, John?"

"I'm saying you went out of your way to make sure Philip Kennedy's death was attributed to a drunken accident."

"That's quite an accusation. What does Professor Donner say? No, hang on a minute—he's not with us, is he?"

"Dod Blantyre is, though—he was there with you when the hip flask came out."

"You been on the sauce yourself, John? Next you'll be telling me about the pink elephants."

"That not-proven verdict really got to you, didn't it? That's why you went to Kennedy's house..."

"Jog on, pal."

"Were we ever pals, you and me?"

"We were more than that—we were Saints of the Shadow Bible."

"But the Shadow Bible was the copy of *Scots Criminal Law* we were given. Big black thing with a leather cover and brass screws. And we all spat on it and rubbed it in till it was dry. I thought it was a kind of oath, but it wasn't—we were saying the rules could go to hell, because we knew better. We were the ones in the field..."

"We absolutely were."

"And it was a shadow bible because it wasn't quite the word of God—it was written by committee, meaning we could disregard it."

"We got results, if you'd care to remember."

"Oh, we got results all right—but at a cost. And it seems to me we're still paying."

"So how come I don't feel bad about myself?"

"It's because as far as you're concerned, there *is* no one else, no one that matters. As long as your money is making you more money, the rest of the world can go screw itself."

Rebus heard a cold chuckle on the other end of the line. "And yet here I am at an adversary's funeral."

"Odd how many of your adversaries end up dead."

The silence lingered, until Gilmour broke it. "I'm going back in now."

"Enjoy your freedom, Stefan. There might not be much more of it..."

Rebus ended the call and headed back to the booth, where Clarke had finished her meal and was holding a hand to her stomach.

"That bad?" Rebus asked.

"Ate too quickly," she explained, stifling a burp.

"So what do you make of Malcolm's theory?"

She looked at both men, then offered a shrug. "A few facts would be nice."

"Wouldn't they, though?" Rebus agreed.

Clarke's eyes were on Fox. "Because I'm not sure any of this gets us much closer to proving who killed Billy Saunders. On the other hand, maybe that's not what's most important to you—maybe Summerhall's still top of your list."

"I don't really see a distinction, and I'm not sure John does either."

"What about Pat McCuskey?" Rebus asked. "Does anyone know if the investigation's still stalled?"

"Far as I can tell," Clarke answered. "And that's driving Nick Ralph spare." She looked at Rebus. "You think it connects to that crash, don't you?"

"Jessica's flatmate was sleeping with him," Rebus stated.

"What?"

"Alice Bell. She had a thing going with Forbes's dad."

"Did Forbes know?"

"I'm not sure—Alice says not."

"And Jessica?"

"Ditto."

"Could that be what happened? They're out driving and they happen to see the pair of them?"

"Might make me put pedal to metal," Rebus conceded. "But Alice is keeping quiet."

"Worth nudging her a bit?"

The look on Rebus's face said no. He turned towards Fox.

"I suppose you'd go to DCI Ralph with it anyway? That way your arse is covered if it turns out to be important."

Fox considered for a moment, then nodded. Rebus turned his attention back to Clarke.

"So maybe that's what you should do."

"Saunders is my priority, John." She checked her watch. "Which means I need to get back and crack the whip."

"Might want to stop off at a pharmacy first," Rebus said, indicating her stomach. "Dose of liver salts will see you right."

"I'll take that under advisement," Siobhan Clarke said.

That evening Rebus drove the full length of Arden Street, seeking a parking space, ending up in Marchmont Crescent. Cursing his luck, he locked the car and crossed Marchmont Road, stopping in at Margiotta's for provisions before walking home. At the top of Arden Street, he saw a figure slumped in a doorway. Heading towards it, he recognized Forbes McCuskey. The young man was dressed in his funeral suit but was missing his tie. The top three buttons of his shirt were undone, and something had been spilled on the shirt itself. He had lit a cigarette and it was still wedged between two fingers, reduced to the filter and an inch of ash. Rebus nudged McCuskey's foot with his own.

"Wakey wakey," he said.

The eyes, when they blinked open, were glassy and unfocused.

"This where you live?" Rebus asked.

Mustering all his strength, the student turned his head to examine the door behind him.

"Looks like," he slurred.

"Bit too much wine?" Rebus guessed. "Or have you been sampling the goods?" He leaned down and started to lift McCuskey to his feet. The student was wiry, almost no meat on him. The jacket of his suit was scuffed, as were his shoes.

"How did you get here?" Rebus asked.

"I didn't drive," McCuskey protested.

"But you were driving that night, weren't you?"

"Had to get away."

"Who from?"

But McCuskey was sagging, eyes closing again.

"Let's get you inside," Rebus said, dipping a hand into various pockets in search of a key.

"What's your game?" Rebus turned his head towards the question. Two men the same age as Forbes McCuskey stood there, carrying grocery bags of their own. "You picking Forbes's pockets?"

"Is he your flatmate?" Rebus said. "Found him sparked out here. Just getting a key to unlock the door."

"He's been to his father's funeral," one of the flatmates explained. "Leave him to us."

"You sure?"

McCuskey's eyes were blinking open again. "Policeman," he said.

"You want us to call the police, Forbes?" the same flatmate asked, wary eyes on Rebus.

"He's telling you I *am* the police," Rebus explained. The two students had taken hold of their friend. Rebus took a step back. "And I've a message for him when he comes back down from space. Tell him his dealing days are over—Deano's not going to be supplying anymore."

"I don't know what you're talking about."

"Of course you don't. But tell him anyway." Rebus peered into one of the flatmates' shopping bags. "Big bag of nachos and a jar of salsa? You might as well get 'munchies' tattooed on your foreheads..."

He had reached the main door of his own tenement when a car horn sounded behind him. A white Range Rover Evoque had pulled to a stop in the middle of the road, its tinted driver's-side window sliding down. Rebus saw that Darryl Christie was behind the wheel, staring in his direction.

"You haven't moved up the property ladder, then?" Christie said.

"How about you?" Rebus countered. "Still living with your mum?"

"Penthouse the other side of the Meadows," Christie corrected him. "Got time for a quick word?"

"Just barely."

"Get in, then."

Rebus walked around to the passenger side and climbed aboard, placing his shopping on the floor by his feet. Christie drove to the bottom of Arden Street and took a right.

"We headed anywhere in particular?"

"I just like to keep on the move. That way there's less chance of anyone listening in."

"You're a bit young to be suffering paranoid delusions."

"What about that guy back there—what was he suffering from?"

"He'd just been to a wake."

"I sort of recognized him."

"Son of the Justice Minister. So what can I do for you, Darryl?"

"One of your colleagues pulled my doorman in for questioning."

"Yes?"

"Second time he's been questioned, so I'm curious."

"Nothing to be curious about—you told us yourself that Dean Grant had been on duty that night. We just needed to know if he'd seen who got into the minicab."

"And?"

"Why not ask him yourself?"

"I have."

"What did he say?"

"He's paid to deal with trouble, not make it."

"Pretty much chimes with the story we got—he didn't see anything. A bit hard for us to believe, him being on the door and everything, so we had to push that bit further." Rebus gauged Christie's reaction to this. If he accepted it, Dean would stay in a job and might end up convinced he owed Rebus a favor at some point in the future. The Range Rover had reached the traffic lights at Buccleuch Street. Christie signaled right, then right again. They were making a circuit. Once the speed bumps on narrow Melville Terrace had been negotiated, they'd more or less be back where they'd started. Waiting for traffic to clear, Rebus couldn't help looking towards the site of Summerhall police station. Here he was, thirty years down the line, still sharing oxygen with villains. But Darryl Christie seemed to represent change. He was young and hungry, yes, and venal too, but he was also clever—not just street-smart but calculating and astute. Having no weight of his own to throw around, he had found other avenues to success.

"The thing is," Christie was saying now, "CID interest is bad for business, and business being what it is right now..."

"Don't tell me the downturn's hurting you?"

"Economy's tough for all of us, Mr. Rebus. There's a lot of competition out there, and when markets contract you try to find new ones, even if that means encroaching."

"Turf wars? Are you being squeezed?"

"Maybe not quite yet."

"But you can feel it coming?" Rebus watched as Darryl Christie nodded slowly. "There was a car crash just over a week back, out by Kirkliston. Midevening. We've got a few theories."

"Yes?"

"One is boy racers."

"And the other?"

"The driver was doing small-time deals right here in Edinburgh. He had a local supplier, but I'm thinking maybe he got greedy or wanted to move up the food chain."

"Was he anywhere near Livingston?"

Rebus stared at the side of Christie's head. "It's possible."

"Only there's someone out that way...Not originally; originally he was Glasgow, but he couldn't hack it there—if you'll pardon the expression. He moved out to Ayrshire, Lanarkshire..."

"And now Livingston? Very much *your* neck of the woods, Darryl."

"Some people think competition can be healthy." Christie was keeping his eyes on the road, when they weren't checking the rearview mirror. Each turn he made, he signaled first, always stopping at Give Ways. Rebus had thought Fox a cautious driver, but this was something else again.

"He's selling drugs?" he asked.

"Just starting to, I think. You'd be doing me a favor if you took him out of the game for a while." Christie allowed himself a thin smile. "Name's Rory Bell."

"I'm a bit busy right now to be doing favors for gangsters."

"Then you're probably not much use to me." As Christie signaled to pull to a stop at the foot of Arden Street, he turned his face towards Rebus for the first time. "Does DI Clarke think I'll ever use Dean Grant again? Whether he told you anything or not, he's off the payroll. Damaged goods, Mr. Rebus—no place for them in today's harsh economic climate, and that's the truth."

Rebus pushed open the door and got out, retrieving his carrier bag. As Darryl Christie drove off, he appeared to have forgotten all about his recent passenger, his focus on the road in front of him absolute.

"Oh well," Rebus muttered under his breath. "Sorry about that, Deano."

"I just wanted to thank you," Fox said. He was sitting with Siobhan Clarke at a table in a boisterous Italian restaurant near the top of Leith Walk. It was early evening, but a coach party was taking advantage of the pretheater menu before heading to the Playhouse.

"For what?" Clarke asked.

"Putting a word in with Rebus."

"Did I do that?" She furrowed her brow.

"You told him you thought I was okay."

"And for that I deserve to be bought dinner?"

"You can't live on cheeseburgers."

"Don't remind me." She made show of rubbing her stomach, stopping as the drinks arrived—a large Pinot Grigio for her, tomato juice for Fox. "How long have you been dry?" she asked.

"Long enough to know it's the way it has to be. Have you ever tried persuading John to stop?"

"Once or twice. He seems to cope, though."

"I think the term is 'functioning alcoholic.'"

"Whereas you...?"

"Come with a history of *mal*functioning." He paused. "Doesn't mean I envy him the ability to keep drinking. It's taking more out of him than he gets back, whether he knows it or not."

"You've talked to him?"

Fox shook his head. "What's the point? But I can see he's worried. Not about the drink, but about his job. He wonders how long he has left."

"And without the job..."

Fox shrugged. "What else has he got?"

"How about you, Malcolm—what have you got?"

"My dad and my sister. Plus my team from the Complaints. We still meet up."

"Might be a bit of distance between you and them now you're CID..."

Fox nodded. "And I know I have to earn my place. Nobody's going to trust me at the start. But plenty of others have made the move before me—it *can* be done."

Clarke nodded her agreement. Their food arrived and they ate in silence for a few moments, while fresh laughter erupted from the table of revelers.

"Nice to know there's another world out there," Fox commented. "Too easy sometimes to let the job smother us."

"Though having said that..."

Fox looked at her and smiled. "You want to talk about the case?"

"I'm wondering if you think there might be a connection. Dean Grant sells drugs to Forbes McCuskey. He's also one of the last people to see Billy Saunders alive. Saunders and Forbes's father both end up dead."

"And Summerhall?"

"Ties to Saunders but not to Pat McCuskey—unless I'm missing something."

"Stefan Gilmour," Fox stated.

"You mean because he was on the opposing team in the independence fight?" Clarke nodded slowly while she chewed. "But I don't sense any animosity between the two men—far from it. People we've talked to say they had a lot of respect for one another."

"Maybe a facade."

Now she shook her head. "I don't think so."

"You want to amalgamate with DCI Ralph? Turn the two cases into one?"

"I don't know. Your money would still be on Summerhall, wouldn't it?"

"Yes. But in the meantime, I'd probably want Nick Ralph to know that Forbes McCuskey's father was sleeping with Forbes's good friend Alice."

"Could the wife have suspected?"

"She might need to be asked that."

"I should phone Nick?"

"I would."

"And if Alice Bell denies it?"

"Then she denies it."

"How did John get her to own up?" Clarke asked, eyes narrowed in thought.

"The man *does* have his qualities," Fox said, reaching for his tomato juice as the table of theatergoers began singing a chorus from *Oliver!* He saw that Clarke was worried, unable to relax. "It's a big case, Siobhan, but you couldn't be handling it any better."

"Thanks."

"I'm not just buttering you up."

"I'm sure you're not."

One of the women from the very vocal table squeezed by them on her way to the toilets.

"Love's young dream," she clucked.

"If only she knew," Malcolm Fox commented.

"John," Maggie Blantyre said, eyes widening as she recognized him. He was standing on the doorstep of the bungalow, collar up against a sudden flurry of sleet.

"Mind if I come in?" he asked.

It took her a moment to decide. "I was just tidying away the dinner things..." She stood back and opened the door a little more. Rebus stepped into the hallway.

"Do you get any help?" he asked.

"Help?"

"With Dod."

"Someone comes in at bedtime, and again first thing in the morning."

"And that's it?"

"It's as much as he'll allow. Here, let me take your coat. Is anything wrong?"

"Just thought I'd drop by."

"If I'd known you were coming." She dabbed her fingers to her face.

"You look fine," he assured her, while she draped his coat over the banister. "Dod's not in bed, is he?"

"In his chair." She motioned towards the sitting room door. "Watching TV while I wash up. Do you want a cup of tea?"

"Tea would be great. I'll just go say hello."

She nodded and began backing towards the kitchen as Rebus headed for the sitting room. Dod Blantyre was in his usual chair, and seemed to be wearing the same clothes as on Rebus's previous visit, but with a stained tea towel draped around his neck.

"Thought I recognized the voice," he said.

"Evening, Dod."

"Get this thing off me, will you?" Blantyre gestured with a trembling hand towards the tea towel. The room smelled of stewed beef. Rebus undid the towel and draped it over the arm of Blantyre's chair. There was a trolley nearby with a beaker of liquid on it.

"Want a drink?" Rebus asked.

"Double whisky, if you're buying." Blantyre tried twisting his mouth into a smile.

"Thought it was your round," Rebus replied, smiling back.

"What brings you here, John?"

"Just wondered how you were doing."

"I'm doing my best not to die—not just yet. I see Stefan's been getting a kicking from your lot."

Rebus nodded. "Silly of him to phone Saunders in the first place."

"Not a crime, though."

"Maybe not."

"They've not talked to me yet, but I know they want to." Rebus nodded.

"And you too?"

"And Porkbelly."

"Are you here to make sure we get our stories straight?"

"I'm here because..."

Rebus broke off as Maggie nudged open the door, carrying a tray. She'd made a whole pot of tea, and added a plate of chocolate digestives.

"Milk?" she inquired.

"And no sugar." Rebus took the mug from her. It bore the Airfix logo and a painting of a Spitfire. "You used to make models," he said to Blantyre, suddenly remembering.

"That's right."

"There were a couple of them on your desk at Summerhall."

"He'd spend hours on them," Maggie Blantyre added. "Tiny pots of paint lying everywhere. Each detail had to be perfect."

"Just like police work, eh, John?" Blantyre said.

"Just like," Rebus echoed.

"John and me need a minute to ourselves," Blantyre informed his wife.

"To do with that man Saunders?"

"Less you know, the better."

She hesitated. Then she spotted the tea towel and picked it up. "I'll be in the kitchen," she snapped, striding from the room. Rebus sipped from his mug and sat on the corner of the sofa nearest to Blantyre's chair.

"How much does she know?" he asked.

Blantyre managed to shake his head. "How much do *you* know?" he said.

"Tell me about Philip Kennedy."

"Care to give me a clue?"

"Slippery Phil. We got him as far as court but the verdict was not proven. Next thing, he's found dead at home with a broken neck."

"Yes?"

"You attended the postmortem examination."

"Did I?"

"According to Professor Norman Cuttle."

"Bloody hell—is he still alive?"

"Good memory on him, too. Remembers you and Stefan being present. Then the senior pathologist—Professor Donner—invents an excuse to get him out of the room. When he returns, Kennedy's stomach has been opened and Stefan has emptied a hip flask of whisky into it. Why would he do that, Dod? You were there, so I'm assuming you know the answer."

"What does Stefan say?"

"Stefan thinks I should mind my own business—but this *is* my business."

"Kennedy was a scumbag of the first order, John."

"I'm not going to argue about that. But Stefan killed him and made it look like an accident. I mean, maybe it *was* an accident. I'm not saying he meant to push him down those stairs. But it happened, and he was quick to arrange a cover-up. Probably left one or two empty bottles lying around the place, but then realized that the autopsy would show Kennedy hadn't been drinking. Donner was a mate and open to a bit of bribery. Cuttle wasn't, and had to be out of the room for it to work." Rebus paused, and leaned forward. "But *you* were there, Dod. So you know how it went down."

"You're jumping to conclusions, John."

"I hadn't been a Saint long enough to be let in on it. But somehow Billy Saunders found out, and that meant he could kill Douglas Merchant knowing Stefan and you owed him one huge favor. Thirty years later, he might be on his way to jail again and he doesn't want that. He'd be happy to trade what he knows. Stefan couldn't let that happen..."

Blantyre was trying to shake his head, his shoulders jerking.

"Remember the gun, Dod?" Rebus asked. "The one taken from Laurie Martin? The Saunders inquiry knows all about it. They think it's the same one they pulled from the canal, the one used to shoot Billy Saunders. Now isn't that neat? It disappears from Porkbelly's drawer and thirty years later turns up again..."

Blantyre fixed Rebus with a heavy-lidded stare. The silence stretched until he broke it.

"Remember your promise, John? That night in the pub? The oath you swore?"

The years melted away. Rebus remembered all right. A bar on Buccleuch Street, just along from Summerhall. The regular haunt of the Saints. Rebus wasn't sure the owner liked this, but he put up with it. A place filled with billowing smoke and curses, the waft of stale urine every time someone opened the door to the toilets. A Friday evening probably, hence the densely packed bar, Rebus having just got in the drinks. Then Dod Blantyre at his shoulder, offering to carry a couple of them back to the table. But tightening a hand around Rebus's forearm first, leaning in so that his lips brushed Rebus's left ear.

I know about you and Maggie. And it's going to stop right now. Do we understand one another?

Rebus nodding mutely. And then the growling voice again.

One more thing—this is the price you pay for me not thumping you. Whatever happens among the Saints, we never talk, we never grass—okay?

Another nod. Rebus with his mouth open, but unable to find the words. The glasses of whisky lifted from him—the usual generous measures—and transported to the corner table, where Gilmour, Paterson and Frazer Spence waited with smiles and a sheen of sweat.

Here's to us...

One for all...

Come on, Johnny Boy, drink up—what's the matter with you? You've a face like a burst coupon...

"I remember," Rebus said, in the sitting room of Dod Blantyre's overheated bungalow, his eyes fixed on a man in constant discomfort, a man with not much longer to live.

"A promise is a promise, John." Blantyre noticed Rebus's eyes flitting towards the door. "Don't worry," he said. "She doesn't know. This is just you and me here."

"You're telling me it's okay to cover up a murder?"

"Nobody's mentioned murder—you said so yourself: Kennedy could have taken a tumble. All we need from you is your silence."

Rebus got up and placed the mug back on its tray, still half full. Then he turned to face Dod Blantyre. The man was mustering as much of his old grit as he could, hands gripping the sides of his chair, as if he might try to rise from it at any moment.

"I'll see myself out," Rebus said.

"We deserve better from you, John—all of us."

But Rebus was shaking his head slowly as he left the room. He had already pulled his coat on when Maggie emerged from the kitchen.

"Cigarette in the back garden?" she asked.

"I have to go."

"What's wrong? What's he been saying?"

"Nothing, Maggie—I just need to be elsewhere."

She reached out to him, but he turned away and opened the front door, glad of the cold air and the squall.

"John?" she was calling as he headed down the path towards the gate. "John?"

He lifted a hand, waving without looking.

We never talk, we never grass...

Come on, Johnny Boy...

It's going to stop right now...

"Too true," Rebus muttered to himself, unlocking his car and getting in. When his phone buzzed, he knew it would be Maggie. He didn't take it out of his pocket to check. Just turned the key in the ignition and got going.

DAY ELEVEN

20

If I didn't know better," Malcolm Fox said, "I'd think you were relishing the chance to get your hands on the Summerhall files now they're not under lock and key." He was removing his coat and scarf and shaking rainwater from both.

Rebus was seated at the desk in Wester Hailes police station, the one with the boxes of folders next to it. He'd already been there over an hour and it wasn't quite half past eight.

"Morning," he said, as Fox hung up his things. He'd bought a coffee from a petrol station on his way into work, but the inch or so left of it was stone cold.

"Maybe there's some other reason why you seem so interested in being here when I'm not?" Fox went on, rubbing at his hair to dry it.

"You're keen," a fresh voice added. Siobhan Clarke was standing in the doorway, paperwork clutched to her chest.

"Maybe it's because you've won me over," Rebus said.

"In what way?" she asked, stepping into the room.

Rebus tapped the sheets on the desk in front of him. "Say you're right and Saunders was killed by one of the Saints. From what I'm seeing here, we're not going to find proof from Summerhall. Any amount of paperwork could have been tampered with or removed. At most we'd find anomalies and things that can be explained away as admin errors."

"Okay."

"And if we go asking Stefan Gilmour to account for his movements on the night Saunders died…well, we're dealing with a pro—you can bet he'll have set something up that's as watertight as it can be."

"Leaving us where exactly?" Fox asked, resting against a corner of the desk.

Rebus looked from him to Clarke and back again. "It might be that the best way to get to him is to go after the others. It worked before. He fell on his sword precisely so that the Complaints didn't tear apart the rest of the Saints."

"We bring in Paterson and Blantyre?" Clarke guessed.

"You sweat them," Rebus agreed. "You let Gilmour know you intend to prosecute all three." He held up a finger. "Blantyre was at the autopsy when it was rigged and he never said anything." A second finger. "Paterson meantime had the gun in his desk drawer. Gives you the opportunity to say you intend taking them all down."

"And you really think that'll be enough to get him to confess?" Fox asked, sounding skeptical.

"With all he's got to lose?" Clarke added.

"You won't know till you try."

Clarke looked at him. "And where are you when all this is going on?"

"I know my place, Siobhan—I'll be nowhere near."

"And if one of them implicates you…?"

"Up to you to decide if they're lying."

Clarke's focus had shifted to Fox. "What do you think?"

"I really doubt it'll work—but right now I'm not sure what else we've got."

Clarke nodded slowly, then turned to leave the room.

"I'd say that's a definite maybe," Fox commented to Rebus. "But you must know this could end up rebounding on you?"

"I can live with that." Rebus leaned back in the chair. "How did we get away with it?" he asked, tapping the tip of one finger against the paperwork again.

"Most of the journalists that mattered could be bought or si-
lenced," Fox surmised. "No social media for the airing of grievan-
ces." He offered a shrug. "How am I doing?"

"On the nail, I'd say. The more we got away with it, the more we
kept doing it..."

"Conscience getting to you?"

"Fuck off, Malcolm." But there was no venom behind the words.
"You really think you can keep your nose out while we question your
pals?"

"I'm busy on the Jessica Traynor crash."

"Still?"

"New name I need to look at—Rory Bell. Villain who might be
a player in West Lothian."

"Same name as Jessica's flatmate," Fox commented.

"What?"

"Isn't the flatmate's name Bell?"

"It's not that uncommon."

"You're probably right," Fox said, walking over to the window
and sliding his hands into his trouser pockets. "Ever since I started
hanging out with you, I seem to be seeing conspiracies everywhere—conspiracies, connections *and* coincidences. Think we're
due a break in this bloody weather anytime soon?"

But Rebus had stopped listening.

"DI Clarke says hello," Rebus told Laura Smith.

"She owes me a favor," Smith retorted.

"She knows that, which is why these coffees are on her."

They were in a spacious modern café near the foot of Holyrood
Road, across the street from the offices of the *Scotsman*. Stripped
wood, the day's newspapers, and workers from the nearby BBC
building. The café sold food, but all Smith had wanted was the biggest latte they would give her. Rebus had paid for a croissant to go
with his cappuccino. He tore a piece off and dunked it before popping it into his mouth.

"Very French," Laura Smith said.

"I've never been."

"Never been to France?" She sounded disbelieving.

"Or anywhere else, for that matter." He chewed and swallowed. "Scotland's always been more than enough to be getting on with."

"And we do live in interesting times."

"Reckon independence will do you out of a job?"

"I doubt we'll go crime-free overnight." She smiled, and stirred her drink.

"Too much to hope for," Rebus agreed.

"You said you wanted to pick my brains?" she nudged eventually. Rebus nodded. "I'm assuming Albert Stout was before your time?"

"I wasn't even born when he was in his heyday."

"Back then, crime reporters drank in the same lunchtime pubs as us. Bought us a dram or two and we'd tell them stories—not necessarily *true* stories, mind."

"Now it's coffee and croissants." She looked at him. "I'm not sure you think that's a change for the better..."

Rebus managed a smile. "I'm interested in a guy called Rory Bell—do you know him?"

"Heard of him," she admitted, eyes narrowing. "Is there something in this for me?"

"Might be, in the long run. Depends on what you can tell me."

"He's early thirties. Used to be muscle for one of the Glasgow gangs. Branched out, but was soon persuaded he'd live longer if he relocated. Lanarkshire wasn't quite far enough. Last I heard, he'd set up shop in Livingston."

"Doing what?"

"Security. If businesses turn him down, they might suffer the odd break-in or arson attack."

"Nice."

"He also has shares in a haulage company. One of their drivers was done last year for smuggling duty-free ciggies."

"Told the court he was doing it off his own bat?"

She nodded and took a sip of coffee, savoring it. "A few trailers have gone AWOL from yards, too—rumor that one of Bell's rigs might have been the culprit. It all adds up."

"But no prosecutions as yet?"

She shook her head, studying him above the rim of her oversized cup. "I'm not doling all this out for the good of my health."

"Understood." Rebus paused. "Any run-ins between Bell and Darryl Christie?"

"They seem to be doing a good job of tiptoeing round one another. Christie's business is predominantly bars and clubs, and Bell hasn't gone there yet. Though he *did* slip up when he tried selling security to one pub in Falkirk... Turned out it belonged to Christie, something that only came to light after its windows had been put in."

Which explained the grievance felt by Christie—and maybe why he wanted Rebus to have his competitor's name.

"Suddenly you've got a twinkle in your eye," Smith noted.

"Might be the onset of cataracts," Rebus explained. Then: "Bell's definitely from Glasgow?"

"That's when he first came on the radar."

"But he was born there? Grew up there?"

"I'd need to check."

"Could you do that and get back to me?" Rebus handed her his business card.

She held the card between the tips of two fingers. "I don't like that this is one-way traffic."

"Think of it more as a contraflow—there'll be a green light on your lane soon enough."

The door burst open and a young woman a few years younger than Smith scoured the room before heading for their table, her eyes fixed on the journalist.

"Your phone's off," she said, catching her breath.

"I'm in a meeting." Smith gestured across the table towards Rebus.

"You'll want to see this." She was holding an iPad, turning its screen towards Smith. "It's from about an hour ago, but it's already gone viral."

"Amusing cats? Infants taking a tumble...?"

"How about a furious widow?" The young woman tapped the screen and a video began to play. Rebus had got up from the table and come around to see. The footage was shaky, presumably taken with a passerby's mobile phone. Looked to Rebus like the university buildings on Buccleuch Place, the uglier edifices of George Square in the background. The clip lasted only fifteen or twenty seconds, but the widow was recognizably Bethany McCuskey. With the sound turned up, her expletives came with a distinct American accent. She was lashing out at a young woman, whose bag of textbooks fell to the ground during the attack.

"Filthy whore! Little goddamned slut!"

Followed by squeals from the victim as she attempted to defend herself from the blows. Then a glower from McCuskey in the direction of whoever was filming, before she turned and marched towards a small silver sports car.

The clip ended and Laura Smith looked at Rebus with widening eyes. "The Justice Minister's widow," she stated.

Rebus could only nod.

"But who was she attacking?" the assistant asked.

"No idea," Smith said.

Rebus cleared his throat. "Maybe that red light you were complaining of has just changed," he said. "She's Jessica Traynor's flatmate."

"Jessica Traynor? You mean Forbes McCuskey's girlfriend?" The crime reporter's eyes widened further. "My God, do you think...?" She had turned towards the screen again. Without looking at Rebus, she asked him if he had a name.

"No name," he lied. Rory Bell and Alice Bell within two minutes of each other—Laura Smith would have sniffed something, something Rebus still wasn't sure was actually there.

"If Pat McCuskey was sleeping with a friend of his son's," the assistant was speculating, "could make the story interesting all over again."

"It could," Laura Smith agreed, getting to her feet and readying to leave.

"You won't forget," Rebus told her. "Rory Bell's background?" He nodded towards the card she was still holding. "My e-mail's on there."

She nodded distractedly and thanked him for the coffee.

"It was DI Clarke's treat," Rebus reminded her, but she was already on her way back to the office, acolyte following in her wake. Rebus sat down again and tapped Clarke's number into his phone.

"I've heard," she said, picking up. "I spoke to Nick Ralph last night and told him about Alice Bell."

"And he took it straight to the widow?" Rebus stared at the ceiling and sighed.

"I know what you're thinking, John—you would have kept it to yourself. But we can't know what's pertinent to an inquiry..."

"Sometimes we can guess, though. This was Malcolm, wasn't it? He persuaded you?"

"He didn't need to—it was the right thing to do. Look, I've got to go."

She hung up on him and Rebus tossed the phone onto the table. Alice Bell would know—only *he* had deduced the affair, and he was the only one she'd admitted it to. The chain began with him and ended with the widow's assault. He would get nothing else from Alice now. On the other hand, if it drove a wedge between her and Forbes—and Jessica—maybe she would open up. Maybe...

But open up to Rebus? The man responsible for all of this? Not a chance in hell.

"Walked into that one, John," he said to himself.

And all because he'd trusted Clarke and Fox, confiding in them. Cursing under his breath, he grabbed his phone and made his exit.

*   *   *

Rebus found DC Christine Esson behind her desk at Gayfield Square. James Page was in his broom-cupboard office, busy on the telephone. He flicked his free hand towards Rebus in greeting, then busied himself writing something down.

"How are things?" Rebus asked. Esson looked up from her computer.

"Dead slow," she answered. "You?"

"The devil seems to find work."

"Have you seen the video?"

"Of Widow McCuskey?" Rebus nodded.

"It had seventy-five thousand hits in its first hour." She opened YouTube and found the page she needed. "Almost double that now, and the comments are pouring in." She showed him where on the screen to look, then began scrolling down.

"They've got Alice Bell's name," Rebus commented.

"And plenty of speculation to go with it. Popular opinion seems to be on the side of the wronged wife."

"But nobody knows for sure she *was* wronged."

Esson gave him a look. "None of that matters online. If they were handing out flaming torches, Alice Bell would be done to a crisp by now. This'll be the tip of it, too—if she's on Facebook or Twitter, there'll be plenty more bile flying her way. I really feel sorry for her. On the other hand..."

"What?"

"Well, doesn't it flag up to you that Pat McCuskey had secrets? Might reenergize the inquiry. I'm not saying poor Alice had anything to do with it, but a spurned lover maybe...?"

"*Spurned?* You been at the Barbara Cartlands again? Anyway, I'm glad you've got your keyboard warmed up..."

"Oh?"

"I want you to check a name for me—Rory Bell."

Esson puckered her lips. "Any relation?"

"Probably not. He's a player in West Lothian. I did have a reporter taking a look, but I might have slid down her list of priorities."

Esson had already typed the name into the search box. "Date of birth? Anything that would help narrow things down?"

"He's in his early thirties, spent some time in Glasgow as an enforcer."

"So he'll have a police record?"

"Reporter says no prosecutions—worth checking, though."

"I'll see what I can find."

"You're a star."

It was a couple more minutes before Page ended his phone call and emerged from his office. He looked around.

"Where's John?" he asked Esson.

"He had to be elsewhere," she apologized.

"I was under the impression he'd come out of retirement—wouldn't know it from his current work rate." He paused. "What's keeping you busy today?"

"Diagnostics and analytics," Esson replied blithely, knowing the effect the words would have.

Sure enough, Page struggled for a moment, then told her to carry on and returned to his room, closing the door after him.

Christine Esson allowed herself a little smile.

Rebus's lunch comprised a steak bake from Greggs, eaten in the Saab with the engine running so the heater would continue to work. Afterwards he brushed flakes of pastry from his clothes before answering his ringing phone.

"This is your fault, isn't it?" Maggie Blantyre's voice asked.

"Usually is," he said.

"They came to question Dod. Right bloody grilling they gave him. Said next time it might have to be at the station. Wouldn't let me stay in the room. You should see the state of him. Last night you left in such a hurry and Dod wouldn't say why. But I could tell he was upset. And now this—it's *your* doing."

"I'm sorry you think that."

"Then tell me I'm wrong."

"Who was it came? DIs Clarke and Fox?"

"I think so. Woman seemed to be the boss."

"That's Clarke. She's running a murder case, Maggie. Gun used may be the same one we kept in a desk at Summerhall—they'll be questioning everybody about it."

"You included?"

"Me included. And not all of us will merit a home visit."

There was silence on the line, followed by a sigh of defeat. "It just seems so unfair."

"Has it really upset him?"

"He's up to high doh."

"Did he ask you to call me?"

"No."

"What about the others—Porkbelly and Stefan? I'm assuming he couldn't make a call without your help..."

"Christ, John, is this you fishing for information? I phone you in a state, and you do nothing but act the bloody detective?" Her voice was rising. "Well thanks for nothing—I'm sure Dod will be touched by your complete lack of concern."

"Maggie, you know I didn't mean—"

But there was no one on the other end. His phone's screen told him the call had ended and wondered if he wanted to reconnect.

"Chance would be a fine thing," he told it, before indicating to the approaching traffic warden that he was about to move off.

There were fewer reporters outside Wester Hailes police station. They were huddled in their cars, cupping hot drinks to their faces. No vans, no TV cameras. When Rebus walked into the building, the first person he saw was Alice Bell. She was seated by the reception desk, looking furious with the world. Recognizing him, she leapt to her feet.

"I know," he said, trying for a pacifying gesture with the palms of both hands. "And I'm really sorry. But our job is to find out why

Pat McCuskey died, and that means piecing together a jigsaw of his personal life. Like it or not, you're one of the pieces."

"She *attacked* me," Bell complained.

"I know she did—are you all right?"

He could tell that she'd lost a clump of hair from her scalp, and there were grazes and scratches to her face and neck.

"I've been getting dogs' abuse—your lot want to know if I'll press charges."

"And will you?"

He watched her shake her head. Then he realized something. "What are you doing here, though?"

"Waiting for DCI Ralph. He's in some meeting or other."

"You'll be all right, Alice. Just tell them the truth—how often you met with McCuskey, that sort of thing. Whether he seemed worried about anything."

"Pillow talk, you mean?"

"Is there anyone I can call? Your mum or dad?"

"They're both dead."

"I'm sorry to hear that. Anyone else who could come sit with you?"

"Jessica and Forbes are hardly likely to oblige, are they?" she complained.

Rebus made show of wincing. "Have you talked to them?"

She shook her head. "What's to say?"

"Any family *at all* I could phone for you?"

"I'll be fine." She paused, her voice hardening. "You've already done more than enough damage, don't you think?"

DCI Nick Ralph appeared through a doorway. He nodded a greeting in Rebus's direction, then apologized to Alice Bell for the wait, leading her towards a corridor.

"There's a way out to the car park," he was explaining. "Means we don't end up feeding the jackals."

"What's left of me for them to pick at?" the young woman asked, giving a final bitter glance over her shoulder towards Rebus.

He watched the pair of them leave, then headed for the Major Incident suite. Fox was behind one of the desks.

"You just missed your pal," he informed Rebus.

"Not quite—I bumped into her downstairs."

But Fox was shaking his head. "I mean Eamonn Paterson. We've just had him in the interview room. He left not twenty minutes ago."

"Then I'm thankful for small mercies." Rebus slumped onto the spare chair.

"You saw Alice Bell, then?"

Rebus nodded. "She was *thrilled* I'd grassed her up."

"She should have come forward," Fox stated. "Might have saved all this grief."

"What was Ralph playing at, telling the widow?"

Fox offered a shrug. "Your chum Paterson wasn't very helpful, by the way."

"And I hear you've already been to see Dod Blantyre."

"Again, with very little to show for it. But then we expected that—it's up to Stefan Gilmour now, *if* you've read him right."

"What was Ralph doing here, by the way?"

Fox leaned back in his chair. "Think about it for a moment."

"I'm struggling," Rebus said after a pause.

"He was asking Siobhan about the night Jessica Traynor crashed her car. Close by the McCuskey house. Not long after, the house is attacked and McCuskey is dead. Turns out he was having an affair with Jessica's flatmate . . . Seems like quite a tight little circle, don't you think? Especially if you remove Forbes McCuskey from the scenario and replace him with Alice Bell."

Rebus shook his head. "I don't see that."

Fox shrugged again. "Well, DCI Ralph thought the question worth asking."

"And how did Siobhan answer?"

"I told him I didn't see it either." Clarke was standing in the doorway, arms folded. She looked tired and dispirited. "Good of you to drop in, John. Means we can get you out of the way."

"Meaning?"

"Your formal questioning, of course. Otherwise it looks like you're getting special treatment."

"Well we can't have that," Rebus said.

"Indeed we can't," Clarke agreed.

21

Do I need a lawyer here?" Rebus asked.

The three of them were seated around a table in the interview room. Fox had produced another of his lined notepads—pristine as yet—while Clarke seemed content to stare at Rebus, her arms folded.

"Think you need one?" she asked.

"I'm sure Stefan Gilmour would lend you his," Fox added.

"Just to clarify," Clarke asked, "could you state your relationship to Philip Kennedy?"

"The guy looked like a cartoon character, but he was no joke—liked to put the frighteners on little old ladies and steal whatever they had."

"That doesn't quite answer my question."

"He was a bad guy and my job was to put him away—*that* was our relationship."

"And as the nickname 'Slippery Phil' suggests, you never *did* put him away."

"Not for want of trying."

"Frustrating for you," Fox added.

"Very," Rebus admitted.

"Ever think of framing him?"

"Personally? No."

"But other colleagues...?"

"You'd have to ask them."

"They'd have told you, wouldn't they? You were a 'Saint,' after all."

"A new recruit."

"All the same..." Clarke paused. "How about William Saunders and Douglas Merchant—any history with them?"

"Give me a break, Siobhan."

"What makes you think you've earned one?"

"You stole that line from me," Rebus said with a tired smile. "Maybe I should sue."

"Soon as we finish with our questions," she retorted. "Now, why don't you tell me what you can about the gun..."

After forty minutes, he was free to leave. He went outside and smoked a cigarette. He was in the car park to the side of the building, the fence and locked gate separating him from what remained of the press pack. At one point he noticed Fox watching from one of the upper windows. One sarcastic wave from Rebus later, Fox was gone.

Could the crash really connect to the Justice Minister's death, and could Alice Bell be the glue? He was debating this when his phone announced an incoming text. It was from Christine Esson, telling him she had news.

"You're a naughty man," she said when he called her.

"How so?"

"Something tells me you already knew there was a connection."

"Between Alice Bell and Rory? Actually, I'd no idea."

"He's her uncle. Alice's mum died six years back—cancer, by the look of it. Then her father was in a car smash."

"A car smash?"

"I know—bit of a coincidence. That was over three years ago, and he died from his injuries."

"Where did it happen?"

"A81, near Port of Menteith."

"I'm no further forward."

"Sounds like it should be on the coast, but it's actually west of Stirling, towards Loch Katrine."

"Geography your strong point at school?"

"Ten seconds on Google," she corrected him.

"So it's right that her family came from Stirling?"

"Rory was born there. Left school at sixteen and moved west soon after. No actual criminal record, though he's sailed close to the wind more than once."

"Does Alice have money?"

"Her dad didn't leave a lot—he worked as a butcher. He was traveling to see one of his suppliers. Van coming the other way tried an overtaking maneuver on a bend and went straight into him."

"Making Alice an orphan at sixteen. Anything else on Uncle Rory?"

He listened, but she hadn't found out much more than he'd been told by Laura Smith. He thanked her anyway and ended the call. He was wondering how close Alice was to her uncle. Maybe he slipped her some money now and then to help with her university bills. *Could* she have been in Jessica's car the night of the crash? She'd shown no injuries of any kind, no whiplash. Was she the kind who would panic and flee the scene? Again, Rebus doubted it—she would have stayed with her friend, phoned for an ambulance. Unless there was something the authorities couldn't be allowed to see. He remembered the car boot—closed when the first officer on the scene had taken his photographs, but open the following morning as the car was winched aboard the flatbed truck...

Rebus called Esson again and asked her to pull up two numbers: that police officer, plus the scrap yard. The uniform's name was Bryan Hall, and when Rebus got through to him he was adamant no one had tried opening the Golf's boot while he'd been present. The owner of the scrap yard was less helpful.

"Reece knocks off at five on the dot," he barked. "You want to speak to him, you get here before then."

His full name was Reece Bairstow, and Rebus stared at it in his notebook after the owner had hung up.

"Well, why not?" he said to himself, stubbing out the cigarette and heading towards his car.

The scrap yard was on the outskirts of Broxburn, so he took the road out towards Edinburgh Airport. Listening to the radio, he was informed that the economic crisis was getting no easier and other European countries were approaching "basket case" territory. Cyprus, Portugal...no one seemed to know where it would end. He switched to a local station; an angry phone-in was debating how an independent Scotland could remain part of NATO if it ditched the nukes. After a couple of minutes Rebus could feel his blood pressure rising. He reached for a CD and slid it home. Spooky Tooth's second album.

"Better," he said to himself.

The yard was behind a chain-link fence, some of it hidden behind a further makeshift barrier of corrugated sheeting and all topped by three separate strands of razor wire. Signs warned of CCTV and guard dogs. Sure enough, a German shepherd got to its feet and bared its fangs as Rebus drove through the open gates and into the compound. The dog was tethered by a length of greasy inch-thick rope and a studded leather collar. The office it protected looked to have been constructed from leftovers of timber and beaten metal. The man who emerged knew Rebus for a policeman straightaway, just as Rebus could tell the man had served time at some point in the past. The rolled-up sleeves of his shirt displayed arms festooned with faded home-made tattoos, the kind prisoners inflicted on each other for want of any other hobbies. Shaky writing and wonky thistles seemed to predominate.

"What's the dog called?"

The owner squinted at Rebus. He was squat, almost hunch-backed, and his bald dome of a head had an oily sheen to it.

"Boris," he eventually answered, at which the dog's ears pricked up.

"Reckon that rope's strong enough?"

"You better hope so." The man allowed himself a gap-toothed grin. "You're the cop who phoned?"

"DS Rebus. I didn't catch your name."

"Eddie Duke. I told Reece you wanted to talk to him, and guess what? He decided to knock off early."

"He's gone?"

"That's right."

Rebus pretended to look disappointed, then gestured towards a compactor sixty yards away. "So that's his twin, then?" he asked. "See, I've met Reece before."

The owner's face fell. Then he placed his fingers to his mouth and let out a piercing whistle. Reece Bairstow looked up from his work and saw his boss signaling him over.

"You've been very helpful," Rebus told the man. "Don't think I won't remember that."

He started walking towards Bairstow, meeting him halfway. Bairstow was tugging at the fingers of his work gloves, pulling his hands free of them. He gave a twitch of the mouth by way of greeting.

"Remember me?" Rebus asked.

"The VW Golf outside Kirkliston? Car's right here." Bairstow nodded in the direction of a meter-high cube of squashed metal. Another vehicle had already been placed atop it.

"Yard's been busy," Rebus commented.

"Way I like it." Bairstow stood with almost three feet of space between his work boots, shoulders pulled back.

"You worried, Reece?" Rebus asked.

"No."

"Your stance says otherwise."

Bairstow looked down at himself and tried to relax, shuffling his feet and unknotting some of his muscles. "What do you want?" he asked.

"I want to know what you took from the car."

The man just stared at him. "Nothing," he eventually said.

"Want to try that again?"

"I've told you."

"Easy enough to pop the boot open—key was still in the ignition. But when we suddenly turned up you had to look busy, and you forgot to shut it again." Rebus paused and took half a step towards the man. "It's not just a case of bad driving anymore, Reece—might end up connecting to a murder. Anyone who holds back from us, there's going to be a price to pay further down the line." He turned his head towards the owner's shack. "I'm willing to bet your boss won't like us coming back here day after day to question you. Probably got a few things he wouldn't want us getting wind of…"

Bairstow's nostrils flared. He was breathing hard, face fixed in a scowl. "I've told you," he repeated.

"So you have," Rebus agreed, nodding slowly. "But this won't be the last time you see me or someone like me—far from it. I suppose I better go tell your boss that." He turned and started retracing his steps. He heard footsteps behind him, Bairstow's voice telling him to hang on a minute. Rebus stopped and waited while the man walked around to face him.

"How much trouble would someone be in, taking something from a wreck? Nothing much, I mean—something they didn't think anyone would want?"

Rebus pretended to consider this, then gave a non-committal shrug.

"Maybe if you were to show me," he offered.

Bairstow dragged his fingers through his beard while he debated with himself. "All right then," he said, adjusting his baseball cap. "It's over here."

He led Rebus behind the shack towards where several cars were parked. One of these was an olive-green Land Rover, and Bairstow opened the back, reached in and held something out towards Rebus.

"It's a crowbar," Rebus said. He took it and weighed it in his hand.

"Nearly new, too," Bairstow added. "Price sticker's still on it."

Rebus studied the sticker. "Bought from B and Q."

"It's not exactly industrial quality."

"But you thought you'd have it all the same?"

Bairstow lowered his eyes.

"And this is all you took?"

"There wasn't anything else."

"Nothing from the car's actual cabin?"

"I've told you."

"And when you brought the VW back here…I'm guessing you stripped it down? Any surprises?"

The man shook his head.

"Just this?" Rebus said, lifting the crowbar.

"Just that," Reece Bairstow agreed. "And if you're asking me, I'd say it's only been used once or twice."

"Once or twice on what, though?" Rebus asked, receiving no answer.

Alice Bell pushed home the key and turned it, opening the door to the flat. She listened to the silence before entering. Closing the door after her, she tiptoed along the hall, holding her breath. She had tried to think of somewhere else she could go, but had come up with nothing. This was all she had.

"Well, well," Forbes drawled as she entered the living room. "If it isn't the Whore of Babylon…" He was seated on the sofa, stony-faced. Jessica was next to him, her damaged ankle resting on his lap, phone held in both hands, as if she'd just finished texting.

"I'm sorry," Alice said, color flooding her face.

"For opening your legs to my old man? It's my mother you should be apologizing to."

"She decided she'd rather tear clumps out of me."

"Can you blame her? Jesus Christ, Alice…"

"You want me to go?" Bell was staring not at Forbes but at Jessica. It was McCuskey, however, who answered, his voice rising.

"Of course she wants you to go!"

"I can speak for myself," Jessica Traynor said, wincing as she removed her leg from his lap and twisted round to face her flatmate.

"Have you seen?" she asked, angling the screen of the phone in Alice's direction. Alice took a step forward. It was a Facebook page, filled with hate for her.

"And Twitter's not much better," Jessica added with quiet sympathy.

The tears came, Alice pressing her hands to her eyes as if to dam them. She stumbled backwards into the armchair and sat with head bowed, shoulders heaving.

"I'm sorry, so sorry, so sorry. Oh God, oh God..."

McCuskey had risen to his feet and started pacing the room, Jessica keeping her eyes on him lest he make a lunge at Alice.

"She's already a pariah," Jessica told him. "I doubt you can bully her half as well as the trolls on here." Waving her phone towards him.

"It's a mess," he said, almost to himself. "Or should I say, one *more* mess."

"We seem to be becoming experts."

"Because of *her*." He jabbed a finger towards Alice, who was still intoning the same words of apology.

"Sit down, then," Jessica said calmly, "and let's think about what we need to do."

He did eventually sit, and listened, and after a little while Alice started listening too.

That night, Rebus was in his armchair at home, dozing, when the bell rang. He got up, rubbing life back into his facial muscles, and lifted the stylus from *Hard Nose the Highway* before heading into the hall. He pressed the intercom and asked who it was.

"Stefan," came the reply. "We need to talk."

"Better come up, then," Rebus said, pushing the button to unlock the main door. He left the door to his own flat ajar and went back into the living room, wondering what the millionaire would make of it.

Entering, Gilmour surveyed his surroundings. "Thought you might have got round to a fresh coat of paint," he commented.

"I did that ten years back."

"Seemed a lot more homely when Rhona was in charge. How is she, by the way?"

"Fine."

"One daughter, right?"

"Right," Rebus said. "Do you want a drink?"

"I'm okay, thanks."

"Take a seat, then." Rebus settled back into his chair. There was an unfinished cigarette in the ashtray, so he relit it, squinting into the smoke.

"I'm not staying," Gilmour told him. "Had a couple of meetings and now I'm headed back west."

"I take it you've heard from Porkbelly and Dod?"

Gilmour nodded. His hands were in his coat pockets. He was dressed for business—suit and tie, gloss-black shoes not yet broken in. "Is it supposed to impress me, John, all this hounding of the Saints? You reckon you're outside the tent now, pissing in?"

"I'm nowhere, Stefan. DI Clarke is the one with the map."

"From what I hear, you used to own her—what happened?"

"You've had your spies check up on me? Better tell them they're misinformed."

Gilmour was studying the room again. "I could find you something better than this, you know. A penthouse in the Grange, maybe…"

"If I play along, you mean? Lead Clarke and her team a merry dance?"

"You're living in the past, John—the fact you're still in this flat tells me that. But Rhona's not coming back, is she? Time you started considering your future—what there is of it."

"Constitution of an ox," Rebus said.

"Even so, another ten or twenty years and you'll be history. You need to think what you'll be leaving behind for your daughter." "If you've come here to bribe me, just mention a sum."

Gilmour seemed to consider this, then he shook his head. "You can't be bought, John. But turning me down would give you a rush, so I'm not going to give you the opportunity." He paused. "But I *do* have something."

"Oh aye?"

Gilmour shrugged. "It's not much. You can take it or leave it."

"I'm all ears."

Gilmour removed his hands from his pockets and folded them in front of him. "That old pistol—the one everybody's so excited about..."

"Yes?"

"Dod was the one who lifted it from Porkbelly's desk." Gilmour paused. "Think about that, will you? Because the last time I saw that gun was thirty years ago, and it was tucked into Dod Blantyre's waistband."

"You spinning me another line, Stefan?"

Gilmour shrugged again. "I wanted it for myself, and Dod knew that. My last day at Summerhall, I opened the drawer to take it, but Dod laughed and wagged a finger, then patted his jacket, letting me know he'd beaten me to it."

"He could have put it back after you'd gone."

"You'd have to ask him. But tell this to your boss—back then I took one for the team because I deserved it. Not this time, though, not this time."

"But you *did* throw Slippery Phil Kennedy down the stairs?"

"No stairs, John, and not me."

"Then tell me what happened. And never mind all the Shadow Bible stuff. Someone killed Billy Saunders and they're doing bugger all to stop you being put squarely in the frame. If you don't want that to happen, I need to know."

Gilmour considered this. Eventually he lowered himself onto the edge of the sofa, leaning forward, elbows on knees. Rebus stubbed out his cigarette and leaned forward too, as if to stress that anything said would be kept in confidence.

"What will you do with it?" Gilmour finally asked.

"I'm not sure," Rebus admitted.

"I'd never testify in court—or a formal interview, come to that." Rebus nodded slowly.

"Well then," Gilmour went on, tapping the tips of his fingers together as he made his decision. "It was Porkbelly. He'd had a skinful and was itching for some action. We'd pulled Kennedy in—found him drinking in a pub near Haymarket. We did it for the hell of it."

"You were angry about the not-proven verdict?"

"I wanted him out of my city. Best bet was to scare him into leaving. Porkbelly agreed with that. Stuck him in a cell, shouted the odds at him, then left him to stew."

"His name was in the custody ledger?"

"Had to get rid of that afterwards," Gilmour said, nodding.

"He died in Summerhall?"

"Porkbelly gave him a bit of a doing. One punch sent Kennedy flying over the back of his chair. Smacked his head and...We thought he was unconscious at first, but you can tell, can't you?"

"You couldn't have him being found like that?"

"Bruised and bloody? Stuck in a cell without good reason? No, we had to get him out of there."

"You took him back to his house and left him at the foot of the stairs," Rebus stated.

"That's about the size of it."

"Then made sure the autopsy report mentioned plenty of alcohol in his system. You and Dod in attendance with Professor Donner."

"Best to keep Porkbelly out of it. Poor guy was in shock."

"How come I don't remember?"

"We didn't know you well enough to let you in on it."

"Donner played along, though."

"Randy old goat—married man, but he did like the occasional call girl."

"Arranged by you?"

"All part of the service." Gilmour took a deep breath and rose to his feet.

"Hang on," Rebus said. "How did Billy Saunders find out?"

"Come on, John—it's not rocket science."

Even so, it still took Rebus a minute. "He was in one of the cells?"

he eventually offered. "Heard or saw what happened? Another reason that page had to go from the custody ledger..."

Gilmour made show of clapping his hands before sliding them back into the pockets of his coat.

"So who shot Saunders?"

"Not a clue," Gilmour said. "Kind of depends on whether it really is the same gun, doesn't it?" He turned to leave.

"You should take this to Clarke," Rebus advised. "It's the only way to clear your name."

"I don't need to clear my name, John—it's enough for me that I know I had nothing to do with it. And I'm a Saint, remember—defender of the faith and all that."

"To the death?"

"Maybe not quite that far."

"You've got plenty of money, Stefan. You could fly off anytime you like."

"Somewhere with no extradition treaty?" Gilmour gave a thoughtful smile. "Like some old-time crook, always looking over his shoulder? Not my style, John. Besides, I've a fight on my hands, if you hadn't noticed."

"The No campaign? Is that what your meetings were about?" Gilmour nodded slowly. "I trust we can rely on your vote?" "I wouldn't rely on anything if I were you, Stefan."

Gilmour's gaze hardened. "Pity," he said, making his way out of the room. Rebus followed him to the front door.

"Any word on the McCuskey case?" Gilmour was asking.

"Stalled."

"So Owen Traynor's involvement is at an end?"

"As far as I know."

"Probably a good thing. I hear his latest venture has gone tits-up, creditors and HMRC on the warpath. The guy's combustible, John..."

"Tell me, Stefan—you seem to know a few shady business types—ever come across a Rory Bell? He's west-coast—or he was."

"Something to do with alarm systems and security guards?" Gilmour paused at the front door. "I know the name. I think a pal mentioned him a while back. In fact I bumped into the pal tonight—John McGlynn. Want me to put the two of you in touch?" Gilmour had lifted his phone from his pocket.

"If it's not too much trouble," Rebus said.

"Is this getting a bit awkward, John, you needing a favor from me?" Gilmour smiled. "Reckon it means you'll owe me further down the line?" Without waiting for an answer, he made the call. "It's gone to answering," he informed Rebus. Then, into the mouthpiece: "Hiya, John. Stefan here. You're probably busy, but an old cop of my acquaintance is after news of Rory Bell. Maybe you could oblige. He's on..." Gilmour broke off to look at Rebus. Rebus recited his mobile number, while Gilmour repeated it, ending the call.

"John's Glasgow-based, but you might get lucky—he's this side of the country for a couple of days."

"And he's legit?"

"Solid gold," Gilmour said. "I don't *exclusively* hang around with wrong 'uns. It's not like I'm a detective or anything." He opened the door. "That stuff I just told you about Slippery Phil and Porkbelly—you really don't know what you're going to do with it?"

"I really don't."

"Any chance you'll let me know when you decide?"

"And afterwards we'll be square?"

Gilmour gave him a hard look. "Afterwards, I never want to see you again. Let's make that absolutely clear." Having said which, he walked through the open door, leaving it ajar. Rebus listened to his footsteps as he made his descent, then closed the door and returned to the living room. He put side two of the Van Morrison album on again and sat down. It played for twenty minutes or so, but he wasn't really listening.

DAY TWELVE

22

Rebus drove to work next morning in what his father would have called "a dwam," unaware of the world around him. As he got out of the Saab, he realized the car park was unfamiliar—or not as familiar as it should have been. A uniformed sergeant was puffing on a pipe in the smoking zone.

"What brings you here?" he asked.

Only then did it dawn: he had driven to St. Leonard's police station. Hadn't worked there in a number of years. It was where he'd been introduced to Siobhan Clarke, where they'd forged their working relationship.

"Meeting," he explained to the uniform, making his way towards the entrance. Didn't want the man to think he'd grown senile. Indoors, he bided his time, pretending to check his phone for texts. When the coast was clear, he headed to the car park again, got back in the Saab and wondered where to go.

Maybe that was the problem right there—Clarke was in Wester Hailes with the Saunders murder; at Torphichen, Nick Ralph was running the Pat McCuskey inquiry. Leaving Rebus with what? The only thing waiting for him at Gayfield Square was an irritable James Page and a workload of desk-tidying. When his phone rang, he hoped to hell the caller might give him some direction.

It was Christine Esson, and she did. "The boss wants to know where you are—he's got a job for you."

"Tell him I'm on my way."

"But are you?"

"Oh ye of little faith. I'll be there in ten minutes."

"You've not seen the snarl-up at the Conan Doyle roundabout—I'll tell him fifteen to be on the safe side."

"Twenty quid says ten."

"Oh aye? Parked outside, are you?"

"I'm at St. Leonard's." Rebus repeated the bet.

"Starting now," Esson said, after a moment's calculation.

"You're on."

Rebus knew better than to head for North Bridge and Leith Street. Instead, he drove through Holyrood Park and out the other side, taking Abbey Hill and Royal Terrace and missing the worst of the congestion. He took the stairs two at a time and was in front of Esson's desk in eleven and a half minutes.

"A good try," she conceded.

"Call it a tenner, then." Rebus held out his hand.

"John!" Page barked. "In here!"

"I'll be back," Rebus warned Esson, receiving only a smirk for his efforts.

"What time do you call this?" Page was asking when Rebus entered the room. He was behind his desk, laptop open in front of him.

"Had to drop into St. Leonard's," Rebus explained.

"Whatever for?"

"Running an errand for Siobhan. But now that I'm here, how can I help?"

"Another errand, I suppose. You heard they pulled a body out of Leith Docks yesterday afternoon?"

"No."

"Adult male. Autopsy is in an hour's time."

"Suspicious death?"

"That's what I'm hoping we'll find out."

"By 'we,' I assume you mean me?"

Page nodded.

"Anything I should know? Got a name for the deceased?"

"Don't think so."

"And you picked me over Esson, Ogilvie or any other poor sod because...?"

"Look, it's simple enough—just go oversee the postmortem exam and then report back. I know it lacks the glamor of a shooting or the death of an MSP, but it's still part of life's rich tapestry." Busying himself at his computer, he flicked the fingers of one hand in Rebus's direction, indicating that the meeting was over.

Back in the main office, Esson was trying not to look smug.

"You might have bloody warned me," Rebus complained.

"You're the one who was in a hurry," she shot back. "Besides, I hear there's a new pathologist—might be fun to be had there."

"Oh, the mortuary's a nonstop riot," Rebus drawled. "You better have my winnings ready when I get back..."

"You're too late," the attendant said. "We had to bring it forward an hour."

Rebus had been to the mortuary many times. There was a large storage area at ground level with a concrete floor that was regularly cleaned with a pressure hose. One whole wall comprised metal roller-drawers where the corpses were stored, with a separate smaller room off for worst-case scenarios. Vans could be backed in through a bay door from the car park, keeping the general public unaware of the building's primary use. Labs and autopsy suite were one floor up, along with staff offices, the viewing room, and a waiting area for next of kin.

"She's probably phoning in her report as we speak."

"She?"

"Professor Quant."

"Any chance of a word with her?"

The attendant nodded towards the flight of stairs. "She's got to be elsewhere in twenty minutes," he cautioned.

But Rebus was already on his way.

The door was ajar, but he tapped on it anyway. Quant had already changed out of her scrubs and was ending a call at her desk.

"You're DS Rebus?" she asked.

"That's right."

"I was just telling DCI Page..."

"You had to bring the autopsy forward."

"I need to be at a lecture." She glanced at her wristwatch.

"I could give you a lift."

"Quicker walking—it's just by the McEwan Hall."

"I'll walk with you, then."

She fixed him with her blue eyes. Mascara coated her eyelashes and thick red hair fell to her shoulders and just beyond. Rebus placed her in her midforties, maybe a touch older. No rings on any of her fingers, but that could have been for professional reasons. The backs of her hands were pink, perhaps from the scrubbing they'd just been given.

"Just so you can update me," Rebus explained.

"Fine then," she said, gathering paperwork into a capacious leather bag before lifting her coat from the back of the chair and putting it on, Rebus resisting a sudden urge to help.

"Always supposing the case is worth updating," he felt it necessary to qualify.

"I'm trying to find time for a second examination later today—if I can locate another pathologist to work with me."

"Oh?"

She was looking around the cramped space, making sure she hadn't forgotten anything.

"It's a strange one," she said.

"He didn't drown, then?"

"Dead when he entered the water. The question is: for how long?" She saw the look he was giving her. "I'm thinking months," she explained. "Possibly even years."

"*Years?*"

"Spent seated, judging by the way the bones have fused."

"Professor, are we talking about a skeleton here?"

"There's skin, but it has all but mummified. Hard to say much more right now. Body probably wasn't in the water for more than a couple of days—the dock isn't exactly tidal, so it almost certainly was disposed of there rather than being washed up from elsewhere." She grew thoughtful. "That's about as much as I was able to tell DCI Page. Sure you still want that walk?"

"I'm sure," Rebus said, holding open the door.

They climbed from the Cowgate to Chambers Street, Rebus working hard to keep up with her.

"So you're the notorious John Rebus?" she asked.

"You must be thinking of someone else."

"I don't think so. You knew Professors Gates and Curt?"

"Worked with them for years."

"I think it was Professor Curt who mentioned you. He used to teach me, back in the day. You featured in a few of his war stories." They were passing the museum, and she asked him if he'd been in.

"Not since it reopened," he admitted.

"You should."

"Are you sure about this corpse, Professor Quant?"

"My name's Deborah. And I'll admit I have more questions than answers right now."

"Nothing to identify the body?"

"He was naked when they pulled him out of the water. No obvious tattoos or scars. Fair haired, five feet ten. I'd say he weighed around a hundred and seventy pounds at one time—bit of a paunch. Someone from Forensics will be there when we do the next examination. There were fibers stuck to the body. I'm guessing he was wrapped in something." She stopped walking for a moment. "I did read somewhere about a similar case—husband couldn't bear to part with his wife, so he left her in the chair where she died, wouldn't let anyone into the room for the best part of five years."

"You think that's what happened here?"

"All I know is there are no immediate signs of violence."

"Who spotted the body?"

"A jogger. Usual story—mistook it for a bag of rubbish at first." She had resumed walking, turning left out of Chambers Street and heading down Bristo Place. "We're almost there," she said, checking her watch again. "And for once I'm going to start on time."

"You lecture in the medical faculty?"

She nodded. "Are you going all the way back to the mortuary now to collect your car?"

"Yes," he admitted, earning a smile. "What time's the second autopsy?"

"If I can find a willing helper, four forty-five. Will I see you there?"

"Hopefully."

They were on Teviot Place now, at the entrance to her building. She held out her hand and he shook it. The hand was slender, and he could feel the bones beneath the skin. Then she headed through the archway and was gone.

"Fucking mummies now," Rebus muttered to himself, readying to retrace his route. His phone rang and he answered it.

"Why is nothing ever simple with you, John?" Page asked.

"I didn't ask for the assignment."

"From what Professor Quant tells me, we have a suspicious death at the very least."

"She told me that too."

"You saw her, then? I hear she's a fine-looking specimen."

"You're misinformed," Rebus responded, ending the call and searching his pockets for his cigarettes.

He met Eamonn Paterson at a lunchtime pub on Raeburn Place. Rebus was seated at a corner table when Paterson arrived. Paterson got himself a pint of lager, Rebus shaking away the offer.

"What the hell is that?" the older man asked, nodding towards the bright green drink in front of Rebus.

"Lime juice and soda—Siobhan Clarke swears by it."

"I'd swear too if you plonked one in front of me." Paterson picked up the menu and studied it. "You eating?"

"I'm fine," Rebus said.

"Just want to get down to business, eh?" Paterson put the menu back and took a mouthful of lager.

"The thing is, Porkbelly, I know about Phil Kennedy."

"Oh aye?"

Rebus nodded slowly, his eyes on his old friend. "You had him on a chair in the cell, giving him a doing. He smacks his head and that's that. To cover your arse, the body's taken back to his house and arranged at the foot of the stairs. The relevant bit of the custody ledger is torn out so no one's any the wiser—except Billy Saunders, who heard everything from the cell next door."

Paterson stared at the table, as if committing to memory the pattern of its grain. He was holding his glass but not drinking from it. Eventually he sniffed and rubbed at his nose. But still he failed to make eye contact with Rebus, finding the window, the walls and the bar staff more interesting.

"Aye," he said at last, stretching the single syllable as far as he could. Then he risked meeting Rebus's gaze. "You found out from Saunders? He wrote it down somewhere?"

"Doesn't matter how I found out."

"It can always be denied, you know. There's no actual proof."

"You're right."

"And it really was an accident, if it was anything."

"The cover-up was no accident, though. It was planned to almost the last detail."

"Almost?"

"The custody ledger, and the presence in the vicinity of Billy Saunders. He cuts a deal: you'll go out of your way to see he gets off next time he's arrested. He knew precisely what he was going to do—batter Douglas Merchant to death. And if you didn't help him, he'd tell everyone what he knew. Wouldn't just be you with your head on the block; it'd be Gilmour and Blantyre too, plus Professor Donner, and

I'm guessing Magnus Henderson had to be in on it—hard to tamper with the ledger without the custody sergeant knowing."

"Magnus Henderson is dead, John. Professor Donner is dead. So is Saunders, and our old friend Dod Blantyre hasn't much longer to go. Ask yourself what any of this—*any of it*—is going to achieve."

"Probably not much," Rebus conceded. "But a man was shot dead in cold blood in the present day. Are you going to tell me that doesn't matter?"

"It matters," Paterson said. "Of course it matters."

"Do you know what happened to that pistol, Porkbelly?"

Paterson considered how to answer. Another mouthful of lager gave him courage. "I always thought Stefan lifted it. It was never seen again after he left Summerhall for the last time." He managed the most rueful of smiles. "When he started making a go of his business, I used to wonder if he maybe produced it at meetings to get the signatures on the relevant documents."

"It's a thought," Rebus said.

"You're not managing to sound convinced. You know, we kept you out of it as a way of protecting you."

"Protecting me?"

"The less you knew, the better."

"What about Frazer Spence—was he in on it?"

"You were still the apprentice back then, John—Frazer had served his time."

"Meaning you didn't trust me?"

"We didn't know how you'd react."

"Thanks very much." Rebus pushed his garish drink aside. "You say Stefan had the pistol? That must mean you think he shot Billy Saunders?"

"I doubt I'm alone in that."

"You're not—doesn't make it the truth, though."

"Is it the truth that's needed here, or just a convincing story? My bet is any one of us would do as far as your friend Fox is concerned." Paterson paused. "That's why we should offer him Frazer."

"The more you and Stefan try to use Frazer, the more I realize how much of a lie the Saints were. And here's the thing—Frazer used to send titbits Albert Stout's way, but never once did he give the press anything on you or Stefan or the rest of us. He went to his grave with whatever dirt on you he had, and now you're offering him up as a sacrifice."

Paterson seemed to have no answer to this. He lifted his glass again, but put it down without drinking. "We're old men, John. You think I'd do any of the stuff I did in Summerhall, knowing what I do now? Every night I lie in my bed and think back on the people we were. But you won't find those versions of us anymore."

"Except for whoever killed Billy Saunders. And it wasn't Frazer Spence."

"Stefan isn't going to own up to it."

"The meeting with Saunders had to be arranged—somewhere traces will exist. Maybe on CCTV, maybe on a phone. Siobhan Clarke won't rest till she's peered into every last corner."

"Good luck to her." Paterson was rising to his feet. "Next time I see you might be Dod's funeral—you realize that?" He took one last look at the contents of Rebus's glass. "Soft drinks and playing things by the book. Who'd have thought it?"

Rebus watched as his one-time colleague left the pub. There was a slight limp—maybe his hip was playing up. And a stoop to the spine, too. But at one time Paterson had struck a fearsome figure— using his heft to intimidate suspects, hardening his face to suggest violence was not out of the question. Rebus could well visualize him tipping Phil Kennedy out of his chair. Maybe that was as far as it had gone. Then again, with Kennedy's head resting against the cold concrete floor, the temptation would have been to haul it up by the hair and thump it down again. Rebus remembered Stefan Gilmour rubbing his hands together as if washing them clean. He had glimpses of entering the CID office and the conversation ending, or changing.

The less you knew, the better...

Still the apprentice...

"Not anymore," Rebus said to himself, heading to the bar for a whisky.

23

Good of you to meet me," Rebus said, shaking John McGlynn's hand. McGlynn was younger than he'd expected and wore a black V-neck T-shirt below the jacket of his tailored suit. They were in the foyer of the Balmoral Hotel on Princes Street.

"I can only offer a few minutes," McGlynn apologized.

"Probably all I'll need."

There were some chairs by the reception desk, so they sat down. McGlynn exuded restless energy, his eyes alive to possibilities. "Stefan said you're interested in Rory Bell," he began.

"I don't know much about him."

"Am I allowed to ask why he's on your radar?"

"I'm afraid not."

McGlynn digested this. "Well I can't say it surprises me. A few businesses got on the wrong side of him when he tried selling them his services."

"I've heard the rumors. Is that what happened to you?"

McGlynn shook his head. "He came to me looking for a favor, actually. Couple of years back, this was. I own a few car parks in Glasgow, and Bell was interested. No way I wanted him as a partner, though—or anywhere near my firm. But I did seem to whet his appetite. Next thing, he'd got himself a couple of multistories—one by Edinburgh Airport and the other in Livingston."

"The airport?"

McGlynn nodded. "Your ears seem to have pricked up."

"Might be something or nothing." Near the crash scene... Bell's niece's pals going off the road...

"Would that be a genuine something or nothing or a policeman's something or nothing?" McGlynn was smiling.

"Do I need to answer that?"

"Not really."

"Anything else you can share regarding Rory Bell?"

"He's left me and mine well alone—I'd hate to think that might change because I've talked to you."

"It won't."

"I'm only here because of Stefan."

Rebus nodded slowly. "You've known Stefan a while?"

"A few years."

"Get on well with him?"

"I've no complaints." McGlynn checked the time.

"He's had a bit of bad publicity lately—you reckon he's coping with it?"

"He's Stefan Gilmour—bullets bounce off him." McGlynn was rising to his feet, extending a hand for Rebus to shake. "Are you telling me his armor might be weakening?"

"Would that cause something of a feeding frenzy?"

"Business is business, Mr. Rebus. Lot of hungry mouths out there..."

With a farewell nod, McGlynn walked in the direction of the restaurant, a member of staff giving a little bow as they met. Rebus headed out front, where his car was parked. The tram works were just as bad this end of Princes Street. He listened to the gripes of the Balmoral's liveried doorman as he smoked a cigarette.

"Place deserves better than this," the doorman told him. "Capital city? Makes what we're doing to it a capital crime."

"So tell me who to arrest," Rebus offered.

"What would be the point? Damage is already done."

"True enough," Rebus said, unlocking the Saab and getting in.

*   *   *

He preferred Glasgow to Edinburgh, though he chose to live in neither. Partly it was the people—too many of them, mostly just passing through. Then there was the narrowness of the streets, which felt claustrophobic. The layout made no sense until you drove into the New Town, and even there the roadworks and diversions meant you could not rely on satnav. No matter how much time you'd given yourself, it almost always took longer to get anywhere.

He was in a white van today, nicely anonymous. A small van, empty apart from a set of overalls, some everyday tools and a liter-sized pot of paint. Reaching his destination, he found a parking space and got out, climbing into the blue workman's overalls. He saw the name on the intercom, and pressed one of the other buttons. Someone was home, and they buzzed him in; didn't even ask his business. That was Edinburgh for you: people kept to themselves, no interest in others. Up the stairs, pausing at the top and listening at the letter box. No hint of life within. It had taken a while to track the place down. The Golf had been registered to an address in London, surname Traynor. But then at the funeral the McCuskey son had been pictured with his girlfriend, named in the media as Jessica Traynor. Simple enough after that, and here he was. He looked around. The skylight above him was covered in protective mesh and bird crap. The interior walls were cream-colored and graffiti-free. And the door was pale green. Pale green was fine. Crouching, he prized the lid from the paint with a screwdriver. The paint was a lighter shade of red than he would have liked—not quite the color of blood. Taking a step back so as to avoid the splash, he made ready to deliver his message.

The same mortuary attendant told Rebus that once again his timing was off.

"They were due to start at quarter to five," Rebus complained, receiving a shrug in response.

Rather than interrupt proceedings, Rebus took a seat in the viewing area. Glass panels separated him from the action, and there were rows of uncomfortable benches to sit on. He had always meant to ask someone about the benches—it seemed to him that a couple of dozen onlookers could be accommodated, but he'd never seen more than a handful at a time make use of them.

Noticing him, Deborah Quant gave a little wave with one of her instruments. She was dressed in scrubs and a face mask, as was her companion. Rebus guessed the man must be the forensics bod Quant had mentioned. An assistant worked in the background, bagging and labeling. The whole procedure looked painstaking, and was being recorded by a microphone which also transmitted to a speaker in the ceiling above Rebus.

"We had to start a bit early," Quant said for his benefit. "Professor Thomas here is a forensic anthropologist. He has to be in Glasgow for a professional dinner."

Without knowing who the visitor was, Professor Thomas gave Rebus a nod of greeting. He looked young—younger even than Quant. He asked a second assistant to take close-up photographs of one patch of skin. The cadaver lay on its front—Rebus could make out the fair hair on its head, and the folds of skin covering the skeleton.

"Difficult to tell how far the injuries predate death," Thomas commented.

"Professor Thomas," Quant explained, again for Rebus's benefit, "has found evidence of bruising. Nothing that would have caused a fatality, unless there were underlying health issues." She paused. "I missed them first time round."

"Easily confused with lividity," Thomas reassured her.

"Death occurred two to three years ago." Quant's eyes were on Rebus. "A DNA fingerprint should be straightforward enough, but someone needs to check the missing persons files—for the whole of the UK."

"No biggie, then," Rebus muttered, knowing she couldn't hear him. She could see him, though, and smiled, sensing what he was thinking. He tapped a finger against the top of one arm.

"Distinguishing features?" she asked her colleague.

"No tattoos. No scars. No signs he was ever operated on. Dental records might be another route to establishing identity. I'd say the work was basic British NHS. Calluses on hands suggest manual labor of some kind. Or maybe he just enjoyed DIY. Ingrowing toenail on left foot, but hard to say if he'd had it treated or not. Nothing very exciting in the stomach or lungs. He was probably a moderate smoker. Might have killed him eventually."

Rebus did a mime of a knife slashing a throat.

"Suspicious death?" Quant asked.

"The fact is, he hadn't been in the water more than a day or two, and died several years before. So whether the death is suspicious or not, there *are* questions that need answering."

Quant turned her attention to Rebus again. "Body was wrapped in something woolen—maybe a tartan travel rug; we have blue and red fibers. It covered the torso and the legs to just above the knees. This would have had to happen soon after death for the skin to adhere to the fibers. Once atrophy sets in, the epidermis is less obliging."

Rebus nodded slowly, then mimed taking a drink. Quant's forehead creased.

"Was he a drinker?"

Her colleague looked up, but Rebus was shaking his head and pointing at her.

"Oh," she said. "No, sorry, I'm busy later."

"Too busy to attend the Glasgow dinner," Professor Thomas added, sounding put out.

Rebus shrugged and mouthed the words "Just an idea." She nodded and got back to work.

It was dark by the time Siobhan Clarke and Malcolm Fox reached the canal. It had been Fox's idea—try to work through the sequence of events. So they had parked on the industrial estate and started off from the alley where Billy Saunders had been sleeping.

"Though we don't know for sure this is where he was," Clarke argued, buttoning her coat against gusts that seemed to have originated in the Arctic.

"We don't," Fox agreed. "But he wanted a meeting nearby, somewhere he felt he knew the terrain. Once he was on the towpath, he would have plenty of notice of anyone coming from either direction."

"He didn't trust the person he was meeting?"

Fox nodded. "Maybe reckoned they'd bring backup."

"Stefan Gilmour and the Saints?"

Fox just shrugged. They were clambering up the slope. The canal wasn't well lit. In fact, the only real illumination came from lampposts beyond its other bank, behind railings and next to the main road.

"Someone could have been watching from there," Clarke surmised.

"Watching, yes. But to get to the nearest bridge and then end up here...that's a walk of a good five or six minutes."

Clarke folded her arms. "And Saunders was shot at close range. So whether he trusted his visitor or not, he allowed them to get close."

"Close enough to talk."

"Talk or listen." Clarke thought for a moment. "Let me know if any of this leads you to believe we're not discussing Stefan Gilmour..."

"Well for one thing, Gilmour's not an easy man to get to. Phone number's not in the book, unlike George Blantyre and Eamonn Paterson."

"You've checked?" She watched as Fox nodded. "And Rebus?"

"Is ex-directory."

She considered this. "It *was* an arranged meeting, right?"

"Had to be."

"And whoever Saunders met wasn't the one who initiated it?"

"Hard to do when they'd no idea how to reach him."

"Unless the plan to meet predated his little vanishing act."

"True," Fox allowed. "But I don't think that's what happened."

Clarke looked at him. "You've been giving this some thought?"

"Trying to think like a detective," he answered, with a thin smile. "And?"

"And we have a man who's terrified of something—so scared he abandons his car in another part of town, far from where he knows he's going to hole up. Hotels won't do, and he can't rely on friends—to be absolutely safe, he needs to sleep rough. Can't use his bank account or phone—both could be traced, or at the very least would indicate he's still alive and kicking. For the same reason he can't contact his wife to let her know he's safe." Fox paused. "But there's *someone* he needs to see. Easiest way to set up a meeting is if he calls them."

"Nearest working phone box is almost two miles away."

"But there's the petrol station. From CCTV, we know he bought snacks there."

"Except that their public phone has been out of order for almost a fortnight."

"Something he might not find out until he tried using it."

She saw now where Fox was going. "Staff knew him. Might have loaned him their phone."

"Of course, they've been interviewed. But do we know they were asked the right questions, shown a good clear photo of Saunders?"

"Worth a second go?"

"I'd say so."

"And we're not just clutching at straws here, Malcolm?"

"Maybe we are."

"Stefan Gilmour *is* capable of it, isn't he?" Clarke was gazing at the surface of the canal. It looked dark and oily, and even in daylight would give no hint of what lay beneath.

"No doubt in my mind," Fox answered. "Way he's built his empire, he takes no prisoners."

"I remember reading once that the successful tycoon sees the world the same way a psychopath does."

"I'm not saying Stefan Gilmour is a psycho."

"He's just a man with goals unachieved and successes to protect."

"You think a forensic psychologist might help us nail him?"

Clarke shook her head. "Let's stick to what we know."

"Meaning?"

"We follow leads, Malcolm. Starting with your petrol station…"

The only other customers when they got there were two licensed minicabs. The drivers had parked next to the shop and were inside, drinking coffee from a coin-operated machine and exchanging gossip. Fox made straight for them, pulling out his warrant card.

"Did either of you know Billy Saunders?" he asked.

"Knew *of* him," one driver said.

"Worked for the competition," his friend added.

"You always use the same petrol station?"

"Tend to," the first driver conceded.

"Fill the tank, break the monotony?"

"That's right."

"Did Saunders use this particular pit stop?"

The second driver shook his head. "Petrol station in Powderhall, far as I know."

"You never saw him here?"

Fox received a further shake of the head from both men. He thanked them and headed for the counter.

"Nice thinking, though," Clarke told him in an undertone.

"Saunders drove a minicab, liked the night shift—petrol stations were a second home to him." He took out his warrant card again and showed it to the assistant.

"You've been questioned about William Saunders?" he asked.

The youth behind the counter appeared no older than a school-leaver. His face was peppered with angry-looking acne and his thick black hair looked like it had been styled with a pair of secateurs and a pot of glue. He agreed that he had already spoken with the police.

"And your colleagues too?"

The youth nodded.

"All of them?"

"All except Patrick, I suppose."

"Patrick?"

"He's on holiday in Ibiza."

"Nice for him. When did he leave?"

"Six days back. Finished his shift at six and was in the air by eight."

Fox looked at Clarke. Like him, she had done the arithmetic.

"So he was working here the day William Saunders was killed?" Fox checked.

"Suppose," the youth agreed, eyes darting between the two detectives, Adam's apple bobbing. "He's not in any trouble, is he?"

"The officers you spoke to—they knew this, right?"

"I think I told them. Somebody would have."

Fox nodded. But he was thinking: maybe, and maybe not. There was just a hint of dismay on Siobhan Clarke's face—someone on her team might have screwed up.

"We need to talk to Patrick," Fox was saying. "Do you have his number?"

The youth shook his head. The minicab drivers were waving goodbye to him through the window as they returned to their vehicles. "You'll have to ask my boss," he told Fox, waving back.

"We'll do that, then. Did you ever see Mr. Saunders yourself?"

The youth shook his head again.

"You always work the same shift?"

"No, but I've been on nights for a few weeks."

"He never came in during that time?"

"Don't remember him."

Fox nodded slowly. The payphone was on the wall next to the toilet. The sign warning that it was out of order comprised a pink Post-it note—easy to miss until you got close.

"Anything else?" the youth asked Clarke.

"Just this," she said, placing a Bounty on the counter.

"And your boss's phone number," Fox added, as the youth got busy with the scanner. "The one kept for emergencies—we need to contact him tonight..."

Outside, as she unwrapped the chocolate bar, Clarke told Fox it could probably wait till morning. He nodded his agreement, and drove them back to Wester Hailes so she could pick up her own car. The car park was near empty. The team would have clocked off. Overtime was available, but Clarke was running out of things for them to do outwith normal office hours. She looked tired, while Fox felt energized.

"See you in the morning," he said, as Clarke opened her door and undid her seat belt.

"That was useful tonight, Malcolm. Thank you."

"No problem," he assured her with a smile.

He drove fully quarter of a mile in the direction of home before pulling over to the curb again, taking out his phone and searching his pockets for the scrap of paper the youth at the petrol station had given him.

Forbes and Jessica had been out all day, Jessica managing with the aid of a walking stick. They'd taken taxis, and avoided stairs and steps wherever possible. She'd felt the need for fresh air, for reminders that a city existed beyond the confines of her flat. A café, a restaurant, a park bench and a bar—and now they were back in Great King Street, climbing slowly but purposefully towards the sound of scrubbing and sobs.

It was Alice, on her knees on the landing, a bucket of soapy water by her side. She was using a brush on the door, trying to get the red paint off. Tears had dried on her cheeks. There were splashes of paint on the wall, and it looked as though she had already sluiced the stone floor.

"What the hell?" Forbes said.

"It was like this when I got here," Alice explained breathlessly. "Your mum and her friends...all that online hate..."

Jessica was gesturing for Forbes to help Alice get to her feet.

"You think that's who did this?" she asked.

Alice stared at her flatmate. "Who else?"

"We both know." Jessica paused. "We *all* know. Now let's get you inside. Forbes will take over cleaning."

"I will?"

"In a bit. First we need to get this straightened out."

All three headed for the living room, Alice drying her hands on the front of her already ruined T-shirt.

"You need to phone him," Jessica told her.

"But then he'll—"

"Know it was you," Jessica interrupted, finishing the sentence with a slow nod. "But maybe he'll back off—right now, it's just me and Forbes, isn't it? And you're the one who can do something about that."

"So the paint wasn't for me?" Alice asked.

"Go call him," Jessica said.

"My phone's in my bedroom..."

Alice went to fetch it, but ended up seated on her bed instead, feeling the sweat cooling on her back. How could she talk to him? What would he do once he knew? What would he do to *her?* She felt a shiver run down her, all the way to her toes. Holding the phone to her ear, she found the strength to head back to the living room.

"Not answering," she said as she walked in. Then she saw that Jessica too was making a call. Forbes's eyes were on Alice. He looked nervous.

"Who...?" Alice began to ask, but she broke off. She knew the answer well enough. It was written on Forbes's face...

DAY THIRTEEN

24

Next morning, Rebus drove out towards the airport. He had got the addresses of Rory Bell's multistory car parks from Christine Esson. He followed the signs from the A8 Glasgow road and found himself just north of the village of Ratho. When he lowered his window, he caught a whiff of sewage and pig farm. An aircraft was rising into the sky with a thunderous roar, not quarter of a mile away. The car park advertised its special long-term rates and twice-an-hour shuttle service. An automatic barrier rose when Rebus took the proffered ticket from the machine. He drove slowly around the ground floor, unsure what he was looking for. Jessica had crashed her car not too far away. She was friends with the niece of the car park's owner. The owner was less legit than might have been the case. Add to that the brand-new crowbar...and Rebus still wasn't sure. There was a cabin staffed by a single uniformed flunky. The ground floor was half full. The cars looked like they belonged to middle management: Beemers, Audis, a couple of Jags and a Merc. He drove up the ramp to the next floor, which was quieter. One Range Rover had a film of dust over its windscreen. Maybe it belonged to someone who was enjoying protracted winter sun elsewhere. Rebus couldn't blame them. The next floor was empty, as was the unsheltered roof, though it too had been laid out in marked bays. Rebus doubted the place ever got full. On the other hand, it was easy money—one member of staff, few overheads.

He stopped the Saab on the roof and got out for a cigarette. He could see the airport runway, an orange-liveried EasyJet plane coming in to land. Jessica's car had crashed somewhere to the west. If she'd started her journey at this car park, she and Forbes had been driving *away* from the city. Towards his parents' place? Possible. If Rebus had possessed more of a head for geography, he might be able to make out the house and grounds. As it was, he saw only a patchwork countryside and snowcapped hills beyond.

"You okay there?"

The voice was amplified, metallic. Rebus looked around and saw a tall metal pole with a loudspeaker and camera attached to it. He gave it a wave and got back into his car. He was approaching the exit barrier when he saw the attendant emerge from his cabin. The man was at the barrier before him, waiting for a word. Rebus wound his window down again.

"Everything all right?" the man asked. He had a pockmarked face and irregular teeth, his eyes milky but wary.

"Forgot something," Rebus explained. "Need to go back to the office."

"You went all the way to the roof."

"Is there a law against it?"

"Maybe." The attendant was examining the scuffed interior of the Saab. Rebus meantime had slotted his ticket into the machine.

"Must be a mistake," he said, staring at the display. "Six pounds fifty?"

"That's the minimum. Gets you four hours."

"I've hardly been four minutes."

"System's automated—nothing I can do about it." The man wasn't managing to disguise his pleasure at Rebus's discomfort.

"You telling me you can't go back to that wee booth of yours and swing the barrier open?"

"Company would haul me over the coals."

"Six-fifty, though."

The man offered a shrug.

"Rory won't be happy when I tell him about this."

"Rory?"

"Your boss." Rebus looked in vain for a flicker of recognition. "He owns this place."

"I'm just doing my job."

"Okay then, tell me this—these cameras of yours, do they film what they see?"

"Why are you asking?" Then it dawned. "You the police?"

"In a manner of speaking. So do they record or don't they?"

"The machine wipes itself every forty-eight hours."

"And is there always a human being on duty?"

"Always."

"So if I gave you a date and an approximate time...?"

"For what?"

"Anything."

The attendant straightened up and folded his arms. "That's something you'd have to talk to management about."

"Meaning Rory Bell?"

"I told you, I've never heard of him."

"So who do you deal with?"

"The office is in Livingston."

"There's a multistory there too—you ever do a shift at it?"

"You need to speak to the management."

"Don't worry, I will. Now are you going to let me out of here?"

"Soon as you pay what's due." The man turned away and walked back towards his booth. Cursing, Rebus looked for coins in his pocket, then realized the machine only accepted credit cards. So he stuck one in, entered his PIN and pressed the button for a receipt.

Livingston.

Rory Bell's base.

Plus he had another car park there.

And...

The driver who had been first at the scene of Jessica's crash—wasn't she on her way home from work in Livingston at the time?

So instead of taking the road back into the city, Rebus headed further out in the direction of Newbridge, and from there onto the M8. It didn't take long to reach Livingston, though once there he was faced with a Mensa-level puzzle constructed almost entirely of roundabouts. Livingston was one of Scotland's "new towns," designed in the 1960s by planners who liked lots of circles in their diagrams. Second only to this passion seemed to be their crush on the word "Almondvale." It cropped up time and again as Rebus sought his destination: Almondvale Boulevard, Way, Avenue and Drive. Not forgetting Parkway and Crescent—plus the football stadium where the local team played. In the end, Rebus conceded defeat and stopped to ask a pedestrian, who gave him directions to *a* multistory, just not the right multistory. Rather than take a ticket, Rebus left the Saab outside, found the security cabin and asked for directions. The attendant was able to help, and Rebus thanked him. Ten minutes later, he was driving into a four-story car park—the top story being its roof. There was no sign of life in the booth, though lights were on inside. Rebus drove around the ground floor, which was full. Mums with toddlers were loading bags into their vehicles, having returned from the nearby shopping center. Next story up there were fewer cars, and fewer again as Rebus climbed. As before, no one at all was using the bays on the roof. Rebus spotted the same setup of speaker and CCTV camera, and maneuvered the Saab back down the ramp. He parked on the next level and got out. He was alongside an unwashed Citroën. Across from it sat another car, covered with a dust sheet. The bay next to that was empty, but Rebus noted clumps of dirt, leaves and sweet-wrappers on the floor. If he were a betting man, he would have said a car had been parked there until recently—and it had been sitting in the multistory for some time. He took another look at the Citroën. Its tax disc had run out the previous year, and similar detritus had gathered beneath its wheels. When he ran a finger down the paintwork, he left a clean line, and his finger came away blackened. He crossed to the other car and began to lift the dust sheet, catching a glimpse of red bodywork.

"Hell do you think you're playing at?" The man striding up the ramp wore the same uniform as Mr. Bad Teeth from the airport multistory, but was a different breed altogether—ex-forces, maybe, and still able to take on a route march. Beefy arms, fists clenched, jaw jutting. The hair had been shaved from the skull and one ear had a chunk missing from it.

"Early for a meeting," Rebus lied. "Just killing time." He made show of checking his watch.

"Like fuck you are," the man spat.

"Okay then," Rebus bristled. "You tell me—what *am* I doing?"

"Whatever it is, you're not staying." The man clamped a hand around Rebus's forearm.

"That could be classed as assault, pal."

"Oh aye? How about this?" A fist crunched into Rebus's stomach, and he felt his knees buckle. The same hand was digging in his coat, then his jacket's inside pocket, tugging free the warrant card and flapping it open.

"Detective Sergeant, eh? DS Rebus? Okay, I've got your name now, *pal*. And if you report any of this, we'll be having another wee chat. So think about that."

As the wallet was pushed back into Rebus's pocket, he found enough strength to take a swing at his assailant. The man blocked it without too much effort, using his elbow, while his grip on Rebus's other arm tightened still further. Then he let go and took a step back.

"Anytime you like, Grandad," he said.

"I could have a squad car here in two minutes."

"I believe you—but remember what *I* said. Won't just be out to wind you next time."

Rebus flashed back to interview rooms down the years, the softening-up of suspects, the "accidental" trips and falls. And now here he was, on the receiving end. He considered his options and found them wanting. Yes, he could call it in, and the scrapper in front of him would be arrested, questioned, cautioned—but to what end? He had learned something, and that was almost worth the short-lived pain and the residual embarrassment. Time was he would have gone blow-for-blow with the man.

Time was.

"I'll be back," was what he ended up saying.

"Best bring a Terminator with you," his attacker said with a lopsided grin, watching as Rebus trudged back to the Saab. "Got your license plate now too," the man added. "Means I can have your address anytime I like."

Rebus held one hand to his stomach as he drove, removing it only when he needed to change gear, which was often — all those bloody roundabouts again. He stopped at a fast-food place and got some fizzy orange. His mouth was dry, heart pounding. When his phone rang, he thought about ignoring it, but saw James Page's name on the screen.

"I'm on my way," Rebus answered.

"Where from?"

"Another errand."

"For Siobhan Clarke? Maybe I should ask her to confirm that."

"Up to you." Rebus slurped the ice-cold juice through a straw.

"I've just spoken to Professor Quant about our floater. Bringing in Professor Thomas seems to have been useful. I think we've got a suspicious death here, and maybe even a murder."

"Murder? Not from what I saw at the second autopsy."

"Nevertheless."

"Look, I can see what you're doing — everyone around you seems to be heading a big case, so you want one too. But the Procurator Fiscal's office will laugh you back to Gayfield Square if you go to them with this. There's no evidence to back you up."

"There are bruises."

"I've got a few of those myself. Doubt very much I'll die from them."

"Are you all right?"

"Tickety-boo."

"And you're really on your way here?"

"Absolutely."

"So what do you think we do about the floater?"

"For starters, maybe stop using that word. Then you set up a trawl of missing persons, going back as many years as necessary. He was white-skinned, fair-haired. We know his height and build. An appeal is a good idea—get his description out there."

"Right."

"Christine Esson's the expert—she'll know where to start."

"Thanks, John."

"Anytime, boss."

"How long till you get here? Twenty minutes? Half an hour?"

"Soon as I can—scout's honor."

"But we both know you were never a scout."

"You've rumbled me," Rebus confessed. Then: "Forgive me for saying, but you sound a bit cheerier."

"News from on high: no plans to scrap Gayfield Square."

"Glad to hear it."

"Aye, me too. But doubtless you'll do *something* to sour my mood before long."

"I dare say." Rebus ended the call and gave his stomach another rub. He had one slight detour to make before Gayfield Square. And some big questions that needed answering.

Great King Street was lined with cars, except for a stretch of single yellow line at the end. Rebus parked and placed the POLICE sign on the dashboard. He was close by Drummond Place, with its central splodge of green space, protected by high railings and available only to keyholders. He walked back along the street until he was outside the door he wanted, pressing the buzzer for the flat marked TRAYNOR/BELL.

"Yes?"

The crackly voice belonged to Forbes McCuskey.

"It's DS Rebus. I need a word."

"There's nothing for you here."

"Let me in or I swear I'll kick down the door."

There was silence. Then a buzzing as the door was unlocked. Rebus pushed it open and managed the stairs fine. The blood was rushing in his ears by the time he reached the top, but he hadn't had to pause for breath. The door was closed, so he thumped on it. His hand came away stained pink. Looking again, he saw that paint had been thrown at the door, then wiped off. Whoever had cleaned it had tried to be thorough, but the stone floor beneath Rebus's feet was stained too. The door was eventually opened, Forbes McCuskey standing there.

"I'm collecting for the UVF," Rebus said, holding up his palm.

"Jessica says this is intimidation. She says I should phone a lawyer."

"Want to borrow my mobile?" Rebus held it out towards the young man. "I don't care what the hell you do, Forbes. And I can appreciate you're scared." He indicated the paint marks on the floor. "You've had a visitor. I think maybe they went to your home too. Expected to find you rather than your dad." He paused. "Can I come in?"

"We don't want you here."

"Maybe not, but I think you need me. How else are you going to be rid of Alice's Uncle Rory?"

"Christ..."

The utterance came from a doorway beyond.

"Hello there, Alice," Rebus said, though he couldn't see her. "You've managed to make it up with Forbes and Jessica, then? I suppose you had to—the three of you have to stick together, too much to lose otherwise." Then, to Forbes McCuskey: "I've just been visiting the multistory in Livingston. You took Jessica there for a look. I'm guessing it must have been Alice who let it slip, maybe one night after a party—a couple of drinks or a toke too many. Alice's scary uncle and some car he'd told her about. Something in its boot? A crowbar would be needed if someone wanted to know what it was." Rebus paused, his eyes fixed on those of the student. "Am I getting warm, son?"

"Tell him to go away!" A different voice, louder, almost hysterical: Jessica Traynor.

"The gang's all here," Rebus said with a smile. "Crisis meeting sort of thing? How come Alice can't just go have a word with Uncle Rory?"

"It's too late for that!" Alice Bell cried out. Rebus tried shuffling into the hall, but McCuskey was determined to block him.

"Come back when you've got a warrant," he said, a determined look on his face.

"Might be too late by then, Forbes. You saw what happened to your dad."

"We don't *know* what happened!"

"We can take an educated guess, though," Rebus argued. "And you three are more educated than me, so *I'm* guessing you've come to a few conclusions." He paused again. "And they're scaring the shit out of you even as I stand here. Oh, and by the way, Alice? Nice touch, putting me on the trail of Forbes's dealer. I'm guessing that was to stop me focusing on the crash, and for a while it actually worked."

Forbes turned away from Rebus towards Bell. "You *told* him?"

"I had to!"

Rebus heard the main door downstairs open and close—a neighbor, returning home, their feet sounding like sandpaper against the stone steps.

"You need me," he persisted. The young man's resolve was crumbling, his whole world in imminent danger of collapse. "You need to tell me what happened."

"Just go," McCuskey said, with something like resignation.

"Who else is going to be there for you, Forbes?" Rebus stretched out his arms to reinforce the point.

"Well there's always me."

This time the voice came from behind Rebus. He turned just as Owen Traynor reached the landing. Jessica emerged limping from the flat, brushing Rebus aside and throwing herself into her father's embrace. He ran his hand down her hair, eyes on Rebus.

"You can bugger off now," he said. "I need a quiet word with my daughter and her friends."

"You can't get involved in this," Rebus warned him.

"Involved in what?" Traynor made show of widening his eyes.

"This isn't your fight."

Traynor, draping an arm around Jessica's shoulders, began to steer her past Rebus into the flat.

"We'll be fine now, thank you, Officer," Traynor said. "Shut the door, Forbes, there's a good lad."

McCuskey had the good grace to look apologetic as he obeyed the Englishman's command. Rebus shook his head slowly, steadily, until Forbes McCuskey disappeared from view. The click of the Yale lock echoed around the stairwell. He cursed under his breath, then took out a handkerchief and began rubbing the paint from his hand.

Christine Esson was busy at her desk when Rebus reached Gayfield Square.

"MisPers," she informed him when he took a look over her shoulder at her computer screen. "Lots and lots of them—so thanks for that."

"Don't blame me if you're the IT wizard around here."

"Judging by the autopsy photos, it's an archaeologist we need."

"Maybe put out a call for tombs that have been raided lately." Rebus patted her shoulder before settling himself at his own desk. He had checked the damage to his stomach, studying it with the help of the mirror in the toilets. The bruise was already forming, but he doubted any real harm had been done, other than to his pride. From what he'd seen of the cars in the multistory, none had been attacked by a crowbar. Just the one then—the one since removed from the scene. Drugs, he was thinking. They were the obvious answer. Could Forbes McCuskey have lifted them? Spotted on CCTV, the guard waking up and bellowing a warning over one of the loudspeakers. McCuskey and Jessica Traynor getting the hell out of there. But the barrier would have stopped them. And the machine only accepted credit cards. Meaning Rory Bell would have their faces and the license plate from the CCTV, plus the card details. Easy enough to trace them. Especially if Forbes McCuskey's card was registered to his parents' home address...

But now Owen Traynor had entered the picture, and that was a complication. If he did a deal with Bell, the case would cease to exist—along with the evidence. Rebus had to do something. He looked towards Page's office, but the man was nowhere to be seen.

"Where's Mr. Happy?" he asked.

"Persuading the upper echelons to give him a press conference. He wants the world to get a good look at Tutankhamun."

"Any idea how long he'll be?"

"I think he went home for a change of shirt—always likes to look his best for the brass."

Rebus pondered his options. He could take what he had to DCI Ralph at Torphichen. The Pat McCuskey inquiry had drawn nothing but blanks—there was always the chance they'd welcome Rebus with open arms.

On the other hand, what did he have in the way of hard facts? Probably not enough for a search warrant for the car park. Nick Ralph's first step would be to interview the three students again, and they would almost certainly stick to their original stories. The paint on the door could be explained as a prank. They had placed their trust in Jessica's father rather than CID.

Rebus couldn't really blame them.

He needed more before he could go to Torphichen, so he sifted through the paperwork he had on Rory Bell, put it back in order, then fired up his computer and got ready to start a Google search of his own.

*　　　*　　　*

It took him an hour to spot what Esson had missed. Missed, or had failed to see as being of importance. Alice Bell's father had died two years back when his car was hit by a van. The van driver's name was Jack Redpath. He had been charged with dangerous driving…but the case had never reached court. Or rather it had, but he hadn't. He'd done a runner.

Such was the assumption of the local paper that had covered the case. Just the one mention. Rebus picked up the phone and managed to get through to someone in Central Region, who eventually connected him to an officer who remembered the incident.

"Guy was divorced, living in a hovel and about to lose his job—maybe even do some time inside. He stuffed what few possessions his wife hadn't taken into his car and offskied."

"You tried tracking him down?"

"We did what we could."

"But he never turned up?" Rebus scratched the underside of his jaw. "Have you got a record of the car he drove? Make and registration?"

"Bloody hell." The officer gave a snort. "It's Indiana Jones you need."

"Maybe so, but *you're* what I've got. It was only two years ago—how hard can it be? Plus a photo or description of Redpath—and whether he was a smoker or not." He looked across to where Esson was still busy at her computer, her head resting on one hand, elbow against the surface of her desk. Rebus gave the officer his phone number and e-mail, ended the call, then filled the kettle and switched it on.

"Just hot water, right?" he asked. "No tea bag or coffee granules?"

"Right," she agreed.

"Having much luck?"

"A lot of people seem to go walkabout."

"Any shortcuts?"

"There are organizations—they have websites, Facebook and Twitter accounts..." She turned to look at him. "You've got something?"

"Maybe."

"Keeping it to yourself?"

"For a little while longer."

He poured her drink and handed the mug to her, before making tea for himself. But instead of drinking it, he went back to the toilets and stared at himself in the mirror. It made sense, didn't it? Something kept hidden in a long-stay car park, where no one would ever come looking. A word or clue dropped to Alice Bell, who couldn't resist telling her friends. They prize open the boot—are spotted—flee the scene. The car has to be moved, maybe got rid of.

Not along with its contents, but separate from them.

Two years since Jack Redpath ran.

Or didn't run.

Was taken.

His room emptied to make it look like he had scarpered.

Calluses on the hands, the result of manual labor. Redpath, a plasterer by trade.

Rebus splashed water on his face, rubbing it dry with a clump of paper towels.

The forensic anthropologist would know—two years in the boot of a car, what a body would look like after. One thing Rebus was sure of: to get a corpse in a car boot, it needed to be placed almost in a fetal position.

Easily misinterpreted as having been seated...

His phone rang. He didn't recognize the number.

"Yes?" he answered.

It was the officer from Central.

"Midnight-blue Ford Escort, eight years old. Used to run something sportier but the divorce settlement took care of that." The man reeled off the license plate. Rebus told him to hang on, then went back into the CID suite and grabbed a pen and sheet of paper.

"Repeat that, will you?" he said, jotting the details down.

"Plus I've e-mailed you a mug shot," the man went on.

"Wasn't so hard, was it?" Rebus said. "But was he a smoker?"

"Ten a day. Do I get to go back to actual real work now?"

"With my blessing."

Rebus put his phone next to the computer and opened his e-mail folder. Clicked on the attachment, then called across to Christine Esson. She studied the face, front and side views. Physical details were listed beneath.

"Height, five-ten," Esson intoned. "Weight, a hundred and seventy pounds. Gray eyes, fair hair..." She retreated to her desk and returned with the autopsy photos. "So who is he?" she said.

"Would you say they're the same person?"

"It's possible."

"No more than that?"

She shrugged.

"I think it's him. He was stored in a car boot, and then dumped in the docks."

"Stored for two years, you mean?" She watched Rebus nod. "So where's the car?"

"Right here," Rebus said, holding up the sheet of paper. "Eight-year-old blue Ford Escort." He thought back to the cars in the multistory. No, it matched neither of them. It had probably been driven to Leith Docks with its cargo still on board. Then got rid of. Rebus picked up his phone and called the Road Policing Unit.

"Any abandoned cars in the past couple of days? Tax disc almost certainly a year or more out of date." He described Jack Redpath's Escort and then waited.

"You think it's out there collecting parking tickets?" Esson asked.

"Best-case scenario."

"And worst?"

Rebus just shrugged. He was listening to news that the information could take some time—the city's traffic wardens would need to be questioned.

"Soon as you can, eh?" Rebus gave his details and put the phone down. "Now we wait," he told Esson.

"Maybe you do, but I'm heading out to the shop. It's lunchtime, if you hadn't noticed—want me to fetch you something?"

"Maybe a sandwich or a sausage roll." He dug into his pocket for change.

"My treat," Esson told him. "A sandwich is probably healthier."

"Make it the sausage roll, then."

She rolled her eyes and shrugged her arms into her jacket. Rebus remembered Deborah Quant doing the same, and his own instinct to help. When he'd suggested meeting for a drink sometime, she hadn't turned him down flat. Then again, he didn't have a number for her, excepting the one for the mortuary.

He headed out to the car park for a smoke, then remembered the phone upstairs could ring at any moment. So after three or four draws he nipped the end of the cigarette and returned it to the packet. He could hear the phone ringing on his desk from the top of the stairs, but it stopped as he entered the office. Cursing under his breath, he sat down and waited. Esson returned and handed him a paper bag. The lack of grease stains meant she'd ignored his request. The baguette contained ham salad.

"It's like being at one of those health spas," he muttered. But he demolished it anyway.

When the phone rang again, he snatched at it.

"Thought you were in a hurry," the RPU officer complained.

"I am."

"So why didn't you answer earlier?"

"Call of nature. Now what have you got?" Rebus listened for a moment. "Taken away to be scrapped?" he repeated for Esson's benefit. "Yesterday?" He reached for his pen again. "Do we know which scrap yard?" He began taking down the details but then broke off. "Yes, I know it," he said. "Thanks."

He finished the call and made another, but no one was answering. Cursing, he stuffed his phone into his pocket and got up from the desk.

"What do I tell the boss when he gets back?" Esson asked.

"That his sartorial elegance has shamed me into doing a bit of shopping."

She smiled and gave him a little wave as he made for the door. Then she left her own desk and crossed to Rebus's, taking her prawn sandwich with her. She studied the photo of Jack Redpath on Rebus's computer screen.

"Maybe," she said to herself. "Just maybe..." She fixed her eyes on the doorway. She hadn't known John Rebus long, but she knew he was good at this, like a bloodhound given a scent and then left to do what it was best at. Form-filling and protocols and budget meetings were not Rebus's thing—never had been and never would be. His knowledge of the Internet was rudimentary and his people skills were woeful. But she would lie for him to James Page, and take the rap if caught. Because he was a breed of cop that wasn't supposed to exist anymore, a rare and endangered species.

And she would miss his kind when they did—as they would—eventually vanish from the world.

It was the scrap yard Jessica Traynor's Golf had been taken to. The same German shepherd rose to its feet and bared its fangs as Rebus got out of his car. Eddie Duke emerged from the shack and snapped at it.

"Boris! Pipe down!"

Then, to Rebus, and indicating the Saab: "Just leave it there. We've got a bit of a backlog, but we'll get round to it when we can."

"That's hilarious," Rebus said, looking as though he'd never found anything less funny in his life. "I've been trying to phone you."

"I told you, we're busy." He gestured towards the compactor, which was squeezing the life out of its latest victim. Rebus could hear the dying gasps of metal, plastic and glass. Reece Bairstow was working the machinery. Rebus noticed a car number plate resting against the wall next to the guard dog. He walked over and picked it up, ignoring the dog's growls.

"This car?" he asked.

"Was blocking a street in Granton. Obviously abandoned."

"And is now...?"

The man gestured once more towards the compactor. "Is there a problem?" he asked.

Granton: just along the coast from Leith. Rebus dropped the number plate and marched towards the machine, yelling for it to be switched off. Bairstow did as he was told. His boss was a couple of yards behind Rebus, repeating his question. Rebus peered into the compactor. He could smell engine oil. The blue Ford Escort had been reduced to a third of its size, and wouldn't be carrying passengers again. Rebus looked at the two men.

"You stripped it?"

Bairstow checked with Duke before answering. "Someone had already picked it clean."

Not that it looked clean—even mangled as it was, Rebus could make out the thick coating of dust.

"Been stored for a while, would you say?"

Bairstow nodded.

"Check the boot?"

"I didn't take anything."

"We removed the tires and hubs," his boss added. "Some of the electrics. The engine was pretty well shot..."

"I want it out of there," Rebus ordered. "A scene-of-crime team will come and examine it."

"For what?"

"Just get a hook or whatever on it and pull it back out. Throw a tarp over it and keep it safe."

"There was a bit of a smell, you know," Bairstow conceded. "Backseat and the boot."

"And the boot was easy enough to open?"

"Lock was bust. Looked like someone had taken a..."

"Yes?" Rebus fixed his eyes on the man.

"A crowbar to it." Understanding now exactly why Rebus might want the car kept.

*   *   *

Nick Ralph listened to the story with arms folded, lips puckered. He was seated behind his desk at Torphichen.

"It's thin, John," he said, after about a minute's thought.

Rebus had walked into the station and straight up to Ralph without any preamble. The first words out of his mouth had been "Can I talk to you?"

"I've seen you before," Ralph had responded, after which Rebus had introduced himself.

Now the two men were engaged in a staring contest, Ralph rocking slightly in his chair.

"Very thin," he eventually said, breaking the silence.

Rebus just shrugged and waited.

"You're saying this man Bell killed Redpath as retribution of sorts?"

"Yes."

"And stored the body for a number of years in a car park? Pat McCuskey's son finds out, so Bell goes after him?"

"That's my thinking."

"And you brought it to me rather than DCI Page..."

"He's not in charge of the McCuskey inquiry, sir. And if I can be frank, without the leads I've just given you, you seem to be stalled."

"Is that so?" Ralph's shoulders stiffened. He took a deep breath, picked up his phone and ordered a scene-of-crime team to the scrap yard.

"And the multistory?" Rebus suggested. But Ralph had already put down the phone.

"One step at a time, John. We need to bring in the students and hear what they have to say."

"They won't have anything to say."

"Still has to be done. And after that, we can talk to Rory Bell. If it went down the way you say it did...did Pat McCuskey smack his head while trying to get away?"

"Either that or he was in a fighting mood—they wrestled him to the floor and he connected with the fireplace."

"Accidental death, then?"

"More like culpable homicide. Plus the initial break-in. There'll be plenty to charge Bell with, don't you worry."

"*If* we find anything useful in the boot of the Escort."

Rebus accepted this with a shrug.

"Well." Ralph was rising to his feet, signaling that the meeting was over. He reached out his hand for Rebus to take. "We'll let you know."

"Maybe I could oversee the SOCOs."

But Ralph shook his head. "I'm not the kind to forget favors done, John, if that's what's worrying you."

"It's not."

"Well then, as soon as I have news, I'll be in touch." He made the gesture again with his hand, and this time Rebus shook it.

He heard nothing until half past five.

Every half-hour he'd been taking out his phone, checking it had both charge and signal. When it did eventually ring, he almost dropped it in his haste to answer.

"Rebus," he said.

"John, it's Nick Ralph."

"Yes, sir?"

"Neither good news nor bad, really. Fibers were found, and the lab will check if they match the ones from the body pulled out of the dock. It's not always an exact science, though."

"Nothing else?"

"The team did comment on the residual smell—definite whiff of decay, though that's unlikely to convince a jury."

"But it *is* Jack Redpath's car."

"Yes, it is. And you may well be right that the chap hauled from Leith Docks is Redpath. That's why I suggested to your boss that one of his relatives is contacted and asked for a DNA sample—

wouldn't be conclusive unless the man boasts an identical twin, but it would let us know we're on the right path."

"You've spoken to James Page?"

"As a courtesy." Ralph paused. "Which is when I discovered that you hadn't said anything to him after our meeting. Hope I've not dropped you in it."

"Not at all." Rebus looked around the empty office. Christine Esson had clocked off, and so had practically everyone else in the building. He wondered if Page would be on his way here right now, full of righteous indignation.

Answer: yes.

Because there he stood, filling the doorway, face reddened, eyes furious.

"Speak of the devil," Rebus said into the phone, before pressing the cancel key. Page was advancing on his desk.

"How dare you!" he exploded. "That floater is *my* case!"

"He's not a 'floater'—if I'm right, his name is Jack Redpath and he connects to the McCuskey killing and a lot more besides."

"All of which should have been given to *me,* so that *I* could decide what to do with it!"

"Granted," Rebus said. "But you were a bit busy grooming yourself for the cameras and the brass. That left me here as the senior officer, and I acted like one."

"You did this to get at me—no other reason! Clear your desk and get the hell out. Go ask your good friend at Torphichen for a job. Or maybe you know someone at Wester Hailes. You better hope you're wanted somewhere, because you're not wanted here!"

"It's been a pleasure," Rebus said.

"It really hasn't. Everyone warned me: Rebus is a loose cannon; he's off the scale; you can't trust him; he's past his sell-by. *Everybody* told me that, and a lot worse too. Ask yourself this: how many cop shops in this town would have given you the chance? Not a second chance either, but a sixth or seventh or eighth? I did it because at heart I thought you were a good cop—a copper's cop, the kind from the old days that I used to hear about but hardly ever seemed to meet." Page paused. The fire had been damped. If anything, he seemed fatigued and—yes—genuinely disappointed.

"Sorry I let you down," Rebus conceded.

"It seems to be your specialty."

"I can't disagree—and you did say I'd sour your mood sooner rather than later. For what it's worth, DCI Ralph knows this is your investigation. He told me as much."

"He shouldn't have had to do that, though, should he?"

"No, he shouldn't."

Page nodded slowly at the admission. Then he turned towards his cupboard of an office, went inside and closed the door. A moment later it opened again. He placed an empty cardboard box on the floor and slid it towards Rebus's desk.

"For your stuff," he said. "I want you gone in ten minutes."

The door closed once more. Rebus sat there for half a minute or so, then got up and fetched the box. Placed it on his desk, then realized that he didn't need it. There was almost nothing here that belonged to him. He hadn't been back in CID long enough to accumulate anything.

"What the hell have you done, John?" he muttered to himself. He stared at James Page's door, willing himself to go knock on it and ask forgiveness and one more chance.

Just one more.

"No chance…"

Forbes McCuskey ended the call.

"That was the police," he said.

He was seated in Jessica's flat. Alice Bell sat at her desk. Her laptop's screen saver had been activated. She was halfway through an essay she hadn't touched in days and had no enthusiasm to finish. Jessica was on the sofa, playing with the last bottle of her prescription pills. Owen Traynor was in the doorway, sleeves rolled up, hands in trouser pockets.

"Which police?" he asked.

"DCI Ralph—he's in charge of my father's case."

"What does he want?"

"He says he needs to see us—me, Jess and Alice."

"Did he say why?"

"No."

"We're finished," Jessica said, voice trembling.

"You don't need to be afraid of the police," her father reassured her. "They've got nothing on you, because you *did* nothing." He looked around the room, making sure he had everyone's attention. "We stick to the plan, and you leave everything to me." Then, to Forbes: "When does this guy Ralph want to see you?"

"First thing in the morning at Torphichen police station."

"No problem, then. Everything will be sorted long before that."

Alice Bell realized that he was standing directly in front of her. She looked up towards his face. He was holding out his mobile phone.

"Punch in Uncle Rory's number again, will you, sweetheart?"

She did so, and he plucked the phone from her hand, pressing it to his ear, listening first of all to the ringtone, and then to Rory Bell's questioning voice.

"It's me," Owen Traynor said. "So do yourself a favor this time and listen..."

25

This was the second place Siobhan said to try."

Rebus looked up from his table. He was seated in the corner by the window in the back room of the Oxford Bar. There were a couple of smokers outside, visible through the glass, and he'd been readying to join them. But now Malcolm Fox was standing in front of him, hands in pockets, a thin smile on his face.

"The first being...?"

"Arden Street."

"So you went there?"

Fox shook his head. "I disagreed with her analysis."

"Am I due a bollocking?" Rebus asked. "Because—trust me—I'm really not in the mood."

"How about a drink instead?" Fox nodded towards Rebus's near-empty pint. Rebus studied the man, wondering what his angle was. Then he nodded.

"IPA," he said.

Fox retreated to the bar and Rebus stuffed his cigarettes and matches back into his coat. The bar was quiet—midweek, midevening. There was a folk night planned for later, but Rebus would be making himself scarce before then. His car was outside and he knew a breathalyzer would do for him. He rubbed a hand through his hair and exhaled noisily, hunching over the table.

"Here you go," Fox said, placing the fresh drink in front of him.

He'd fetched a can of Coke for himself, plus a glass filled with ice.
"Cheers."

Rebus watched him fill the tumbler, the ice cubes crackling.

"Do you go to AA?" he asked.

"Not anymore."

"And you can come into a pub and not feel tempted?"

"Of course I'm tempted." Fox settled himself on a chair. "I'm only
human—despite what you might think." He lifted his drink. "You
look like you've had a day of it."

"Did Siobhan send you to play Good Samaritan?"

"Is one needed?"

"You've really not heard? Page has had enough of me. I took
something to the McCuskey inquiry that was rightfully his."

"Oh."

Rebus stared at him. "I'd've thought Page would have been
straight on the blower."

Fox shook his head again. "I don't think Siobhan knows."

"So why are you here?"

"The Saunders case."

"Hauling me in for further questioning?" Rebus took a mouthful
of beer, hanging on to the glass while he stared Fox out.

Fox rested his arms against the edge of the table, leaning in towards Rebus. "Saunders set up a meeting with his killer. He wanted
to use the phone at a petrol station, but it was out of order. There
was a kid behind the till—he'd got to know Saunders's face from the
few times he'd been in buying food. So when Saunders offered him a
tenner for the loan of his mobile, the kid agreed. Saunders promised
it was a local call and took the phone outside. The call lasted six and
a half minutes."

"That precise?"

"I was able to get the records. Took me most of today. Pinpointed
the exact time the call was made. Not quite three hours before Saunders was killed."

"That sounds suspiciously like proper detective work." Rebus raised his glass in a silent toast. "So let me guess—he was phoning Stefan Gilmour?"

But Fox shook his head. "It was an Edinburgh number, a landline. Listed in the phone book, so easy for Saunders to track down."

"Eamonn Paterson?"

Another shake of the head. "George Blantyre."

"Dod?" Rebus's eyes narrowed.

"Saunders spoke to him for six and a half minutes."

Rebus was recalling Stefan Gilmour's words: *That old pistol... Dod was the one who lifted it...*

"You're telling me a man who can't get out of his own armchair managed to haul himself to a canal path halfway across town?"

"Seems improbable," Fox agreed. "But there is another explanation..."

He let his words drift off, knowing Rebus would see what he meant.

Rebus gnawed at his bottom lip, then arched his neck to stare at the ceiling. No matter how often they painted it, it seemed to retain a nicotine sheen.

"Bloody hell," he said eventually. Then: "So why aren't you there right now?"

"Thought you might want to tag along."

"Siobhan's idea?"

Fox shook his head. "Mine, actually. She needed a bit of persuading."

"Why is she staying away?"

"She's in a meeting with the bosses, laying it all out for them." Fox finished his drink and gestured towards Rebus's. "You going to drain that, or would you rather take a clear head with you?"

Rebus looked at the drink, pushed it away and got to his feet.

They rang the doorbell of the bungalow in Murrayfield and waited. Maggie Blantyre answered. She was dressed in a white T-shirt and baggy gray joggers, almost no makeup on her face.

"Can we come in?" Rebus asked, no warmth in his voice.

"John..." She placed a hand to one cheek. "If I'd known..."

"We need to talk to you, Maggie. This is Inspector Fox." Rebus broke off. "*Detective* Inspector Fox," he corrected himself, earning a faint smile of thanks from his colleague.

"What's it about?"

"I think you know." Rebus was already brushing past her into the hallway.

"Don't you need a warrant or something?" She was sounding flustered.

"Want me to fetch one?"

"I still don't really see why you're here."

But she had relented, ushering Fox inside and closing the door. "Dod's having a bit of a nap in his chair."

"It's you we need to talk to, Maggie." Rebus fixed her with a look, and she seemed to sense that he knew. "Maybe if we go into the garden." Then, to Fox: "Can you go sit with Dod?" He indicated the living room. Fox looked ready to protest, but eventually relented. Rebus led Maggie Blantyre through the pristine kitchen and out onto the patio. He lit a cigarette for himself and offered her one, which she refused.

"You spoke to Billy Saunders," he stated. "He called the house. I'm guessing it's always you that answers. No need to deny it—we have the phone records. He was scared of what Stefan might do to him, wasn't he? But that wasn't going to stop him giving evidence against the Saints—anything to save his own skin from another stretch in jail." Rebus sucked on the cigarette. His hand was trembling and he wasn't sure why.

"So I spoke to the man—what of it?"

"But you did more than that, Maggie." Rebus let the words lie between them. After a moment, Maggie exploded.

"You and your bloody Saints! They're all Dod can ever talk about. He lives more in the past now than ever before—maybe because he's got no future. And here's this man ready to tell everyone Dod was a killer, and that he'd covered the whole thing up and got away with it."

"It wasn't Dod who killed Phil Kennedy."

"But he was *there!* And he helped carry the body from the cell and everything." She stared across the garden and seemed to see something. "Wait here," she told Rebus. But he followed her to the shed, watched her open its door and start rummaging in the darkness, between and behind paint pots and unused tools.

"This where you kept the gun?" he asked.

"Dod thought I'd destroyed it. I told him I had. Same as I was supposed to have thrown this out." She was handing him something. It was a well-worn copy of *Scots Criminal Law,* with the distinctive leather cover, faded gold writing and brass screws. Its pages were damp, curled at the corners.

"The Shadow Bible," Rebus said, turning it over in his hand and rubbing at the spot where they had all added a gobbet of saliva, cementing their loyalty to the cause.

"It's just a bloody book," Maggie said. "But it was more than that to Dod. You all meant so much to him, and he was going to spend his last days seeing it all torn apart in front of him."

"Did you mean to shoot him?" Rebus asked quietly.

She nodded, tears forming in her eyes. "I did it for all of you—because Dod couldn't."

"You don't have to tell them that. You can say the gun went off by accident. Maybe your finger slipped, or he tried grabbing it from you..."

"More lies, eh, John?" She turned her head to look at the house. "What will he do without me?"

"Is there someone you can call?"

"Now, you mean?"

"You'll have to come with us, Maggie."

She thought for a moment. "His nephew's been very good."

"Maybe him, then."

She nodded. "My phone's in the kitchen."

"Let's go in." He tried placing an arm around her shoulders, but she shrugged it off. Snatching the book from him, she spat on its cover, wiping her mouth with the back of her hand afterwards. Gently Rebus took the book from her and led her indoors.

While she made the call, he went into the living room. Fox was standing in the middle of the floor. Dod Blantyre was awake, and wanted to know what was going on.

"Where's Maggie?" he demanded of Rebus.

"She's on the phone. We need to take her to the station."

"No." The man was attempting to rise from his chair, head bobbing, legs twitching.

"Nothing you can do, Dod. Your nephew's coming to look after you."

But Blantyre had fallen to his knees. With Fox's help, Rebus got him back into the chair, just as his wife appeared in the doorway, carrying her coat.

"Oh God," she said, her hand going to her mouth.

"Don't leave me, Maggie," Blantyre implored. Then, to Rebus: "She didn't do anything."

"We still need to talk to her," Rebus said gently.

"You don't! You don't!"

"Give me five minutes with him," Maggie said, gripping Rebus's forearm. "Wait in the car and I'll come out." Her eyes were pleading. "Just a few minutes."

Rebus looked towards Fox and nodded, the two men filing out of the room and making for the door. Outside, as they walked down the path, Fox asked if she'd confessed.

"Pretty much," Rebus said. He was carrying the Shadow Bible in one hand. Fox asked if it was what he thought it was. Rebus nodded. Fox unlocked the car and they got in.

"I'll text Siobhan," he said, taking out his phone. Then, after a pause: "This must be hard for you, John. Made me think about what I'd do if a close colleague went too far."

"You'd turn them in, wouldn't you?"

"Maybe." Fox concentrated on the text he was composing. "Probably," he eventually conceded. "But twenty or thirty years ago..." He offered a shrug. "Different game, as all you old people keep saying."

"Bloody hell, Malcolm, you're not exactly a spring chicken."

Fox gave a twitch of his mouth and finished the text. "So what about you and Mrs. Blantyre?"

"What about us?"

"You needed to talk in private—makes me think there's history there."

"Is that right?"

"I'm good at reading people, John. I have to be."

"Well you're wrong this time."

"Am I?" Fox's phone let him know his text had received a reply. He looked at the screen. "Siobhan will be waiting for us at Wester Hailes." He paused. "But she says..."

"I can't play any part in the interview?" Rebus guessed.

"You're too close to the case, John."

Rebus nodded his agreement. He peered in the direction of the bungalow.

"How long do we wait?" Fox asked.

What will he do without me?

Don't leave me, Maggie...

"Shit," Rebus said, pushing open the passenger-side door and breaking into a jog. The bungalow's front door was closed, held fast by a Yale lock. Rebus banged on it, then realized Fox was standing next to him. He gave the door a kick with his heel, then tried shouldering it.

"The two of us together," Fox said.

Eventually the wood split, the door bursting open. Rebus flew into the living room and saw Maggie looming over her husband, shoving tablets into his mouth and her own. Painkillers of some kind, empty blister packs lying on Dod Blantyre's lap, tears streaming down both faces. Rebus pulled her away and hooked a finger into her mouth. Without the aid of liquid, the tablets were proving hard to swallow. Fox got busy with Dod, flicking tablets onto the floor.

"Can't let you do it," Rebus told Maggie as she crumpled, wailing. "I'm sorry, but I just can't."

Fox was already on his phone, requesting an ambulance. Rebus was on his knees in front of Maggie, stroking her hair as she wept, her face buried in the carpet. He turned and saw that Dod Blantyre was watching him through his own tears. Fox was asking for the address, so he could give it to the switchboard. Rebus told him, and began to clamber back to his feet.

Rebus was slumped in the public waiting area of the Royal Infirmary's Accident and Emergency department. The row of hard plastic seats was fixed to the floor and not intended for long-term comfort. Fox was feeding coins into the drinks machine. Somewhere behind the reception desk, in adjacent curtained cubicles, husband and wife were being examined. As Fox returned with two small plastic cups of coffee, Siobhan Clarke arrived. She sat down next to Rebus.

"Hell of a thing," she said.

"Isn't it, though?"

"Lucky you were there."

He fixed her with a look. "If we *hadn't* been there, it wouldn't have happened in the first place."

"I know it can't be easy, John..."

Fox handed Rebus a coffee and asked Clarke if she wanted one.

"Maybe a tea," she said, watching as Fox retreated to the machine, digging into his pocket for more loose change.

"You sent Malcolm," Rebus said. "Is that because he needed it or I did? I should probably warn you, I make a poor patient but a worse therapist."

"It's not therapy Malcolm needs. He'd done all the work tracing that number. I thought he deserved to be there at the end."

"So it wasn't just a case of you steering clear?"

"How do you mean?"

"Maybe you've been on hand at too many of my fuck-ups. And here you are outranking me, running your own major incident." He paused. "Maybe letting me know I'm history..."

"That wasn't my thinking."

"No?"

"No," she stated.

"I wish I could believe you." Rebus stopped as Fox returned with her drink. She took it from him with a muttered "Thanks," then asked if there was any news.

"Neither one of them's in any danger," Fox obliged. "And John's already heard Mrs. Blantyre admit to shooting Saunders."

"Accidentally," Rebus added. "I told you how it is with Brownings." His eyes met Clarke's, willing her to challenge him.

"She took it with her to the canal, though—and ended up pointing it at her victim."

"To scare him off, so the last few months of her husband's life wouldn't be spent in an interview room or police custody."

"You sound like her lawyer." Clarke shifted her attention to Fox. "Solicitor General's going to be happy, wouldn't you say?"

Fox just shrugged, and Clarke stared at her drink, her shoulders slumping. "Look at the three of us," she said. "A result in the bag and feeling no better for it."

Fox made to sit down, lifting the big black book which Rebus had left there. He rested it on his knees, and Clarke could just make out the lettering on its cover.

Scots Criminal Law.

DAY FOURTEEN

26

You okay?" Fox asked.

"Sure. And thanks for coming."

"You really think I'm required?"

Rebus threw him a glance. "You've got heft. That's what I need."

"Not my brains or beauty, then?"

Rebus concentrated on the road. They were in the Saab, heading for Livingston. "Anything to report?"

"They were kept in overnight. Neither one of them had managed to ingest many of the tablets. Maggie Blantyre will be interviewed formally this afternoon."

"And her husband?"

"At a date to be decided, once we've had a medical report." Fox looked at Rebus. "For what it's worth, she's sticking to her story. Saunders tried taking the gun from her and it went off."

"You believe that?"

"I'm not sure. Do you?"

"Any evidence to disprove it?"

Fox studied him. "You know there isn't. But she'll still go to prison. Best lawyer in the land couldn't prevent that."

"She'll have the best, too."

"Oh?"

"I spoke to Stefan Gilmour last night when I got home—he'll make sure of it."

"How much did you know?"

"I knew Phil Kennedy died in custody and it was covered up."

"From what little George Blantyre has been saying, he's keen to shoulder the blame."

"Is that right?"

"Says he pushed Kennedy off his chair. Thought he was unconscious but then noticed he wasn't breathing, so he took the body back to Kennedy's place and made it look like he'd fallen over while drunk."

"He acted alone?"

"That's his story. The man's not long for this world, so what has he got to lose?" Fox paused. "Looks like Stefan Gilmour and Eamonn Paterson can breathe easy, even though *we* know that's not the way it was."

"Will anyone bother charging Dod?"

"I get the feeling the inquiry will drag its heels, let nature take its course."

"What a mess. Have you taken the news to the Solicitor General yet?"

"I'm trying to decide what to tell her."

"That's easy, isn't it? You tell her what you know."

"Which isn't half as much as I suspect."

"She won't thank you for anything that can't be proven."

Fox nodded as if in agreement, then studied their surroundings. "Lot of roundabouts. I'm impressed you're not resorting to satnav."

"We're nearly there."

They arrived at the barrier of the multistory. Rebus reached out and plucked the ticket from the machine. Passing the security cabin, he saw that his attacker wasn't on duty. Another uniform had taken his place—skinnier and older.

"Might not need you after all," Rebus commented, taking the ramp to the next floor. When they reached the third, he pulled into a bay and started swearing.

"What is it?" Fox asked.

"They've moved the cars."

Fox looked out at the vast, empty concrete space. "What cars?"

"Exactly. When I was here yesterday, there were two cars, dusty and abandoned. There'd been a third, but that was already gone. Jack Redpath's body was in the boot. They dumped him in the docks and left the car to be towed and scrapped."

"Okay." Fox was frowning, concentrating hard as he tried to catch up.

"But there were two other cars still here, one of them under a dust sheet." Rebus got out and walked to the empty bays, Fox following suit. "See? Yesterday there was a lot of leaves and stour. The cars had been here for months, maybe even years... What are you smiling at?"

"It's such a great old word, 'stour'—my dad uses it."

"They've swept it all away, every last trace."

"That's thorough."

"The cars are used for storing stuff—stuff that needs to be kept away from prying eyes."

"And a public car park is the place for that?"

"On a level no one ever has to use, with CCTV and a guard."

"Okay, so you think there are other bodies in these cars?"

"I've no idea." Rebus thought for a moment. "This has to be Owen Traynor. He meets with Rory Bell, they discuss what happened. Traynor knows we might come looking and persuades Bell the cars need to be moved."

"Traynor?"

"Jessica's father. He's got a sharper brain than Bell. Even after Forbes and Jessica saw what was in that boot, it still took Bell a while to decide he needed to ditch car and body both. Traynor comes to town to broker peace and asks Bell if there's anything else the police might find if they come looking..."

"You came looking yesterday."

"And word got back—so the cars had to be got rid of."

"Moved where, though?"

"How should I know? But sweeping up—that's the sort of detail someone like Traynor would think of." Rebus scratched a hand across his head. "Maybe in a lockup somewhere. He wouldn't take them to the car park at the airport—too obvious."

"What makes of car are we talking about?"

"One was a Citroën; the one under wraps I'm not sure about—red bodywork is all I saw."

"You didn't get the license plates?"

"I was interrupted by a punch to the gut."

"What?"

"Different security baboon from today."

"That's why you thought you might need heft?"

"Yes."

"I'm almost flattered. Why didn't you report it?"

"Some things you keep to yourself."

"Like being bested in a fight?"

"Did I say I was bested? You should see the other guy. Maybe that's why he's off work this morning."

"I'll take your word for that."

As they headed for the exit, Fox asked if it was worth questioning the new guard. Rebus shook his head. As he slotted his credit card into the pay machine, he shared his thinking about the night of the crash.

"When Jessica and Forbes took a crowbar to that Ford Escort, CCTV was watching. Guard would have come running, but by then they'd seen enough to be freaked out..."

"Yes?"

"Still, there's one exit and it only takes cards. Forbes was driving, so he'd be paying, too."

"Meaning they'd have his details...leading them straight to Patrick McCuskey?"

"No sign of young Forbes, so they gave his room a going-over to let him know the score."

"And the attack on his father?"

Rebus grew thoughtful, then offered a shrug.

They pulled into a service station for petrol. In the shop, Rebus bought a fresh packet of cigarettes, Fox a bottle of water.

"Biggest rip-off going," Rebus counseled as Fox tipped the bottle to his mouth.

"I was about to say the same." Fox gestured towards the twenty Silk Cut.

They were on their way back to the Saab when Fox asked: "These cars, would they be daft enough just to dump them like they did with Redpath's Ford?"

"I'm not sure."

"Only, it ended up going for scrap..."

Rebus stopped with one hand on the driver's-side door handle. "You think they might have...?" Rather than finish the question, he got into the car and called the scrap yard in Broxburn. He was expecting to hear Eddie Duke's voice, but it was Reece Bairstow who answered.

"It's DS Rebus," Rebus told him. "I'm after a favor."

"Aren't you always?"

"Anytime you want to explain that crowbar to my colleagues, Reece..."

There was a sigh on the line. "So what's the favor?"

"Scrap yards within easy distance of Livingston."

"Apart from us, you mean?"

"Yes."

"There aren't any."

"None at all?"

"Only players in town. So can I get back to work now?"

"Soon as you answer one last question."

"Which is?"

Rebus took a deep breath. "Two cars, one a Citroën with an expired tax disc, the other a medium-sized saloon with red paintwork..."

"Yes?"

"You wouldn't have seen them, by any chance?"

"They came in last night."

Rebus blinked a couple of times. "Tell me they've not made it into the compactor yet."

"I was just about to get started. But something tells me you're not going to want that to happen."

"Correct," Rebus said. "We'll be there in twenty minutes. Nobody touches them until then—understood?"

"Getting to be a familiar refrain," Bairstow was muttering as Rebus ended the call. He stared at Fox.

"I owe you a large drink," he said.

"Got one, thanks," Fox replied, shaking the bottle of water.

Eddie Duke had taken Boris the guard dog to a vet's appointment.

"Nothing trivial, I hope," Rebus said.

As Bairstow explained it, the cars had arrived around closing time. One—a red Renault—was cleaner than the other. The drivers of the two vehicles weren't the ones in charge, however.

"There was another car—the one they all drove off in afterwards. Guy behind the wheel was the one who did the talking and handed over the cash."

"What did he look like?" Rebus asked.

"Maybe six feet, well built, short black hair with sort of a widow's peak."

Rebus had only seen photos of Rory Bell, but that was just how he would have described him.

"No name?" he inquired.

"Not that I heard."

"What was he driving?"

"New-looking BMW X5. Black bodywork and tinted windows."

"You didn't happen to get the license number?"

Bairstow shook his head. "Wasn't personalized or anything."

They were standing in front of the cars. Rebus recognized the Citroën—the line was still there where he had dragged a finger across its bodywork. The dust sheet that had been covering the Renault was visible through its rear window.

"What about the other drivers?"

Rebus listened to Bairstow's description. One was almost certainly the guard from the multistory, the one who had left Rebus with a bruise the size of a tea plate.

"They left the keys?"

Bairstow dug in his overalls and held them up.

"Have you taken a look yet?"

The man shook his head.

"Sure about that?"

"Completely."

"Then let's get both boots open and see what we've got."

They unlocked the Citroën first. Rebus could smell some sort of oil. There were strips of cloth inside and he lifted one to his nose.

"What do you think?" Fox asked.

"Been wrapped around something. Maybe guns."

"Guns?" The blood drained from the mechanic's face.

Rebus lifted the carpeting but found nothing except a spare tire. Fox meantime had opened one of the rear doors and was feeling around beneath the seats.

"Got any plastic bags?" he asked.

"In the office," Bairstow said.

"Go fetch some."

When the mechanic had moved off, Fox told Rebus they really needed a forensics team.

"Agreed. You finding anything?"

"I'll show you in a minute."

Rebus opened the driver's door and reached across to open the glove box. Nothing inside but a spare set of bulbs. The floor was clean and the door pockets were empty. Bairstow had returned with some small clear bags, the kind bank staff used when counting coins. Fox placed his hand into one of them and used it to pick something up from the floor, folding the bag back over the item, trapping it.

Then he held it up for Rebus to examine. An unused shotgun cartridge.

"Boom," Rebus said, patting his colleague on the back. He took the second key from Bairstow and unlocked the Renault. Again, there was nothing obvious in the boot, other than the remains of some fine white powder.

"Looks like a bag maybe burst," Rebus commented.

"Or someone needed a taste," Fox added.

Rebus dabbed at a little and rubbed it against his gum. "Bit of a burn," he said.

Bairstow's eyes widened further. "I didn't...If I'd known...They'll kill me, won't they?" He was beginning to twitch.

"Your name won't even feature, Reece—don't worry." Rebus took out his phone. The signal was weak, but he got through to Torphichen and asked to speak to Nick Ralph. "And I know you probably hear it all the time, but this really *is* urgent."

When Ralph was eventually found, Rebus laid everything out for him. "Bell is in a black BMW X5 with tinted windows. We need to grab that car. There's a good chance it'll have some goodies in the boot. Plus a few baddies in the front."

Rebus watched Fox roll his eyes at the pun. He mouthed the words *Get used to it* and added a wink. Then, to Ralph: "We also need a search warrant for the multistory in Livingston. Has to be right away, because there's some CCTV footage there we can use, if we get it before it self-erases. It'll probably show the stuff being transferred from the two cars to the BMW."

"I'll see to it, John," Ralph said. "And a forensic team to the scrap yard, yes?"

"Absolutely. Checking for prints and trace evidence."

"And you're sure you've cleared this with DCI Page?"

"He agrees with me, sir—it's all the one case."

"Then I'll get onto it. Thank you, John."

"Yes, sir. Oh, by the way—have you pulled the three students in for interview."

"They were supposed to be here at nine. Tried their phones and sent an officer to Ms. Traynor's flat—no joy."

"Keeping their heads down."

"Pretty much as you predicted. Any more tasks for me before I get started with this lot?"

"No, sir." Rebus ended the call and tapped his phone against his chin.

"Job done?" Fox asked him.

"Not quite," Rebus decided. "But it's up to you whether you want to see it through. Could get messy."

"I can always clean up after," Fox told him with a shrug.

"Getting to like CID, Detective Inspector?"

"It has its attractions," Malcolm Fox conceded.

Every parking space on Great King Street was taken, so Rebus ended up on the single yellow again. He had explained to Fox that they were going to have a word with Owen Traynor. If he wasn't there, hopefully Jessica or Alice Bell could provide his where-abouts.

"Alice knew about the body in the boot?" Fox asked.

Rebus nodded. "Her uncle's way of letting her know he was tak-ing care of her."

"Not quite a birthday card with a tenner in it."

"Not quite," Rebus agreed.

Rebus pressed the bell but there was no answer. He was trying a second time when Fox tugged on his sleeve. "Isn't that...?"

He was pointing along the street, towards a black 4x4. Rebus led the way, walking around the car. Tinted windows. BMW X5. No parking fee had been paid and the wardens had already stuck a ticket on the windscreen.

"Shall I phone it in?" Fox asked.

Rebus nodded, then tried the boot, though he knew it would be locked. Pressing his nose to the glass, he couldn't see anything on the backseat. No boxes or bags.

"Someone should stand guard till the cavalry gets here," he said, once Fox had ended the call.

"And let you go upstairs on your own?" Fox was shaking his head. "If Rory Bell is in there, his sidekicks might be too. What do you think they're doing?"

"Best-case scenario, having a powwow with Traynor."

"And worst-case?"

"I don't really want to think about it."

"Nobody's answering anyway," Fox commented.

But as they approached the building, a neighbor emerged, maneuvering a bicycle ahead of her. Fox sprinted forward, holding the door open. The woman thanked him with a smile as she strapped on her helmet.

"Thank *you*," he replied, ushering Rebus inside.

They climbed the three stories in silence. When they got to the door of Jessica Traynor's flat, Fox indicated that it wasn't quite closed. Rebus pushed it open an inch and listened.

Silence.

Another inch and he had a view of the hallway.

No sign of life.

He let it swing wide and walked in, calling out "Hello?"

The varnished wooden floor creaked beneath him as he made his way along it, passing the bicycles belonging to Jessica and Alice. Again, the door to the living room wasn't quite closed, so he opened it. Owen Traynor was seated in one of the chairs, head leaning back, hands draped over the sides. He was in shirtsleeves and looked pale and almost drugged.

"Mr. Traynor?" Rebus said, eyes taking in everything around him. No students, no Rory Bell.

"How did I know I'd be seeing you again?" Traynor's mouth seemed parched, his voice brittle.

"Any bother here?"

Traynor looked at Rebus and shook his head. His eyes were hollow from lack of sleep.

"Been here all night?" Rebus asked.

"Maybe."

"Jessica and Alice?"

"I sent them elsewhere. Forbes too."

"So you could talk to Rory Bell in private?"

Traynor's gaze grew more focused, but he decided not to answer. His fingers were beating out a silent rhythm against the sides of the chair. Rebus turned his head towards Fox and indicated that he should take a look around. Then he moved towards the chair and crouched down in front of it.

"It didn't do any good, you know—moving those cars out of the car park. We got them anyway."

"I don't blame Alice, even though she told me I should—after all, she's the one who got Jessica and Forbes interested."

Rebus heard the sound of a vehicle squealing to a stop in the street outside. He straightened up and walked to the window, peering down onto the roofs of two patrol cars, their lights flashing.

"We had a good long talk, all four of us," Traynor was saying, almost for his own benefit rather than Rebus's. "Cleared the air. Alice really liked Forbes, but he belonged to Jessica. That was why she started seeing his father—it was the next closest thing. They're just kids, yeah? They don't always know what they're doing. Forbes said he was sorry for leaving Jessica in the lurch the night of the crash. He was planning to run to his folks' place and fetch help. There was nobody home, and by the time he got back to the Golf, Jessica was already on her way to A and E..."

"John?" It was Fox's voice. He was standing in the doorway. "Bathroom," he said.

Rebus walked back along the hall until he found it. Rory Bell lay in the empty white porcelain tub. Fully dressed, his neck twisted at an unusual angle, eyes open and glassy. Rebus felt in the man's pockets and pulled out a set of car keys. One trouser leg had ridden up, showing a pale, hairless calf. He tugged the material back down again, as if to add the smallest touch of dignity to the scene.

A scene that would be photographed, swabbed for prints and gone over by a team of SOCOs. The SOCOs Rebus now needed to call. Heart pounding, he walked slowly towards and into the living room. Owen Traynor hadn't moved.

"Nobody scares my daughter like that, Rebus. Not if they want to live."

"He didn't bring anyone with him?"

Traynor shook his head. "Had to be the two of us—I was adamant about that."

"This was last night? Late last night? And you've been sitting here ever since?"

"What else was I going to do?"

Rebus turned towards Fox. "Get a couple of the uniforms from downstairs, will you?"

Fox nodded and turned to leave. Rebus walked over to the window again.

"He can't hurt her now," Owen Traynor was intoning. "I've made sure everybody's safe."

"When my colleague comes back," Rebus explained quietly, "you'll be cautioned. Do you want to call Jessica first and tell her what's happening?"

"It was easy, you know. Almost too easy—there was no strength in the man. And it almost wasn't me at all; I was watching it happen from somewhere else..."

"You should call your daughter."

"I already did—maybe an hour ago. She said she'd come and help me. She said we could hide the body, or get rid of it somehow. But that wouldn't do any good, would it?"

"It wouldn't," Rebus said. "Not in the long run."

"I thought about doing myself in, you know."

"Jessica will be happy you changed your mind."

"She's the one thing that stopped me." Traynor had joined Rebus at the window. "That his car?" he asked.

"Yes."

"What's so interesting about it?"

"We're hoping to find out. The man you killed was no saint, Mr. Traynor."

"Can't say I've encountered too many saints in my life."

"Me neither," Rebus agreed.

Outside, he used Rory Bell's key to open the boot of the X5.

"Bloody hell," Fox gasped.

A couple of shotguns and their cartridges. A holdall filled with bags of white powder. Thick bundles of what looked like counterfeit cash. Plus a laptop, Rolexes, necklace and brooch—the proceeds from the break-in at the McCuskey house.

"If I didn't know better," Fox mused, "I'd say Owen Traynor just did the world a favor."

"Lucky you know better, then," Rebus responded, closing the boot and readying to wait for the SOCOs.

"You two look pretty chirpy," Siobhan Clarke said as Fox and Rebus marched into Torphichen police station. She had been waiting for them, so that all three could report to DCI Ralph.

"How's Maggie Blantyre?" Rebus asked.

"Shell-shocked."

"And Dod?"

"His nephew's coping. Meantime..." She fixed her eyes on Malcolm Fox. "Solicitor General wants a nice long debrief from you—Philip Kennedy, Billy Saunders, Summerhall..."

Fox tried not to look in Rebus's direction. "There's not much actual evidence. A lot's going to remain circumstantial."

"Tell *her* that," she said, leading the way to Ralph's office. He was behind his desk, but got up to shake hands before gesturing for them to sit down.

"We picked up Rory Bell's goons," he said. "They're in interview rooms one and two. With the charges hanging over them, I reckon at least one will end up telling us the story of the visit to the Justice

Minister's house. Looks like we all got results to be proud of—with the possible exception of DCI Page." Ralph was focusing on Rebus. "I know you've had your share of run-ins with him, but there'll be a job for you *some*where. Meantime, I hope the three of you have planned a celebration of some kind."

"On Police Scotland's tab?" Clarke asked.

"Doubtful—we're supposed to be *saving* money, remember."

"Then it'll probably be a Greggs pasty and a bottle of pop."

"As long as it's not in office hours." Ralph smiled, flicking a hand in the direction of the door to let them know the meeting was over.

Instead of leaving the station straightaway, Rebus went in search of the interview room he wanted. He walked in, identifying himself to the officers who were questioning the guard from the Livingston car park. The man was no longer in uniform. He wore a camouflage jacket and matching trousers. His arms were folded and he was scowling. Seated alongside him was a lawyer, a downtrodden-looking individual holding a cheap ballpoint pen over a lined notebook. Rebus asked the detectives if he could have two minutes. They didn't look happy about it, but he stood his ground and eventually they exited the room. The lawyer stayed, but that was fine with Rebus. He leaned his knuckles against the edge of the table and loomed over the man who had punched him.

"Remember me?" he asked.

"You want to take a shot at me, go ahead."

"In front of your solicitor? No, I'll get my satisfaction watching you in the dock. Only thing that'll help you is grassing your boss. It'll feel like a blow to the guts, but you'll do it anyway, because it'll bring your sentence down. But all the time you're inside, the cons will know what you did. They'll know you blabbed. That feeling in your guts won't ever go away..." Rebus straightened up, his attention moving to the lawyer.

"Don't knock yourself out," he said, turning to leave.

*   *   *

That evening, when he returned home, the only parking space on the street was next to a white Range Rover Evoque. As Rebus got out, so did Darryl Christie.

"I heard about Rory Bell," Christie said.

"He won't be trying any more landgrabs," Rebus acknowledged.

"I also hear you had something to do with his demise." Christie held out a hand. Rebus stared at it until the young man lowered his arm. "Whether you like it or not, I owe you a favor. Anytime you want to call it in, I'm at the end of the phone."

"Right," Rebus said, locking his car and heading for his tenement. He paused at the door, key not quite in the lock, and turned his head back towards Christie.

"Is that a serious offer?" he called out.

EPILOGUE

At four the next afternoon, like clockwork, Peter Meikle emerged from the bookmaker's on Clerk Street with a disappointed look on his face, a look which only intensified when he clocked Rebus.

"Again?"

"Again," Rebus agreed.

"What if I say no?"

"This is the last time, Peter. Just take this ride with me and that's us."

"Promise?"

"Promise."

Meikle got into the passenger seat of Rebus's Saab and fastened his belt. "Holyrood Park?" he guessed.

"Holyrood Park," Rebus confirmed. Then, signaling to move into the stream of traffic: "It was a long time ago, wasn't it? Has there ever been a day it didn't prey on your mind?"

"I didn't kill Dorothy."

"Ach, Peter, of *course* you did. And in the old days, there would have been ways of dealing with that—for the police, I mean. But things have changed."

"You still seem to enjoy a bit of intimidation."

"Is that what this is?" Rebus glanced at Meikle. "But I'm not smacking your head against a wall, am I? And I'm not framing you—planting evidence, altering paperwork. This is just the two of us, out for a drive, having a little heart-to-heart."

They were heading towards the Commonwealth Pool. Left at the lights and they would enter Holyrood Park.

"Some stuff's happened lately," Rebus went on, "and it's got me thinking. The good guys are never all good and the bad ones never all bad." He offered a shrug. "I know that's not exactly news. But there's a place where the two meet, and that's when it can get interesting. It's like we're all standing on the same carpet, without bothering to look down at the pattern." He glanced towards his passenger again. "Does that make sense?"

"Maybe to you—but then you've been drinking."

"Just the one whisky, Peter. Call it Dutch courage."

Meikle was staring at him. "What are you going to do?"

Rebus offered a cold smile. "We're just driving," he repeated.

And so they were—snaking around the foot of Salisbury Crags, with the Dumbiedykes estate on their left, then passing Holyrood and taking a right at St. Margaret's Loch, beginning the ascent around Arthur's Seat. Meikle knew where they would stop—opposite the gateway that led to Willowbrae, just like before. There was another car parked up, and Rebus drew to a halt behind it.

"We've not got long, Peter," he said, checking his watch as he turned off the ignition. "You carried her body up here, yes? Buried her somewhere in the vicinity." He paused. "Did you find your phone, by the way?"

"Took me almost half an hour, scouring those bushes."

Rebus nodded his satisfaction. "You'd had a bit of marital strife. Neighbors knew it, Dorothy's sister knew it. Dorothy had gone to her saying she was terrified of what you'd do to her if she tried walking out. Maybe she was packing a case when you came home. Maybe you thumped her and she decided enough was enough. Lots of ways it could have played out, Peter. The one way it *didn't* play is her jumping on a bus or train and leaving town for pastures new."

"You're barking up the wrong tree."

"Am I? All right then, fair enough." He tapped his hands against the steering wheel.

"Eh?"

"I've done what I can." Rebus sounded the horn and the doors of the car in front opened. Two men emerged. One was Darryl Christie, the other a huge, shaven-headed creature who had presumably taken over Dean Grant's role.

"What's this?" Peter Meikle asked, his left hand gripping the Saab's door handle, as if to stop it being opened from outside.

"This is where we say goodbye."

"That's Darryl Christie," Meikle spluttered.

"Darryl owes me a favor, Peter, and I've decided you're it. Now out you get."

"What?"

"You're going with them." Rebus nodded towards the Evoque. "I'm too old and too tired. All the stuff I used to be able to do to you, *they* still can. And afterwards, there'll be a nice quiet spot for your bones."

"You can't do this!"

"Why not?"

"You're the police!"

Rebus leaned towards him, face tightening. "I'm from the eighties, Peter—I'm not the newfangled touchy-feely model. Now get out of my fucking car!"

When Meikle, wide-eyed, looked through the passenger window, he saw Christie and the man-monster standing right there. Then his door was being wrenched open, despite his best efforts, and Rebus was helpfully unclipping his seat belt.

"No!" he pleaded as he was hauled out of the car. One of his cheap slip-on shoes came off and lay there on the floor. He was dragged to the Evoque and shoved onto its backseat, the bodyguard climbing in next to him. Rebus wound down his window and got a cigarette going. Then he watched as Christie pulled shut the driver's-side door and the car moved off. As it disappeared around a bend, his phone rang.

"Hiya, Siobhan," he said. "We still on for tonight?"

"Can we not find anywhere more salubrious than the back room of the Ox?"

"That's a deal-breaker for me."

"Fine, then." She sighed. "Eight thirty?"

"I might be first to arrive."

"You're on your way there now?"

"Not quite. Can Malcolm definitely come?"

"Says he's looking forward to it."

"The management might feel differently if he sticks to drinking Coke."

"I dare say you and me can make up for him."

"I dare say." Rebus allowed himself a smile, flicking ash from the window.

"You somewhere with a breeze?"

"Taking the air."

"Next few weeks might be uncomfortable. Lot of questions are going to be asked."

"I'll be ready."

"Maybe we can compare notes when we meet?"

"Are you sure that isn't against the rules?"

"I suppose it might be. Lucky we've got Malcolm to keep us on the straight and narrow."

"Best place to be, Siobhan."

"I've called Laura Smith and given her a heads-up. Reckoned she just about deserves it."

"You never know when you might need a friendly journalist. I'll see you tonight."

"Tapas afterwards at Café Andaluz?"

"Couple of drinks is all I can manage."

"Other plans?" She paused. "Don't tell me you've got a *date?*"

"You better not be about to tell me I'm too old."

"Who is it?"

"Am I not allowed a private life?"

"You know I'm going to keep digging."

"I'll see you tonight."

"Best suit, remember. And don't take her anywhere cheap..."

Rebus was smiling as he ended the call.

He kept his eyes on his wing mirror as he finished the cigarette. Then he got out of the Saab, lifting something from the backseat. The wind whipped around him as he started tearing methodically at the loose-leaf pages of the Shadow Bible, gusts scooping them up, sending them flying. He had just finished, nothing left but the leather covers, when the Evoque crawled past, settling in the same spot as before. The three men got out, the man-monster holding Peter Meikle upright while Darryl Christie walked towards Rebus.

"He'll show you," he said. "Right now, if you like."

Rebus opened the passenger door of the Saab, threw the remains of the Shadow Bible onto the seat and picked up Peter Meikle's shoe.

ABOUT THE AUTHOR

Ian Rankin is a #1 international bestselling writer. Winner of an Edgar Award, a Gold Dagger for fiction, a Diamond Dagger for career excellence, and the Chandler-Fulbright Award, he lives in Edinburgh, Scotland, with his wife and their two sons.